DIFFUSE

BRIDGET L. ROSE

This book is dedicated to everyone who has ever felt alone during their mental health journey. You're not, I promise. Adrian, Nevaeh, and I have your back.

Trigger Warnings

This book contains explicit sex scenes, as well as F1 crashes which might be scary for some readers and vulgar language. It contains topics of grief, violence, mental health, and more that may be triggering for some readers.

Author's Note

Hello, my dear reader,

Thank you so much for reading Diffuse. I am so excited to share this book with you! I know we have all been anxiously awaiting this second part of Adrian and Nevaeh's story and I hope it's everything you were hoping for and more. I hope you have fun, and I cannot wait to hear your thoughts.

Again, I would also like to note that you will see Nevaeh with anxiety. Her experience with anxiety is taken directly from my experience with it as well, just like it was with Scarlette in The Inside of a Rainbow. I want to clarify that her experience is not a universal experience and that anxiety can appear in many different forms. This is merely my own personal experience. It doesn't devalidate anyone else's. It's just the way it is, different perhaps or similar too.

I also would like to point out that Adrian has more panic attacks in this book. There is a big chunk of the book that is about his mental health journey. He goes through A LOT in this book, and I'm sorry for all the pain in advance, but I do think that it's a necessary step for him in his healing process as well.

If you have anxiety/panic attacks and other mental health struggles too, I hope you will feel seen through Nevaeh & Adrian. I know they have made me feel less alone too in my mental health journey, and bringing their character's journeys to life was very therapeutic for me.

Also, in case no one has ever told you before, you're amazing. You're doing your best. I am so proud of you.

Bridget

Pitstop Series
Team Names

Spark Racing

Prologue

Adrian

"I DON'T WANT YOU to go," I say, grabbing my mother's hand as she packs a suitcase for some trip she only told me about ten minutes ago.

"I'll be back before you know it," she assures me, ruffling my hair once before disappearing into her closet again to grab more clothes.

"Does Dad know you're leaving?" I ask because I know something isn't right. I can feel it deep in my gut. My mother is acting weird, and I need to find out why. Maybe then I can stop her from leaving.

"Of course he does, Adrian. I wouldn't just go without telling him," she promises, but her left eye twitches a little, something it always does when she lies.

"Mom, please, stay. At least until Dad gets back," I beg and pull on her shirt again. She yanks her arm away and grabs both of my shoulders.

"Go ask Tini if she wants to play with the new Carrera track and remote-controlled cars your father got you," she says, leading me out of her bedroom and toward my sister's. I knock on Valentina's door as I look over my shoulder at my mother one last time.

My little sister, the most important person in my life, opens her door to show me she's wearing one of Dad's Velocità Rossa baseball caps and a bright smile on her face. She's holding the remote in her hand, already playing with the gift our father got us.

When I ask if I can join her, she grabs my hand and pulls me into her room, leading me to where the track is set up.

Valentina hands me the other remote and settles down on the ground again, patting the spot next to her to get me to sit with her. Tears fill my eyes as I take a seat, *watching my sister's mop of dirty-blonde curls dance as she wiggles from side to side in excitement. I try to swallow them back down, but they fall when I wrap an arm around her, knowing that I won't be able to protect her from what's about to happen.*

I won't be able to protect her from all of the pain our mother will inflict because I can't even spare myself.

I let the tears fall down my cheeks as I press a kiss to the crown of her head, hating that my little sister will know heartbreak before she even knows what that word means.

CHAPTER 1

Nevaeh

ADRIAN'S BEEN GONE FOR a long time.

Whenever I try to text him, he doesn't respond. I'm getting more anxious with every passing second of silence. I think about going to my office to see if he's still there, but if he comes back here and I'm gone, he'll be confused. Maybe his phone just died. That's a logical explanation, not one of the what-if scenarios my anxiety has come up with to torment me.

I stare at my phone, my tired and broken heart beating faster and faster. It's been a long day filled with pain and betrayal. It's normal that I'm more anxious, more on edge. But Adrian is fine. Everything will be fine. He'll come back with some food and my wallet. He'll kiss me and reassure me he's alright after I tell him I was worried. He'll tell me to eat so I can feel better because I usually *do* feel a lot better after I've eaten.

Adrian will say all of those things to me because he knows me so well.

And yet, I sit on my bed, feeling that something isn't right. He would never ignore me for this long, not when I texted him I was getting worried.

I pace around my room, tapping my phone against the palm of my right hand as I wait for Adrian to text me or come back here.

My phone lights up from an incoming call, but as soon as I read my father's name, I hit Decline. I don't want to talk to him. I'm not ready to hear the elaborate story he's going to spin to talk himself out of taking responsibility for what he did. For making *Griffin Sports* hire me even though they didn't have a spot open. To pay for my salary instead of them paying me. To bribe almost every F1 team into letting me interview their drivers and write articles about them that I was actually proud of. I almost laugh at myself for being so naive, for believing I could make it that far in *my father's sport* without his help. Because that's what it feels like. *His sport.* Not mine. Never mine. Not while he's there and has his hands in everything.

I hit Decline because he doesn't deserve anything from me, not even my anger.

He was trying to help me, but all it did was make me realize I was not good enough to make it on my own. And I wanted to do just that. *Make it on my own.* Away from my parents' money and influence.

But there's nowhere to run.

And my only escape from all this pain is currently not answering my messages.

So, I go back to pacing, hoping everything is okay with Adrian because I don't think I'd survive if anything happened to the man I love right now.

Or ever.

CHAPTER 2
Adrian

"Mom?"

I know it's her, so I really don't know why the fuck I'm asking this question. This woman in front of me, although aged, looks exactly the way my mother did when she left us. Her hair is now more gray than dirty blonde, but it's just as long as Valentina's. Her eyes are the same as mine and my sister's. She's as short as Val, too.

She looks so much like us, I'm not surprised my father couldn't handle looking at Valentina and me after she left.

"My sweet boy, I've missed you so much," she says, but I raise my hands to keep her the fuck away from me. I don't want her to come closer. I don't want her to touch me. I don't want anything from this woman.

"What the hell are you doing here?" I ask, fighting back tears by swallowing hard over and over again. She takes another step forward, *toward me*, so I take another back.

Everything hurts. My heart hurts. My head hurts. My body hurts. My fucking soul hurts. I loved her so much. I begged her to stay before she left. I did everything to be the perfect son, and it wasn't enough. All the pain I felt when she left and every day since seems to hit me all at once like an electroshock.

It paralyzes me.

I can't breathe as all of my grief overwhelms me.

She can't be here. I can't be looking at my mother right now. It's not possible. She *left*. She vanished into thin air, never to be seen again. And I've hated her ever since.

I've hated her for all of the pain she's caused this family with her disappearance. My father became an alcoholic. Valentina lost her mother. I lost my mother and struggled with committing to another person for years until I met Nevaeh.

Until the woman I love more than life itself changed everything for me.

"I work at *Griffin Sports*. I'm the COO," she explains, and I feel even sicker.

"All this time, you were so close to us. You were so fucking close, you—" I cut off as a humorless laugh escapes my lips. "Never mind. I'm glad you didn't come back into our lives, and you're not going to now. I never saw you here. You will not bring us more pain," I say, my entire body shaking from how tensed up I am.

"I don't want to bring you more pain. I want to talk to you, get to know my son again," she replies, tears filling her eyes like she actually means those pathetic words.

"Have you been spying on us? Is that why you're working at *Griffin Sports* without ever showing your face? So you could hide from us while observing us?" I want to walk away, want to never speak to her again because she doesn't deserve a second of my time.

But I have so many questions.

I wish I didn't. I wish it meant nothing to me that she's standing here. But she was my mom. She meant the world to me once upon a fucking time. How do you ever truly let go of those feelings, especially when everyone else in your family is dead?

"I haven't been spying, Adrian, but I have been checking up on you. I got this job years ago, and I didn't hide myself. You could have Googled this company and seen my name, my face. I just didn't think you wanted me back in your life, so I kept my distance, but seeing you here, I couldn't help myself. I had to say something. It's just so good to see you," she says, her voice breaking off as tears stream down her face.

It becomes infinitely more difficult to swallow back my own because, fuck, I've always hated seeing my mom cry.

Why is she doing this to me?

What the fuck am I going to tell Val?

Am I going to tell Val?

She has a right to know. She deserves to hear that our mother has been hiding in plain damn sight. But I can't tell her this, can I?

Shit, fuck, shit.

What am I going to do?

If I tell her, I'll bring her even more pain. Val has made peace with the fact our mother is a heartless, conniving, and disgusting excuse of a parent. I don't want to add "Oh, by the way, baby sister, person that I've always done my best to shield from the horrors of the world, our mother has been keeping tabs on us all along *and* she's been right here without ever showing her face."

"You had no right to do this. You had no right to show yourself *now*, after all this time, without allowing Val and me to decide if we were ready for this. You had no fucking right. You made your choice. You decided to leave. You broke our hearts, but you don't get to break my sister's again because I know you. You would just weasel your way back into our lives to disappear again. And I won't let that happen. You can crawl back into the hole you came out of, and we'll pretend today never happened."

As the words slip past my lips, I know I can't tell anyone. I know this will have to be something I take to my grave so I can spare my sister. I won't be able to talk to Gabriel, James, Leonard, or Cameron either because they'd convince me I have to tell my sister. They wouldn't understand how much pain this would cause her.

So, who the fuck can I tell?

I want to talk to Nevaeh, but after the day she's had, how could I pile on even more?

Which only makes this so much worse because I want her to hold me and tell me everything is alright. I want to speak to her about this more than anyone else.

I just want her.

But I can't do this to her. Not after everything.

My breathing picks up speed, a familiar panic filling me until my lungs constrict and my chest hurts.

Realizing what could happen any moment now, I attempt to walk past her when she grabs my arm to get me to stay. Alarm bells go off in my head, so I yank my arm away and take several steps backward.

"Please," Cecilia pleads before I have a chance to speak, that single sound so raw and full of emotion, it brings tears back into my eyes. I swallow them down, straightening out my back as I let anger consume me.

"Do *not* touch me. You are not my mother, you haven't been for a very long time. You don't have the right to touch me," I say and attempt to rush outside, holding onto my girl's wallet because it's the only physical piece of her I have with me.

"I didn't want to leave you and Valentina. I wanted to get away from your father, but he didn't want to let you go with me, so I had to leave you behind." Curiosity and fear spike in my chest.

"Did he abuse you?" I ask because I wouldn't put it past my father. We were kids, so there is a high chance we wouldn't have seen it. But then he also loved our mother more than life itself. He devoted himself to her.

"No, but he was gone so much, it used to feel like I didn't have a husband at all. I was unhappy and leaving seemed like the only way to get him to let me go," she explains, which only makes more anger shoot through me.

"Let me make sure I understand you right. He loved you too much, but he was traveling too often for work, so you left him and your children? That makes perfect sense. Why didn't you just say that in the first place? Now, I can forgive you." Sarcasm drips from my words, and she catches it, causing a frown to settle on her face. It's the same one she always gave Val and me when we were kids and did something she didn't like.

"You're twisting my words, Adri," she says, the nickname she used for me as a kid sending a lightning bolt of pain through me.

"No, Cecilia, you know what I'm doing? I'm refusing to listen to any more bullshit coming from you. You left. No reason will ever be good enough to explain why, so *I'm* leaving, and I don't ever want to see you again."

This time when I walk past her, she lets me. She doesn't grab my hand again, and I almost sigh in relief when I make it out of the building and back to my car.

Relief quickly turns into more pain as I sit in my car, my breathing uneven. I burst into tears, hitting my steering wheel over and over again.

All of the years of heartbreak and anger and betrayal and fuck-knows-what-else hit me so hard, my breath catches in my throat. Sobs have my body trembling, but even as I cover my mouth, they don't slow.

I've lost family members. My dad. My grandfather. My grandmother. I've lost people I loved for far longer, so I know how to deal with that. I compartmentalize until my grief becomes bearable, but this? I have no clue how to fix this, ignore it, or do anything other than fall apart.

I've always done my best not to be selfish. I've tried putting everyone else before me my whole life because most of the people I love have never been placed first, ever. But as I take deep breaths to settle my heartbeat into a steady rhythm and drive back to Nevaeh's, I go against that very nature.

Knowing the day she had, I should wait until everything stops hurting and I've gotten a hold of myself so I can hide what the fuck just happened. I should think about her and only her, but I need her so much right now that I'm acting without thinking.

Parking my car, I run all the way back to her apartment, ignoring the voice in the back of my head as it screams at me to lie to the woman I love.

I won't lie to Nevaeh.

I *can't.*

I burst through the door and, when I see her pacing the room, I collapse onto my knees, sobbing even harder than before. Panic crosses her features as she rushes toward me, her hands finding my face as she cups it, catching my tears with her fingers.

"Adrian, talk to me, *mein Mond.* What happened?"

I try to answer, but, instead, all I manage to do is fling my arms around her and drag her onto my lap so I can bury my face in her chest and hide from the world.

CHAPTER 3

Nevaeh

I don't know what's happening.

Adrian has been clinging to me, crying, for a long time without saying a word. He just barged into my apartment and broke down. Whatever happened can't have been good, but until he calms enough to speak, all I can do is run a soothing hand through his hair and hold onto him. His entire body shakes with sobs, so I make the arm I've slipped around him a steel band, hoping to steady him.

"I don't know what happened, but whatever it is, I'm here for you. We will get through this together."

Adrian takes a deep breath, his body relaxing against me. It takes him another moment before his sobs stop. He sits up and turns to me. His eyes are bloodshot and tears run down his cheeks, but he's still so painfully beautiful. I cup his face again, wiping away the physical representation of his pain.

He lifts his fingers to my wrists, snaking them around me while my thumbs caress his cheeks.

"Do you want to talk about it?" I ask, but he merely stares at my lips before shifting his gaze to mine.

"In a minute."

He kisses me without another word. He kisses me fiercely and with need, almost desperate to get us as close as possible. Adrian's lips are soft and demanding as they glide over my mouth. I can taste the saltiness from his tears, but it's replaced by his taste when his tongue slips past my parted lips and into my mouth. He explores until we both have to come up for oxygen, him more reluctantly so than me. I place my forehead against his as his hands run over my arms and neck, settling on my nape.

"Talk to me," I whisper, but he shakes his head, his nose brushing over mine in the process. "Why not?"

"Because I can't burden you with this, not after everything you've been through today." But he pulls me closer and closer anyway.

"Adrian, you won't bur—" He cuts me off with a chaste kiss.

"Yes, I would. I would burden you to keep this secret from everyone. Pile onto everything that happened today. I'd—" It's my turn to cut him off, but instead of kissing him, I place a hand over his mouth so I can speak.

"Adrian, when will you get it through your head that I love you? That I'd do anything for you? That whatever you're going through, I want to go through it with you? We're a team. Your pain is mine. My pain is yours. This is how relationships work. I know it's all new for you, it is for me, too, but we can figure it out together. First step, tell me what happened."

The way his eyes soften breaks my heart all over again because he's never let anyone take care of him. He's always taken care of everyone else. But he's letting me in, letting me be there for him, and I won't ever take it for granted.

"I just saw my mom at your office," he says.

It feels like a cold bucket of water gets dunked over my head a second before somebody electrocutes me. My hand slowly lifts to my mouth as I fall backward onto my butt. My heart stumbles all over itself as I try to process his words, but where do I even begin? Adrian's mother, the woman who traumatized him and gave him trust issues, commitment issues, and a fear of abandonment is back. The woman who broke my best friend's heart when she was barely four years old is *back*.

I feel nauseous.

"Who?"

I know the answer before he tells me. I know because there's always been something about Cecilia Martin that seemed so familiar.

Her eyes.

Her smile.

Her hair.

"I think she's the Cecilia you were working for. She must have changed her name to Martin, but I don't know why. Her maiden name was Gastaud, and she took my dad's name when she married him," he explains, but all I can do is nod. No words leave me, none at all as I stare at my boyfriend.

"Do you think that's why she kept meddling? I know my job forbid me from dating a driver, but it was only her who enforced that rule. She was the one who called me the second she heard the rumors about us," I say, making shock lace his features before his eyes grow dark with anger.

"That better not be the reason why because, if it is, I might actually commit a crime," he replies, grabbing my hand and lifting it to his cheek. I place my palm flat against it, and he immediately leans into the touch. "What the fuck am I going to do now? I want to pretend I never crossed paths with her. I want to keep this from Val so she doesn't get hurt again. But it feels like protecting my sister from pain is the wrong choice," he admits, and I wish I had an answer for him.

If I'm being completely honest with myself, I have no idea what I'd do if I were in his shoes. I don't even want to speak to my own family after what happened. I can't imagine how Adrian must be feeling. All of that grief, all the days spent wondering why he wasn't good enough, why she left, all just so she could come back into his life without warning or giving him the opportunity to decide when he was ready to see her.

It was cruel of her to do this to him.

"Do you think you'll ever see her again?" I ask, watching his light eyes close as I rub my thumb over his lips.

"I don't know. She blindsided me today, and I have no idea if she'll do it again." His vulnerability is reflected in his gaze, and I suck in a sharp breath at the ache in my chest from seeing him this way.

So hurt.

Feeling so broken.

So lost.

"How about this? If she doesn't get the hint and shows up again, then you can tell Val. Until then, there is no need for her to know if Cecilia decides to disappear again."

My words seem to settle him a bit because his shoulders sag in relief and the tension in the rest of his body also subsides a little. He didn't want to make this decision by himself, and I'd never let him go through this on his own if he didn't want to. Hiding Cecilia's appearance from Val might seem equally as cruel as Cecilia showing up in Adrian's life, but if she's just going to disappear again, there is no reason to throw Val off course during her first F1 season. She might disagree if she ever found out, but we will cross that bridge when we get there.

For now, we've found a way to make Adrian feel less overwhelmed, and that's all that matters to me.

We get up and slip into bed when both of us are tired of being on the cold, wooden floor. His arms wrap around me, holding me against his chest. My ear presses against the area above his heart, listening to its quick beats.

"I'm so sick of fighting. First with my mother, now with my father. I'm so, so done with having conflicts without any way to resolve them," I admit, so he brushes his nose over mine and lets out a deep breath. "We should find ways to make up quickly when we're in a fight," I suggest. He thinks for another moment, kissing my face as he does.

"Okay, we will resolve them in one of three ways. Number one: we talk about it until the conflict is resolved. Number two: we take some time to cool off, but only with the promise of going to dinner after. And number three: we fuck our anger away. Personally, I'm pretty sure three will become my favorite," Adrian says and licks his lips, sending a wave of heat through me.

"It's already mine," I say, giggling when he tickles my sides. As soon as the sound leaves my lips, his eyes fill with the first sign of happiness I've seen since yesterday. He smiles at me, and my heart stutters at the sight. I lift my fingers to his lips, tracing the shape of them. "You are so devastatingly beautiful, Adrian." He presses his lips against the tips of my fingers as a blush paints his cheeks a wonderful pink.

"Funny, that's what I think every single time I look at you." My blush mimics his.

"If only our beauty would protect us from backstabbing, horrible people," I say, causing a snort to escape him.

"What a couple of messes we are," he mutters against the crown of my head, and I burst into laughter.

It dies out as soon as the realization that I have to be around my parents constantly again, to live under their roof as I look for a job, settles deep inside me. Tears replace my laughter, and I let them fall down my cheeks.

"What a fucked up day. One emotional blow after another. Life truly doesn't hold back, does it?" I ask, gripping Adrian's shirt as he pulls me even further against him.

"I've realized long ago that life on Earth is a constant flow of bullshit." His dry response has me chuckling again.

"Then what do we call what we have?" I challenge, so Adrian grabs my chin between his thumb and index finger to tilt my head up. My gaze locks onto his in an instant, letting me see the love in his eyes.

"Heaven."

He kisses me, long and soft and sensual. Until the waves of pain in my chest finally slow, replaced by pure adoration for the man touching me. One last tear rolls down my cheek, but he kisses it away, his mouth moving back onto mine so the salty taste lingers between us.

There is so much emotion in a tear. So much agony and joy. So much desperation and need. So much of the feelings I never know how to deal with.

There is a lot I don't know how to deal with, but all of it will have to wait until tomorrow. I have no more strength left in my body and mind to do anything but nuzzle myself against Adrian's side, turn on *Doctor Strange*, our comfort movie, and let his warmth hug me like a blanket.

Neither one of us manages to fall asleep for a long time. We order some food and eat until both of us are full before we go back to cuddling and escaping our pain through the movies we love.

We make it all the way to the second one, and when Stephen tells Christine, "I love you. I love you in every universe," my boyfriend shifts until his eyes meet mine.

Then, he says, "I love you, Nevaeh. I love you in every universe."

He kisses me before giving me a chance to answer, but I wouldn't even know how to put into words how much I love him. Yet he doesn't expect an answer. He merely smiles as he leans back again, turning his head to the movie.

Soon after, I fall asleep in the only arms I've ever felt safe in.

But I should have known better. I should have known I'm defenseless against my anxiety in these moments, when I'm drained of energy and have no strength left to fight with my mind. Every what-if scenario spirals and spirals until it consumes me with panic. I lose myself to every dark thought. I've got nothing left but the man holding me and the family I made with Val, Gabriel, and the rest of the drivers. And while that is more than most people have, I can't help but grieve my career. I grieve everything I worked for in the same way I grieved my dream of becoming a professional tennis player.

I fall right into the dark hole of my anxiety, even as Adrian clings to me and tries to calm me. I fall and fall and fall without ever hitting the ground. It's an uncomfortable panic snaking around my throat, squeezing until I'm breathless.

Until it feels like I'm dying.

CHAPTER 4
Adrian

SINCE WE DON'T HAVE to hide our relationship anymore, Nevaeh and I have decided to wait another day to deal with our problems and spend some time at the beach. I asked Valentina and Gabriel if we could borrow their boat, and they—very reluctantly—told me I could take it out. Under the condition that Nevaeh is in charge. I gave them the fakest laugh I could muster before flipping them off, snatching the keys out of Gabriel's hand, and leaving again.

Being near my sister brought me too much pain to ask them to join us. Plus, I know Nevaeh doesn't want to be around anyone yet. It hasn't even been a day since everything happened, and, because no one knows, she wants to keep it that way for a bit longer.

Nevaeh also told me this morning how much it hurts her to stay at her place right now, so I asked her to pack a bag and come with me. I prefer to have her at my place anyway. She belongs here, with me, 24/7. She didn't hesitate. She threw everything she needed into two bags and followed me out of the apartment without a word. Then, she sighed in relief as soon as she stepped through the door of my place.

I think she loves it here.

"Nevaeh, mon ange, we should get goi—"

I cut off when I see her standing in front of the mirror in my bathroom, tracing her stretch marks and then the scar on her shoulder. She looks unhappy, but I'm having a hard time keeping my eyes from tracing the shape of her body over and over. The curve of her ass, the thickness of her thighs, the swell of her breasts. Her strong, soft body and beautiful face.

God, she's *everything*.

"What's wrong?" I ask when I notice the frown on her face.

"With everything that's going on, I think I'm just feeling very uncomfortable in my own skin. Insecurities I haven't felt in years are resurfacing and I'm having a hard time swallowing them down," she explains, running a hand over her stomach. She squeezes it, then lets out a small sigh. "I love my body. So, why do I feel this way?" she asks, grabbing a towel to hide.

I step into the bathroom with her, reaching for the fabric. She lets me peel it off her, but when she averts her gaze to keep from looking at her reflection, I grab her chin and lift her head. She meets my eyes in the mirror.

"You're allowed to have bad days. Even I do, and I'm one arrogant asshole," I say, but she merely frowns at me. I grin at her in the mirror. "All I'm saying is that you're allowed to feel this way. Just because you feel confident most days doesn't mean you're not entitled to feel less so on others. Your feelings are valid, baby, and I'll be here every single time to remind you just how beautiful you are."

"Adrian—" she starts but cuts off, shaking her head.

"I've never wanted to study a woman's body as much as I do yours, *mon paradis*," I say, gliding my hands down her arms, over her stomach, and then up her breasts. "Your beautiful body," I add, hearing a little whimper escape her as I guide her ass against my groin.

"What about my scars and stretch marks?" I click my tongue, shaking my head.

"Do you not remember what I told you when I first saw your scar?" I replay the moment, and she must do the same because a smile dances onto her lips.

"'It's your battle scar, a part of you and your journey,' I remember," she admits, and I slide down her bikini top just enough to press a kiss to the sensitive skin above the scar on her shoulder.

"I also said there is nothing ugly about it. If anything, I think they're beautiful, the scar and the stretch marks," I say, my accent slipping through as my voice drops an octave. It happens sometimes when I stop concentrating. And it's hard to concentrate when Nevaeh's body is pressed against mine, her ass grinding against my hardening cock as she looks for any sort of friction. "When the sun sets and the sky divides into different colors, do you think it looks ugly?" I ask, but she shakes her head. "No, because it's the world painting the sky. So, why do you think your body's artwork is ugly?" She smiles at my choice of metaphor.

"It's not," she mumbles while I trace every single stretch mark my fingers can find.

"Don't worry, I'll worship you until the day you believe me. I'll kiss every centimeter of your body until my lips are tattooed on your skin so that when you look in the mirror, you'll see the way they cover every part of you."

My hands cup her breasts again, my thumbs rubbing over her pebbled nipples until she moans. My body gives an agreeing hum, my cock grinding against her perfect ass again.

"Do you feel how hard you make me, Nevaeh? Can you feel what you do to me? This will never change. I will forever be desperate for you, for this body," I say, gliding one of my hands down her chest and toward her pussy.

Right as the tips of my fingers brush her bikini bottoms, her phone rings. Since it lies face up on the bathroom counter, both of us see her father's name on the screen. Nevaeh visibly tenses, so I remove my hands to place them on her hips in silent support instead.

"Do you want to answer it?" I ask, kissing the side of her head as she picks up her phone.

"No, but I have to, if only to say to stop calling me." She stares at the screen for another moment, then slides up on the Answer button before putting her phone on Speaker.

"Nevaeh," her father starts, but he finishes the rest of the sentence in German.

"I don't want to speak to you right now. You hurt me, and I'm not ready to hear your excuses for why you did what you did. Stop calling me." Nevaeh hangs up without giving him a chance to yell at her.

"What did he say before you answered?" I ask, squeezing her hips. She meets my gaze in the mirror and laughs. Actually laughs.

"He was scolding—he was scold—" She cuts off to laugh more, and I'd join her if I didn't know that her laughter comes from a place of overwhelming sadness and disbelief. "Oh God, I'm sorry, I just can't believe him. He was scolding me for not answering my phone and not informing him I was fired." She covers her mouth to get herself to stop. "This family of mine, Adrian... I can't do it anymore. I cannot be the perfect daughter who does everything they want me to. I cannot be someone I'm not. I can't be who they've tried to mold me into being. I'd rather disappoint them than hide who I am any longer."

She spins around in my arms, grabbing a hold of my shirt.

"Becoming a journalist for a big company like *Griffin Sports* isn't what I wanted. It's what they expected of me, so it's what I became. If it were up to me, I'd spend my days doing photography and writing articles I actually care about, like the ones I was writing for the drivers. I enjoy freelance work, being my own boss. I don't enjoy getting manipulated and treated like shit," she explains, her lips falling shut when she realizes she just voiced something she must have never said to anyone before.

"I'm proud of you, Nevaeh. I'm so proud of everything you've achieved and will achieve in the future. You can do anything you set your mind to without anyone's help. Your father might have gotten you the job, but you were the one who wowed every popular tennis player's PR manager. They wanted you, not because of your father but because they loved the pictures you took and the words you wrote. *That* is all you, and I know whatever you set your mind to next will be another success."

Nevaeh studies my face for another moment, then leans away from me to say, "Your unwithering belief in me might be misplaced, *mein Mond*. I'm still jobless and a huge disappointment to my parents."

"Well, your parents don't deserve you. *I* think you are the best journalist I've ever come across. You're kind and fair, don't spread lies to spin a story. You are compassionate and always put the subject of your stories first." Her gaze softens at my words. "Your parents only measure success in accomplishments that can be touched. They're wrong. Success comes in many forms. Don't listen to a word they say."

She kisses me as soon as I'm finished talking. Only when she steps back do I see the determination in her eyes.

"I don't want to hide us anymore, Adrian," she says, patting my left pec.

"Isn't that why we're going on the boat? For everyone to see?" I challenge with a small smirk, but she shakes her head, a serious expression lingering on her lips.

"No, I don't want there to be rumors. I want people to know for certain that you and I belong together. How do we do that?" she asks, so I step around her to lean against the marble counter, pulling her against me while I think.

"There is a dinner gala Velocità Rossa is hosting tonight. I wasn't planning on going because it's not mandatory, but we can. There will be cameras and lots of people who will see us. It's more official than anything else we could do," I say, smiling a little at the thought of the world finally knowing this woman is mine and I'm hers.

"I'm going to need a dress."

CHAPTER 5

Nevaeh

I RUN A NERVOUS hand down my light orange evening gown. After deciding we were going to the gala, Adrian made a few phone calls that led to Gabriel appearing at the front door holding a box with the name *Rush* written across the lid. He didn't want to go alone after Valentina had to attend a last-minute Zoom meeting with Leonard for their driver academy.

Knowing Evangelin, the owner of the small boutique Val took me to before the casino event months ago, probably picked out the dress makes my heart flutter in the best way. In all the chaos and heartbreak, I desperately want to cling to the feeling of happiness surging through me because of such a small yet thoughtful gesture on Adrian's part.

The sleeves are made out of lace and the heart-shaped neck doesn't reveal much. It's tight at the top and loose at the bottom, my favorite kind of dress. I run my hands over the silky fabric again, replaying what happened only an hour ago in my head.

Before I took the dress out, when I was reaching for the hem of my shirt, Adrian made his way to the door.

With an amused smile, I said, "You don't have to leave," but he shook his head with a laugh.

"If I stay in here while you undress, I can assure you, we won't make it to dinner," he explained, and I pressed my lips together to force the smile away, but it crossed my face anyway.

"Thank you," is all I said in response, but he shook his head again.

"Don't thank me. It'll be a present for me to see you in it and show the world that I belong to the most drop-dead gorgeous woman on the planet."

"Are you sure you're ready for everyone to know we're dating? I know I am, but I want you to be ready as well. We can still decide against it if you have doubts or—" He cut me off before I went into full rant-mode.

"Nevaeh, I love you. Simple as that. I'm ready if you are," he said and took a few steps toward me.

"I want this," I admitted, making him let out a sigh of relief.

"*Phew*, good, because it would be pretty embarrassing to show up by myself after I just emailed everyone I was bringing the most beautiful date," he teased, and I nudged him in the side. He attacked my lips, making me giggle uncontrollably.

"I'm so in love with you," I blurted out after he gave me a serious, long, and firm kiss that made my knees weak.

"Which is why I'm the luckiest man alive."

Although I do my best to hurry, Adrian and Gabriel are waiting for me on the sofa after I finish putting on the dress and applying my makeup. It's a simple look, but anxiety has settled in my chest and stomach at the thought of the whole world watching me tonight. I want to do this. I want to make our relationship public, but I'm not foolish enough to believe I won't be hated by some for merely being with the heartbreaker of F1. My life will be analyzed and dissected until everyone knows more about me than I even know about myself.

Everything will be upside down after tonight, but I'm done hiding.

I just have to wrestle my insides into behaving because this will be difficult enough without having to fight off an anxiety attack.

Gabriel gives me a small smile as I step into the living room, but Adrian's eyes go wide with awe when he sees me. Mine must do the same because he put on an all-black suit without a tie, looking like a Greek god. His hair flows in a dozen waves all over his head and his eyes look lighter than ever before. They almost shine as I make my way toward him.

"I was thinking I'd want to rip the dress right off you, but you look so stunning, I could stare at you for hours," Adrian says, and Gabriel lets out a snort that makes Adrian's and my eyes drift to him.

"Sorry, it's a little difficult to believe those words would ever come out of your mouth," he explains as he stands up, his accent thick. "But it's nice. You finally understand how it feels to be wrapped around an incredible woman's finger," Gabriel goes on and straightens out his tie. He's wearing a black suit with a white dress shirt underneath.

Adrian replies something in French that makes Gabriel roll his eyes before he walks toward the door.

"I told him I might be wrapped around your finger, but I'm also leading the championship," Adrian translates for me, and I shake my head at him.

"You're impossible," I reply, but amusement is evident in my voice. Adrian grabs my hand and leads me to the door.

"Impossibly good-looking?" he asks, so I place my hands on my forehead while giving him a look of disbelief.

"Who made you so full of yourself?" He chuckles as he locks his door before taking my hand again.

"You did," he replies and kisses the top of my head before following Gabriel toward the garage of his apartment complex.

"And how the hell did I do that?" Adrian leans down, making sure only I can hear his answer.

"Two ways actually. The first you've been doing since we've met and that's looking at me like I'm a meal to be devoured," he says, but I feel the need to protest. Adrian goes on before I can deny it. "The second was every single time you've fallen apart on my mouth, fingers, and cock." I can't argue with that point. "So, you see, it's your fault I'm this way," he points out like it's the most logical thing anyone has ever said.

"Like I said, you're impossible."

"Impossibly good at turning you on?" he asks, and I cover his mouth.

"No more, Adrian, no more," I say, but my laughter gives away how much I'm enjoying his playfulness. It distracts me from the way my breathing turns more uneven with every step we get closer to the venue. It also warms my insides because he looks so much happier and lighter than he did yesterday after... well, we all know what happened yesterday.

Adrian opens the door of his Velocità Rossa for me. He plants a quick kiss on my lips while I sit down in the passenger seat. It's so very easy to get lost in all of this. In the extravaganza of tonight. In what we're about to do. It's easy to push away the thought of being jobless as well as soon-to-be homeless because there is no way I can pay for my apartment and groceries. Unless I move back in with my parents, which is— I shudder.

"There is something we need to talk about, something serious." Adrian turns down the radio to hear me better. "With everything that happened, I don't think I can stay in Monaco anymore. Without my job, I won't be able to afford the life here," I explain, his eyes completely fixated on the road as his jaw clenches. He's thinking about what to say, and, more than anything, I hope he'll tell me we will be fine no matter where I go.

"You're thinking about moving back into your parents' house?" he asks, and I nod, although it's the last thing I want to do.

"Well, I just lost my job, which means I lost any means to pay for my apartment and the lifestyle here in Monaco. That means I'll have to move back home and be with my parents unless I find another job within the next few weeks. Since that's impossible too, I will really have to find a way to tolerate being in the same room as my father, so I don't have an option and—" I cut off when I see Adrian's concerned expression.

"I don't want you to move back to England," he blurts out, surprising himself. I notice it in the way his eyes slightly widen. "I'm sorry, *mon ange*, that's incredibly selfish," he adds, his hands gripping the steering wheel even harder.

"It's not, not when I don't want to move back there, either. I don't want to live with my parents again."

"I know." His finger reaches out to play with one of my curls, determination in his eyes.

"But I don't think I have another choice."

"We'll figure it out, *mon ange*, I promise," he says, and I tilt my head.

"How can you be so sure?" I ask as he parks the car in front of the valet.

"Because I'd do anything to be with you, no matter what," he says, grabbing my chin and leaning forward to kiss me. "If you don't want to move back, you won't. We will find a way."

Something tells me he already has an idea in mind, but he doesn't elaborate, merely kisses me again. He gets out of the car and rushes over to my side, but, this time, I stay seated so he can open the door for me. His words from last time ring in my ears, and I can't help but smile.

"You don't open your own doors when I'm around, Nevaeh."

Another wave of anxiety creeps in as I take the hand Adrian stretches out for me. One more step, and all the camera flashes that appeared as soon as my boyfriend got out of the car will be directed at me. My parents will be so disappointed, especially Mama. The world might not mind it as much considering journalists date racers all the time, but Papa? He's going to fucking lose it. Twenty-one years of trying to do everything my father wanted, trying to fit his perfect image, will be ground to dust in one evening.

But I take Adrian's hand anyway.

My F1 driver pulls me out of the car, camera flashes appearing all around us. Sensing how anxious all of this is making me, Adrian steps in front of me, taking a very subtle deep breath to get me to take one, too.

"It's just me. No one else. Focus on me, and once we're inside, everything will be alright," he assures me, pressing a soft kiss to my forehead. My eyes flutter shut at the warmth of his lips for a moment.

Then, I refocus on the paparazzi taking our picture.

Adrian places his arm around me, his hand on my hip as he guides us toward the entrance of the building where Velocità Rossa is hosting the dinner gala tonight.

There is a red carpet leading up the stairs, dividers on our left and right where the people taking pictures stand behind. I do my best to smile as naturally as possible, but it's getting harder to breathe the longer we are out here.

My boyfriend gives my hip one more squeeze before whispering sweet things into my ear that have my cheeks heating, probably painting them a deep red. I place a hand on his chest as he guides me toward him, both of us now facing only the left side of photographers. They're shouting things I can't make out, but they don't matter anymore, not while Adrian kisses my lips in a way he's never done with anyone in public before. He's showing everyone we're together, that the heartbreaker of F1 finally found the one person he'd change his mindset on romantic love for.

I kiss him back, fighting to keep the tears inside at the realization of how much this man loves me.

"I don't think I can smile for much longer without my face permanently getting stuck that way," I whisper to Adrian, who bursts into genuine laughter.

"Let's go," he says and guides me all the way up the stairs and out of the view of all of those cameras. He kisses me all over the face, then says, "Your smile is my favorite type of sunshine, and I'm selfish enough to want it all to myself, so best not to get your face stuck that way." I shake my head at him, but he merely grins down at me as we walk inside.

High ceilings, marble floors, and extravaganza beyond measure decorate the room. For a moment, I'm too mesmerized to do anything but study the intricate designs woven into the walls and ceilings to move, but Adrian doesn't rush me either. He lets me take in the artwork hung on the walls, the people in designer clothing as they pass us, and the way the floor is so squeaky clean, I can practically see our reflections in it.

"Nevs!" I hear my friend's familiar voice, causing me to spin on my heels to see Valentina Romana approaching.

She looks breathtaking. Her blonde locks are loose and her curls look more defined than I've ever seen them before. She's wearing a long, red evening gown made out of a velvet fabric. There is no slit on the side, nothing at all that would allow for better movement in a tight dress like hers, and yet, she moves with more grace and ease than anyone else ever could. Her lips are painted red, and her light eyes shine brightly in contrast to the dark eyeshadow she's wearing.

"I thought you couldn't come," I say as I move over to hug her. Adrian is still holding my hand, keeping me back, so I feel it as soon as his eyes find his sister. He tenses visibly, yesterday's events too raw in his mind to ignore the stinging in his chest. I don't have to look inside his head to know what he's thinking or feeling.

"The meeting with Leonard ended early, and I didn't want Gabriel to have to go through tonight by himself. He hates these things without me," she explains as she wraps her arms around me, forcing me to look away from Adrian. "Hey, big brother. What's with the serious look on your face?" Val asks with a little snicker.

"Nothing. Nothing at all. You look beautiful," is all he replies, so Val steps out of the hug to do a little curtsy.

"Thank you. Squeezing into it took much longer than I'd like to admit." I chuckle, but the sound is cut short when Adrian pulls me back against his chest. The air *whooshes* out of me as he bands his arm around me, clinging to me like I'm the only cure to his pain. "Are you sure you two are okay? Wait, did you come here together? What happened to not being seen?" she asks when realization dawns on her. I let out a dry laugh.

"Well, I got fired from my job yesterday because Lincoln took a photo of Adrian and me kissing and shared it with my bosses, so it's not like they could fire me again," I rant because I've always found it easier to quickly rip off the bandaid than linger on what hurts. Valentina's mouth falls wide open, so I add, "But I came here to enjoy my night with my boyfriend and friends. We can save the tears for a lunch date later this week," I offer, but she doesn't look convinced in the slightest.

"Nevs, I don't think you should—" Gabriel appears beside her, grabbing her waist and pulling her away from me.

"You heard the woman. She doesn't want to deal with it tonight," he says, guiding her toward a group of people while she frowns at him but doesn't argue.

"I hate keeping things from her," Adrian whispers, drawing my attention back to him, so I place my hand over his where it rests on my stomach.

"I know." He lets out a long sigh before shaking himself a little and plastering a forced smile on his lips.

"Let's mingle." Adrian holds out his hand for me, and I place mine in his.

"Nevaeh, I want to introduce you to someone," Val says and grabs my hand as soon as we're close enough again, pulling me away from Adrian.

I look over my shoulder to see him watch after me while Gabriel attempts to make conversation with him.

"I think you're going to like her," my best friend adds while she leads me to a tall, brunette woman with long legs and a warm smile.

Her green eyes shift to us while mine move to a man who looks like her twin. His eyes briefly scan Val's face before he finds me, his gaze dropping to my body. I almost shudder at the way he looks at me, an uncomfortable feeling settling inside me.

Instead of lingering on it, I turn to the woman beside the strange man.

"Nevaeh, this is Lucie. Lucie, this is my friend Nevaeh," Val introduces us, and I shake her hand with a smile. "Lucie and I were training at the Velocità Rossa Academy together."

"It's nice to meet you," I say with a smile.

"The pleasure's all mine. Val has told me a lot about you," Lucie says, making me blush. "Oh, and this is my brother, Brandon," she informs me, and he holds out his hand for me to take, which I do hesitantly.

I don't like the way he's smirking at me or how he holds my hand longer than necessary. I don't give him another glance, but his eyes stay on me. Mine, on the other hand, shift over my shoulder again to look for Adrian to see what he's doing. He's speaking to Gabriel but catches my glance as if a single look is all it takes to call his attention to me.

I fake a smile and turn back around.

"Nevaeh, tell me about yourself," Brandon says when Lucie and Val fall into their own conversation. I let out a nervous breath and take a step back when he tries to close the distance. "I'm just trying to be polite. You don't have to be rude," he scolds, causing anger to spread through me. Out of respect for Val and her friend, I swallow it down.

"I apologize if I've offended you." It goes against my nature to say this to him, but I manage to make it sound sincere enough. Brandon's green eyes scan my face.

"You did, but you can make it up to me by telling me about yourself," he replies, and my breathing speeds up.

"Actually, I should probably go back to my—" He cuts me off.

"What are you so afraid of? A good conversation?" he asks, stepping toward me. I instinctively take a step back again.

A familiar body moves against mine from behind before I can say another word. I lean back, enjoying the comfort his touch brings.

"She doesn't owe you anything, Brandon, and I suggest you back away from my girlfriend before I forget who I am," Adrian warns, his voice low, threatening.

"Girlfriend? You don't do girlfriends, Romana, don't be ridiculous," Brandon replies.

"You're right. Girlfriend sounds too plain for how I feel about Nevaeh. How about this," he starts and steps around me to move toward Brandon before adding, "Get the fuck away from my future wife, or you'll see me lose my composure, and I assure you, it isn't a pretty sight."

I slip a hand on top of his shoulder, signaling for him to come with me.

"Come on, Mr. Possessive-Protective. Let's go sit down," I say, flashing Brandon another frown before focusing on Adrian as we walk away. "Also, don't you think it's a bit early for the 'wife' talk?" I ask with a smile, but Adrian gives me a serious look.

"My grandmother used to tell me that saying the things we want out loud helps manifest them," he says, taking my hand to lift it to his mouth and kiss the back of it.

"Mine always said it jinxes things," I tease, so he throws me a playful scowl.

The tables are spread out around the room, red decorations everywhere, along with the horse symbol Velocità Rossa is known for. Adrian and I sit down at the same table as Gabriel and the team principal of Velocità Rossa. Adrian briefly introduces me to him, but Lorenzo's attention is on Val when she settles down next to Gabriel. He asks her about how she's being treated at Alfa Adrenalina as soon as he can. His eyes reveal how much he cares about her, and I have a feeling he's already planning the day he can get her on his team.

"I'm sorry you got fired, Nevaeh," Gabriel says, pulling me back into the moment.

"Don't worry, I'll figure something out," I assure him, and Adrian squeezes my thigh. His intention might have been to comfort me, but it sends a wave of shivers down my spine instead. He notices the goosebumps spreading over my skin and smirks to himself, his tongue briefly darting over his lips to wet them.

"We're leaving as soon as this fucking thing is over," he tells me in a low whisper, his grip on me tightening.

"If we make it that long," I reply, making Adrian touch the roof of his mouth with his tongue to conceal his horny smile.

"That's a big *if, mon paradis.*"

# CHAPTER 6

Adrian

WE'RE HIDING FROM OUR problems. I know we are. It's hard not to when our lives have become giant messes.

And it's oh so easy to ignore it all when I've got my face buried between my woman's legs, my tongue flat against her pussy.

Nevaeh quivers and moans, grinding herself against my face.

We left the gala right after dinner finished, which earned us several disapproving looks from my boss, sister, and Gabriel, but I didn't care. I'd have thrown Nevaeh over my shoulder and carried her to the car if I could have done so without causing a scene.

I hardly had her through the door of my apartment before I pulled her dress off, slipped my tongue into her mouth, and guided her into the bedroom. In the next breath, she was naked with my face buried in her beautiful pussy.

"Right there, Adrian. Fuck, yes, right there," she chants as I flick my tongue over her clit faster with every lick.

I smile before sucking on her clit and pushing her right over the edge. Her hips push off the bed, so I shove them back down to keep fucking her with my mouth, letting her ride out her pleasure for as long as possible. She screams my name and grips the sheets, her entire body trembling from pleasure.

"Adrian, baby, no more. I—Oh shit," I remove my mouth instantly, kissing the inside of her left thigh instead.

"If I could, I'd spend all my time between your legs, Nevaeh." I place gentle kisses all over her legs and pussy, enjoying the way she shudders in response. "I'd spend all my time fucking *mon petit paradis* with my mouth."

"Adrian," she whimpers, covering her mouth to muffle a breathless laugh. "But there is something else I want, Adrian," she says, and I lift my head to see her sit up to look at me where I am between her legs.

Shit, if I wasn't already achingly hard, that look would send all my blood south.

"Whatever it is, all you have to do is ask, *mon ange*, and it's yours."

I would lay the world at her feet if I could. I'd buy every single piece of it only to gift it to Nevaeh as if it were nothing more than a pair of shoes. There isn't a line I wouldn't cross for her, a place I wouldn't go.

She grabs my chin between her fingers and says, "I want you to fuck my mouth. I want to suck your cock and make you feel good." Shivers of pleasure run down my spine until I'm almost shaking.

"Are you sure?"

Usually, I prefer being the one to give head. I have this awful fear of not tasting good for whoever puts their mouth on me, but the way Nevaeh looks at me right now makes all that fear dissipate into thin air.

I sit up and run a thumb over her lips, parting them and pushing it inside slowly. Nevaeh sucks on it without hesitation, making my cock give a needy, hard throb.

"Yes, I'm sure. Now, be a good boy and put your dick in my mouth."

I almost let out a very inhuman growl as I move off her to tear my clothes off. Nevaeh watches me with rapt fascination as she crawls toward the edge of the bed to get close to where I'm standing. She's completely naked, and, for a moment, I get lost in tracing her beautiful figure when she kneels in front of me, her hands running over her breasts and stomach. I give my cock a rough jerk, the build-up almost painful, but I can't look away either. I love watching her play with herself.

"You look so pretty on your knees, Nevaeh," I say and stroke her jaw until her eyes flutter shut. "But I'm going to need you to get on your knees on the floor so I can do as you've asked," I add, reaching for a pillow and placing it on the ground in front of me.

My woman wastes no time moving onto it, an excited moan leaving her when she lifts her hands to my thighs, when her face comes closer to my cock. She licks her lips, and I almost come on the spot without her even touching it. I'm not used to a woman giving me head—I've only ever had one woman do it and I didn't enjoy it—and I have a feeling Nevaeh's mouth wrapped around my dick will be another weakness added to the growing list.

1. My family's well-being and happiness (which now includes Nevaeh)

2. Nevaeh's smile

3. Nevaeh's laugh

4. Nevaeh's freckles

5. Nevaeh's sense of humor

6. Nevaeh's teasing

7. Nevaeh's heart, mind, and soul

8. Nevaeh's body

9. Nevaeh's...

Well, you get what I mean.

"I'm excited. I've been dying to suck you off for months," she says, dragging me back into the moment. She runs her nails down my abs and thighs, then brings her hands to the base of my cock.

"Don't make me come. I want to come while I'm inside of you," I say, making a naughty twinkle appear in Nevaeh's eyes.

"Then you take charge. Fuck my mouth," she says. "But just go slow. You're huge, so I don't know how much will fit," she adds with a dirty smile that has another wave of pleasant shivers running down my spine. She parts her lips and grabs a hold of my thighs, inviting me to do whatever I want.

"Tap my thigh twice if it gets too much." She answers with a single nod before sticking her tongue out, her grip on my thighs tightening.

God, this woman.

I place one hand on her chin while using the other to guide my cock into her mouth. She wraps her lips around my head for a moment, a moan slipping past her lips as she flicks her tongue over it.

"Fuck me." I moan as my head falls backward, the warmth and wetness of her mouth another type of heaven entirely. "Yes, Nevaeh, that's it. Relax your jaw for me so I can go deeper," I say, and she obeys immediately, letting me in. I'm a little more than halfway inside when she pulls away from me, clearly overwhelmed.

I pull back, only moving halfway inside her mouth again when I push back inside. She moans around my length, one of her hands falling to her pussy as I continue thrusting in and out.

"You're my dirty woman, you know that? Fucking yourself with your fingers while you take my cock in your mouth." Her eyes flutter shut at my words, another low, guttural moan escaping her. "Fuck," I murmur, my grip on her jaw loosening the closer I get to my release.

"More, Adrian. Give me more. I can take it," Nevaeh says a few thrusts later, opening her mouth even wider as she looks up at me through those thick lashes of hers. I pump back inside her mouth, and she meets me halfway, taking me deeper. I give her a content groan as I let wave over wave of pleasure consume me. My balls tighten uncomfortably because I'm so fucking close, but I don't want to stop just yet.

This feels way too good, and the way she looks up at me is like a drug, making me high.

It's addictive.

Nevaeh moans again when I'm almost fully inside her mouth, sending a vibration so strong through my cock, it travels all the way into my toes. Her fingers move more frantically now, and I realize she's close to another orgasm. Man, I fucking love that having my cock in her mouth turns her on to the point that she just has to touch herself and make herself come.

She rolls her hips in time with my thrusts, and when she cries out as she falls apart, I pull out. Nevaeh grinds against the palm of her hand while I capture her mouth in a firm kiss, groaning at the taste of myself.

Why did I wait so fucking long to fuck her mouth?

Nevaeh kisses me back so hard, I tumble backward, a laugh escaping me when she merely crawls on top of me to keep kissing me.

"Nevaeh, bed," I say when her mouth moves onto my jaw and neck, another little laugh slipping past my lips.

"No time. Need you inside of me," she says, reaching for my suit pants to grab the condoms she knows I carry with me whenever we're together. She slips one down my length, then goes back to kissing me, clearly too distracted by my mouth to remember she was about to sink down on me.

I guide my cock to her entrance right as her tongue slips into my mouth, tasting me.

"Fucking hell," I say when I'm buried deep inside of her, eliciting a gasp from my angel.

"Yes, Adrian, you feel so good. You feel as good as you taste," she says, rolling her hips to grind her clit against my pelvis. Fireworks go off inside of me.

"Yeah?" I ask with a cocky smile, placing an arm under my head so I can watch the way her breasts bounce as she rides my cock.

If I'd die right now, I'd die a happy man.

"Yeah, *mein Mond*," she replies, an equally arrogant smile on her lips when she adds, "Probably as good as I taste to you."

"Oh, my sweetest Nevaeh, no one tastes as good as you." I lift my free hand to her breast, squeezing her hard nipple until she cries out from pleasure.

"Don't stop," she begs, bouncing up and down.

She leans forward a little, her mouth hovering over mine while she rolls her hips. My orgasm is dangerously close, and if she keeps going this slow, I doubt she'll finish with me, so I grab her hips, driving upward hard and fast until she screams my name.

I love how fucking vocal Nevaeh is when we make love.

"Don't stop, don't stop, don't stop," she repeats over and over until her entire body trembles through another orgasm.

I fall over the edge at the same moment, trying to keep thrusting up to ride out our pleasure, but it's so intense, all I can do is dig my nails into her thighs and moan louder than ever before.

Nevaeh collapses onto my chest moments later, our breathing ragged and our hearts racing perfectly in rhythm, fast and equally as uneven as our breathing. My arms fling around her as I kiss the top of her head, my eyes falling shut at the feel of her warm, sweaty skin pressed against every inch of mine.

Nothing could ever make me let go of this woman.

She's it for me.

My future.

My impossible desire.

Everything I never thought I wanted, never thought I could have.

She's all of it.

And I'll protect what we have from everyone and everything that threatens to destroy it.

And no, you don't have to remind me. I know I'm pathetically in love with Nevaeh, but we all knew I'd be the most in love.

Just ask my family.

They've been saying it for years.

CHAPTER 7
Nevaeh

A HAND RUNS OVER my arm, gently waking me from my deep sleep.

"*Mon paradis*," Adrian's voice fills my ears, and I can't stop the smile from spreading across my face.

My eyes open to see him sitting on my side of the bed, his fingers still trailing over me. I reach for them to wrap my hand around his and bring it to my lips, to place a kiss on his soft skin. My eyes shift to his shirt on my chest, and warmth spreads through me. I love wearing his clothes, even when I don't remember putting them on because we had sex until I passed out. Not literally, but I fell asleep right after going for my pee—don't want to risk getting a UTI.

"Your phone is going crazy," Adrian says and hands it to me, allowing me to see the twenty missed calls from Mama, Papa, and Nova.

There are countless messages, too, but I simply throw my phone to the side and sit up to get closer to Adrian. I suck in a sharp breath when I realize how sore my body is and then let out a small laugh.

"God, I haven't been this sore in a long time," I admit right before my mind replays the events of last night, sending a thrill through me.

I lost count after the first two condoms we used, but, by the way my body aches now, I realize it must have been at least another two. We also didn't go to sleep until early this morning because every time we decided to talk, we ended up having sex again.

The thought makes me smile.

Adrian grabs my chin with his thumb and index finger, slowly leaning down to press his lips against mine.

"It feels too good to hear those words coming out of your mouth," he says after he leans away again and runs his thumb over my bottom lip. "You need to speak to your sister. She's been calling me because you haven't answered her calls or texts," Adrian says, and I roll my eyes.

"Can't we just enjoy this peaceful morning? No drama, simply us having some breakfast and sitting on your balcony?" I ask and fall back into bed, the pillows cradling my head.

Adrian tickles my sides, and I squeal before I can stop myself. He keeps going until I move onto his lap and push him backward, pinning his wrists to the bed. His tongue slides over his top teeth while he lifts his hips off the bed to bring his groin against me.

The sound of my phone ringing interrupts us, and Adrian sits up to hand it back to me.

"Answer it, and then join me on the balcony," he says and gives me one last kiss before lifting me off him and walking away. I stare down at my sister's name and sigh as I hit Answer.

"What do you want, Nova?" I ask, misdirecting my anger, which I quickly realize. "Sorry," I add, but she doesn't say anything at first.

"Do you know how worried we were? You don't speak to us and then, this morning, we see a photo of you and Adriana Romana making your relationship public? Are you kidding me?" she screams into the phone, making me hold it away from my ear.

"Would you calm down?"

"Were you fired?" she asks next, and I play with the hem of Adrian's shirt.

"Yes, but it's quite a surprise really, considering I was only hired because our father bribed them to," I reply and get out of bed to walk into the bathroom.

"You found out," she says, and I stop dead in my tracks.

She knew...

It feels like she just stabbed me in the back and stomach with two separate knives.

I hang up without giving her another chance to speak.

All of them knew.

This betrayal runs deeper than I thought it did.

Tears flood my eyes before I sink to the floor, trying to fight the pain, but it's useless. It doesn't stop until it reaches my heart and spreads through my bloodstream.

"No. No more," I scold myself and stand up, my gaze shifting to my tear-stained face. Anxiety creeps into my chest, but I wipe my tears and brush my teeth to give myself something else to focus on.

My sister knew. My father did it. And my mother most likely knew, too.

"Remember, be glad you got this job. It took you forever to find one."

"Your father may baby you and hand-feed you as if you were still a child, but I won't."

I didn't see it when she said these things to me, but, suddenly, it's crystal clear. She didn't want me to be glad I got the job, she just didn't want me to fuck up the opportunity my father paid for. And she meant he babies and hand-feeds me because of the job opportunity he bought me. I almost laugh. At least my mother gave me hints. My sister didn't tell me a thing. The one person I thought I could count on to always be honest with me, no matter how much it hurt, lied to me.

Adrian's on the balcony when I join him. A croissant rests on the plate in front of him, another on the plate next to his. A cup of orange juice is in front of each, and I move over to him to wrap my arms around him from behind, placing a dozen kisses on the right side of his face. His hand lifts to my arm so his fingers can snake around it. His lips brush over it before he tilts his head to bring them to mine. I kiss him back, enjoying the warmth of his mouth.

"You need to eat something," he says, so I sit down next to him, taking a bite of the food he bought me. "I'm sorry I didn't make breakfast, but I wanted you to actually have something to eat," he explains with a soft laugh, and I smile at him.

Adrian leans toward me, his hand grabbing mine on the table.

"I may not be able to cook, but I can do laundry, empty the dishwasher or wash dishes, take out the trash, wipe the floors, whatever needs doing."

I give him a confused look, so he decides to elaborate.

"If you go back to England, you're right, we'll hardly see each other, and I don't want that. I want to fall asleep every night with you in my arms and wake up with you draped across my chest. I stop chewing as soon as the words sink in, barely reminding myself to keep my mouth closed.

"Adrian—" I start, but he cuts me off.

"I'm sorry, Nevaeh, but I'm not done. Give me one more chance to finish explaining."

It's ridiculous how sweet he is to me. It's something I always realize in moments like these, but it's also something that'll never not make me fall even harder for him.

I don't deserve him.

"We can do it on a trial basis. *If* it doesn't work out, then we will find a different solution for you to stay here. When it does work, well, then it works," he continues with an adorable grin.

"May I speak now?" I ask, and he apologizes again before assuring me he's finished.

His offer swims around in my mind, and the fact that I have a clear answer already should be alarming, but it feels strangely peaceful. Whenever we're together, through all the bad and the good, I feel invincible. He makes me feel like we can get through anything and find happiness at the end of the dark tunnel.

"You want to live with me?" I ask instead of answering because I can't wrap my head around it yet.

"More than I've wanted anything in a long time," he replies, squeezing my hand where it rests on the table. "When you told me you had no other choice but to move back to England yesterday, I felt like somebody knocked all the air out of my lungs. And when you told me you didn't want to go back, I knew there was only one way that'd make us both happy. So, what do you say? Move in with me?" he asks, a nervous laugh slipping past his lips once he's done talking.

I stand up to straddle his lap and hug him tightly.

"You're going to be sick of me within a week," I mumble into his neck, making him chuckle.

"Yeah, probably. Damn, I didn't think about this," he says, but when I lean back to look at his face, the biggest, most teasing grin rests on his lips. "You're the first woman I've ever fallen for, the only woman I ever want to fall for, and there isn't a doubt in my mind that I want this. The only reason I didn't suggest it yesterday is because I didn't want to overwhelm you before we went to the event. But it's a new day, and I still need an answer," he reminds me, and I lean forward to kiss him all over the face.

"I want to move in, but only if you'll let me cover half the rent. I was dependent on my parents' money for too long. I don't want to be dependent on you that way, too," I explain, and he gives me an understanding look.

"No." I frown, but he merely takes my wrist to place a kiss on it. "I'm a millionaire, *mon ange*. I am not taking a cent of your money. When you get your new job, you can take whatever you would have chipped in and place it in a savings account. A safety net in case of anything," he says, but my face falls in the same way his does.

A safety net for what? In case we move in together and we don't work out, after all?

The thought is ridiculous, but just because I'm already planning a future with him doesn't mean he's going to feel this way about me for the rest of his life. He doesn't want me to regret anything, so he's encouraging me to save my money in case we change our minds or... fall out of love. I almost shudder and burst into very irrational tears at the thought.

"Sounds fair?" he asks with a firm expression, and, although I keep frowning, I nod. "Good." Tears jump into my eyes before I can stop them, making his features soften. "I." He starts and kisses me. "Love." *Kiss*. "You." Kiss over kiss follows until I giggle, wiggling on his lap and making him smile, too.

I wish we could stay like this forever, not give a damn about the rest of the world, but I have to find a job and get my life together. I have to confront my family about the shit they pulled. I have to find a way to get rid of this bubble of anxiety lingering in my chest because I'll never truly feel at peace if I simply ignore it.

Adrian has to confront his grief, too. He has to figure out a way to deal with having seen his mother. He has to find a way to regain balance before the season restarts in a month.

Too much is on the line.

Our mental well-being.

His first championship title.

Our happiness.

CHAPTER 8

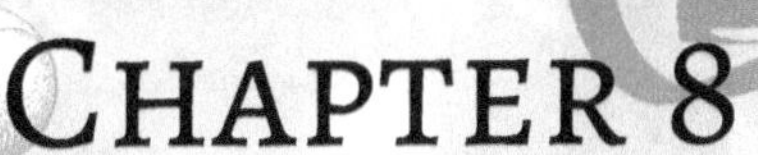

Nevaeh

"Tell me why I'm more nervous for this than I am before my actual races," Cameron Kion says as we all get ready for the biggest Mario Kart competition the world has ever seen.

Scarlette, Julián, Chiara, Leonard, Gabriel, Val, Cameron, Elijah, James, Damian, Adrian, and I are all sitting in front of the massive television my best friend and her fiancée have in their living room. Each of us has a remote, and we're all connected through the online multiplayer thing Adrian and Cameron set up. In order to play all together, we had to bring two more screens here so that four of us can see on the big screen, another four on the smaller one to the left, and the remaining three can watch on the screen to the right.

"I'm going to destroy all of you. I've been playing Mario Kart since before I could walk," I announce, and Adrian flashes me a bright smile in response while Scar, Cameron, and Val burst into laughter, Gabriel, Elijah, and James chuckle, and Leonard and Julián give me an unimpressed quirk of their brows.

"Cocky woman. No wonder we're perfect for each other," Adrian says and kisses my cheek without a care in the world.

It's been a few days since we made our relationship public. My parents have been ridiculous about messaging and calling every chance they get, but my sister has respected the boundary I've put in place, which is something, at least. Val almost got up and hunted Lincoln and my father down to "bring them excruciating pain in a way they've never felt before," but I managed to redirect her focus by asking her to help me find another job.

We were looking and applying all day, even to jobs that have nothing to do with journalism or sports, but I'll take anything right now to make some money and regain my independence.

One position I applied for today would be an amazing job opportunity.

Official photographer for the Alfa Adrenalina F1 team.

I probably wouldn't have to write any articles, which means the whole bias thing my old job was worried about wouldn't be an issue, and I could do what I love for a living. Take photos. Capture moments that will be written into history. Make people feel everything through a single picture.

This afternoon, I sent in my portfolio, along with the work I've already done for the F1 teams. Whether my father paid *Griffin Sports* to hire me and the teams to let me write the articles doesn't matter when it comes to the positive attention they received. A lot of people, the majority of them, loved my work. They adored how much closer to the drivers they felt by getting an inside scoop like never before. And I've always followed every rule of the NDA the teams made me sign in case I witnessed anything I wasn't supposed to, which I never did anyway. They were too careful and I never snooped around.

Since my dad doesn't know I applied for this position, I'm also not worried about them giving me the job, if they decide to do so, because of him. Well, that's a lie. I think I'll always be worried about that now, but I'm not *as* worried.

"Should we do a cup, or should we do races?" Valentina asks, wiggling in her seat from excitement. Chase looks up at his mom when she talks, but Adrian pets the dog's head until he's wagging his tail from excitement.

About ninety percent of the people in this room are extremely competitive, my boyfriend and best friend perhaps the most out of everyone, so I almost feel bad that I'm about to crush all of their hopes of winning. I know this game too well. I know which bike to choose, which setup, how to drift perfectly in the corners. I know this game like the back of my hand, and I'm going to win.

But I do feel a little bad.

A very, very little bit.

"I love the determination on your face, but you won't beat me, Nevaeh," Adrian says, leaning toward me to whisper, "And if you do, I'll let you drive my car home." Excitement replaces the smugness I was feeling before.

"You haven't let me drive your car yet," I point out after he places a soft kiss on my cheek.

"Well, mostly because we were hiding our relationship, so we couldn't risk being seen, but I love my car, and you drove the Velocità Rossa SUV like a person who has lives to spare," he says, making my jaw drop dramatically.

"I did *not*," I reply, but he gives me a look that says "come on." "Well, guess what, I can drive however I want in this game." I turn to my screen without giving him another glance. James is chuckling at our conversation, clearly having overheard everything, but Adrian merely nudges his shoulder before focusing on the game as well.

"Nevs, I hope we can still be friends after I make you eat your words," Val says, and I shoot her one last smirk before we get to choosing our vehicles.

Five minutes later, the countdown numbers appear on the screens, all of us inching closer to the screens like it'll help in any way.

If anyone had asked me a year ago if I'd ever see myself competing in a Mario Kart competition with seven motorsport racers, I'd have laughed.

Now? Now, I'm ready to follow through on what I said and win this race.

James and Adrian have a bad start and can't drive at first while all the rest of us shoot forward and into the first corner of the track they chose. My boyfriend lets out a "FUCK" that makes James smack him upside the back of his head for swearing in front of his kid. But Damian doesn't care at all. He's holding the extra remote Valentina gave him, sitting in her lap and shaking it like it'll do anything.

Val is ahead of me, and Chiara is right next to me, with the rest of our friends behind us, but in a matter of two more corners, I overtake her by drifting longer and more on the inside line. She mumbles something in French that I'm pretty sure are curse words, but I don't celebrate just yet.

Val attacks me with everything she gets. Green shells, red shells, bananas, anything at all. I'm dreading the fact that one of them is probably about to get a blue shell, so I keep scanning the screens to make sure I see it before it happens. The blue shell only targets the first person, so I'll have to be second when anyone gets it.

Right as we cross the line to go for the last lap, Adrian gets a blue shell. I don't even have to see it because I hear his quiet "Aha." He releases it at the same time I release the forward button to slow down, letting Val overtake me.

"Why did you do that?" she asks, frantic, but the blue shell comes into view a second later, taking her out.

I chuckle to myself while she lets out a gasp as Gabriel, Leonard, Julián, Scar, and Chiara overtake her. Adrian, James, Cameron, and Elijah were too busy fighting each other with everything they got to have made it very far to the front, so I hardly have competition during the last lap before I make it over the finish line in first place, the rest of my friends behind.

"That was sneaky, Nevaeh. God," Val complains once she's done, too.

"Sneaky or strategic?" I challenge as I face her, and, even though I can tell she tries to fight it, she cracks a smile anyway. "I told you I'd win. I tried to warn you."

"Let's go again," is all she replies while Gabriel nuzzles his face into the crook of her neck until she giggles. I catch James' face fall a little before he turns his attention back to the screen, his jaw muscles flexing. Adrian gives my knee a squeeze, probably to make me look away.

"Later," he says in French, and I almost pat myself on the back for knowing that word.

"What happened to you, anyway? How did you end up in last place?" I ask, and he glares playfully at me.

"It was James' fault. His bad start made me have a bad start, like a domino effect," he says, so James smacks his best friend's arm and frowns at him.

"Don't blame me for your lack of skill," he complains. "And how were we all beaten by someone who has no experience racing in real life?" James asks, so everyone turns their attention my way for a moment.

I simply smile at all of them, and they shake their heads before going back to their own conversations. My attention shifts to Leonard and Chiara, who are discussing something about their daughter who is currently with Leonard's parents. Then to Cameron and Elijah, who share a sweet kiss and smile, clearly unbothered about their low results in the race. Lastly, I take in Scar and Julián, who are teasing each other about their results.

People say you can't choose your family. They say the ones you share blood with are the ones you're meant to call "family." But I think they're wrong. Family is blood, yes, but it's also *this*. The group of people sitting here with me, enjoying an evening of laughter and happiness. I didn't *choose* them either. They came into my life, and each of them took their own little piece of my heart, but I do *choose* to see them as the family I want more than anything. People who love you without manipulating and lying to you. People who fight for your happiness and don't tear it away from you. People who support you unconditionally, even if you choose a path they wouldn't have chosen themselves.

"You okay, beautiful?" Adrian asks, nudging my chin with the back of his fingers.

"Yeah, I really am."

We played for another hour and a half, most of the races won by me until Adrian took me on his lap and started distracting me so other people could win.

My boyfriend stayed true to his word, too, so I'm currently behind the wheel of his bright-red Velocità Rossa sports car, singing along to one of Kane Brown's songs as we make our way to... our apartment.

When we reach his floor, I stop dead in my tracks at the sight of Aileen leaning against the front door of the apartment. Adrian gives me a confused look, but I don't give him an explanation before I make my way toward her. Tears flood her eyes, causing my heart to skip a beat.

I swear, I had no idea, she signs, and I almost let out an audible breath. A wave of relief washes over me as I pull her into a hug. *I would have told you,* she adds once we step out of the hug.

That's why they didn't tell you, I point out, and she nods a few times in agreement.

I'm so sorry. I can't imagine how you must feel, Aileen signs. Her eyes shift to my boyfriend, who is now standing next to us with a very confused expression. When he catches me looking at him, a small, comforting smile slips onto his lips.

"Can you tell her it's nice to finally meet her and that she's more than welcome to come inside? I don't want her to have to stay out here," Adrian says, so I translate the words for Aileen, and she offers him a grateful, teary-eyed smile. He unlocks the door and brings his hand to my face to briefly caress my cheek.

For the record, he is smoking hot, and I fully support this relationship as long as he keeps making you glow with happiness, Aileen signs as we walk inside, and I let out a small laugh.

I'm not glowing, I argue, making her cock an eyebrow.

Please. The sun doesn't even shine as brightly as you do when you look at him. A blush settles on my cheek, catching Adrian's attention.

"What? What did she say?" he asks with a smile.

"She said you're smoking hot," I say and sign at the same time. Aileen's eyes go wide, but I add, *What? You did say that. It wasn't a lie.*

Yeah, but it wasn't the whole truth either, she points out, but I merely press a kiss to her cheek, reveling in the fact that at least one person from the family I thought I knew didn't betray me.

Can I get you something to drink? Water? Tea? I ask to change the subject.

Maybe some tea, chamomile? I give her a small nod before attempting to make my way to the kitchen. Adrian steps in front of me so I run into him, his hands moving to my hips to hold me steady. I laugh as I look up at him while he stares down at me.

Aileen is right.

No star burns as brightly as I do for my moon.

"Where are you going?" I furrow my brows at him.

"To make Aileen some tea?"

"I'll make it so you can talk to her. Would you like some as well?" I almost snort.

"I could use something stronger," I reply, and a deep chuckle vibrates off his chest.

"I'll bring you exactly what you like," he says and gives my forehead a brief kiss before skipping into the kitchen.

This man...

I laugh to myself before turning to Aileen and leading her onto the balcony. We sit down, the view of the sea clear and beautiful.

I can't believe I'll get to see this every night.

How did you know where to find me? I ask after a few moments. Aileen pulls her lips into a thin line.

Adrian gave Nova his address in case of an emergency. I don't think I'll ever get used to how much he loves me or how thoughtful he is. *I got into a big fight with her, even said that I'd break up with her,* Aileen goes on, her eyes drifting to the sea.

No, Aileen, please tell me it wasn't because of me, I beg, but I can read on her face that I was the cause.

She kept something huge from me, something that had a horrible effect on you. If I can't trust her to be honest with me, what can I trust?

I don't want to have to be the one to defend my sister right now. She doesn't deserve me stepping in and seeing things from her side, but, in order to save her relationship with Aileen, I have to.

She didn't tell you because she knew you'd never lie to me. This was Dad's way of 'helping me,' and, while I can't forgive him, I understand why he did it. None of the places I applied to wanted me, so he thought he'd push the odds in my favor using the one thing I wanted to get away from: his money. Explaining it brings a wave of deep anger forward, one I haven't been addressing because I wanted to focus on how happy I am with Adrian. *His intentions were good, even if it was exactly what I didn't want.*

His intentions don't justify his actions, Nevaeh. You have every right to be upset with him, Aileen signs.

Her validating my anger makes me feel a lot less like I'm overreacting. Because that's exactly what my father would say I'm doing.

Adrian steps outside, slipping a cup of tea toward Aileen and a good, German beer toward me.

"Come on, you really think I don't know my woman?" he says when I give him a shocked look. He hands me the beer, and I grin at him.

Adrian, sit, please. I'd like to grill you to learn about your intentions with my Nevaeh, Aileen signs.

"Aileen can read lips, so you can talk normally," I assure him after I'm done translating what she said.

"Your Nevaeh? Alright, how do I make her my Nevaeh in your mind?" he asks as he settles down in the seat at the head of the table. Aileen smiles at him before leaning her head back to think. Adrian gives me an amused wink before concentrating on her again.

If your intentions are pure, I'll allow for a chance to change my perspective, she signs, and I translate again. He looks away to shake his head.

"That depends. What do you mean by 'pure'?"

"Oh no, I don't want to be a part of this conversation," I say and sign, and they both laugh.

"If by 'pure' you mean honest, loving, and willing to do anything to make her happy, then yes, I have only pure intentions. However, if you mean 'pure' in the sexual way, then it's a big no, unless, of course, Nevaeh says otherwise." Aileen reads his lips closely, disbelief on her face.

Oh, he's one of the good ones, she signs and takes a sip of her tea as I tell Adrian what she said. *But let's get one thing straight. You hurt Nevaeh, and I'll kick your ass.*

It's an empty threat because Aileen is the sweetest and most non-violent person on planet Earth, but Adrian doesn't know that, so his cheeks go a little red once I'm done translating.

"If I hurt her, you have my blessing to rip me a new one," he replies, and both of them grin, bonding over their love for me.

I can't help but join them.

Chapter 9

Nevaeh

Aileen falls asleep on the couch, and Adrian takes my hand to pull me into the bedroom. He gently closes the door, then wraps his arms around me from behind before I can move to the bed. Warmth radiates off him and onto me, a sigh slipping past my lips in response. His mouth moves to my neck where he places soft kisses that make my head spin.

"I'm sorry for all the drama," I say as he trails his lips over my shoulder, brushing them slightly over my scar. I love it when he does that. It's as if he's acknowledging it's there while reminding me how special he thinks the ripped skin is.

"Don't be," he mutters against me. I run my hands over his where they are on my stomach. "Being a part of your life, chaos and calm, I want it all. I want to get swept up in everything you offer and be there at the end of the day to remind you that when everything feels rushed, I will be your brake to slow things down," he says, and I smile at his racing reference. I spin around in his arms to put my fingers on the back of his head.

"You *are* my brake," I reply, his hands moving to the top of my ass as I say the words. "And I need you to do something for me," I add, watching confusion flit over his face.

"Anything and everything."

"I have to talk to my family. Ignoring them won't make any of my problems go away. If all I can get is closure, I need to get answers to the millions of questions I have," I explain, and he nods thoughtfully.

"We can go whenever you're ready. I'll be by your side."

"Thank you." Adrian leans forward, his nose brushing against mine before he hovers his mouth over mine.

"Take a bath with me," he whispers as his lips graze over mine, sending a thrill through me.

Adrian steps into the bathroom with my hand clasped in his. He removes his shirt in one swift move, then his pants before moving toward his enormous bathtub. As he bends over to turn on the water, I let out a low whistle.

"What a perfect view," I drawl, and he starts shaking his ass for me, making me fall to the ground with laughter. He joins me until we're both trying to catch our breaths. "I was trying to be genuine," I manage to croak out, but I haven't found a way to compose myself again. Adrian rolls onto his back, his hand moving to his chest as more laughter falls off it.

"My stomach is cramping," he says a moment later, and, for some reason, it makes me laugh more. He sits up to shake his head, and I finally wipe away the happy tears from under my eyes.

Adrian's face turns serious as his gaze shifts to my clothes, his bottom lip moving between his teeth.

"'Undress, Nevaeh,' yeah, I know," I say, imitating him and making him chuckle. "You're so bossy," I add, so he smirks at me.

"You love it," he reminds me.

I remove my clothes before crawling over to where he is on the floor. My legs move to each side of him before my fingers slide into his hair.

"As long as you keep respecting me," I reply and smile. Adrian would never disrespect me. He worships me, and I him.

"That will never fade," he promises, his hands moving to my hips while he does his best to only look into my eyes.

I grab his chin between my thumb and index finger like he usually does with me, tilting his head down so his gaze drops as well. He moves his hands upward to my breast at the same moment I realize the bathtub is getting too full.

"Oh shit!" I exclaim and stand up to turn the water off.

Adrian gets up too while I dip my toe into the water to check the temperature. Perfect.

"Wait," he says before I can get in, his fingers moving to the stretch marks on my hips. I feel my insecurities wash over me as he traces the indents on my skin. "You know, I've never paid much attention to the small things on a woman's body before. The way it responds to the slightest touch, how all of its birthmarks, scars, and stretch marks are arranged, or even in which direction hair grows, but with you, I want to study it all. You're so beautiful, Nevaeh," Adrian says, his eyes shifting from where he is touching me to my face.

"I love you with everything I am," is the only thing I reply because it's the one thing dominating all other thoughts in my mind.

Adrian beams at me before letting go and stepping out of his boxers. He settles down behind me so my back touches his chest and his knees stand out of the water on either side of me. I place my hands on top of them while his move under my breasts.

We stay like this for a while, talking about everything and nothing until silence fills the room. Adrian caresses different parts of my body, feeling it underneath his fingertips as if he wants to memorize it all.

"Why do I love this so much?" he asks, his voice low and quiet as it hits my ear. I run my fingers over a tiny scar he has on the right side of his left knee and lean my head back to look up at him.

"Because it's intimate in a different way than you were used to in the past." He gives me a confused look, brows furrowed and lips turning a bit downward. "You know the intimacy of sex, but I don't think you'd ever experienced the intimacy of sharing emotional stories while simply being naked with each other, soaking in our own filth, before I came along," I say, and he chuckles against my back, vibrations rushing through me.

"This *is* very intimate, and I've never done it with anyone except you, but it feels like more than that. It feels like I'm connected to you this way, like you're glued to my chest and I don't ever want to let go," he says, making my heart do tiny flips.

"I know it sounds silly," he mumbles a moment later, but I shake my head while turning around in the bathtub until my legs straddle his and I'm on his lap.

"It's not silly at all, *mein Mond*. It's beautiful, and I want you to know you can always share your feelings with me. You might think they're silly, but I happen to love them," I say and lean forward to press my lips to his. He stops me right before I can do so, a serious expression on his face.

"I'm so scared, Nevaeh," he admits, and I furrow my brows in confusion. He evades my gaze and sucks in a sharp breath. Tears fill his eyes, so I take his face between my hands.

"Of what, my love? Talk to me," I beg, and his eyes shift back to me as he clearly fights his tears.

"Of making you leave me."

Pain is laced in his words, and I lean away from him in surprise. He lets out a frustrated groan when the tears drop.

"Fuck, see, this is why I've avoided getting attached to anyone romantically. One mistake is all it takes. One fuck up, and I'll lose you, and I'm surprisingly good at messing things up," he rants, and I cross my arms in front of my chest with a scolding frown. His eyes drop to my boobs, now pushed together, and a little smile slips onto his face. "That's not fair. I can't keep warning you when you do that," he says and reaches out to run his index finger over my left nipple. I would enjoy his touch more if his words didn't make my heart skip a beat.

"You're warning me? Adrian, I know who you are. I know you've been hurt, and we've been through enough for me to understand that things won't be easy. But I love you beyond all rationality. Beyond all words. I love you *endlessly*. In every universe."

He looks away, but I force his gaze back to my face as I place my thumb on one of his cheeks and my index finger on the other. The approach I was taking wasn't right, which is why my next words take a different route.

"Your mom leaving was not your fault. You are not the reason why she abandoned your family, Adrian, and I won't let you blame yourself any longer." This hits the nail right on the head for him, I can see it in his eyes as they grow softer from my words.

"What if she left because I wasn't the son she wanted? Because I was too loud and didn't listen?" he asks, but I shake my head again.

"I have never met a man in my entire life who is as kind, compassionate, selfless, funny, and loving as you are. Cecilia left because that woman is cold-hearted and cruel, and she was incapable of realizing you would become a better man than every single other one in the world. Call me biased, but I've experienced being loved by you first-hand, and there is nothing more beautiful than the way your heart has enveloped mine to keep it safe."

Adrian hangs onto my every word, his fingers digging into my thighs like he wants to make sure I don't go anywhere.

"Is that what my love feels like for you?" he asks.

"Yeah, it is, my love." His tears have finally dried, and he grins at me again.

"Kiss me," Adrian says, so I cock a brow.

"So now you want my kiss again?" I ask and cross my arms once more, making him smirk.

"I want more than a kiss," he admits and pulls me closer by my hips.

CHAPTER 10
Adrian

NEVAEH LOOKS TERRIFIED. THIS is the first time she will see her parents and sister since everything happened, and I can't imagine how anxious she is right now. The pressure to make up with her family while fighting her anger keeps making her suck in a sharp breath. Her legs are bouncing up and down in her seat, her gaze stuck on the movie she's trying to watch. Mine has been on her for the past five minutes, but she hasn't noticed my inquiring gaze.

She's too nervous.

I slide my hand onto her thick thigh, squeezing it until her head falls backward against the seat. Her eyelids flutter shut as she pushes her legs together, her bottom lip slipping between her teeth. I'm trying to distract her from what's bothering her, but I have to remind myself that we're surrounded by other passengers on the plane. I can't lose my composure and *really* make her forget about the rest of the world. Right?

No, fuck no.

I'm not slipping my fingers inside her on a plane with other people around.

Now, a private jet would be a different situation.

It makes me think of a conversation I had with Leonard years ago when we were on his private jet.

"Fuck me, this is so nice," I say, stretching my long legs out in front of me in Leonard's private jet. "I've never been on a private plane before, but I could definitely get used to this," I add, smirking at one of the stewardesses as she walks by. She blushes immediately, looking over her shoulder at me as she walks away. "Definitely," I repeat, mumbling more to myself than speaking to Leonard.

"Do you ever turn off that... that part of yourself?" he asks, pointing at all of me. I cock a curious brow.

"Are you jealous?"

"Of what?"

"My attention drifting to someone else. You can have it all, mate, but you're gonna have to entertain me for the next ten hours if you want my undivided attention." I cross my arms in front of my chest, my eyes staring directly into his.

"Nah, go for it. But I should warn you, the bathroom is not the most comfortable of places to fuck," he says, and I straighten out my back immediately as a bright smile covers my face. Regret fills his eyes.

"And how the hell do you know that?" I ask, the toe of my shoe poking his shin. Leonard stays silent, so I kick him again. "I have ten hours and you have limited space to avoid me, so you might as well fess up." He leans back in his seat, crossing his legs over one another as he watches me for a moment.

"Everywhere in here. Especially where you're sitting." All amusement leaves me.

"Please tell me you had it cleaned."

He shakes his head with a hint of a smile touching the corners of his mouth. The color drains from my face as I undo my seatbelt to stand up.

"That's very unhygienic, Leonard. What the fuck?" He bursts into laughter at my disgusted face, the sound such a surprise, I freeze in place to just stare at him. "Did you just—" I cut off, disbelief filling me. "I need to sit back down, but I don't know where," I say, which only makes him laugh even harder. "Stop, you're scaring me."

"The whole jet got a deep clean, kiddo, relax," he says right as Val steps out of the washroom.

"This bathroom is huge! It's bigger than the one I have at Aunt Carolina's house," she says, smiling to herself before directing her happy expression at me.

"Leonard and I were just talking about the bathroom actually." It's his turn to kick me under the table then. "Ow. Dickhead," I say, rubbing my leg and glaring at him.

The memory makes me smile. Leonard can be such a hardass, but I'm the kryptonite to his Superman-type of impenetrable wall he built around his heart to protect himself.

My thoughts are interrupted when I notice Nevaeh taking deep breaths to calm herself.

"Spiraling will make it worse, beautiful," I say as I use the back of my hand to brush her hair off her right shoulder. I place my index on her pulse point on her throat, feeling her accelerated heartbeat.

"I'm scared. I don't want to face my family, even though I have to. I'm so sick of the drama."

Her mother, who's been fighting with her about her career and life choices for months. Her father, who wasn't home a lot when she grew up but has been trying to make up with her in the worst ways. And her sister, who's been lying to Nevaeh for months.

"Listen, *mon ange*, I know this is going to be difficult as hell, but I will be right with you the entire time," I say, my fingers caressing the skin on her neck before my thumb pushes her chin up and tilts her head. Her lips are mere centimeters from mine now, and I barely hold back from kissing her. "And you'll feel a hundred times better once you get closure."

Part of me doesn't want her to make up with her family so she doesn't have to deal with the shit they keep throwing at her head, but most of me wants her to feel complete again. That only comes from figuring out how to forgive the betrayal.

Her eyes soften from my words.

"I need you to know something," she whispers, and I can't resist bringing my lips to hers once. She tastes like coconut, always so sweet and full of flavor, and I let out a little groan.

It takes all of my willpower to pull away again, especially when Nevaeh flashes me a shy smile.

"Tell me," I say when she doesn't speak again.

"I've found the real meaning of family in you."

Fuck me.

Fuck me, fuck me, fuck me.

I've found it in her, too, and it still scares me. I already laid my fears bare for her a few days ago in the bathtub. I've told her everything, so I don't *have to* say it back. She's not expecting me to, I can see it in her eyes.

I think I'd be really lost in her forever if I said it back now. It's not happening. Nope. There's no way.

"I've found it in you, too."

Nevaeh's eyes light up, and she puckers her lips, telling me she wants a kiss. I wrap mine around hers, unable to deny her a single thing. I wonder if I'll ever feel like I've given her everything she deserves. Probably not, but I plan on trying until the day I die.

"You're so corny with me," she says, and I let out a snort that makes her eyes sparkle with amusement.

She didn't have to point out how cheesy I am. It's a fact I am well aware of and struggling with. Struggling because I love the way she reacts to it and because it goes against my very nature. Well, it used to go against my nature. Before Nevaeh.

My heart is racing like it does every time I look at her. It's telling me, "She's perfect for you. You were made for her, and she for you. You've found your future. Don't fuck it up. I can't beat properly without her anymore."

I wasn't looking for her. I didn't want a relationship that led to feelings, which in turn led to moving in together, marriage, babies, and growing old together. Now it's all I want, but only with Nevaeh. Only ever with Nevaeh.

I finally let go of her face and turn to my tiny television, unable to process all of the emotions whirling around in my heart and chest.

"You're too dangerous," I say in French, shutting my eyes. I want to give my mind a moment to catch up with everything I'm feeling because of Nevaeh.

Then again, there isn't enough time in this world to process *everything*.

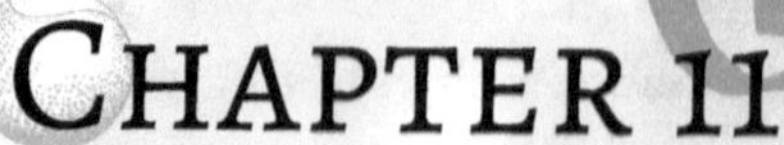

CHAPTER 11
Nevaeh

THERE IS NO INCENTIVE big enough to make me knock on this door. No part of my body is capable of ringing the bell either. Flying to England to confront my parents and sister was my idea, but I regret it now.

Luckily, Adrian's fist connects with the door for me when he senses I won't be able to do it. Aileen is on the other side of me, a nervous expression on her face. All three of us decided to fly here this morning because we knew we couldn't avoid this forever. Well, Adrian only came to be my rock even though he has responsibilities, but he didn't accept that as the reason not to come, because I'm "more important."

I wanted to fall hopelessly in love with someone who I could love in every way. Not just as a partner, but also as a friend, as an inspiration, as a favorite person.

I wanted the kind of love where you fall and fall and fall, never hitting the ground.

I wanted the kind of love where your partner is right there beside you, holding your hands as you drift among the clouds.

I wanted the kind of love that isn't easy but oh so worth it.

Now, I have it all.

Mama opens the door, pulling me back to reality. Confusion and surprise jump onto her features as she looks each of us in the eyes. Her gaze lingers on Adrian before she takes a step back, anger consuming her when she looks at me again.

"Du hast ganz schöne Nerven hier aufzutauchen, Nevaeh. Nachdem du unsere Anrufe und Nachrichten ignoriert hast, tauchst du einfach hier auf? Weißt du wie besorgt wir waren?" she yells at me in German, and Adrian immediately takes a step forward, his protective instinct taking over.

"I don't know what you said, but I suggest you calm yourself before I lose my nerve. You've put Nevaeh through enough, and she might be too nice to say something, but I can be a dick, especially when it comes to protecting the woman I love. Now, with all due respect, back off and start apologizing by inviting us in," Adrian says calmly, and I keep my jaw from dropping at the very last second.

The parent pleaser in me wants to tell him he took it too far, but the version of myself I've become since moving out of their home, since finding Adrian and a family who loves me in a healthier way, wants to kiss Adrian for defending me.

Mama takes a surprised step back, and my eyes shift to Nova. She is behind our mother now, her shoulders sinking as she walks toward us. Anger ripples through me, so I take Adrian's hand for support.

"I don't want to speak to you or see you. I want you to leave," Mama says, making my heart ache.

"I'm not here to speak to you," I say, watching my sister sign something to Aileen before they move into the kitchen.

"Good, because there is nothing you can say to make up for what you did."

What I did? What about what you did?

"Okay," is the only thing I say before Adrian pulls me close to him, and we move past Mama and into the living room. I don't want to fight with her anymore. She gave up on me long ago.

There is no need to fight for a relationship when she isn't ready to speak things through and work it out together.

Papa lifts his eyes and lowers his phone as soon as he hears us come in.

"Nevaeh," he says and gets up, his hands reaching for me.

"I'm not comfortable with you touching me right now," I say, so he stops dead in his tracks.

"Let me explain, honey, please. In private," Papa begs, and I'm so taken aback by the genuine regret and hurt in his eyes, I feel my heart sink.

"Okay."

I signal for him to follow me to my room, but Adrian holds onto my hand before I can leave.

"If he does anything to upset you, call out and I will come," he says and shoots my father a warning glare. I step on my toes to plant a kiss on his jaw before walking up the stairs, feeling my father close behind me.

Anxiety has my hands shaking, but I'm not planning on starting a fight or confrontation. I came here to get answers, not to yell at my father. I still hate confrontation. It makes me feel like I could throw up, so I'll try and keep this conversation as calm as possible. And if that doesn't work, I guess I'll feel sick to my stomach while I scream at him. But I need to resolve this so I can finally have some peace and fewer battles with my father.

I shut the door and turn to him, raising my hands to tell him to stay quiet.

"After everything, the nights I cried and told you I needed to get out of here, that I needed to start my life without your influence, how could you do that to me? How could you let me think I achieved something when you were behind it all along? How could you lie to me for months?"

All of the anger I haven't been able to let out is coming through in the form of tears. Papa settles down on my old bed, rubbing his face with his hands out of frustration.

"Listen, Nevaeh, I know this might seem like the biggest betrayal of your life, but all I wanted was to help you. You didn't get a job anywhere else and asking them to give you one in Formula One was to make sure you'd succeed. I knew Formula One would be better than—" I cut him off as pain shoots through my chest.

"Wait, wait, wait. So, not only did you bribe them to employ me, but you made sure I wouldn't get a spot in the tennis department?" Papa nods, and I involuntarily sink to the floor.

"But it was only because I could help you succeed there. In tennis, you would have been all alone, and I didn't know if you—" He cuts off, but I know where his sentence was going.

Papa stands up to move to me but stops when I speak again.

"You didn't know if I could succeed by myself," I finish for him, more tears flowing from my eyes. He nods once more. "You had no faith in me. You're my father, you're supposed to believe in me! Was I not capable enough for you either when I trained every single day of my life to become a professional tennis player? Was I not strong enough when I was healing from my injury and had to change my whole life? Was I never fucking good enough for you that you did this to me?" I take three strides toward him, pushing at his chest. "All I wanted was to start my own life." I shove him again. "Why couldn't you believe in me?" Shove. "I did everything to prove I'm worthy of creating my own happiness, why couldn't you let me try?" One last shove.

He grabs me by the shoulders and shakes me.

"I did! You were getting nowhere, and I couldn't watch another one of your dreams die without being able to help you, okay? It was selfish, but I didn't have it in me, Nevaeh. It was hard enough once, no matter how strong you were throughout. I would have done anything and everything to make sure you would succeed in journalism, and I'm not sorry because look where it has gotten you! You made a name for yourself. They can't stop bringing you up in every meeting I'm in."

He stops to squeeze my arms.

"I gave you the tools to make a scooter, and you build a fucking car. Please realize that no matter what I did to help, you're the one who made it all by yourself." His rant comes to an end before he steps away and takes deep breaths.

I've never seen him this frustrated with a situation, which is probably because he and I have never fought like this, and I hate it. I hate the way my heart feels like it's suffocating and the way my brain tells me his words make sense. I hate that I can't stop my hands from shaking or to stop crying.

"I love you, Nevaeh, and I'm sorry for lying to you. Forgive me. This world is a cruel place, the world of journalism included. Buying you an opportunity had nothing to do with me not believing and everything with the world denying you the chance to prove yourself," he says, but I shake my head.

"No, Papa, you crossed a line. You made me become everything I hate. A nepotism baby. I don't have the right to something just because you have the money to buy it for me. I would have waited for another job opportunity. I would have kept trying, but you took that journey from me by—by hand-feeding me everything." I hate using my mother's words, but they do make sense now. "It's like Lincoln getting his F1 seat. You gave it to him because George is your best friend. Money doesn't equal being deserving. Money is a privilege." He moves back over to sit on my bed.

"I don't know how to fix this. I thought I was doing something right."

"If you truly believed that, you wouldn't have hidden it from me." He nods in agreement, dropping his face in his hands again. "You made me believe I was achieving everything I'd dreamed of. I moved into a place I can no longer afford now. I lost the job on my own, I'm not saying I didn't, but I shouldn't even have had it in the first place. You do realize that now, right?"

Papa sucks in a sharp breath, fighting back tears.

"Can you tell me why you got fired? They wouldn't tell me," he says, so I settle down in front of him, fighting the shame that comes with remembering my failure.

"Well, I wasn't allowed to date a driver, and Lincoln sent them a photo of Adrian and me kissing, so I got caught, you could say," I explain, but my father furrows his brows immediately.

"What do you mean you weren't allowed to date a driver? It didn't say that in the contract they gave me to read over." My heart drops all the way into my stomach. *Cecilia.*

Another wave of nausea hits me, but I swallow it down to refocus on what's more important right now. Trying to find a way to stop being so angry with my father.

"I want to stop being so upset with you, but I think it'll take some time. I hope you can understand that," I say, so Papa grabs both my hands in his and squeezes them.

"Your happiness means everything to me. I'm sorry I hurt you, truly. I see now there are no excuses, no good enough reason. You wanted to get away from our money and make a life for yourself, and I ruined that, too. So, yes, I understand. Take as much time as you need. I won't rush you." He presses a kiss to the back of my hand, then he lets go entirely.

"Don't ever bribe anyone for me again. And don't lose faith in me. I'm your daughter. I learned how to kick life's ass from you my entire life," I say as I look into the pair of eyes he gave my sister.

"I promise I won't lie to you or bribe for you ever again," he assures me, and I let out a sigh. "Okay, now, I have to ask. You and Adrian Romana? Since when?" Papa asks after a brief moment of silence.

"Since the day I met him," I admit and smile to myself.

"So, you're in love?"

"He makes me feel more loved than I ever have before. No matter what, I come first with him. He doesn't lie or play tricks. Adrian just..." I trail off for a moment. "He's everything good in the world wrapped into one person," I finish and wipe away the remainder of my previous tears.

Papa chuckles before getting up.

"Good. If he hurts you though, I'll get him suspended from many, many races," he teases, and I shake my head with an eye roll. Papa's hand moves to my shoulder before he gives it a squeeze. "I really am sorry about everything," he repeats.

"I know." He gives me a small smile and walks out of my room.

My eyes close for a moment, but I smell Adrian before he even settles down next to me. I lean my head on his shoulder while he takes my hand to lace his fingers through mine.

"So, this is your old room, huh?" I smile before opening my eyes and tilting my head to look at him. He presses a kiss to the tip of my nose, making a blush heat up my cheeks.

"Yeah," I simply reply, and he nods while looking around the room some more. A smirk slips onto his face as he studies every corner and inch, realization filling my thoughts. "You're imagining the best places to fuck me, aren't you?" His gaze continues to flit around the room.

"I think you know the answer," he says as if it is the most obvious thing in the world.

Standing up, I pull him with me before guiding him toward my artwork.

"These were once my most prized possessions," I admit, and he switches from inspecting the one of Serena Williams to looking at me. "You know, since my injury, I haven't been able to hit a single ball, let alone pick up a racket. I used to love playing tennis, but I'm so scared nowadays, I can't bring myself to," I explain. Adrian runs his fingers over my scar while thinking of the right thing to say.

"You don't have to be ready yet, Nevaeh. Your physical wound may have healed, but it's okay for your emotional one to need a bit more time," he says, making me smile up at him.

He always manages to find the right words.

"Elena! It's nice to see you," I hear Mama say, the blood rushing out of my face.

Adrian gives me a confused look, but anger courses through me a second later when I hear Lincoln's voice. I storm past Adrian, who attempts to hold me, but I'm too strong for him to do so. My feet rush downstairs where I find the man I hate most in the entrance. His eyes go wide, but he doesn't step back as I approach him, allowing me to release some of my anger by pushing him as hard as I can.

"You backstabbing, two-faced piece of shit!" I yell, and Mama gasps in response. I ignore her as I continue my attack. "You fucking photographed me kissing Adrian so you could send it to my boss? You revolting dirtbag!"

"Nevaeh," Mama warns, putting a hand on my shoulder to stop me. Adrian moves in front of her to break the skin contact.

Lincoln takes a step back to observe the situation, but there is no remorse on his face. At best, his hazel eyes show a hint of guilt, but I couldn't care less. He deserves my anger.

"You were my best friend years ago, but you're nothing to me now. You're not my enemy, not my friend, you're nothing. I don't love you nor do I hate you. I'm indifferent about you." It's a lie because I despise him, but those words are worse than any other I could have said. Indifference has always bothered him more than my hate.

Anger grows in Lincoln's eyes, but it's not directed at me; his glare is focused on Adrian.

"This is all your fault, asshole. If you could have just stayed away, Nevaeh and I would have been happy," he states as if I'm not in front of him.

"Nevaeh has long realized all you have to offer is immaturity and chaos." Adrian is cool and relaxed, but I feel my blood boiling from anger. Lincoln stares down at me before bringing his eyes back up to my boyfriend.

"You know what? Have at it. Just remember all you're getting is my sloppy seconds." Papa grabs my hand before I can deliver a well-placed punch in Lincoln's face. Meanwhile, Adrian smirks confidently as he steps closer to Lincoln.

"You degrade Nevaeh like that one more time, and it will be the last thing you do on this planet," he says and bends down to make sure Lincoln hears every word since he's a lot taller than him. "You may have kissed her," Adrian goes on in a low voice. "But that's all you'll ever have. That, and a messy past you caused. I get everything. I get her *future*. So, I suggest you don't come near her again."

Adrian picks off an imaginary lint from Lincoln's shoulder before flicking it away.

"I've warned you before, Lincoln, that I'd do anything to get you kicked out of F1. But I doubt I have to do anything now. I wonder if Robert is going to renew your contract for next year after the shit you've pulled. You know, considering you only got your seat because of your daddy's connection to him," is the last thing Adrian says before turning to me and taking my hand. "Ready to go, *mon paradis*?" he asks.

"With you, always," I reply.

CHAPTER 12

Adrian

MY TEAM ASKED ME to test a new upgrade they made to our car, so, despite having promised Nevaeh we'll take the next two weeks of summer break to relax and move her things out of her old apartment and into ours, I dragged her with me to Maranello. Gabriel was also asked here, and Valentina came along to be around us.

She's been teaching Nevaeh everything there is to know about testing sessions while I'm in the car, and Lorenzo even gave my girlfriend permission to take as many pictures of the car while it's on the track—some even in the garage—as she wants. I gave her permission to take as many of me as she wants, too. She's taken what feels like a hundred thousand pictures over the past few days. Me with my fireproofs hanging low on my hips. Me with my racing suit fully on. Helmet on. Helmet off. Only with my balaclava. In my jeans and team shirt.

I can't help but smile every single time I catch her camera on me, but it dies out as soon as my eyes land on my sister. While Cecilia hasn't shown her face again, I still feel bad keeping this from her. She deserves to know. But she looks so happy. I don't want to ruin that.

Especially when I see the same happiness on Nevaeh's face as she smiles at Val. If all I ever got to see in this world were these looks of joy on the faces of the people I love, I could die a very happy man. Unfortunately, life has a way of destroying every good thing. And if it's not life, then it's me. I find a way to mess it up.

I swallow hard but can't bring myself to look away from Nevaeh's beautiful face.

"Adrian," my boss warns, and I realize he must have been speaking to me for a while without me hearing a single word.

"Yeah?" I ask, my gaze lifting to Lorenzo Mattia's exasperated expression. "Sorry," I add with a grimace.

"Did you hear a word I said or was your girlfriend's face more interesting?" he asks with a teasing smile, which I return.

"I know how in love you are with your wife. Don't even try to act like you don't stare at her every chance you get," I remind him, but he merely shrugs.

"That's why I don't bring her to work. I'd never get anything done." *Fair enough.* "Will you be able to focus?"

"Sir, yes, sir." I place my index and middle finger on my temple to demonstrate I'll be a good soldier now.

"You're a strange man, Mr. Romana," he says, making me snort. "I wanted you to look at this data. When you move into corner three, you lose a lot of momentum by braking too early. Don't be afraid to hit the corner a bit faster. We're trying to test how quickly the car can go now that we've made some updates on the power unit, but our results won't be conclusive until you push the car more," he says, so I nod several times, pulling on the zipper of my racing suit to put it on properly again.

"Adrian," Chloe says, waving me over to her. "I have a few ideas on how to maximize the car's performance."

She goes into detail while I listen attentively, doing my best to understand the more technical terms she's throwing at me. If Val wasn't racing for another team and was allowed to hear any of this information, I'd ask her to translate it for me. While I do understand it—mostly—she's always made things sound simpler than Chloe. My race engineer just expects me to understand everything as soon as the words leave her mouth, which I appreciate most times, but sometimes I also absolutely hate because *what the fuck?* What does any of this even mean?

"So, I'll go fast?" She frowns at me as soon as I've said it.

"You're a dumbass," she complains, shaking her head before shoving my earpiece into my hand. I handed it to her earlier because I was hearing some weird static sound whenever she spoke. "It's fixed now. Try not to break it again," she scolds, and I let my jaw drop dramatically.

"Me? I didn't do anything. I just put it in my ear," I defend, but she merely waves me off.

Daniel walks toward me, handing me my helmet and balaclava, waiting to offer me my gloves, too. He looks awfully joyful for someone who had to wake up at six this morning to fly all the way to Maranello to help me over the next few days.

"What's up with you?" I ask, giving him an unsure grin.

"Your girlfriend just showed me the most unflattering picture of you ever taken," he replies, making a shocked gasp leave me.

"No, she didn't. Nevaeh! Tell me you didn't," I say as I look around Daniel to see my woman grinning at me. "Oh, I'm going to pay you back for that later," I add, but she merely cocks an unimpressed brow at me.

"Do your worst. It's worth it," she says with a chuckle.

Oh, I'll do my worst.

"Get in the car," Daniel says, redirecting my focus. I roll my shoulders and take a deep breath as I slip my balaclava over my head.

For a moment, I stare at the helmet I spent hours designing with Val before the season began. It's orange, with music notes swirling all around it. The number eight is painted on each side, but it looks more like an infinity symbol. I think about all the times I've traced this exact symbol on Nevaeh's skin and smile to myself as I slide the helmet on.

Then, it's tunnel vision.

I slip into the car, listening to Chloe reminding me of everything I have to do during this practice run. See how the car does in the corners with the new update. Attempt to set faster lap times. Manage tire degradation at the same time because if the new update fucks with the tire lifespan, it's useless to us.

I buckle my seatbelt, feeling a bit uneasy for a reason I don't want to decipher right now. The same sensation keeps flooding me every time I get into a car these days, a deep fear of failure threatening to consume me. As much as I don't want to blame Lincoln and his words, I think they're the cause.

"You're not good enough for the trophy. Your grandfather and father were champions in their time, I used to watch them when I grew up, and you're nothing like them. You don't have what it takes to win. It's why Gabriel won last season. It's why I'll win this season. They'd be so disappointed to know you don't have what it takes. Luckily, they're too dead to watch you fuck up your second chance."

Fuck him. Fuck the fact his words have left a mark on my confidence. Fuck the world for taking my family from me.

I shake my head, pushing my grief to the back of my mind. Nevaeh made me promise I'd address my grief during this break, and I will. Once I'm out of this car, I'm taking a long vacation and sitting down to actually address my feelings for once. Therapy wasn't for me when I tried it. I know it helps a lot of people, and I'm so happy they can find a way to heal, but I've tried five separate therapists who couldn't help me. My journey working through my grief needs a different approach.

I just wish I knew what approach will help me most.

Lorenzo gives me one last thumbs-up before I head out of the garage. I probably shouldn't race while I'm feeling this way, but I have no choice now. Plus, it's not like there is anyone else on the track.

It's just me.

All alone.

In my darkness.

Fuck.

Snap out of it, Adrian.

For the first lap around the track, I go slow, warming my tires. On the second lap, I push, just like Chloe told me to. I brake later into the corner, using the momentum. The new upgrade helps a lot when it comes to a smoother exit, and on the straights, I also see improvements. When I tell Chloe that, she merely gives me an unemotional "Copy" before telling me to go for one more lap.

I hit the throttle and push the proper buttons to shift gears. Speeding over the main straight, I slow even later as my car glides through the corner, but, this time, I did it too late.

The rear slips away as I lose control, my car spinning at high speed before it hits the gravel and twists all over itself.

All I can do is tense every muscle as I flip over and over until I finally hit a barrier.

"How are you feeling?" Nevaeh says, her hands on her hips and worry in her eyes.

"I'm fine," I lie, holding the ice pack the paramedic gave me to my throbbing head.

"Perfect, if you're fine, do you mind doing a handstand and twirling twenty times in a circle for me." Both of her brows are cocked in challenge, but I can't help but snort at her words.

Using my own horrible sense of humor against me is as mean as it is hilarious.

"Do I have to do a handstand? Or can I just do the twirls?" Nevaeh frowns, and if she didn't look so worried about me, I might keep lying, but she knows me so well, she sees right through it. "My head hurts, and I'm pretty sure I bruised one of my ribs, but I'll live," I assure her, and even though she keeps frowning, she nods several times. "Come put your hands on me, Nevaeh. It'll make me feel better." That finally brings a hint of a smile back.

She lifts her hands to my face, cupping it. Her thumbs run over my cheeks, making my eyes flutter shut. It feels like the throbbing in my head is instantly dulled by the thrumming in my veins. I love Nevaeh's touch. If I didn't know better, I'd think it has a superpower. Or magic. I wonder if that's where the saying *magic touch* comes from.

"That was fucking terrifying." I nod, grabbing her wrist and leaving my eyes closed so she doesn't see the tears jumping into my eyes. Tears of fear because it will never not terrify me when things like this happen. Tears of pain because my entire body hurts. Tears of guilt because I can't begin to imagine how scared she was.

"I'm so sorry," I reply, opening my eyes to see tears have jumped into hers, too.

"It's not your fault. Chloe told me that the rear tires didn't have enough grip because they were too old. They should have told you to change them," she says, still caressing my cheeks, probably to reassure herself I'm still here. A shudder shakes my body at the realization. "Are you okay? What can I do to make you feel better?"

"You existing is everything I'll ever need."

Chapter 13
Nevaeh

NOVA HAS BEEN SILENTLY packing up my things, helping me put them in suitcases to take to Adrian's apartment. We've barely spoken since she offered to come to Monaco, but neither one of us is forcing a conversation either. The speaker in the room plays a song we both love, and she gives me a small smile, which I return with difficulty. We've always been close, but now? Now it feels like there is an entire ocean between us instead of mere meters.

Adrian and Gabriel keep walking in and out of the apartment, grabbing more things to put in the truck my boyfriend rented. Every time he walks past me, he grabs me from behind and quickly nuzzles his face into my neck to make me giggle. He's been gone for half an hour now, unpacking my clothes to bring the suitcases back for me to reuse. I don't have a lot of belongings, but it will take two trips.

"I'm sorry for lying to you, Nevi. Dad told me not to tell you, that it would protect you, but I should have said something. I'm truly sorry," Nova says after a few more moments of silence, and I lower the dress I was about to fold to look at her.

"Out of all the people in the world, I always thought you'd be the one to never lie to me. I don't trust anyone the same way I do you, which is why it hurt a lot to hear you'd betray me so easily. However, I understand now why you did it, and, honestly, I don't want to fight anymore. It's exhausting enough with Mama, and the fights with Lincoln have used up all of my energy to hold a grudge."

I chuckle at my last comment, but a strange stinging sensation shoots through my chest at the mention of his name.

"Speaking of Mama, when do you think you'll make up with her?" she asks, and I pick up the clothes again to neatly place them inside the luggage.

"When she's ready to accept I'm grown up," I reply at the same time as Valentina skips into the room. She makes her way to me with a laugh that fills my heart and wraps her arms around me, pulling me close.

"Okay, I have a big favor to ask, and you can say no, but I would absolutely love it if you said yes. Ready?" Val asks and steps back, her hands holding onto my arms while she continues to build suspension. "Would you, please, be my maid of honor for the small wedding ceremony Gabriel and I want to have in a few months?" My eyes go so wide, it feels like they're about to pop out of my head.

"Are you kidding me? Of course! You didn't even have to ask." I pull her in for another hug, barely able to contain my excitement.

"Okay, cool," Val says and wipes under her eyes to get rid of the tears that slipped from them. I feel some sting mine too, but, luckily, Adrian walks into the apartment with one of my bikini tops strapped to his head, making me laugh instead.

"What the hell are you doing?" I ask him when I see Gabriel slip past him, shaking his head while amusement plays on his features.

"We accidentally dropped it at the car, and he's been wearing it like that since he found it on our way back here," Gabriel informs us, his accent thick, and chuckles at the same time. I look at my boyfriend. He reaches for the piece of clothing and drops it in the suitcase.

"You're so weird," I tell him, but he simply grabs me by the hips and pulls me against his chest. Adrian leans down, his lips next to my ear while his hot breath sends shivers down my spine.

"Those yoga pants you're wearing are killing me, baby. Please tell me we're almost done so I can take them off and bury myself in my heaven," he begs, and I forget how to breathe. Pleasure coils in my stomach at the way he looks at me.

"Yeah, we're almost done. A few more items, then we can go home," I assure him, and he lets out a satisfied moan.

"Say that again," Adrian says, and I lean back to see happiness written all over his features.

"We can go *home*," I repeat.

He picks me up so my feet dangle in the air, his lips briefly crashing onto mine before he drops me back down and helps me pack the rest of my things.

"But, don't forget, Nova is coming with us. So, no *petit paradis* for you until she's asleep," I whisper when I'm next to him, and he lets out a groan that turns everyone's heads. Adrian's eyes go wide when he realizes, and I press my lips together to keep from laughing.

Soon, everything is packed, only the furniture left, which the landlord bought off me for the next tenant.

Adrian takes the heavy suitcase I was holding and hands me a lighter one. I'm about to complain when he starts singing a Dylan Scott song so loud, he makes sure he can't hear me. I simply laugh and make my way out of the door. Nova, Gabriel, and Val are already downstairs loading up the truck. I walk toward the elevator, Adrian following behind me.

His eyes burn my backside, but I can't help but smile.

"How closely are you watching my ass right now?" He chuckles deeply, a sound full of filthy promises, sending a thrill through me.

"So closely that I have tripped over my feet twice already," he replies, and I shake my head yet again. "Have you seen your ass in those pants? Fuck me, there is hardly a sight more delicious."

"You are one horny man, do you know that?" I ask, pushing the button for the elevator to get to our floor. Adrian lets go of the suitcases to stretch, revealing his V-line as his shirt lifts. I suck in a sharp breath, which I cover by clearing my throat.

"Says the woman who eye-fucks me more times in a day than I can keep count of," he replies, grinning at my shocked laugh.

The elevator *dings* and I step inside without giving him the satisfaction of a lame comeback. Once the doors close, he steps against me, wrapping his arms around me in a sweet hug.

He only lets go when we have to step out of the elevator again. Someone rushes past me, and Adrian quickly pulls me out of the way, preventing the teenage boy from running into my bad shoulder. Panic courses through me as I choke on my own breath.

"You're okay," he assures me, and I give him a small nod, my hand lifting to the scar. Adrian says something in French to the boy, but I don't even try to catch any of the words. My mind is stuck on the paranoia I feel about something I should not be scared of anymore.

"Adrian?" He steps in front of me, his attention on my face. "I'm sick of living in the fear of something happening with my shoulder. Will you help me face this fear?" A small smile instantly spreads over his face.

"Yes, and I know just where to start. Give me a bit of time, and I'll arrange something, okay?" I give him an unsure "okay," but he kisses me so fiercely, I don't ask any questions.

This is one of his more dangerous gifts, but it's as much a blessing as it is a curse. It takes my fears for the briefest moment and turns them into seconds of happiness.

It's time I face my fears. Adrian took a big step this morning when he went through some of his grandfather's things at Val and Gabriel's house, and I can no longer hide from what is holding me back either. I want both of us to grow, and just like I was holding his hand this morning, I know he'll be holding mine every step of the way.

CHAPTER 14

Adrian

"WHEN WAS THE LAST time it was just you and me?" Valentina asks, and I let out a small sigh, sliding my arm across her shoulders to tug her against my side. Chase is running around on my balcony with his toy, and I enjoy his company, too.

I love that little guy.

"Too long ago," I reply as we stand on my balcony, staring at the water as the sun sets behind it in a sea of colors.

We stay silent for a moment, but there is something I want to get off my chest, I *need* to tell her.

"Your entire life, I've watched you struggle. I've watched you trying and fighting and never giving up. Now, you have your F1 seat, and you've been doing an incredible job. Dad and Grandpa would be so proud of you," I say. She leans her head against my shoulder. "I'm so proud of you. You've exceeded expectations that never existed in the first place. You're slowly becoming the best race car driver of the Romana family, and, when the time comes, you will win your first Drivers' Championship, just like I will, just like Gabriel has."

She smacks my stomach, and I let out a surprised gasp.

"Hey, what's that for?" I complain, watching her wipe away tears.

"You're making me cry, that's what it's for," she complains, and I kiss the top of her head with a laugh.

"You deserve to hear how special you are, Val, and I haven't said it enough, not recently. Almost everything and everyone was against you, but you didn't lose yourself. You didn't lose your determination. It was deep inside of you the whole time, even during the darkest days. I admire that about you. Then again, I admire everything about you. You are my little sister, after all, and I pretty much raised you so, in reality, I'm the awesome one," I joke to ease the emotional tension, and my sister bursts into heartfelt laughter.

"You're unbelievable, Adrian," she complains and steps away from me, dropping onto the seat behind her.

I join her at the table, shuffling the cards she brought over. It's a new game she wants to try out called 'Monopoly Deal,' and I'm already dreading it.

I fucking hate the board game version.

"You know, you always tell me how proud you are of me, but you're the one leading the championship right now. You're the one who has worked harder than ever before to be an even bigger competition for Gabriel. I have absolute faith you can win this year," she says, and I halt my movements.

Damn.

The thought courses through my entire being like venom, lacing my cells, muscles, and blood with hope, hope I shouldn't cling onto as much as I am right now.

"Gabriel is a fantastic driver, he proved it last season, but you will win this year. You will hold the trophy, you will have the title." I refuse to let tears shoot into my eyes, no matter how strongly they're burning my throat. "You've believed in me my entire life. You've held my hand all the way to my success. Now, let me hold yours." It's a metaphor, but she slides it toward me anyway, waiting until I press my palm to the back of it.

"Can we talk about something else? I'm not in the mood to cry." I almost did yesterday already when I saw Nevaeh twirling around in our living room, dancing to a song after we unpacked her last suitcase.

"Talk to me about Nevaeh then," Val says, and I smile immediately. There is no fighting it. Any mention of her, and I'm a mess of smiles and laughs and...joy.

"She's perfect. The end," I say, and Valentina snickers to herself.

"You know, I always knew you'd fall hard, but I didn't expect this."

"Well, you can only blame yourself. All that talk about how in love you are and how great it is made me think I could have it, too," I defend, and my sister tucks her lips between her teeth until her mouth is pulled into one thin line.

"And? Now you have it, too. Aren't you happy?" she challenges, and I let out a shaky breath, which turns into a laugh midway.

"Never been this happy," I admit. Valentina raises an amused brow before focusing on the cards I just handed her.

"I know. I see it every single day. Nevaeh is good for you in all ways possible. She's healing you."

Yes, she is. She's helping me fight my demons, and they've been defeated every time they've resurfaced so far. Together, we're undefeatable.

"Just promise me one thing, Adrian." I nod, letting her know I'd promise her almost anything. "Don't push her away. No matter what happens. Don't pull the same shit Gabriel did. Don't ever think there is something too big for you to figure out together. As cheesy as this is going to sound, a love like this doesn't come twice in one lifetime. Hold onto it, please. I don't want to see you lose her, not ever." Valentina shudders for a moment. "Man, I think Gabriel is starting to rub off on me."

We both burst into laughter.

"I promise, Val, I will hold onto Nevaeh with everything I've got." My sister gives me half a smile, then focuses on her cards again. "Enough about me. I wanna know how the wedding preparations are going."

"Great. My maid of honor and I are going to start working on it soon, and Gabriel already has lots of ideas," she says, so I give her a confused look.

"Maid of honor? Who? Evangelin?" I ask because I didn't know Val and Gabriel were doing the whole maid of honor/best man thing. She shakes her head. "One of Gabriel's aunts?" Amusement slips over her face then.

"Nope. But that would have been cute, too."

Who else?

Nevaeh.

"What did she say?" I blurt out so loudly, Val leans away from me a little. "Sorry." I laugh.

"Obviously she said 'yes.' I just told you we were going to start planning soon. A bit of a stupid question there, Mr. I-Think-Of-Myself-As-Perfect." *Touché.*

"Neither of you talked to me about it," I defend, but Val responds with a shrug.

"I asked her *yesterday*, and you two were probably busy 'unpacking' last night." My sister lifts her fingers to show the quotation marks she put around the word.

"We did unpack," I say, but a smirk slips onto my face before I can stop it.

Nova went to do some sightseeing by herself, so we were all alone in our apartment. We were done organizing her things within an hour, then spent the next couple naked and sweaty.

The memory sends a wave of heat through me.

When the hell will Nevaeh be back from dropping Nova off at the airport?

"Yeah, I'm sure." She snorts, and I keep smiling at my cards. "You should know, Gabriel will be here any minute. He said something about wanting to discuss a work-related issue with you."

Have you ever seen a child lie? They give you that look that says whatever they claim they didn't do is exactly what they *did* do. Well, that's how Valentina lies. She's terrible at it, and I've always seen right through her.

I'm just glad she can't tell I'm hiding something from her. Something huge. Something I haven't even dealt with yet.

Nope. Ignore it, Adrian. We're not thinking about Cecilia.

Gabriel knocks on the door minutes later, walking in without waiting for permission. His gaze is on me, determination in his eyes. *Oh no.* I almost burst into laughter when he stands in front of me with note cards in his hands.

Then, he starts his speech.

"Adrian, from the moment I met you, I was unsure about you." *Okay, we're off to a strong start.* "You were so full of yourself, arrogant, and a complete dick at times, to be completely honest," he goes on, and I cock an eyebrow.

"I hope this is going to take a more positive spin, if not, I'm—"

"As a teammate, you're unbearable a lot of the time. You always think you're right and—"

"Okay, thanks, mate. I get it," I say, slightly offended but mostly amused. Gabriel frowns at me.

"I'm not done yet, so I'd appreciate it if you'd shut the fuck up for once. I know you love the sound of your own voice, but *shush*." I drop my head, my shoulders shaking as I chuckle.

"Fine, please, proceed." Gabriel straightens out his back.

"You put up this façade, pretending nothing can get to you because you hold yourself on a high pedestal, but you're so much more than that. Getting to know the real you has been an honor and a privilege I know you don't bestow on many people, and I need you to know that you're one of the best guys I've ever met. I would love it if you were my best man for our little ceremony," Gabriel finishes, touching the back of his hand to Val's cheek with the last sentence.

I lean back in my chair, cross my arms in front of my chest, and watch him with humor spilling onto my face.

"Cameron didn't want to do it, did he?" Gabriel laughs.

"No, he didn't. That's why I'm asking you," he replies, and the corner of my mouth curls into a smirk.

Dick.

"How much does it pay?" I ask, and Gabriel's hand drops from my sister's face and onto her shoulder, squeezing it.

"*I* have to pay *you*? I don't think so. You're more work than anything I will ask of you," he replies, and I burst into laughter again, standing up to give him a quick hug.

"It would be my pleasure to tell you everything you're doing wrong."

"I know." I place my hand on his shoulder with a smile when the front door unlocks again.

Nevaeh steps through the door, holding the key I gave her. Noticing three sets of eyes on her, she turns our direction and grins.

She's finally home.

CHAPTER 15
Nevaeh

I HAVE... A JOB interview.

With the head of Alfa Adrenalina's social media team.

This is the job I was hoping to get an interview for, and today is the day. We're only a week away from the season restart, so I've been growing more anxious with every day I remain jobless. But the opportunity Alfa Adrenalina is giving me to even come in for an interview has hope spreading through my chest in dangerous waves.

They already emailed me, and I spent half an hour on the phone with the head of the team yesterday, discussing how much she loved my portfolio and the articles I used to write. We talked about my skill-set and my availability, and I told Samira I'm available to travel anywhere she needs me to as well as being flexible about what type of photography she wants to fit the social media aesthetic they've already created.

She really liked that answer because it was directly afterward when she asked me to come in today.

"How's my outfit?" I ask when I step into the simulator room where Adrian is training. I waited until he was done with a race so I could have his undivided attention.

His head tilts my way, his eyes lighting up at the sight of me. His lips part, and he sits up a little straighter, even though he looks exhausted enough to pass out any second. Sweat drips down the side of his face, which is the color of a tomato.

"Baby," he starts, leaning forward to get closer as he adds, "you look so beautiful." He shakes his head in disbelief, his eyes tracing me as a smile curls the corners of his lips.

"Yeah? I feel a bit silly," I admit as I run a hand down my pencil skirt. The blouse I'm wearing feels unnecessarily tight. "Actually, I feel like my stomach is going to fall out of my ass because of how nervous I am," I admit, and he stands up to close the distance between us.

"Is that what it feels like to have anxiety?" He scans my face, placing his hands on my shoulders for comfort.

"Honestly? Sometimes, yes. Other times, it just feels like I'm dying," I explain, my palms starting to sweat at the same time my breathing hitches.

He kisses me before I can spiral, redirecting my attention to him instead of the swelling anxiety in my chest. My shoulders untense as I lean into him for a moment, but this interview is important, so I can't procrastinate leaving any longer. The German in me is too paranoid about being late to spend another second kissing Adrian.

No matter how much I want to keep doing it.

"Okay, I have to leave. I love you. Bye," I say and attempt to step away, but he holds on to me to kiss me until I giggle.

"Say it again," he replies, nibbling on my bottom lip for a second.

"Bye." He frowns, making me giggle even more. "I love you."

"I love you endlessly, *mon paradis*. In every universe."

I should have stayed home. My heart feels like it's about to explode, that's how quickly it's beating. Two other jobs I applied for emailed me the positions were filled already, so I really need this interview to go well.

I just wish my anxiety could calm the fuck down to make this easier.

But how could it? When my thoughts are spiraling until tears shoot into my eyes and my breathing turns labored? When I feel like this interview is the only chance I have left to stay in the sport I fell in love with? When failure makes me want to crawl into a hole and hide from the world forever?

"Ms. Fuchs? Ms. Chandra will see you now," the person at the front desk says, and I stand up without hesitating. The faster I get to start this interview, the sooner my anxiety will find a way to settle down.

The *before* of a situation is always worse than the *during* and *after* for me.

Samira Chandra is a tall woman with warm brown skin, long brown hair that reaches all the way to the small of her back, and light brown eyes that welcome me as soon as she sees me. Her smile is just as kind, and the way her entire face lights up at the sight of me already makes me feel more at ease.

"Nevaeh, how are you?" she says, holding out her hand for me to shake.

"I'm as excited as I am nervous for this interview, if I'm being honest," I say, hoping a bit of candor will break the ice. The way she smiles at me lets me know it does.

"Well, being nervous means you care, and I only hire people who are passionate about the jobs they apply for." I return her smile with a genuine one.

We spend the next hour speaking about my strengths and weaknesses along with my previous work in F1 and my father.

"May I ask, what happened with *Griffin Sports*? When I called to ask, Mrs. Lu spoke very highly of you, so I don't quite understand why you decided to leave," Samira says, and I barely stop my jaw from dropping.

Why would Mrs. Lu lie? Saying I was fired would have been much worse than telling Samira I left on my own terms. Why would she help me?

"Honestly, they had a no-dating the drivers rule, and I fell in love with the most popular one," I explain, which isn't the entire truth, but it's also not a lie. Samira gives me a kind, understanding look.

"You chose love." It's not a question, so I just smile to myself. "A job shouldn't dictate who you can or cannot date. If they were worried about bias, they should have had an editor look over your work. Someone unbiased, which should happen regardless," she continues, staring at the papers in front of her for a moment as silence fills the room.

"So, it's not a problem for you that I'm dating Mr. Romana?" Samira shakes her head immediately.

"If I'm being honest, Nevaeh, it's one of the reasons why we want to hire you. The fans love Adrian and you together. You have given the sport a lot of good publicity, and if Alfa Adrenalina hired you, we would also be a recipient of that good PR." That makes sense. "Not to mention, we primarily want to hire you for your photography, even if we can't deny that having another article written on Leonard Tick and a few on Valentina Romana is something we are interested in as well."

"I'd love to. Writing the article on Leonard was a pleasure, and I've been waiting to write one on the first female F1 driver since the beginning of the season," I explain, my face lighting up at the mention of my best friend.

"I must say, Ms. Fuchs, your resume is impressive. Your previous work for us was as well. We've had a very good experience with you in the past, and since our photographer quit, we're in desperate need of another. The season restarts soon, and we haven't had anyone nearly as talented as you apply. Plus, your name has fallen in a dozen conversations I've had since you started working in F1. You'd be the perfect fit." A shimmer of hope makes my heart flutter.

"I'm honored to have even gotten an interview with you. Alfa Adrenalina has had my respect for a long time, and it doubled after the team signed Valentina," I say, grinning when Samira flashes me a smug smile.

"I *am* very proud to work with a team as diverse as this one," she replies. "And I hope you'll feel the same way, too."

My knees are shaking a little as I make my way through the gate of Valentina and Gabriel's home. Tears keep filling my eyes, but I do my best to swallow them down because there is no reason to cry.

I won't allow the tears to fall.

At least that's what I tell myself before I see Adrian, Val, and Gabriel sitting at the table on their veranda, playing a game of cards as they wait for me. Chase runs up to me to greet me, and I only barely register petting his head.

"Nevaeh! How was the interview?" my best friend asks as soon as she sees me, and I cover my mouth as tears track down my face. Adrian's back straightens and he moves, ready to stand up and close the distance between us.

"Alfa Adrenalina offered me the job," I explain, and all of them jump up, cheering as they rush toward me.

Adrian pulls me off the ground as I start crying even harder. Val gives me a big hug before Gabriel wraps his arms around us followed by Adrian until we're four idiots standing on the veranda, hugging like we just won the lottery.

"I'm going to get a bottle of champagne to celebrate," Valentina eventually says and breaks up the hug. Gabriel follows her inside, probably to help her carry the glasses and bottle. Adrian turns me to him, his palms sliding onto my neck.

All the tension and pressure finally slide off my shoulders to give way to pure, unfiltered happiness. After all of the shit we've been through over the past couple of weeks, it's time something good finally happened again.

Besides having each other, of course.

"I did it," I say, swallowing down another wave of tears. Adrian nods, his thumbs caressing my cheeks.

"I'm so proud of you, *mon ange*." I lean into his left hand as his face reveals the slightest hint of sadness. "I guess you don't have to move in with me, after all." I close my eyes and bite back my smile.

"No, I don't *have* to," I reply and slip my hands under his shirt. He cocks an eyebrow, but my gaze drops to where I'm touching his body. "But your apartment has a kitchen, which my old one didn't. It also has a room with a piano and a killer view," I say before bringing my eyes to his. "Most importantly, it has you," I add, and he grins like a happy child.

"I'm going to make you so happy, you'll see," Adrian informs me before leaning down to bury his face in the crook of my neck and wrapping his arms around my waist.

Adrian is about to kiss me when Gabriel and Val walk back outside, interrupting us.

"Don't stop on our account. I know how difficult it is to keep your hands off the woman you love," Gabriel says and pinches Val's ass as she walks past him toward the table.

She squeals in surprise and puts the glasses down to roll up her sleeves and jump at him. Adrian pulls me into the air at the same time and spins me around until all of us are laughing.

CHAPTER 16

Adrian

Nevaeh is having a hard night.

A few months ago, she told me she has nights where she has a light case of insomnia and simply cannot sleep. She also told me it's hormone-related because it always happens right before her period.

Tonight is one of those nights.

She's been tossing and turning for hours, even sitting up in bed with her face in her hands and rocking back and forth. I've never seen her so frustrated before, and I have no idea how to help her.

I've been laying next to her, awake and wondering what I could do, for hours. I keep rubbing her back in hopes it'll help her fall asleep, but nothing is working.

Then, it gets even worse.

She starts crying.

"I'm sorry," she says, her face in her hands again. "I'm so sorry. I'll go and be on the couch," she adds, but I snake my arm around her middle and pull her into bed again.

"You're not leaving because of your anxiety-induced insomnia, my beautiful Nevaeh. Stay with me." I'll tell her a story, rub her back, and hold her until she falls asleep. "If you can't fall asleep, then we will stay awake together, okay? You and me, we've got this."

More tears fall down her cheeks as she nuzzles herself against me. I wrap my arms around her, my fingers trailing up and down her back in soothing strokes. Her hands press against my bare chest as she tries to slow her breathing.

"What story?" she asks after a moment of silence.

With every moment we spend awake, the more tired I get. I love my sleep, but I love my Nevaeh more, so I'll fight sleep with every fiber of my being.

"When I was a little boy, my dad sat me down and told me that my mom was pregnant with Valentina," I start, my fingers still running up and down her back to soothe her. "I didn't know I could love anyone as much as I loved my sister before she was even born. I used to touch my mother's belly and ask if she could hear me. My mother used to say, 'Every time you speak, she moves' and I knew right then that my sister would be everything to me."

Nevaeh's expression softens at the story, and I press a kiss to her forehead before I go on.

"Then, she was born, and my dad let me into the hospital room after my mom had gotten some rest. He let me hold Val, and I remember crying at the sight of her. She was so small, so fragile, and I wanted to protect her with everything I had. All it took was me holding her one time, and I knew if anything ever hurt her, I'd die a little. Dramatic, I know," I say when she chuckles against me.

I notice her eyelids are falling shut more and more frequently with every word until she doesn't even open her eyes anymore.

"And now? Now I still feel the same, but my sister has Gabriel, and most of my focus has shifted." I take a deep breath, but she doesn't look up at me, which makes saying my next words easier. "Now, if anyone ever hurt you, Nevaeh, I'd rip this world to shreds, burn it until nothing but ashes remain, and rebuild a more beautiful one with you." A small smile tugs at the corner of her mouth.

"Violent and romantic. You do it all," she says, and I snort.

"I'd do anything and be everything for you."

"I love you just as fiercely," she replies, silence filling us as her words settle deep inside of me.

Nevaeh finally falls asleep, making relief flood through me at the sight of her evenly rising and falling chest. Her hands are still lying flat against my chest, but her fingers twitch against me every few minutes, as if she wants to pull on me to get me closer but then remembers I'm not wearing a shirt, even in her sleep.

"I love you, I love you, I love you," she mumbles over and over after a few more minutes, and I study her face to see the creases between her brows.

Her words warm everything inside of me, but I don't say a single thing. Nevaeh needs to sleep, and I won't wake her because I think it's wonderful that even in her sleep she's telling me how much I mean to her.

Nevaeh proves it to me every single day. She just said it ten times in her half-sleep, not even knowing I was awake to hear her. It proves without a doubt how deeply she cares for me, but my brain won't let me believe it. It won't allow my insecurities and issues to wash away.

What if she leaves me?

What if I make her leave me?

Fuck, I couldn't handle it if Nevaeh ever left me. She's everything I could have ever asked for. She's the type of perfection my brain has been looking for subconsciously. No one else has compared to her, nor will there ever be someone who will. Soulmates, true loves, fated lovers, whatever concepts society has fed its people, I never believed in it. I never believed there was someone out there in the world made for me. I didn't think I was made for someone else.

Now, after Nevaeh, I believe in it all.

I guide her further against my chest, unwilling to ever let her go again. She said something recently, two things, that I haven't been able to get out of my head.

"There is nothing more beautiful than the way your heart has enveloped mine to keep it safe."

It's all hers. My heart lives in her chest, wrapped around hers to protect it from any harm. I want it to stay there. I don't ever want it back in my body. She needs to hold onto it forever. I don't think it would even return to my chest. It would stay with her no matter where she goes.

The second thing is the one that hit me the hardest.

"Your trust is safe with me. I'll keep it in my heart and fight off anyone that comes close to it."

I don't ever trust anyone. I keep them away because of the shit my mother pulled, leaving like her children never meant anything to her. But Nevaeh? For fuck's sake, there was no pushing her out of my head. There was no question whether to trust her after she told me she loved me. I'd never doubt her loyalty to me, her devotion. My past makes me believe no one could love me as much as she does, but my heart knows.

That's why it can't let go of hers, why it will never be able to.

Nevaeh Fuchs is the end of Adrian fucking Romana. I'm drifting further into my heaven, never to be seen again.

Fine by me, Nevaeh will be there.

Shit, I'm so happy.

CHAPTER 17

Adrian

THE SEASON HAS OFFICIALLY restarted.

As it currently stands, I'm the leader of the Drivers' Championship with Lincoln in second, Gabriel in close third, James in fourth, Valentina—being the badass she is—in fifth, Leonard in seventh, and Cameron in eighth.

I'm leading. Only by a few points, but I *am* leading the championship, and I'm ready for the rest of the season.

With Cecilia nowhere to be found, I also feel more at ease again.

Lying by omission with my sister is still a heavy weight on my shoulders, though.

"How are you feeling?" Daniel asks, so I nod several times. It's all I can manage to do while I attempt to make my mind focus on the race.

But then my attention drifts to Lincoln, and I almost growl at the mere sight of him as if I were an animal. Fitting enough considering I'd like to rip him to shreds.

"Hey, focus. You can kill him after the season is over and his contract wasn't renewed," Daniel reminds me, and I shake my head with a smile.

But since you're in my head and I really need to tell someone, I'll tell you: I don't think I can wait until the season is over to bring this man some pain. Physically or emotionally, at this point, I don't care anymore.

"He's starting second, and it pisses me off," I admit, reaching for my suit where I tied it around my waist.

"Yeah, but Gabriel is in third, which means there is a good chance he'll overtake the rookie at the start of the race." I crack a smile at the word "rookie," pleased that Daniel has adopted this name for Lincoln as well.

"Unless he plays another dirty trick and costs my teammate his race."

"And then he'll have so many penalty points, he'll get a race suspension. He's already more than halfway there. Don't worry, mate, karma always comes to collect," he assures me, and the thought of Lincoln getting punished for all his crimes settles me enough to let go of my anger.

At least until he marches over to where my sister is standing with Nevaeh. A red light goes off behind my eyes, and I make my way over to the two most important people in my life as I try to fight the rage inside of me. Nevaeh is working. My sister is working. He needs to fuck off, disappear into his car and wait for the start of the race, which is in fifteen minutes.

Instead, he approaches Nevaeh as she takes a picture of Val in front of her car as my sister gets ready for the race.

Strike one of the day.

"Give me one minute, Nevaeh, that's all I ask." Of all the times to approach her, so close to the start of the race is not only stupid of him but also damn inconsiderable to Val's crew, my sister, and my woman.

"Get the fuck away from me, Lincoln." *That's my girl.*

"No, just talk to me, I—" I cut him off when he grabs Nevaeh's arm.

"Get. Your. Hand. Off. Her." He doesn't let go, merely turns to me with an irritated frown.

"Lincoln, you should really let go," Nevaeh says, and while I can't see her facial expression, I know it's filled with concern because of the way I'm staring at Lincoln.

She knows what's about to happen.

If Lincoln were smarter, so would he.

But he isn't.

"Go deal with your own business, Romana, I'm not hurting her."

"Yeah, but she doesn't want you to touch her, and you're interrupting Nevaeh's and Valentina's work," I say at the same time Nevaeh tries to wrestle out of his grasp, but he only holds on tighter.

Strike two.

"What they're doing is child's play. Valentina isn't going to win, and no one will see Nevaeh's photos anyway."

Strike. Number. Fucking. Three.

"Go. Away." It's my last warning, and when he still doesn't let go, I take a step toward him.

"No. You can't—"

My fist colliding with his face cuts him off.

Pain lances my hand, but finally letting go of my restraint and doing what I've wanted to do for months overpowers the ache.

It's a clean uppercut, much like the ones I've practiced with James and Val during our boxing sessions in the past, and it catches Lincoln so off-guard, he falls on his ass at the initial contact. At least his hand is finally off Nevaeh. But Lincoln won't leave the humiliation resting on him this way. He scrambles to his feet and flings himself at me, but two of Val's crew members hold him back before he makes contact with me. Leonard appears in front of me and places a warning hand on my chest, but I wasn't planning on doing anything more than punch him.

Will this have consequences with the FIA?

Yeah, definitely.

Do I give a shit?

No.

And the fucking satisfaction I get when I see a drop of blood running from Lincoln's nose is worth all the warnings in the world.

Plus, he couldn't take "no" for an answer, and I believe every man who refuses to understand that word deserves more than just a single uppercut to the face.

"You're fucking dead, Romana," Lincoln says as he fights against the grip the crew members have on him.

"You've already tried to kill me on the track several times, Lincoln." This shuts him up because, no matter what he pulls, getting called out for the dangerous shit he does is obviously a sore spot.

"Adrian," Nevaeh says, and I turn to see her shaking her head. Her look says, *it's not worth it*, but I do notice the proud glimmer in her eyes. The right side of my mouth lifts a little.

"Mr. Romana and Mr. Nash, the FIA demands your presence right now."

I shift to look at the member of the FIA team who's speaking to us, and I simply give them one nod before turning back to Nevaeh. In three strides, I'm in front of her, cupping her arm where Lincoln held onto her.

"Are you okay?" I ask in French, but rage returns when I see the red marks around her wrists.

"Yes, are you?" she replies in my mother tongue, but I merely give her a curt nod. My eyes drift to my sister, who is doing her best to keep from laughing at this ridiculous situation.

Lincoln didn't let go. He keeps harassing my woman. And he attacked my sister's ability as a racer.

He had it coming.

"You shouldn't have done that. I don't want you to get into trouble because of me," Nevaeh mumbles, but I simply kiss her sore wrist and grab her chin for the briefest moment while I think of the best response.

"Don't worry. He's not getting into trouble. I've had about enough of Lincoln's behavior as well." Nevaeh's father's voice startles her, and she steps away to look into his eyes as the man she admired more than anyone else most of her life approaches us.

"What are you going to do?" she asks him, her attention divided between Robert and me.

"I'm going to speak to the FIA on Adrian's behalf. Let's go."

No one argues with the team principal of Grenzenlos.

We all simply get our asses to the FIA head office, but I do it with a smile on my face.

In my head, I'm singing, *"Lincoln's about to get fired. Lincoln's about to get fired."*

CHAPTER 18

Adrian

FUN FACT, A FORMULA One driver punching another F1 driver before a race had never happened before today, so the FIA doesn't quite know what to do with us.

They've postponed the start of the race here in The Netherlands by half an hour so we can a) cool off, b) listen to their lecture of how violence is never the answer and should anything like this happen again, it will result in a race suspension, if not more, and c) allow me to ice my hand and Lincoln ice his face.

I was fined 10,000 Euros for punching Lincoln, but after Robert Fuchs opens his mouth to *defend me*, Lincoln ends up getting fined 50,000 Euros for harassing his team principal's daughter and my sister. Robert has also announced to the FIA that Lincoln's contract will not be renewed by the end of this season, which made me absolutely fucking giddy.

Like I predicted, besides the fine, all I got was a warning.

Lincoln, on the other hand, was told that if he does anything even slightly beyond the rules today, it will result in an immediate three-race suspension. Apparently, they are as sick of his bullshit as the rest of the drivers. They may have also let it slip that Lorenzo Mattia complained about the amount of damage and money my team has had to fix and pay because of Lincoln, so today was the last straw for them.

"We suggest you become a stellar driver, Mr. Nash. Otherwise, Grenzenlos won't be the ones in charge of your future for the rest of the season. We will be," the head of the FIA, Martin Albert, says, causing a smirk to break out across my face. "And you, Mr. Romana, wipe that smug smile off your face."

I merely shrug.

"Honestly, I'm trying, but I can't help it," I admit, earning a murderous glare from Lincoln. "Is he allowed to even look at me like that? I'd hate for him to get a race suspension," I taunt, trying my best to rile him up so he'll do something stupid and actually earn a suspension.

"You piece of fucking—" Robert stands in front of Lincoln, shaking his head and cutting him off.

"That is *enough*. Do you know how ashamed your father would be if he knew how you're behaving? Everything he worked for down the drain because you just couldn't leave my daughter alone. You couldn't earn the seat that he worked so hard to help you get. You are a failure and a disappointment."

The entire room goes silent when Robert pauses. Lincoln's anger has washed away entirely, leaving only shame in its place.

"I can't believe I ever defended you to Nevaeh. You didn't deserve that. You don't deserve anything more from my family."

These last three sentences are so quiet, Martin and the rest of the board can't hear them. But I do, and I grimace because *fuck* am I glad this speech isn't directed at me.

"I understand," is Lincoln's only reply before he storms out of the room and away from this situation. Robert looks over his shoulder, nods at me once, and then leaves as well.

I'm about to step out myself when Martin says, "Mr. Romana?" I turn my head his way, smiling my charming smile.

"Yes, sir?" He frowns at my smug expression.

"Try not to punch anyone else this weekend or any other weekend for that matter." I give him a simple shrug.

"As long as no other driver touches my girl without her consent, I promise you, I won't."

Every member of the board dismisses me with a nod of their own, and I step into the summer heat here in The Netherlands. As I make my way back to the grid where every member of every team is working on the cars and getting ready to race, I flex my hand a little, trying to ignore the way it stings.

Still worth it.

I stop at Valentina's car to check on her and Nevaeh, but my girlfriend is nowhere to be seen.

"She went inside to take some pictures of the crew," Val explains before I even voice my question.

"Are you okay? I know what he said was a low blow." I place a hand on her shoulder, looking directly into her eyes to see if Lincoln's words have affected her confidence or mood even in the slightest.

"If I let every man who ever said something negative about me drag me down, I'd be at the center of the fucking Earth," she says, and I snort at her comment. "Don't worry, big brother, I've got thick skin, and Tiny Dick Lincoln's words aren't going to penetrate it." This time, a real laugh bursts free.

"God, you're truly the best sister anyone could ask for, you know that?" The words make the guilt inside of me spike about hiding Cecilia's appearance, but I swallow it down, ignoring it.

"I know," Val replies, wiggling her brows at me with a cocky smile.

A moment later, Daniel drags me away and toward my car. I throw a quick, "Breathe, race, and win, as long as it doesn't cost you a limb," over my shoulder at my sister, but then I focus on the task at hand.

Winning today's race.

"Nevaeh wanted me to wish you a safe race. She also told me to tell you she is rooting for you always and that if you win, to meet her in your private room for a quickie," my performance coach and close friend says, and my heart stumbles all over itself. Heat rushes into my cheeks, and I forget how to breathe. I open my mouth to respond, but it falls shut again. "I'm kidding about the last bit, mate," he adds and laughs as if it's the funniest thing he's ever said. "I don't want to hear that again. Once was enough." Embarrassment makes my cheeks burn hotter.

"You heard us?" I hiss, and Daniel booms out another laugh.

"Her? No. You? Yes." He clears his throat before adding, "'*Fucking hell, baby,*'" he imitates me, so I shove my elbow into his side, making him grunt in pain.

"I hate you."

Daniel laughs again, entirely unbothered by my words.

"You should focus on getting into your race mindset," he says, and I feel like punching a second person today.

It's easier said than done, especially when images of Nevaeh on the table in my private room with my face between her legs resurface. When I remember how she crawled toward me. When I replay the sound of her falling apart over and over.

My body hums with need, and I hurry to get into the car before anyone can see how tight my racing suit has gotten in the front. I mean, it's always *tight* in a way because my dick doesn't really fit, so any less space, and it feels like it's suffocating in there.

After slipping on my balaclava and helmet, I jump into the car, taking the gloves Daniel hands me to put them on, too. He winks at me once, and I pray that my muscles won't hate me for the next three months for not properly warming up again after what happened with Lincoln and the FIA. The warm up is essential to prevent being extremely sore the following days, but actions have consequences.

After the formation lap, I line up at the first place grid position again, taking several deep breaths and focusing solely on racing. Chloe is in my ear, reminding me of the strategy and letting me know the rain is still an hour or so away.

One by one, the red lights flicker on above me, and I watch them like a hawk, ready to release the clutch and press down on the throttle. As soon as all the lights disappear at once, I do exactly that. My reaction time and Lincoln's are almost identical, but my car stays ahead in the first corner. He gives me a lot of space, more than he would have if the FIA hadn't threatened him, and I almost smile at the way he brakes earlier than I do to avoid running into me, too. For anyone else, that's a given. You're supposed to drive the way Lincoln is now, which is exactly the opposite of what he usually does.

If I wasn't pushing my car to its limits to stay ahead, I'd actually smile, but I'm having a hard time keeping control in the corners because we've been struggling with grip all weekend.

I'm not looking forward to the rain.

The dark clouds above me look angry after a few laps of Lincoln and me fighting. Not nearly enough to match the plan my team and I made.

"Chloe, talk to me. What's going on with the rain? Do we change tires or wait to see what is gonna happen?" I ask, but it could be risky.

If it starts pouring and I'm not on either wet tires or intermediate ones, I'll have no grip. I could crash, or I could lose a lot of places by spinning, drifting into the gravel, or other horrible scenarios I'm going to try not to think about.

"The radar doesn't say anything we haven't been staring at for the past twenty-four hours, Adrian," she assures me at the same moment a single drop hits my visor.

Then another. And another.

"Chloe," I say, my voice breathless as I guide my car through another tough corner. Lincoln is barely more than a second behind me, which is dangerous.

"I see it," she says as I push through the last corner and then race down the straight again.

More rain follows. My heart stutters a little.

"Yellow flag! One of the Tempête drivers is in the wall," Chloe says as we approach the second to last corner again. "Can you describe the track conditions now?" I almost laugh.

"Fucking wet, Chloe. I can't see shit."

"Copy."

"Well? Do I box?" I yell because in about ten seconds, it'll be too late for me to go in.

"Not yet. We're not ready with the tires. They only have a set for Gabriel."

Lincoln, Gabriel, Val, pretty much everyone behind me stops to go onto intermediate tires for the rain. Everyone but me.

"FUCK," I curse, slamming my hand on the steering wheel once as I slow down behind the safety car. I keep slipping as the track gets wetter and wetter from the rain, and it takes extra concentration not to slide into the gravel.

"Gabriel is ahead of Lincoln now. Box, box. You'll come out in front of them if everything goes smoothly." Chloe's words send another wave of anger through me, but only because I don't want to be in this position. *If* everything goes well.

After taking a deep breath, I steer the car toward the pit entry. My crew is waiting with four tires. Good. Four tires is good. If they're the right tires as well, that is.

Right as I drive past the Grenzenlos crew, they release Kyle Hughes unsafely. I swerve to evade him, slamming on the brakes at the same time, but it costs me a lot of time. Too much time.

"What the fuck was that?" I scream into my radio, not angry with Chloe or my team but with Grenzenlos.

"Focus. I'll deal with it," Chloe says as I guide my car to where my crew is, the rain now coming in faster and harder. "We'll be on wets, Adrian. Everyone else will be on intermediate, which won't be enough if the rain continues like this. In three laps, they'll all have to stop again to go on wets. It'll be okay." I take another deep breath, letting her words calm me.

My pitstop goes smoothly after the fuck up with Grenzenlos, and I rejoin the race behind my sister. I'm in fourth now, and instead of screaming and getting angry, I trust Chloe. I'll still get that win, and the more it rains, the surer I am. The radar didn't show this heavy of a rainfall, which is probably why everyone else went on intermediates.

The safety car ends a few laps later, and I fight my way past my sister within another three laps. I look at her as I pass her on the straight, her midfield car no competition to my championship-leading one. She throws her pinky up at me, our way of saying "fuck you," and I chuckle to myself before braking to take the first corner. The track is flooded with rain now. I hear Chloe telling me that all the other teams are talking about changing to wet tires because none of them have any grip. Wet tires were not part of the strategy we came up with, but Chloe's instincts about what this would turn into and the fact the rain started much earlier helped us a lot.

Unless something like another yellow flag or a red fl—

"Red flag, Adrian. Huge crash between the Klein drivers."

You've got to be fucking kidding me.

CHAPTER 19

Adrian

I HATE RED FLAGS.

While they're a great invention to clean up the debris and cars in a way that keeps everyone safe, coming off the adrenaline rush and then having to go back in the car after is hell. Not to mention, everyone who wants to change their tires to wets or intermediates—depending on how badly it rains when the race restarts—can. Chloe's strategy has gone down the drain. Everybody will be equal as soon as the race restarts. Everyone will have fresh tires.

"You'll have to overtake them the old-fashioned way," Chloe says, as stoic and grumpy as ever.

"Yeah, I got that," I say with a smile that I hope looks more real than it feels.

"If you want to cry about it, better let it out now instead of in the car. You've had enough problems with the FIA today," she teases, but I'm so happy about her trying to be playful to ease the tension, I smile anyway.

"You're such a ray of sunshine, Chloe, I don't know what I'd do without you." That earns me a "suck my dick" from her in Portuguese, a phrase she loves to use with me when I piss her off, and I chuckle as I walk away and toward my car again.

I notice Nevaeh standing in the corner with the head of the Alfa Adrenalina social media team, discussing something related to the pictures she took, but when my beautiful girlfriend catches me staring at her from outside the garage, a blush settles on her cheeks. She gives me the cutest little wave, and I wave right back at her because I love her so, so much.

How can anyone be so gorgeous and adorable when they're doing the smallest thing like waving at me?

Do you know how many people wave at me a day? Thousands.

But Nevaeh waves at me once, and I feel weak in the knees and turn into a puddle.

"Have you already planned out how you're going to propose to her?" Gabriel half-teases. The other half comes from his own experience. He told me once he'd planned to propose for years because Valentina has always been the woman he wanted a future with.

"That's none of your business," I say with a grin.

I meant what I told them all just recently. Whatever Nevaeh wants, she will have. She wants to marry me? I'll propose as soon as she says the word. She wants five children? I'll give her five. She wants no children? We will get dogs. She wants a mansion in France? I'll build it myself. She wants to stay in our apartment forever? I'll fucking buy it.

Planning a future with her comes as easy to me as breathing.

"Come on, *mon frère*, you can tell me," Gabriel encourages. I turn to him, crooking my finger for him to come closer and pretending I'll share my secrets with him. Excitement fills his eyes as he does as instructed, tilting his head so his ear is near my mouth. I almost burst into laughter.

"It's none of your fucking business," I repeat, and he frowns at me. Disappointment laces his features.

"You know, I've seen something very clearly since you met her," he starts, piquing my interest. "You're not lost anymore. You found her and yourself in the same heartbeat."

Dammit, Gabriel.

"You're so disgustingly cheesy. Go make out with Val or something," I say and walk away, the sound of his laughter following me all the way to my car.

The race is announced to restart in ten minutes, so I get back inside the car, preparing for the standing start. The rain has slowed and the clouds are slowly clearing, the blue sky replacing them. Everyone is on intermediates now since the track is still wet, but it's highly likely all of us will have to pit again.

Winning this race has just become infinitely more difficult, if not impossible. Gabriel and Lincoln are my biggest competition this season, and they're both ahead of me on a track where my car and I struggle for grip in the corners.

"Ready?" Daniel asks, and I nod before hopping into the car again.

Ten minutes later, we're given the green light to take another formation lap starting from the pit lane and moving to the starting places on the grid. My heart is thundering. I don't remember a day it hasn't been. I've always put so much pressure on myself that when I fail, I beat myself up about it for weeks. When I lost the championship to Gabriel last year, I fell into a hole of doubt and regrets, constantly thinking there was something I could have done better.

I don't think this will ever ease, but I'm not as hard on myself anymore. Not when Nevaeh takes any excuse to tell me just how amazing she thinks I am. I lose a race, she sits me down and looks over it with me, showing me how well I did even if I didn't win. Nevaeh puts things into perspective for me, and I'll never take that for granted.

"Clean overtake at the beginning. Get your lead back," Chloe says, so I inhale deeply, hold my breath, and exhale at the same moment the lights turn off and I release the clutch. My car speeds forward, attempting to chase down Gabriel, but he overtakes Lincoln in the first corner. My teammate takes the lead, but Lincoln stays closely behind him, using the slipstream to create a gap between them and me.

I fight hard. I stay within a second of Lincoln so when the DRS is enabled, I get that extra speed advantage.

We fight for laps over laps.

I attack, he defends.

There are twenty laps of the race left, and I'm so close, I can smell the second-place trophy. Gabriel is almost five seconds ahead now so catching him will be difficult, but I can overtake Lincoln. I *will* overtake him.

"Try to avoid taking the curb in corner fourteen, Adrian. You're losing a lot of time there," Chloe says, and I curse a few times.

"I'm aware, thank you." I can practically hear her snort.

"Can you be aware and fix it?"

"Oh, is that what I'm supposed to do?" I ask, sarcasm dripping from my words. "I thought I should let all the other cars pass and be first from the back."

"Just avoid the curb," she grumbles, and I do my best for the next few laps to be extra cautious of that turn.

And damn, as soon as I figure out how to avoid it, I gain time on Lincoln.

With every lap, I get closer.

With every lap, my heart races faster until finally, I overtake him.

But what happens next is even more wonderful.

Valentina closes the gap between Lincoln and herself. I'm driving away, but I ask Chloe to give me updates.

"She's in his DRS zone," she informs me, and I hold my breath. "Point-six seconds behind him now." A lap later. "She just attempted an overtake, but it didn't stick yet."

Come on, Valentina Esmèe Cèlia Romana.

Get. Him.

"She did it! She overtook him. Last lap. Push for fastest lap now." My head spins from the excitement of my sister being third and her instruction as the words leave her lips in a single breath.

I'll celebrate later.

For now, I want the extra point that having the fastest lap of a race gets a driver.

A sense of victory blooms in my chest as I cross the line in second place. I may not have won, but our second pitstop went well and the rest of the race also went smoothly after I overtook Lincoln.

Gabriel and I drive side by side on the track, celebrating the beautiful one-two our team just secured. He gives me a thumbs up, and I open my visor to wink at him. He shakes his head, but I only see his helmet moving from side to side. I slow down even more to wait for my sister, who came third in the race.

I'm so proud of her, I could explode.

Making a fist, I shake it a little at her as a way to say "fuck yeah," and she does the same motion, celebrating this achievement. It's her second third place of the season, which is incredible for her first year in F1 as well as racing in a midfield car.

She deserves all the glory in this sport, and I can't wait for the day she wins her first race.

I hope it's soon.

The three of us hop out of our cars as soon as we park them at the first, second, and third place sign, and Gabriel and I run over to Val immediately, picking her up and jumping up and down to celebrate her accomplishment as well as ours. Leonard, James, and Cameron eventually come over to shake her hand and pat her shoulder, too.

After the interviews, the celebration on the podium takes place. We're handed our trophies after listening to the Monegasque and Italian anthems. Velocità Rossa and Alfa Adrenalina belong together, which means they're both Italian teams. And all three of us podium sitters are Monegasque. It's the most perfect celebration our teams could have today.

My eyes dart toward where Nevaeh is standing with Valentina and Leonard's team, winking at her when I catch her camera facing me. She lowers it to throw me a kiss, then lifts it up again for a few more pictures. Knowing she's watching me, I tilt my head back and close my eyes, hoping the post-race glow makes me look extra sexy to her.

Once we're finally allowed, I pick up the champagne bottle, slam it on the ground, and let the liquid shoot up in the air before directing the spray my sister's way. Gabriel is already pointing his bottle her way, so all Val can do is laugh and let herself get completely drenched in the champagne.

Today is a good day.

Well, at least it was until I had to look at Gillian fucking Fender's dumb face.

"Mr. Romana, it's nice to see you," he says as I approach him. All I give him is a nod, the straw of my bottle between my teeth as I take a sip of the electrolytes Daniel gave me.

As predicted, because of the lack of warm-up, my body now feels like I've been hit by several trucks.

"I'd say this was your best race of the season so far," he adds. I choke on my drink.

"I beg to differ, but okay," I reply, furrowing my brows at him.

"Is it because you didn't come in first?" he asks, but the question is so fucking stupid, words leave me for a moment.

"Among other things." God, I hate him.

"When do you think you lost the chance to win today?" *What is it with the idiotic questions today, Gillian?* I almost voice the question. Almost.

"Obviously during the red flag. It messed with our strategy, but you don't have to ask me this question. You know when I lost the chance to win today," I say with a humorless laugh.

"It could have been somewhen else. For example, during the first safety car," he says, and I shake my head at him.

"But it was *not* then, and you know that." With my arms crossed in front of my chest, I stare him down. "Are you only going to ask me questions you already know the answers to?" I smile at him, smug when he sputters out a string of words to recover. "Alright, then we're done here."

His camerawoman lowers the device, turning away to hide her amused smile.

Fatima, my PR officer, shakes her head and stops recording my words, and I use that opportunity to close the distance between Gillian and me to say, "Maybe if you'd kept Nevaeh on your team, you'd actually have interesting and good questions to ask. It seems like when the responsibility is on you to come up with them, the only thing we drivers get is a load of bullshit. If I were you, I'd feel the utmost regret about alienating Nevaeh right about now."

I walk away without another word, sick and tired of Gillian and every other person who has ever dared to hurt the woman I love.

Chapter 20
Adrian

GABRIEL AND VAL GAVE me the key to their boat... again. This time, Nevaeh and I have actually managed to take it out of the harbor though. She's currently lying on one of the benches at the front, her body covered by a tiny bikini I've envisioned removing with my teeth since she slipped out of her dress. I've been sitting on the bench across from hers ever since, pouting because she put sunscreen on without asking me for help. Granted, she only put it on her front so far, so there is still hope she'll want to even out her tan and turn around, which means she'll ask me to put some on her back. But still.

I took us far enough out of the harbor to make sure we're all alone, no prying eyes anywhere near us, so she could touch me as much as she wanted and vice versa. Nevaeh loves having sex in places where we could get caught. I've started to become a big fan, too.

So, why isn't she touching me very inappropriately right now?

"What's wrong, *mein Mond*? You look like someone told you your hair doesn't look good today," Nevaeh says, and as much as I want to smile at her witty comment, I keep frowning. She sits up, furrowing her brows at me. Even though she's wearing sunglasses, I know there's a hint of amusement sparkling in her eyes.

"You did something much worse," I reply, crossing my arms in front of my chest and leaning against the back of my seating area.

"Me? What did I do?" she says, sitting up and lifting her sunglasses.

"You didn't ask me to put sunscreen on your body. You did it yourself." Concern turns into more amusement as she looks at me. Nevaeh picks up her sunscreen bottle before walking toward me.

"How rude of me," she replies, making her way onto my lap until her crotch hovers perfectly over mine. Almost on instinct, my hands fly to her ass, squeezing until she lowers herself completely.

That's better.

"Very."

"How can I make it up to you?" she asks, looking around once as if checking for any boats, people, or cameras, just in case, before rolling her hips to grind herself against my hardening cock.

"Well, what are the options?" I ask, smiling as a wave of pleasure spreads through me when she keeps rolling her hips.

"We're out here all by ourselves. Sky's the limit, baby. You tell me what you want, and I'll fuck you exactly that way." God, her filthy mouth is one of the most wonderful things.

"All because I was pouting like a brat for not getting to put sunscreen on you?" I ask, moaning when she grinds harder against me. My fingers dig into her round ass as I reflexively thrust up against her pussy.

"Well, the question is, Adrian, are you going to be my good boy now and do as I say?" she asks, and, fuck me, I'd let her do anything she wanted just so she calls me her good boy again.

"Yes, ma'am," I say with a smile.

"Good boy," she praises, and somehow, my cock gets even harder.

A groan escapes me, but Nevaeh's hip movements become agonizingly slow, almost like she knows how hard her words have made me and now she wants to tease me. Deny me the pleasure of both of our releases.

Good thing I fucking love it when she teases me.

"Take off my bikini top," she says, her hands lifting to my shoulders to hold onto me while she keeps grinding against my cock.

"What if someone sees?" I ask with a smirk.

"No one's here. It's just us," she assures me, leaning down to brush her lips over mine. "And even if, let them watch. Let them see how good you make me feel with your magnificent cock," she says, and my composure slips through my fingers.

"Can I flip you onto your back, *mon paradis*? Will you give me permission to do that?" She nods, but right before I stand up to flip us, she grinds down harder, forcing a moan out of both of us. "Fuck, Nevaeh," I curse, leaning forward to gently bite down on her bikini top, pulling the triangle covering her right nipple to the side. Her grinding becomes more frantic as I wrap my mouth around her pebbled nipple, sucking until a low moan slips out of her.

"Don't stop," she says, rolling her hips even faster as I softly bite down on her other nipple through the fabric still covering her left breast. "Yes, God, there," she calls out, her hands flat against my pecs while mine stay on her perfect ass.

"Make yourself come, beautiful. Let me see my dirty girl get off on being so exposed while dry-humping me." I slide her bikini bottoms to the side to place my thumb on her clit and rub, but she's so worked up that within seconds, she's trembling through her orgasm. My mouth finds her exposed nipple again, sucking it into my mouth and making her whimper.

"Right there, right there," she says as I flick my tongue around her sensitive, hard nipple. One of my hands wraps around her throat, squeezing either side a little until she smiles.

"Yeah?" I press my thumb hard against her clit, smirking up at her.

"Ah, yes, that feels so good." Her bottom lip slips between her teeth, her eyes closed as she rolls her hips a little, riding out the pleasure for as long as possible.

I use that opportunity to take her in, admiring her. The way her pale skin on her chest and cheeks has turned a beautiful pink shade. The way she looks wonderfully unruly with one of her breasts no longer covered by her bikini top, her pussy exposed, and her hair a mess from the wind blowing through it. The way her freckles are perfectly painted onto the bridge of her nose and cheeks. The way she smiles from pleasure, still grinding against my hand. My hand is still wrapped around her throat, but she grabs my wrist to guide it to her lips, sucking my thumb into her mouth and eliciting a low groan out of me.

"You want to suck my cock again, *déssee*? Is that why you're doing that?" I ask and slip my thumb further into her mouth to show her what I mean.

She gives me an eager nod.

"Then get on your knees, baby."

She kisses me, excitement flowing from her and straight into me. Within seconds, she's on her knees, fumbling with the strings of my bathing suit to undo them and suck me down. Once she's undone the knot, Nevaeh pulls my cock out, moaning as she runs her thumb down my hard length.

"So eager," I say with a smile, grabbing her chin to make her look up at me. Her honey-brown eyes are full of lust.

"You've denied me the experience of fucking you this way for months. Now that I've had a taste, I find it hard not to suck your cock every chance I get." This. Fucking. Woman.

I let out a breathless laugh because her words—her filthy, perfect words—are followed by her tongue playing with the head of my dick.

"Would you like that, Adrian? If I just dropped to my knees to take you in my mouth whenever I want? Let you fist my hair and shove your cock down my throat," she adds the last sentence but sucks me down before giving me the chance to respond.

I almost fall apart right then and there. For someone who has always done what was asked of her, has been a good girl most of her life, Nevaeh certainly has a side to her she's never been able to explore with anyone before I came along. Getting fucked in a semi-public place where anyone could see. Saying the dirtiest of things before giving me head. Doing whatever she wants now. I'm so proud of her and love her even more for every side she shows me.

"I'd like that very much," I admit, wrapping her hair around my fist and thrusting up into her mouth. Nevaeh moans as she wraps her hands around the base of my cock, sucking hard on the head of it.

"Is this how you like it?" she asks, but she knows I'm under her complete control right now. She knows I'm obsessed with her and the pleasure she gives me. Her hands slip behind her back, undoing the clasp of her bikini top before slipping it off.

I lose my composure.

I pull my cock out of her mouth and guide her to the floor of the boat, slipping between her legs.

"Impatient, are we?" she asks as she wraps her arms around my neck and drags my mouth down to hers.

"Yes. Need to be inside you, Nevaeh," I reply, reaching for my swim trunks to retrieve a condom, but she puts a hand on my arm to stop me.

"You know how we discussed not using a condom anymore?" she asks, bringing me back to our conversation from a week ago.

We both got tested and are all clear, and Nevaeh is on birth control. Not to mention, I don't ever want to be with anyone but her again. I'm committed to her. She's it for me, my everything, and this was a step I wanted to take, so I asked her if she was ready for it as well.

"Leave it off. I want to feel you without a barrier. My walls wrapped around you without anything in the way. Please," she begs, reaching for my cock and stroking it.

"How could I ever deny you a single thing, *mon paradis*? When you beg so pretty."

She's so wet for me, so ready, I slip inside of her in one swift, effortless stroke. "Fuck me," I breathe out, pleasure weakening every limb, every muscle until my arms are shaking as they hold me up. This is unlike anything I've ever felt. Being bare inside of her... *Fuuuuck.* There are no words to describe how perfect she feels, her walls clinging to my cock, hugging it. I could get used to this so fucking easily. Become addicted.

Just when I thought Nevaeh couldn't get any more dangerous.

"Oh my God. Why haven't we done this from the beginning? This feels so good," Nevaeh says, rolling her hips a little in search of friction. I place my thumb back on her clit, still trying to recompose myself. "Fuck, Adrian, don't do that. I'm gonna come too fast," she says, but I keep going because there is no way in hell I'll last. I'm not used to this overload of pleasure, and my balls are already tightening like I'm about to come without doing anything other than having my dick inside my woman. Out in the open. Where anyone could catch us.

I'm gonna come.

Fuck.

"Come, Nevaeh. Let me feel it while I'm inside of you with nothing between us." My chest rubs against hers as I slide out of her, driving in harder and quicker than before. God, why does this feel so good?

A boat honks, but it sounds far away, so I don't stop yet. We're both so close, just a little bit longer.

"What if they see us, Adrian?" Nevaeh asks, but she's also moaning and clinging to me like she doesn't want me to go anywhere.

"Don't care. Need to feel you like this for a little longer," I manage to say through the cloud of pleasure blurring my thoughts.

"And here I thought I was the one who loved the thrill of this more than you," she says, and I let out a breathless laugh that turns into a low groan when I fuck into her again, this time so hard, I see stars.

"You're a very convincing woman."

"Hmmm," is Nevaeh's only response, her walls tightening around me.

I fucking lose it. I come with a groan so loud, she slaps a hand over my mouth, even as she trembles through her own orgasm. My hand slips onto her mouth when she cries out as well, our bodies shaking in perfect harmonization as I pump her full of my cum. Full of... *me.*

If I could, I'd come all over again.

"Adrian, we should get dressed. The longer we stay like this, the more likely it is for someone to catch us," Nevaeh says, which is the only reason I am able to peel myself off her and slide out of her perfect pussy.

I tug my swim trunks back on, but my angel doesn't move at first. She merely lays there, propped up on her elbows, her eyes glued to her lower half. I follow her gaze, noticing the way my cum is dripping out of her. I smile while running a single finger down her pussy.

"You like this, *mon ange*? Watching me drip out of you," I say, loving the way she throws her head back and smiles shily.

"Yeah," she admits. "It means you're mine." I almost cock a brow.

"I could argue it the other way around," I reply, placing my hand back on her chin to tilt her face toward mine. A challenge sparkles in her eyes.

"No, this means you're mine. You've come inside *me* and only *me*."

"You're forever going to be the only one," I say and lean forward, kissing her while cleaning her up and placing her bikini bottom back on. "You're my only one, for everything." Nevaeh wraps her arms around me, and I kiss her, both of us laughing a little, maybe from our lingering post-orgasm highs or maybe simply because of how happy we are.

"Val and Gabriel are going to kill us if they ever find out we fucked on their boat," she says once we've put her bikini top back on, but I merely laugh.

"They'll never find out." Nevaeh gives me an unimpressed look.

"There aren't many secrets between you and Gabriel, Adrian. How long can you keep this from him before he does something stupid and you blurt out, 'Oh yeah? Well, Nevaeh and I fucked on your boat so *ha!*' in retaliation?"

The laugh that rips out of me is so violent and loud, it makes me fall over. Nevaeh joins me and soon we're both laughing, tears collecting at the corners of our eyes.

Once we've both calmed down, her nuzzled against my side while my back is flat against the floor of the boat, I have a strange realization. One I try my best to keep from her, but the words tumble from my lips anyway because as much as my brain doesn't want to say them, my heart feels them too strongly to keep them bottled up.

"I think you're my soulmate, Nevaeh Fuchs." She looks up at me, tears shooting into her eyes, which makes some shoot into mine.

"Adrian Romana," she starts, and I hold my breath. "I think you're my soulmate, too. In every universe. In every version of us that exists. In every lifetime." Her lips find mine, sealing this moment with a kiss and a single tear.

A tear that escapes *me*.

She leans back after a few more seconds of tasting me, teasing me, and I go back to tracing her features with my eyes. Her freckles. Her eyes. Her lips. Her nose. Her hair.

All of it is just so perfect. She's so perfect.

"Come on, old man, let's go," she says, standing up and walking toward the edge of the boat, obviously wanting to go for a swim.

"You're three years younger than me," I remind her with a frown. "You're turning twenty-two next month, then it's like we're only two years apart." She snorts at that.

"And three months later you're twenty-five, so it'll be three again."

"Still, I don't think you should refer to me as 'old man,'" I reply with a frown. I already feel triple my age sometimes, I don't need my angel to start calling me that.

"Then come get me," she says, jumping off the side of the boat and diving into the water.

I follow her, laughing all over again.

I'm so far gone for her, I truly am in heaven.

CHAPTER 21
Nevaeh

THE RACE I'VE BEEN anxiously waiting for is finally here.

Monaco.

Adrian, Valentina, and Gabriel's home Grand Prix.

I'm so excited.

My boss has asked me to exclusively follow Valentina and write an article on her like I've done with the other drivers in the past. It makes me even more excited for the weekend.

It's Thursday, which means she is mostly busy with her track walk that I get to join her on, and then press conferences that I don't get to go to. But I'm loving the fact that I'm wearing Alfa Adrenalina's team shirt every race weekend I'm working now.

It makes me feel like a true member of the team.

I walk around the different stands they have provided where merchandise is sold and artwork, too. I don't mind being by myself for a little, exploring the track and its attractions like a true fan.

I love it.

It feels like I finally have a moment of complete silence, even with the chaos of people screaming around me, to think about what the hell my life has become. I have a job I adore, friends that mean the world to me, a boyfriend I love more than everything, and my family is somewhat functional at this point. Mama still isn't speaking to me, but that's my new normal, so I'm okay with it.

I buy an official Valentina Romana cap and Adrian's team shirt, already hearing them complain to me about this. But I want to be a fan for a moment, spending money on normal things as others do. Then, later, I can ask them to sign them and feel even more like a supporter.

The man at the stand gives me a confused look, but I simply take the merch from him with a smile and push through the crowd of people. A lot of them give me funny looks, almost as if they're wondering if it's really me, Adrian Romana's girlfriend, but I don't linger long enough to let them make up their minds. I merely hide under my cap and continue walking.

"I would have never expected the girlfriend of a driver to have to buy his team's shirt. Don't you get those for free?" That voice is so familiar, but it's only when I turn around that I see who it belongs to.

All the color drains from my face.

"I was married to a driver many years ago, and I always got everything I wanted," she adds, but I'm already taking a step away from her, almost stumbling over my own feet.

"Cecilia," I blurt out, my voice barely audible.

"Can I ask you something?"

"No," I reply, taking another step back, but she wraps her hand around my wrist to keep me close. Anger, fear, pain, it all washes through me at once at the sight of her familiar eyes. The green and blue and brown that she gave to her children. Panic grips me, bringing a lump to my throat that I can't swallow.

"Please, Nevaeh, I just want to know, does he treat you well? Adrian, I mean," she clarifies, although she didn't have to.

"You don't deserve to know anything about your children that they don't want you to know," I say without hesitation. "You're the woman who abandoned Valentina and Adrian. You're the person who has caused the man I love and the woman I've become best friends with more pain than words can describe. Then, you played boss and meddled in their lives from your hiding place. You *forbid* Adrian and me from dating. You fired me for not following your rules. You're a horrible person." My insides turn upside down before I cover my mouth to keep the nausea at bay. Cecilia's eyes narrow.

"How did you find out it was me who came up with that rule?" She studies me like I'm a threat.

"Because it was obvious. Mrs. Lu and my father had nothing to do with it, and you were the one who always enforced the rule. No one else." This makes her smile, but it isn't kind.

"Clever thing, aren't you." My heart shudders in fear when she sneers at me, but she pushes her irritation aside to plead with me instead. "Don't tell them I was here. Adrian wouldn't forgive me if he found out," she begs, and I let out a laugh that I don't mean one single bit.

"You're asking me not to tell my boyfriend and best friend that their mother approached me to ask me if her son, if you can even call him that, treats me right?"

The cruel woman nods like there is nothing wrong with that, and I laugh again, this time truly amused by her lack of emotional intelligence. I walk toward her, my face close to hers. My hands are shaking, but I swallow past the anxiety to focus on my next words.

"I never thought I'd get the chance to say this to you, but burn in hell. I don't know or care why you left, just that you did, and I would never, ever hide your appearance here from Adrian or Valentina. If I were you, I wouldn't come close to me again," I warn before storming away from her and toward Adrian's garage.

The first person I run into is Gabriel—actually run into because I wasn't looking where I was going—whose hands wrap around my arms to catch me.

"Nevaeh? What's wrong?" he asks, making me realize the tears I was trying to hold back have run down my face. He searches my features for an answer.

"Cecilia is here," I explain without meaning to, and his eyes go wide immediately. He lets go of me to take a shocked step back.

"No," Gabriel mumbles, and I cover my mouth. This will bring Val and Adrian more pain than either of us can even imagine. My boyfriend was convinced Cecilia would disappear again after almost a month of radio silence. He was so sure.

This is going to break him all over again.

"How do we tell them?" Gabriel asks as I wipe my tears and fixate on his green-brown eyes. He shakes his head before running his hand through his hair.

"Tell them that the woman who abandoned them has decided to come back into their lives? I don't know! How the hell *do* you tell them that?" I reply with frustration laced in my voice.

"This is one way to do it, I guess," Valentina says from behind me, and I turn to see them both standing a few meters away, shock on their similar faces. Then, my boyfriend's fills with sadness.

"Fuck," Adrian curses, squatting down and dropping his head.

"*Mein Mond?*" I ask, but he doesn't even bring his eyes to my face.

"I should have told you," I hear him mumble, but his words are for his sister and his sister alone. Well, maybe a little bit for Gabriel, but mostly, they're for Valentina.

"What the fuck are you talking about?" my best friend asks, and I notice the tremble in her hands, even if she's doing her best to let anger be the only emotion showing. Gabriel takes a step toward her, but she raises one hand to keep him back. "Adrian? What are you saying?"

"I knew she was back. I ran into her at Nevaeh's old place of work. She was her boss for months, hiding behind a new name as she meddled in our lives," he explains, and I watch the color drain from Val's face.

"You kept this from me?" Adrian finally looks up at her, nodding with shame filling his eyes. "Why?" For someone who just had their whole world turned upside down, she's surprisingly calm.

"I wanted to spare you pain in case Cecilia vanished again. And she had left. For a month, we heard nothing from her. I was so sure she'd disappeared," he admits, but Valentina shakes her head, more disappointed than anything else.

"I'm so sick and tired of you treating me like a child that needs protecting, Adrian. I'm a grown woman. Stop keeping shit from me!" Her frustration radiates off her in waves that make my stomach feel uneasy.

"I'll always protect you, Valentina. I'll do everything in my power to spare you pain. Cecilia manipulating herself back into our lives through Nevaeh is not something I wanted you to know about until I knew for sure that's what she was doing." Val considers her brother's words for a moment, then turns to me with tears of anger in her eyes.

"You knew?" My heart shatters into two at her pain-filled tone.

"I—" I cut off, not sure what to say.

"I asked her not to say anything. It was my decision. Be mad at me," my boyfriend says, putting himself between Valentina and me.

"That's the thing, Adrian, I can't be mad at you because you're hurting just as much as I am, if not more. That woman meant everything to you. I understand why you didn't tell me. But I want you to stop carrying all this weight by yourself," Valentina says, her tears finally falling down her cheeks.

"I wasn't carrying it by myself," Adrian replies, turning to me to take my hand. Val tracks the movement with her eyes, but she merely shakes her head. "I'm sorry."

"So am I. I'm sorry you feel like you can't trust me with these things." Valentina turns away, but Gabriel immediately moves in front of his fiancée, cupping her face in his hands and mumbling some comforting words.

"Let's go home, please," Adrian says before wrapping his arms around me and pulling me so close, it almost knocks the air out of me.

"You have work to do," I remind him, but he shakes his head against me.

"I don't want to. I want to go home with the woman I love and forget I heard that my mother is back. *Again.* That my sister is disappointed in me," Adrian says as he steps back. "Please, *mon paradis*, let's go," Adrian begs.

"If it were up to me, my love, we'd already be in the car, but you have responsibilities." I hate to be the one to remind him, but he can get into serious trouble if he goes home early during a media day. He still has interviews to attend, questions to answer. If his boss finds out he disappeared, it would have consequences.

"Screw my responsibilities, Nevaeh. My mother showed up here. If I want to go home, I will."

His tone is so harsh, I take a step away from him. I'm not scared, but the surprise coursing through me must be evident all over my face. When he realizes, he covers his mouth and stumbles away from me.

"I'm sorry," he says, but I shake my head and hold out my hands for him to take. "I should cool off. I will see you at home." Panic floods me as he creates more distance between us.

"What? No, Adrian, you shouldn't be alone. Let me grab my things, and I'll go with you," I suggest, but he immediately shakes his head.

"No, I can't—I can't breathe." He sprints away without letting me say another word, but when I attempt to go after him, Val grabs my arm.

"Trust me, when he gets like this, you need to give him some space," she says, but my heart is following Adrian anyway, beating unevenly at the thought of him alone after finding out the woman who abandoned him as a child won't stop trying to weasel her way back into his life.

"I'm sorry I didn't tell you." Valentina waves my apology away with her hand.

"Don't be. I meant what I said. I understand why," she says, squeezing my arm.

"How are you feeling?" I ask because pain is written all over her features.

"I'll be fine. That woman means nothing to me, she never has." I pull her into a hug.

My family might be dysfunctional, but I cannot imagine what they are going through right now. After all of the loss and grief they experienced, the only person who could come back into their lives is the one they never wanted to return in the first place. Valentina holds onto me, a sob escaping her that shakes right through me and settles deep within my chest.

"I'm so sorry," I say against her cheek before pressing a kiss there and turning her to Gabriel, who is patiently waiting to comfort her.

I leave them there and make my way toward Val's garage. I grab my things before sprinting to the taxi area. Adrian will come home to a dinner prepared with love and a girlfriend who will be there for him, through anger and pain and tears.

I'm going to be everything he needs right now, no matter what that may be.

CHAPTER 22

Adrian

I'M GETTING SICK OF these fucking panic attacks.

Especially because it's not just panic. It's pain. It's unfiltered, raw, inescapable pain.

And I don't know how to make it stop.

What's even worse is that my family's voice always reappears during these times.

Grandpa saying, "You're completely out of balance. You're letting your emotions affect your body and mind. It's why you can't breathe."

Grandma saying, "Think about why this is causing you so much pain. Try to understand why it hurts, and then address it. You will be able to move on."

Worst of all, Dad saying, "Drown your sorrows, son. Forget about the rest of the world and grab a bottle. It always helped me. It can do the same for you."

I know Gabriel was drowning his sorrows through alcohol. He even admitted that it gave him some kind of relief at first, but how everything was worse when it wore off. My entire life, I've stayed away from it. My father was an alcoholic, so I've been too scared to go near this stuff. But I'm just in so much pain.

And Dad's voice is getting louder.

"It will let you forget."

I let the engine of my car roar to life, driving to a liquor store and grabbing a six-pack of Nevaeh's favorite beer. I settle back down in my car and drive until I'm in the parking garage of my building. My eyes fixate on the bottles, wondering if it could truly help me or if I'm being stupid. If I was breathing, if enough oxygen was getting to my brain, I'd have a clearer answer for myself, but I'm already close to passing out.

I take a sip of the beer, regret shooting through me immediately. It's disgusting. It feels wrong as it slides down my throat, and the taste is horrendous, which is why I chug it in one go. I wait a few minutes, the buzz eventually settling in. It's not enough. Close, but not enough. I empty another bottle and then one more without thinking. I'm drunk so quickly, it's embarrassing. Three beers, and everything is spinning. My lungs may finally be able to breathe now, but I feel worse than before.

I cry even harder, having lost all control over my body. My hands slam against my steering wheel a few times to let out some of my frustration, but it turns into a breakdown of sobbing and screaming.

This needs to stop.

How the fuck do I make this stop?

Alcohol didn't work.

Acknowledging what's bothering me didn't help.

Breathing didn't help.

Nothing is fucking helping.

"Please, please, I can't take it. Make it stop." My voice sounds broken in the car. "It's too much. It's too fucking much."

"Come home." Nevaeh's voice fills my ears. She isn't here. I know I'm imagining it. But I revel in the sound anyway. "Come home to me."

Nevaeh.

I'm coming.

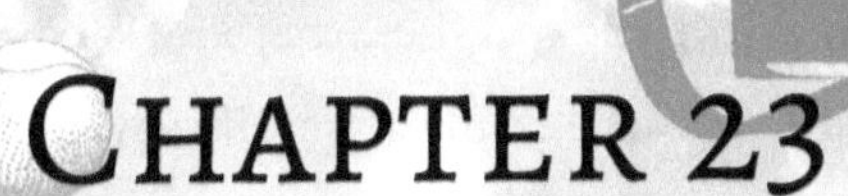

I WATCH THE STEAM fade from the homemade lasagna I made, the minutes ticking by as I do. Either Adrian didn't see my message to come home for dinner, or he doesn't want to be with me right now. Either way, disappointment fills me as I gather the utensils to bring them back into the kitchen.

Suddenly, Adrian stumbles through the door. My senses go on high alert as I rush toward him, catching him before he can hit the floor.

"Adrian, what the hell is—" I break off when the scent of beer hits my nose. "You're drunk," I mumble more to myself than him, but he snorts out a laugh anyway.

"Next thing you're going to tell me is that I have great hair, Sherlock," he replies, and I feel the urge to let him drop on his ass for the sassy remark.

"Alright, *Arschloch*, let's get you to bed," I say because insulting him in English while he's in this state isn't a good idea, but I also needed to let my anger out in some way. He's in pain, hurting from his mother's return, and part of me understands why he got drunk. Yet, a much bigger part has no idea who this man in my arms is.

"*Arschloch*? What is '*Arschloch*'?" he asks, butchering the word while I drag him to our bedroom and plant his ass on the bed.

"It's you right now," I scold while bending down to remove his shoes.

"Are you angry with me?" Adrian says softly, taking me by surprise. His thumb and index finger grab my chin, forcing me to look up at his bloodshot eyes.

"Why did you do this to yourself?" I ask. Adrian pulls me onto his lap, his arms wrapping around me while his eyes stare into mine.

"I wanted to see if it would help me breathe. Since you told me she showed up again, I just—I couldn't fucking breathe, and alcohol, well, they say it's supposed to help you forget." All of my anger, if it even was that, vanishes, and I run my fingers through his hair, tugging a little on the roots, which makes him smile.

"And? Did it help?" Almost immediately, he shakes his head and guides me closer.

"No. I had three beers, but my tolerance is so low, I felt it go straight to my head. Nothing about this is pleasant to me. It didn't stop me from overthinking nor did it help me breathe," he explains, his gaze dropping to his thumbs as they caress my hips. "I should have come home earlier. I should have realized my only remedy to pain is you," he admits, making a warm feeling spread through me. "I'm sorry I stood you up tonight. It won't happen again," he promises, and I lean down to touch my lips to his cheek.

"You need to go to sleep as soon as possible. You have work tomorrow, and we can only hope you're not hungover. If you are, you're calling your management team and telling them you won't make it for the free practices. I won't have you racing if you're not a hundred percent up for it," I instruct, and he chuckles. His tired eyes close as I run my fingers over his eyebrows, down his cheeks.

"Under one condition," Adrian says, and I cock an amused brow.

"I'm not having sex with you while you're drunk," I warn, and he gives me a "seriously" type of look.

"No, I just need you to tell me something." I wait patiently as he guides my hips even further toward him, my breasts now almost touching his lips. My breathing accelerates out of habit, bringing a drunken smirk to his face, but only briefly. "Do you see me differently now?"

"Adrian, no. I understand what you were trying to do, and you realized on your own that it doesn't help." He nods before pressing a kiss to my chest, right above where my heart is. "Just promise me you won't do something this stupid without me again," I say.

"I promise," he replies, dropping his forehead against my sternum. "Nevaeh? Why is everything spinning?" he asks, panic spreading through my chest at the question.

"Bathroom, now," I command, and he lets me guide him to the toilet.

A few groans escape him, but besides him feeling dizzy, nothing happens. His eyes simply flutter shut as he leans against the wall next to his toilet. I wet a towel and place it on his nape, hoping it will help with his circulation.

"I don't understand how he could do this," Adrian mumbles, and I tilt my head to the side before wiping the hair off his sweaty forehead.

"What do you mean?" I ask when he doesn't offer an explanation. His bloodshot eyes skip to my face.

"My dad. He got wasted a lot, and I don't understand. There's nothing pleasant about this," he explains, and I sink down on the floor next to him to place my palms flat on his neck.

"Some people like to forget their problems this way, and, from what you've told me, that man had many. The consequences after maybe didn't outweigh the pros of it during, but I don't think anyone can really know his motivation." Adrian runs his fingers up my leg and down again, listening attentively to my words.

"Do you think he did it because my mom left him?" My hands drop from his neck, but he picks them up and places them back there, not ready for me to let go yet.

"Maybe. Love can make you do stupid things." Adrian nods before leaning forward to touch his forehead to mine.

"Yeah, like you agreeing to date an *Arschloch* like me," he says, and a bit of the anger from before returns to my chest.

"Adrian, one drunken moment of you being a sarcastic asshole does not mean you aren't still the man who loves me better than anyone else ever could. Do not start doubting yourself, it goes against your cocky personality," I joke, and he chuckles.

A moment of silence passes as his fingers lift to my wrists near his neck, and a desperate frown slips onto his usually confident face.

Panic returns to his body. I can see it in the way his chest rises and falls too quickly. The way his eyes unfocus.

"Tell me what you need," I say softly.

"You," he manages to croak out, so I wrap my arms around him. He clings to me while I start to hum 'Can't Take Her Anywhere' by Dylan Scott, the song that has become ours in every way a song can be. He calms a little from it, my voice a soothing distraction for him.

"Have I ever told you that, before we even met, you already took my breath away?" I ask, and he shakes his head against my shoulder.

I run my hand over his forehead, then through his hair before continuing my story.

"It was years before we met. My father was showing me the drivers he was interested in signing for Grenzenlos, which included a picture of you," I explain with a small laugh.

His breathing slows, and, when my hand slides on top of his chest, it allows me to feel the same happening to his heart rate.

"Man, you were so cocky the day I met you. You still are, but, for some inexplicable reason, it's one of the things I love most about you. You've never shown any sign of jealousy, and you don't pretend like you're better than me. I'm your equal in every way, which, considering how full you are of yourself, means you love me a lot," I joke, and he gives me a slight chuckle.

His fingers run over my arm before he takes my hand and lifts it to his mouth to press a kiss on the back of it. He trails the figure eight on top of where he just placed a kiss, making me smile.

"You've been drawing an eight with your fingers since our first dinner. Why?" Adrian sits up to turn to me, his hands sliding onto my neck to force all of my attention to him.

"Because from the moment *I* met *you*, I've felt this need to have you in my life, no matter how. That's why I couldn't let you go, even when your job forbid anything from happening between us. Because when you looked at me, I felt oddly complete.

I wanted you in my life as a friend, a girlfriend, or whatever title you gave me. I draw the infinity sign because I hope it will somehow manifest that you never, ever step out of my life again," he says, making me speechless.

He's said many beautiful things to me over the course of our relationship, but this? This makes the top three. Number one is taken by "*Je suis amoureux de toi, mon paradis,*" and always will be.

"I don't think I ever could," I whisper, wiping the sweat off his forehead.

He digs into his pocket to take out a small box. He stares at the blue package before handing it to me.

"I planned on giving this to you after the race on Sunday, but there is no point in waiting." My heart races uncontrollably, even though I know it's not what I think it is.

"Adrian, you shouldn't have," I say before lifting the lid and discovering another charm to add to my bracelet. It's an infinity symbol. "I love it, Adrian. Thank you," I say and lean forward to kiss him. He breaks it soon to place it on my bracelet.

"Let this be a reminder that you're it for me. That I want forever with you," Adrian says and grabs my hand to squeeze it. "I love you," he adds.

"*Ich liebe dich mit meinem ganzen Herzen,*" I reply, and he cocks an eyebrow. "I guess you have to learn German."

Adrian playfully wrestles me to the ground, tickling me and making me squeal in a way I've never done. A sound of happiness with the hint of dread of the darkness I feel coming.

"Kiss me, please."

I pull his head down, his lips enveloping mine immediately. He breaks the kiss soon, a sob leaving him before he sinks against me and allows his inner child to cry about the one person who was meant to love him more than anything in the world. He cries because the hurt he never dealt with has resurfaced and hits him a hundred times harder every time she shows up.

Adrian pulls me onto his lap to close the distance between us, and I hold onto him while he lets me in completely, all of his emotions flooding my system in a heartbreaking wave.

I hold on even tighter because there is no reason strong enough to ever make me let go of this man.

CHAPTER 24
Adrian

YESTERDAY, NEVAEH MADE ME walk in a straight line and list the alphabet backward to make sure I wasn't drunk anymore before heading to work. Apart from a pounding headache, which I got rid of with some painkillers, I felt fine.

Well, apart from the heartache.

I did well in the free practices yesterday. I was second and first. This morning, in the third one, I came tenth. It was a horrible run, my team trying to fix whatever is making us so slow in the straights, but they're still working on it right now. Hopefully, it'll be fixed by the time we have to get ready for Qualifying.

However, right now, Valentina is at my motorhome, and we've been sitting in complete silence for a while instead of talking about what happened. Pain hangs heavy in the air, on our chests and shoulders, but neither one of us has acknowledged it out loud yet.

Where the fuck do you even start?

Val doesn't need me to point out something blatantly obvious to start a conversation. Then again, I don't really know what to say. My sister simply stares at the bottle with electrolytes in front of her while I try to come up with a way for us to talk through our trauma.

So, easy shit.

"What the fuck?" Valentina blurts out eventually, and the simple question, probably because my emotions are all over the place, makes me burst into uncontrollable laughter. She joins me after a moment of hesitation until we're both crying tears of amusement neither one of us means.

"I don't know. I wish I did, but what the fuck indeed." I reach for her bottle, taking a sip because I forgot my own and need some energy. My brain is still a bit fuzzy.

"Hey!" she complains, but I've already emptied half the bottle. "All jokes aside, Adrian, what are we going to do? It looks like she's planning on staying." Frustration laces her words. I can identify it as easily as breathing because it's the same strain I feel in my voice when I speak about Cecilia.

"She won't stay, I will make sure of it," I reply, but Val gives me a frown so instantly, I feel stupid for believing I could get her out of our lives.

"Your optimism is misplaced in this case, Adrian. She so desperately wants to be in our lives, she took a job that would allow her to be around us constantly if she wanted. Cecilia is determined."

"Yeah, but so am I," I defend, and she raises both of her brows. "I need her gone. She's messing everything up, and I won't let her take my happiness from me. I won't let her cost me Nevaeh." I slump into my chair, fear taking over my body.

"What do you mean? Nevaeh would never leave you because of Cecilia," Val replies, but I shake my head, wiping my face.

"I got drunk the day before yesterday," I admit, avoiding the piercing eye contact my sister is trying to have with me.

"Okay. And? Were you a dick to her?" I nod, finally bringing my gaze to hers. Compassion is all over her face.

"I stood her up. She prepared this wonderful meal for me, to comfort me, and I made her sit at the table, waiting for hours. I'm horrible," I explain, biting back the pain bubbling up in my throat.

"You're hurting, Adrian, and Nevaeh knows it. She knows you're trying to process all of this, and she'd never leave you because of it. Just don't push her away. I know this is one of our darker times, but you need to let her be there for you. You don't have to go through any of this by yourself." The door opens behind us a second before my best friend steps into the room.

"Yeah, mate, you're not alone," James says, his hand slipping onto my shoulder. He squeezes it, trying to comfort me.

"Good, you're here. I need to go, but you stay with him and remind him we all get to be human." I frown at my sister, but she simply presses a kiss to the top of my head and leaves the room.

James takes her seat, the one across from me, and crosses his arms in front of his chest. He's studying me, trying to understand what's going through my head.

"Why didn't you come to me?" is his first question when I don't speak. Ashamed, I can't bring myself to give him an answer. "Whenever something's wrong, I'm always the first person you come to, but not this time. Why?"

That's a very good question, one I don't have an answer to at first. Then, I share what I did instead, telling him every detail about two nights ago and the emotions I felt.

"You bloody idiot," is his only response.

"Yeah, no shit," I spit back, and he gives me a small chuckle.

"After all those years of watching your father, you learned nothing?" I stay silent, more shame slipping into my chest. "I need you to answer my question, Adrian. Why didn't you come to me?"

"Because I didn't want to be the cause of more problems. You have enough to worry about with Damian, Nicolette, and Domi, and I didn't want to add to that. Is that so hard to believe?" I challenge, and James shakes his head, disbelief making his eyelids flutter shut.

"It's stupid, that's what it is. No matter what is going on in my life, no matter the problems I deal with, you come to me. End of discussion. My door is never closed to you. You're my brother. You are my family, and I expect you to start acting like it, for fuck's sake. Don't make me repeat myself again." I smile for the first time in minutes. He's so angry with me, I'm touched.

"Sorry," I say, and he gives me a firm nod.

"If you want to get drunk, you come to me," he replies, and I let out a small chuckle.

"Don't worry, I'm never going near that stuff again. It was disgusting," I say and mean every word. There was no pleasure in it for me, no relief except that it distracted me from my panic.

"Good." He stares at me for a few seconds, unsure what to say next. I think about changing the subject, but the silence between us works like a relief. My ears appreciate the quiet, even if it doesn't last long. "Do you want to tell me how you're feeling about Cecilia being back?" he asks, and I suck in a sharp breath.

"I'm not entirely sure how I feel." I should probably figure that out, and maybe he can help me. Maybe it's time I let him. "I'm angry in a way I've never been. There is so much pain whirling around in my chest, it's hard to focus on anything else. I want her to vanish, the same way she did before, but I'm simultaneously terrified of how broken I'll feel afterward. On top of it all, my emotions are out of my goddamn control, and I'm scared of what that'll do to Nevaeh and me."

My rant comes to an end, and I almost laugh when I see James' eyes have widened and his lips have parted. He wasn't expecting me to say any of this, but he also seems proud I did.

"I didn't know you could ever be so emotionally complex." I bite back a laugh. "I'm afraid I don't have any advice to magically make everything better, but I'm here for you, always. Time will ease the intensity of the feelings you're experiencing right now. Just be patient," he says, and I shake my head.

"When have you ever known me to be a patient man?" I challenge, and he snickers at my response.

"With Nevaeh, you were the most patient man in the world. What happened to him?" There is a fake sadness in his voice now.

"She calls me hers, and I call her mine. I don't need to be patient anymore," I reply. James lets out a snorting sound, which makes me tilt my head as I study his disgusted expression.

"You're so in love. *Ugh*. I'm going to be sick."

"Says Mr. Romantic himself. All right then," I reply, taking another sip of the bottle Val left for me.

"Well, Mr. Romantic is getting a little sick of watching everyone around him finding the love of their life while he's stuck on—" James cuts off abruptly, and I stop every single one of my movements. I'm not even breathing anymore. "I can't believe she's getting married. They're so young," he blurts out, dropping his head into his hands. I lower the bottle back onto the table, swallow what's left in my mouth, and then answer his unspoken question.

"They're already connected in every other way possible, James. They just want to have this because they know it would make our late families happy. Gabriel's mom always wanted him to get married to the love of his life, and so did Grandpa for Val. This ceremony is mostly for them, and a little for Gabriel and Val, I guess. I don't know. I only know I want to marry Nevaeh one day to be able to call her my wife, to have her call me husband. That's the best title I could ever ask for." Fuck. That came out of my mouth way too quickly and easily.

"I have a son I share with his two mums. I have been in love with the same girl for over a decade. How am I ever going to find someone who will love me for me?" he asks, and I'm a little surprised by his self-doubt.

"Whoever that person is, mate, they will knock you off your feet so fast, you won't have time to doubt how they can love you. And no one, absolutely no other person, loves as fiercely as you do. You always make the best out of the worst situations, and you protect the ones you love with everything you have. You're loyal and kind, and I'm going to stop talking now because this is getting emotionally heavy, and if you start crying, I'll probably break down, too. It's been two way too fucking long days." I'm breathing heavily by the time I'm done talking, which we both laugh at.

James simply nods before standing up and signaling for me to go with him.

"It's time to work."

If there's one thing I struggle with a lot as a driver, it's beating myself up when things go wrong. Today is one of those days when I just want to hide under a rock and pretend the rest of the world doesn't exist.

"Track limits. Your lap was deleted," Chloe says right as I cross the line again, entering my cool-down lap for Q2.

"I didn't go off!" I argue, but there's a feeling deep inside of me that knows I messed up. Not for the first time today. In Q1, I almost crashed into a Zeitgeist driver on their cool-down lap.

"They've deleted it, Adrian. You are now ninth and have no more time to go for another lap."

"What does that mean?"

"It means hold your breath and pray nobody kicks you out of Q3." Chloe's answer is so dry, I kind of want to shake her.

Bringing the car back into the pits, I'm going over every corner in my mind, analyzing every mistake I made.

Okay, fine, *over*analyzing, but it's almost the same thing.

"So far, no other car has overtaken your spot, but there are two Zeitgeists, two Carousels, and one Klein still on their fast lap." More panic floods my system. Five cars. Five drivers who can push me below tenth place and kick me out of the chance to partake in Q3.

"Fuck me," I mumble under my breath, but my radio isn't on, so Chloe and the rest of them can't hear me swearing.

I shouldn't have gone so fast into the chicane because who the fuck even gets track limits and their lap deleted in Monaco? On a fucking street circuit?

Answer: me. The idiot who is currently leading the championship and wants to win his first title.

Well, I'm not going to win like this.

"Stop beating yourself up, Adrian," Chloe says, my silence apparently speaking volumes.

"Hard not to when I'm the one who fucked up."

She doesn't say anything for a while, but I know what she's thinking. That there is nothing she can say to cheer me up until I know for certain I'll have made it into Q3.

"Both Carousel drivers are out. Just waiting on the last three," Chloe says, my car getting dragged back into my garage so my team can work on it while we wait.

"Klein driver is out."

I only need one more driver to be slower than me. To set a slower time.

"Come on," I say, placing my hands on the front of my helmet to shift my visor up and wipe the sweat off my brow.

"Both Zeitgeists didn't make it into Q3. You're safe."

A breath of relief escapes me, and I ball my hands into fists to stop them from shaking.

There is so much pressure on my shoulders. I'm leading the championship. This is my home race, a race I've won in the past in a car that was much slower than my own. There are so many expectations. My mother is here, too, taunting us with her presence. There is too much happening, and my brain can't keep up with everything.

I—

A hand appears on my arm, pulling me back into the present. I turn my head to see Daniel beside me, grabbing my hands and holding them in his to stop them from shaking. I hadn't realized that balling them up didn't help.

"It's alright, Adrian. I've got you," he says, his voice muffled because of my thick helmet padding. "Ten more minutes of pressure, then you're done for the day, okay?" I don't know why, but I needed that reassurance, a timespan. Ten minutes. A little while longer, and I'll get to see Nevaeh again, too.

Deep breaths.

After a short break, the countdown for Q3 starts, and I listen to Chloe as she tells me to go set a lap time now and then we'll go for another run with different tires closer to the end. Focusing entirely on the task at hand instead of worrying about everything I did wrong previously helps my panic settle a lot. Shocker, I know, but I'm trying to figure out my panic attacks and their origins. It'll take some more time to find coping mechanisms, but I won't pressure myself to have everything figured out immediately.

The first lap time I set is good, but not nearly good enough. Lincoln has been silent this whole weekend, but it's his silence that unsettles me now. When he's setting lap times so fast, he's on provisional pole.

"You lost point two seconds in the chicane. You can go faster, Adrian. Don't be scared," Chloe encourages me during my cool down lap where I make my way back into the pits. "You're P4. You can go faster."

A few minutes before the end of Q3, I drive out of the pitlane again for my last attempt. The outlap lets me warm up my tires and charge up my battery for my fast lap. I speed up as soon as I make it to the start line.

"Gabriel has provisional pole," Chloe says, and I nod. At least Gabriel is better than Lincoln. I'd rather lose to a man I consider my brother than a dude I have considered running over with my car on several occasions.

I take a deep breath and release it as soon as Chloe tells me my time has started.

I weave through the turns more smoothly than before, picking up speed as I go through the chicane again. Fear grips me, but I ignore it and fixate on being the fastest on the track.

I almost brush the wall on the exit, but only almost.

It might have cost me pole, though.

"Chloe," I say, but she makes a disapproving sound before responding. "Focus."

I grit my teeth and push up until my tires cross the finish line. The breath I've been holding for the last few corners rushes out of me, but not in relief.

Not until I hear Chloe's next words.

"You got pole. You did it!"

A scream of joy erupts from me, and I slam my hands against my steering wheel repeatedly as I celebrate this win after a tough day.

I'll probably still beat myself up over what happened before, but adrenaline and ecstasy flow through me in steady waves at the moment. I'm going to ride them out for as long as I can.

"Gabriel P2, Lincoln P3, and—" Chloe cuts off, and my heart tumbles all over itself in anticipation of her next words. "Valentina is P4."

"Fuck yeah!" I celebrate all over again.

There are three Monegasque drivers in the top four places.

Monaco explodes into celebrations.

Now, we just have to hope we can carry this momentum into tomorrow's race.

CHAPTER 25

Nevaeh

VALENTINA HAS BARELY SPOKEN to me since she found out about Cecilia. She's given me enough content for my article and posed for some pictures, but speaking about her feelings has been at the bottom of her priority list.

She wants to win her home Grand Prix.

It's a dream she's never been this close to reaching, and I won't remind her of her mother while she's trying to go into game mode. A midfield car fighting for the win when three of the fastest cars on the grid are ahead is nearly impossible.

Valentina needs every piece of concentration she can get.

But, no matter how desperately I want her to win today, I'm not sure it'll be possible. Not with her head all over the place and Monaco being one of the worst tracks to overtake.

"Even when you're frowning you're gorgeous," Adrian's voice fills my ears, and I can't help but smile. He gently takes my chin between his fingers to guide my lips toward him and plant a single kiss on them.

"Breathe, race, and win," I start.

"As long as it doesn't cost you a limb," he finishes before leaning down to brush his nose over mine. His fingers wrap around the bracelet he gave me as a naughty smirk slips onto his features. "What do I get if I win this week?" he asks, his thumb trailing over the charms. He's starting from pole with Gabriel in second, Lincoln in third, and Val in fourth.

This is going to be the race of the year.

"What would you like?" I reply, my hands sliding onto his stomach. His race suit prevents any skin contact, which frustrates me.

"You, in front of a mirror, watching me finger fuck you until you come all over my hand," he says in a low voice that sends a thrill through me. Excitement settles between my legs, and my breathing hitches at the thought. "You like the idea of that, don't you?" Adrian asks with a smug smile.

"You should get back to your team before we end up in a closet somewhere and you miss the race," I croak out, not half as confident as I would like to be. Adrian closes the distance between us until his nose is buried in the crook of my neck. He takes a deep breath in just to let it out with a sigh. I giggle a little before I can stop myself.

"Fuck, okay. I have to leave. I love you," he says and quickly presses another kiss to my lips. He rushes out of the room without giving me the chance to say it back or tell him anything else.

As much as I'd like to linger on our kiss or the fact that Adrian keeps telling me he loves me so freely when he's never done so with anyone else, I can't. I can't concentrate on anything other than Val running toward her private room, tears streaming down her face.

Following her is not a conscious decision. It's a reflex. An instinct.

"Val?" I ask as my fist briefly connects with the door leading to her private room.

"Nevaeh?" she says, her voice filled with pain.

"Yeah, it's me. May I come in?"

"Please," she replies, and I open the door to see her curled up in the corner, countless tears falling from her eyes. "Cecilia just spoke to me," Val explains, and my shoulders sink in defeat.

"I'm so sorry," I say while settling down next to her and wrapping my arms around her shoulders. She immediately hugs me back, sobs slipping from her. They are muffled since her mouth is pressed against my shoulder, but her pain is loud and clear. "Cecilia had no right to approach you before you were ready, and I'm so sorry she took that choice from you, Val."

Another sob skips off her lips and settles deep within my chest.

"How could she do this to me? After all this time, she came back right before the most important race of my season!" Tears shoot into my eyes at the devastation coming off her in steady, unstoppable waves.

"She has no regard for your feelings," I state, a realization more meant for myself than for the woman I call my best friend.

"She doesn't. It's all about her and her feelings. It always has been. It's the reason she left."

Silence engulfs us as Valentina clings to me and continues sobbing. I shoot Gabriel a quick message because, as much as I want to be there for her, I know Val needs her fiancé more than me. He's been there longer, knows more about her pain and undealt with heartbreak, how it all affects her now.

Gabriel is what she needs.

"*Ma chérie*," he says softly as he steps into the room and approaches his fiancée. Valentina lets go of me when his hand wraps around her arm before pulling him close to her. Gabriel gives me a small nod, signaling that he's got it from here, so I stand up to give them some privacy.

"Shit," I mumble to myself as soon as I've closed the door to Val's private room, fighting the urge to hit a wall.

Cecilia has messed with my family one too many times, and I don't want to know what she has planned for the rest of the season. Plus, now Adrian is going to lose it. He warned Cecilia about getting close to Val—at least that's what he told me after the first time he saw her at the office—and she didn't listen.

My feet bring me to his garage where I watch him get into the car, his concentration mode activated. Under any other circumstance, I'd be really turned on by the way his hands look grabbing the halo or how smoothly he lowers himself into the car, but I have no mind for that.

I'm trying to think of a way to tell him his mother is the biggest asshole to ever walk this Earth.

But I can't tell him when he's so close to winning another race at his home Grand Prix.

There is going to be enough drama with the Romana siblings fighting each other for the win, along with Adrian's two biggest rivals—the man he hates the most, and the man who's become his brother in every way that matters.

I'm terrified of this race.

"How do you deal with the anxiety before the races?" I ask Scar, but she merely shakes her head and blows out a breath.

"I put on lots of lavender oil and do my best to focus. Usually, when I'm in work mode, my anxiety isn't as bad," she explains, and I nod several times, trying to get my own anxiety under control.

It's too much. Everything that's happening is too much. I haven't been sleeping well, too worried about Adrian to close my eyes without seeing the pain on his face. My heart hasn't been beating evenly since Cecilia reappeared. There is so much pain, and Valentina's earlier interaction with her was the cherry on top.

My anxiety level is officially skyrocketing, and not even the thought of work can calm me, not like it helps Scarlette. My hands are shaking and my breathing is painfully uneven. The uncertainty surrounding the race and the nerves on top of it only make everything worse.

"Here, take this," Scar says, handing me a small bottle with a bouquet of lavender painted onto the sticker. "Rub it on your pulse points and under your nose so the scent can calm you," she adds. "It won't be a magical cure, but maybe it'll help a little." She gives me one of her beautiful smiles, her blue eyes shining brightly.

"Thank you," I reply, doing as instructed and letting the delicate floral scent fill my nose.

"Everything will be okay. Take deep breaths. You're more powerful than your anxiety. It may control you at times, but you can control it, too. With a willpower as strong as yours, it doesn't stand a chance." I don't know what comes over me, but I pull Scar into a hug, letting her comfort sweep through me.

No one's ever truly understood my anxiety the way she does because no one in my family has anxiety. It's a comfort like no other to know I'm not alone. That there are people like Scarlette who understand me.

Neither of us speaks again. She merely gives my shoulders a squeeze before moving back to her desk and putting her headphones on. Isabella, Val's performance coach, hands me some headphones as well, and I place them on with shaky hands.

The formation lap takes place half an hour later, and I can barely sit still.

Here we go.

Chapter 26
Valentina

I push all thoughts of my mother and our conversation earlier aside to focus on one specific task: win my home Grand Prix with a slower midfield car and the three fastest cars on the track ahead of me.

So, easy peasy.

Setting this unrealistic goal for myself may have been ridiculous, but some people would have argued that a woman becoming a Formula One driver is just as ridiculous.

But I proved those fuckers wrong, too, so I'm not giving up hope.

"Take a deep breath, Val. I know you're nervous. I can see your hands shaking on my screen," Scarlette says, and I almost smile.

"Care to sit in this car and sweat your ass off waiting for the rest of the drivers to line back up on the grid?" I ask but inhale anyway, trying to calm my nerves.

"No, I'm happy where I am, enjoying the cool air from the little fan Riley gave me," she says, making me snort so hard, I temporarily forget about my nerves. Riley is Leonard's race engineer, and they've befriended Scarlette almost as soon as she started working for me.

"I hate you," I reply, not meaning the words in the slightest.

"Go get that trophy."

The first light turns on, causing my breathing to hitch.

The second light turns on, and Grandfather's voice fills my ears.

"You will be a champion one day, and no one will be able to take that away from you. You, Valentina Romana, will go down in history as the first female Formula One World Champion."

I've already made history, but that goal, the dream he had for me and I had for myself, I still have to find a way to make it come true.

Winning today wouldn't just be a massive step in that direction. It would mean so much more to have my first win be here, in Monaco.

The third light turns on, and it finally feels like I'm shutting out the rest of the world for good.

The fourth light turns on right as I take a deep breath in and hold it.

The fifth light follows, but I only release the breath when all lights disappear and I hit the throttle.

My reaction time is better than everyone else's ahead of me, but Adrian and Gabriel shoot away, leaving me to fight a slow Lincoln. His start is awful. I push beside him into the first corner. He fights me, but there is no point. I'm already ahead of him.

"Good job. Keep pushing. Try to stay close to Gabriel so you can take advantage of the DRS as soon as it's enabled," Scar informs me, and I appreciate her grounding me again because as thrilled as I am to have overtaken Lincoln, it's overwhelming to claim third place with a Grenzenlos on my ass.

Lincoln chases me for the next few laps, but Gabriel and Adrian are fighting each other for first, so neither is driving away. That means I can stay in Gabriel's DRS and fend off the angry Brit in the car behind me.

Man, he would be so pissed if I kicked his ass and won.

When.

"Your lap times are great, Val. The rest will stop for new tires soon, but I recommend we stay out for a bit longer. You've been managing your tires well," Scarlette says almost halfway through the race.

"Agreed." It's risky. Fuck, it's so risky to stay out, but we have to take risks.

What Scar didn't say on the radio is, "Stay out, pray for a safety car."

Well, I'm praying for the safety car after Adrian and Gabriel get called in by Velocità Rossa for their pitstops, leaving me to take first place.

Lincoln goes to pit as well, so the nearest car, Adrian's, is now almost an entire pitstop length behind me. Almost.

He has fresher tires and will be able to set faster lap times, which means he'll catch me in no time at all. But I have the fastest lap right now. I can do it.

Maybe if there is just one safety car, I could—

"Box, box, Valentina. Adrian is chasing you too quickly. You need to come in," Scarlette says a few laps later, and my heart sinks in defeat.

"Copy."

I start the next lap, preparing to make it to the pits. This was my only chance, but, often, strategies don't play out the way a team hopes. That's why we've got several different ones, and they're most often named after letters of the alphabet. At least, that's how we do it at Alfa Adrenalina, and, according to Gabriel and Adrian, at Velocità Rossa, too.

Right as I slow down to enter the pits, Scarlette's voice fills my ears again.

"Lincoln has hit the wall in corner five. Safety car is being deployed. Everyone has to slow down."

Hope blooms in my chest like a sunflower as the sun shines on it during the warmest summer day.

"Will I be P1?" I ask, but Scarlette doesn't answer me again until after my pitstop, which goes as smoothly as it possibly could.

"Yes, you will come out in P1."

Her voice is emotionless, but I know she's as excited as I am. I have fresher tires. I'll come out in P1. Overtaking is difficult on this track. All of these factors roam around in my mind until I feel a sense of determination I didn't feel before.

I *can* win.

This race has played into our hands. If only I can keep my brother and husband—well, soon-to-be husband—back, I can take this trophy home.

I can, I can, I can.

Maybe if I think it often enough, it'll come true.

When I re-enter the track, with my pace significantly reduced to follow behind the safety car, I'm ahead. Adrian and Gabriel are behind me, and as we drive by corner five where Lincoln hit the wall, I suck in a sharp breath. If I cared about him, I'd ask if he's okay despite seeing him walking behind the fence toward the nearest marshal on a moped, but I hate him, so I don't ask Scarlette.

He's hurt Nevaeh and my brother one too many times for me to feel anything but satisfaction because he's out of the race.

It takes the marshals some time to completely clear the debris. By the time this whole ordeal is over with, there are only twelve laps left. The safety car leaves a lap later, making me the leader of the restart.

Every single car is close behind me, and I have to find a way to stay ahead of the two people I love the most in the world.

Fuck, there is no way my little Alfa Adrenalina can hold off the two bulldozing Velocità Rossas behind me for eleven laps.

"Defend, defend, defend," Scar says before I shoot ahead, ultimately restarting the race. I've caught my brother off-guard enough to make it through the first corner without a threat from him, but it doesn't last long.

He's fighting me for first place half a lap later.

"Well then, come on, Adrian. Come get me, if you can," I mumble to myself, smiling in a way that would be perceived as a challenge in and of itself if anyone saw it. If my brother did.

My body is tired, but I clench my teeth and fight through the exhaustion. Adrian's front tire almost touches mine as we head into the first corner with nine laps to go, but I brake later than he does and manage to stay ahead. We keep battling, cars almost touching, but Gabriel is right behind us, too. And my husband is still fighting for second place.

With Gabriel fighting Adrian, my brother has to focus on defending instead of attacking, something I'm sure Lorenzo Mattia, the team principal of Velocità Rossa, is getting furious over right about now.

"Gabriel disobeying team orders?" I ask Scarlette, five laps to go now.

"Maybe a little," she replies, making a breathless laugh escape me. Of course he is. He doesn't just want second place. He wants first place... for me.

My brother could never just hand me the win. It isn't in an F1 driver's nature to give up a chance at victory for anyone, be it a friend or family. But Gabriel can distract him. The love of my life can make sure I bring this home while potentially securing himself second place.

I smile even harder.

Then, I notice Adrian getting closer again.

"Gabriel was told to back off," Scarlette informs me right as my brother attempts another overtake on me that I barely fend off.

Four laps left.

I can hold him off for four more laps.

"Try getting a better exit in corner three. You're losing a lot of time there," Scarlette suggests, and I do my best to follow her instructions, braking later to get a better exit. Checking my mirror, I see Adrian even closer.

"Scarlette," I say, but the rest of my sentence never leaves my lips as my brother pulls next to me, about to overtake. "Fuck." I try to give him as little space as I can without ending both of our races, and he backs off when he realizes what I'm doing.

He makes a mistake.

He brakes so hard that he's further behind me now, still in DRS range, but less of a threat.

Four laps later, I cross the finish line for the last time, officially a Grand Prix winner of Formula One.

And not just that, a winner of the Monegasque Grand Prix.

"P1! You got P1! You did it, Val, you won," Scarlette cheers, and I hear in her voice how tears are streaming down her face as well.

"*We* did it, Scarlette. We won," I say, but everything else I want to tell her disappears as a wave of emotions constricts my ability to breathe, let alone speak.

Monaco is roaring with excitement. They're screaming for me. For Adrian and Gabriel. For their three drivers as we bring home podium finishes all around.

I wave at every single fan as we drive by them, but Gabriel soon pulls up next to me, punching the air in excitement and pointing at me. He's cheering for me. I place my hand on top of my helmet where it covers my mouth before blowing him a kiss. He catches it and plants it right on top of where his mouth would be, and I can't help but cry even harder.

It's only when I park my car in front of the first place sign that I take a moment to breathe properly, letting the realization sink in. Then, I take off my steering wheel and get out of the car, stepping onto the front of it before placing a single hand on top of where my number rests on my helmet, the other forming a fist I punch the air with.

More tears stream down my face as I run toward my crew, throwing myself into the crowd they form. They catch me with ease, patting my back and legs and shoulders. They release me only so I can make my way to Scar and the rest of my crew, celebrating with them as well. Lorenzo Mattia, the man who took a chance on me and gave me the opportunities to make it where I am today, comes up to me and hugs me.

"Well done," he says in Italian, and I can't help but hug him tighter.

As soon as I step back, strong arms wrap around my middle, Gabriel pulling me into the air and against his chest. Adrian hugs both of us from the side until the three of us are standing together and jumping on the spot in excitement.

There is nothing like winning your home Grand Prix.

There is even less when your home Grand Prix is one of the most fabulous ones in Formula One.

I turn to see Nevaeh taking pictures of the three of us from the side, so I sprint toward her and fling my arms around her neck, too.

"You drove beautifully. You deserve this win more than anyone," she says, her arms like bands of steel around me.

"I love you, Nevs," I say, my emotions running so high, I can't keep the words at bay, especially when I mean them. I do love her. She's become my best friend, a part of our family, and now that she's in my heart, I don't think I'd ever be able to let her go.

"I love you, too," she says, tears stinging her eyes.

They fall down at the same time some more fall from mine.

I'm ushered away and toward the little podium where water, towels, and a cap are waiting for me. After taking off my helmet, I meet Gabriel's gaze, puckering my lips until he lets out a small chuckle and presses his mouth to mine.

It's merely a brush of our lips, but tingles spread down my spine anyway.

"My sister won her first race!" Adrian says to Nevaeh, and I notice tears streaming down his face before he grabs her face and kisses her senseless. "I gotta go," Adrian adds right after releasing her and then skips over to me again to pull me into the air.

He drops me back on my feet so I can get interviewed, and I'm pleased to find motorsport legend Hana Yoon standing in front of me. In her day, she was breaking barriers and paving the way for women like me to make it into F1.

"Valentina Romana, congratulations on your first win in Formula One," she starts, and I barely keep from breaking into more tears.

"Thank you," I croak out, taking a deep breath to fight back my emotions.

"What an achievement. You should be very proud of yourself." The crowd screams my name, cheering for me at the top of their lungs.

I think I might pass out.

"You are the first woman to win a Grand Prix. You are the first to win her home one, at that. You've been making history from the day you set foot in a kart, but today you have taken it a million steps further. How does that make you feel?" Hana Yoon asks, her brown eyes filled with pride.

"I have no words. All I want to say is that, to all the girls and women out there who don't think they can achieve something because a man told them they couldn't, you can. You are powerful and you are capable. I hope I can serve as a reminder of that," I say, waving at everyone who bursts into more cheers.

Hana asks me a few more questions before I end my interview speaking to my home crowd in French, stepping aside to let Adrian and then Gabriel be interviewed.

In the cool-down room, my two favorite people start bombarding me with compliments and telling me how amazing I drove. Adrian doesn't even seem to be mad about the stunt Gabriel pulled. I worked my ass off my entire life for this moment, and he would have never forgiven himself if he'd taken today from me.

When I step onto the podium, it feels like the whole country is screaming for us. Their three drivers.

First, they play the Monegasque anthem. Then follows the Italian one. All the while, tears continue to track down my face, but I don't care. This has never happened before. I'm allowed to cry as much as I would like.

Thomas Crovetto, crown prince of Monaco and brother of my former rival Christian Crovetto, hands me the trophy with a cocky smirk that must have people fall at his feet. He winks at me before moving on to Adrian. I notice Gabriel shooting the prince a deathly glare, but his expression softens when he notices me grinning at him.

Once everyone has received their trophies, we put them down and pick up our champagne bottles. Adrian slams his on the ground, making the liquid shoot into the sky, but I can't linger on the sight of it because Gabriel sprays his champagne my way, drenching me in alcohol. A surprised gasp leaves me, but Adrian and Gabriel direct both their sprays my way until I can do nothing but stand there and let it happen, just like when I got third place in the Dutch Grand Prix.

The crowd roars with excitement.

Cheering for us.

Cheering for *me*.

I've never been this happy.

Chapter 27
Nevaeh

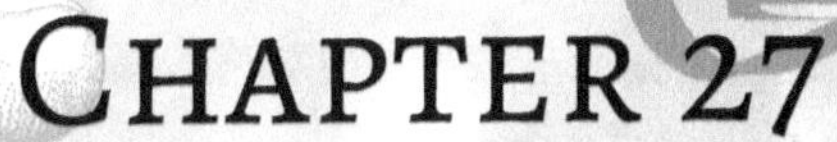

Valentina and Gabriel are dancing to the slow music that is now playing in the restaurant. James, Leonard, and Cameron are having a heated conversation about which one of them would win in a one-on-one race while my boyfriend is listening to them with the biggest smile on his face. His curls are perfectly styled, and his light eyes are practically shining from happiness, their color only brought out more by the polo he's wearing. He looks too gorgeous for me not to take my phone out and snap a few photos. He notices it and turns to me so I can get a better angle. I grin at him as he pulls my chair closer to his.

Adrian's hand slides onto my leg and then slightly under my dress, making my heart race and the ache between my legs unbelievably persistent.

"How wet are you for me right now, *mon ange*?" he asks as he brings his lips next to my ear. My head falls backward, goosebumps spreading all over my body.

"Dry as the desert," I lie. "Feel it for yourself."

He chuckles, his hand lifting higher and higher until his index finger runs over my soaked panties. A satisfied moan leaves him when I press my legs together to ease the throbbing, trapping his hand between them.

"You didn't win today, so you won't get your wish," I tease him. Adrian removes his hand, even though that's the last thing I want him to do. A naughty grin spreads over his face.

"You're glad I didn't win today, don't pretend otherwise," he replies, and I let out a little laugh. "Now, let's go home, beautiful, so I can take that dress off. It should be illegal for you to even wear it." His hand squeezes my leg, and I push forward out of reflex, barely able to keep my gasp quiet.

"You think every type of clothing should be illegal on me," I defend when I find my voice again. Adrian gives me an easy smirk.

"That's because with a face, body, and confidence like yours, anything becomes the sexiest piece of clothing I've ever seen. It gets me into trouble," he says while his thumb traces an infinity sign onto my leg.

"So you'd rather I'd walk around naked?" I challenge, which makes him run his tongue over the right side of his top teeth.

"At home, yes. Anywhere else, no. I don't want anyone to see your body the way I do," he admits before placing his fingers on my chin, his thumb running over my bottom lip. My breathing hitches slightly, making him grin. "I really think we should go home," he whispers, and I nod in agreement.

There is nothing I want more right now.

Valentina and Gabriel sit back down at the table before we can leave. She takes my hand in hers and squeezes gently, smiling brightly. I return it, hopefully just as happily.

"Thank you for comforting me after what happened with Cecilia. I'm very thankful to have you in my life, Nevaeh, I hope you—" Adrian cuts her off before she can finish that sentence.

"I'm sorry, Val, I hate to interrupt, but what happened with Cecilia?" He shoots me a weird look and then focuses on his sister again.

"She approached me, but it's not a big deal, don't worry," she assures him and turns to Gabriel, who cocks an eyebrow at her and winks. I'm pretty sure he's signaling her to go home and spend some alone time together, something I would love to do with Adrian as well. But looking at his upset face lets me know he has a bone to pick with me.

"You should have told me," he complains, so I give him an apologetic smile.

"I didn't want to spoil the mood of Val's win."

He shakes his head and stands up, walking over to his sister to press a kiss to the top of her head. Adrian squeezes Gabriel's shoulder before turning to me with a stern look.

"Let's go, *mon ange*." His voice is firm, letting me know he's not asking but telling. It bothers me, but I stand up and follow him regardless. He's upset with me, with Cecilia, with God-knows-who else, and I will tell him in a calm tone to never speak to me that way again. The only thing I agree with right now is that this needs to be settled in private.

We don't speak until we're in the apartment, where he throws his jacket on the couch and storms into our bedroom. I pick it up and hang it in the closet—because it would bother him if he wasn't so worked up since he's very particular about everything going in its proper place at home—while he walks back out and rubs his face in frustration.

"You should have told me," he repeats, and I nod.

"I agree. I should have told you on a day that isn't as special as today, like tomorrow or the day after. I should have told you, and I would have, but, first of all, it was Val's experience, and, secondly, look at your reaction. You're angry with Cecilia and letting it out on me. Do you think that's fair?" Adrian drops his arm and frowns at me.

"I should be able to count on you to tell me something like this as soon as possible, Nevaeh. You're my girlfriend."

"Exactly, I'm your girlfriend. I protect you. I made the decision for us to enjoy this victory tonight, and I'm sorry you feel like I betrayed you in some way, that wasn't my intention. All I wanted was for you to have tonight. Does that really make me the bad guy here?"

This shuts him up for a moment. He stares at the ground while I wait patiently for him to find words.

"It makes you dangerous," he replies, and I raise both eyebrows.

"Excuse me?" I ask and cross my arms in front of my chest, catching his attention. "You better have an explanation for that, and a good one, too." Adrian takes a step toward me, his eyes still on my breasts before he shifts them to my face.

"You're dangerous because you protect me. You shield me from the bad, and I have never had that before. I'm already completely and irreversibly under your control, and I can't stop myself from getting tied to you with more knots. I don't want to. Control me, *mon paradis*," he says, and I shake my head while trying to ignore my uneven heartbeat. He's in front of me then, lowering his lips to my neck. "You were right. My anger is misplaced. I have so much of it and don't know how to deal with any of it. But I'm so sorry for getting angry."

"I was just trying to protect you," I whisper as his hands find my hips.

"I know. I'm sorry. You deserve better than me getting upset with you for something I've done with everyone I love all my life. Please, forgive me, *mon paradis*," he apologizes and starts to nibble on my soft spot.

"Has no one ever told you how to properly ask for forgiveness, Adrian?" I ask, my breath hitching in anticipation. "Get on your knees," I command, and he chuckles against my neck. "You wanted me to take control? Get on your knees, Adrian, and make it up to me there," I add, and he brings his hands to the side of my tits, running them slowly down my body as he sinks to the ground.

His fingers slip underneath my dress, leaving goosebumps in their wake. He curls them around the waistband of my panties next, pulling them down painfully unhurried.

"I," he starts, pressing a kiss to the top of my right thigh. "Am," he goes on, another kiss, this time on the inside of my leg. "So." Adrian trails kisses toward my aching clit, his mouth hovering over it as his eyes drift to my face. "Sorry." His lips wrap around it as he gently sucks on my clit, immediately weakening my knees.

"Fuck," I breathe out and slide my hands into his hair for stability.

I tug as he licks and thrusts his fingers into me, curling them at the perfect spot like he always does.

"Adrian," I moan so loudly, it makes him chuckle against me. "Shit."

He sucks on my clit again, and I almost lose it. Everything inside of me and my skin is on fire, and the build-up in my lower stomach is unbearable. It tenses with every movement of his.

"Wait!" I call out and grab his face to bring it to mine, making him stand up. Adrian leans down enough so our lips are barely apart. "I need you inside me."

He bites down on his bottom lip before crashing his mouth onto mine, devouring my lips in the same way he always does when he craves me most.

"Where?" he manages to ask before placing his tongue back into my mouth and bringing his fingers to my clit, rubbing it gently.

"Sofa," I reply, but it sounds more like a moan. He guides me toward it, his lips never leaving mine. He sinks down onto the couch and then pulls me on top of him for the briefest moment, only to push me backward and slip between my legs.

"I'm so sorry for being a dick," Adrian says between kisses, and I let out a small laugh when his mouth moves to my jaw and neck.

"Luckily, yours is big enough to back up your attitude," I tease, and he lets out a combination of a laugh and groan.

"Fuck, Nevaeh, why are you this perfect?" he asks before taking out his cock and giving it a rough jerk, aligning himself with my entrance moments later. "I want to get lost in you forever," Adrian says as he looks deep into my eyes and slowly slides inside of me.

My back arches off the couch, which he takes advantage of and removes my dress. My breasts bounce free, and his lips almost immediately wrap around one of my hard nipples.

"You taste like candy to me, do you know that?" he asks, and I shake my head, rolling my hips to bring the head of his dick to my G-spot.

"Oh my God," I almost scream, and Adrian lets out a satisfied moan.

"I was fucking made for you, and you for me, Nevaeh," Adrian blurts out, his fingers wrapping around my neck to force me to keep eye contact. He loves to look into my eyes while he fucks me, and I love watching him lose his composure every single time.

His thrusts turn shallow for a moment, quickening and slowing in turns to make my head spin. He drives into me hard and deep for a while, both of us moaning messes by the time I feel my build-up return. Adrian drops his head into the crook of my neck, inhaling once before picking up speed. He won't last much longer, but neither will I. Shivers run down my spine as my hands slip onto his back, my nails digging into it when pleasure consumes me.

"Sorry," I say, but my orgasm is about to overwhelm me, and I have to find something to hold onto for stability.

"Mark me all you want. I'm yours, Nevaeh Fuchs," he says, hitting the perfect spot inside of me even faster now.

All the tension releases at once as an orgasm takes over my body, shooting through me like adrenaline.

"Fuck," he moans, both of our bodies shaking, trembling through our pleasure before he collapses on top of me.

"I love you," I say while my breathing slows and my hands run through his hair.

"I love you endlessly. Please, forgive me about earlier," Adrian begs and pushes off me to look at my face.

"I already did."

Because a small thing like earlier, which he apologized multiple times for, will never be a reason for me to stay mad at him.

CHAPTER 28
Adrian

I LOST MY TEMPER with Nevaeh.

She tried to protect me, and I got angry with her.

Fuck, how did I let that happen?

How could I have been so stupid?

She does everything for me, and I show her gratitude by being an asshole. Nevaeh deserves better. I've thought that since I met her, but I'm too fucking selfish to let her go. For a while, I thought I was enough. I thought I could be the man to give her everything, the universe and all of its cosmic features. Since Cecilia's return, I've started to doubt it again. After all, I'm behaving like a real *Arschloch*. She deserves better, and I know it. Even right now, as I'm sitting here in front of my piano, playing a melody that sounds just like her while she's on the couch with a book in her hands, I know she's everything I don't deserve. When she fucking smiles at the ink on the pages, I become undone all over again.

Nevaeh is the love of my life.

I've known it for months, planned out our entire future, but every time I realize it, it affects me like nothing else ever has. It hits me deep in the chest, scaring every cell and bone in my body.

How would I even continue living if I ever lost the love of my life?

I've been dancing around this thought, and it sends a wave of panic through me every time it reappears.

We're scared to lose her, dumbass, of course we're going to panic, my subconscious chimes in, and I can't even argue.

I'm so terrified of losing Nevaeh. I've been keeping my distance for days because I'm scared she'll see how wrong I am for her...

No, I'm not. I'm not wrong for her. I'll be everything good in the world for her. There is nothing I wouldn't do to see Nevaeh filled with joy, and, no matter what happened in the past, I will do everything to become a better man. A better version of myself.

I stop playing the piano, walking toward where she is and dropping my entire body weight on top of her. My hands grab onto her curves as she giggles beneath me, placing the book on the table in front of the couch. Her fingers slip into my hair, and I fight back the tears of exhaustion.

There's no use with Nevaeh.

It's like her very presence releases me of all barriers I've built in my mind until I'm bare in front of her, feelings and emotions on a serving plate. I know she can feel my tears as they drop onto her naked, beautiful thick thigh, but she doesn't make me speak. All she does is hum our song while I nestle my head into the area between her legs.

Warmth spreads through me everywhere.

"Have I told you about the first time I understood you calling me *'mon paradis'*?" she asks, and I smile to myself. I love it when she tries to distract me by sharing our stories with me from her point of view. "I couldn't breathe, I couldn't think. You held me on such a high pedestal, I wanted nothing more than to kiss you. The only reason I didn't was because I was still too good at lying to myself. But I should have known. I should have known how desperately in love I was. I should have known there isn't a better man than Adrian Romana out there in the world." I'm about to shake my head when her fingers hold me in place. "You are. You're just in pain right now, my love, but you're everything to me," she says, and I sit up, looking directly into her eyes.

"But I'm broken," I reply. She grabs my chin in the same way I usually do hers.

"You're not broken, *mein Mond*. People don't break. Our bones may, but we don't. Our souls will always stay whole, and so will our hearts. Those two for you might be a little bruised from all the pain you've had to endure, but they're not broken, Adrian. They're still perfect."

She kisses me so fiercely, so deeply, I believe every single word. She convinces me of them with the sincerity of her kiss, and the coconut taste coming from her makes my head spin.

"You make me feel safe," I say when Nevaeh leans away from the kiss.

"You make me feel at home," she replies, and I tug her body closer against mine, her breasts squeezing against my chest and resting just below my chin now. Perfect. This feels like perfection to me. "Will you ever tell me what went through your mind when you first saw me? I mean, did you actually think I was taking photos of you?" she asks, and I keep my head on her chest as I chuckle.

Then, I share the story with her.

It's fucking freezing. England has outdone itself again with these temperatures. No wonder James moved to Monaco. I wouldn't want to have to endure this every winter either.

I'm making my way back to my car, cursing under my breath at the stinging sensation the cold is inflicting on my exposed skin when, suddenly, everything warms. My face heats up and so does my body.

Without hesitation, I move closer to the woman photographing my car. Her light brown hair flies in the wind, strands of blond almost glowing in comparison to the rest of her locks. Her curves are hidden under layers of clothing, but I can see the silhouettes of them, and fuck, they're beautiful. Burning honey-brown eyes, so bright I actually forget how to breathe, focus on my car.

She steps away from the car and stares down at the little screen of her camera. I approach her without another thought.

"So handsome," she whispers at her photos, and I chuckle to myself.

"Thank you," I reply, and her head snaps up. She lowers her camera, and I watch the color drain from her face for a moment. I wonder if she knows who I am. "But if you wanted a picture of me, you didn't have to hide behind my car to take it." I'm teasing her, but she looks confused.

"Excuse me?" she asks, freckled cheeks turning a deep red now. I look her up and down for a moment, trying to drink in her appearance from closer. God, she's gorgeous. I don't think I've ever found anyone this attractive. My heart is racing in my chest because of the excitement coursing through my whole body.

"I saw you squatting and standing on your tiptoes to get a better angle of me while hiding at the same time." I see her trying to protest, so I go on. "Listen, I don't mind, I just wanted to let you know you could have asked for one, you didn't have to go through all this trouble." I'm trying to get her to smile. I'm trying to see if it will have me on my knees because the rest of her is already pretty damn close. She only lifts her tongue to the roof of her mouth and shakes her head.

"I'm sure you don't hear this very often, but I wasn't taking pictures of you. Your car caught my attention, and, to be honest, I didn't even notice you were behind it," she says, and I raise both brows. So, she doesn't know who I am.

I take a step closer now, needing any reason to keep this conversation going. She doesn't seem interested in me, and it surprises me a little. I usually have a very different effect on people.

"I think I need to see some proof," I blurt out, my words soft because she leaned in a little, smelling my cologne. Her eyes flutter closed for a moment, and I almost let out a happy laugh. She likes the way I smell.

"Fine," is her only reply before determination takes over her face. She's ready to prove me wrong, I can see it. I already know she's right. I'm full of myself, but I never thought she'd actually shove her camera toward me to prove me wrong.

I take it, looking through the photos of my car. There are no words for how talented this woman is. Momentarily, I completely forget about her standing next to me, breathing heavily because I'm close to her, and fixate entirely on the details of her photographs.

"These are incredible. You are a very skilled photographer," I say without hesitation.

"Thank you," she says, surprise evident in her voice.

Talent doesn't come close to describing what she has, and neither is subtlety. Her eyes are fixated on my lips, and I have this urge inside of me to ask her out right then and there. Instead, she makes me so nervous, I say the stupidest thing.

"If you want to take a picture of them, you can." I was hoping she'd finally smile at me, but, instead, she rolls her eyes.

"You're an arrogant man, do you know that?" she asks and crosses her arms in front of her chest.

"Perhaps, but do you know what you are?" I ask, focusing entirely on her now.

"Please, enlighten me. I'm dying to know what you think of me." It might be wintertime, but the fire inside of her burns so brightly, I've never felt this hot in my entire life.

"You are devastatingly beautiful." God, Gabriel would be proud of the cheesiness coming out of my mouth. Her cheeks turn an even darker shade of red, but she doesn't reply to my comment.

Instead, she says, "Can I have my camera back?" and holds out her hand so I can give it back to her.

"Yes, of course." I can feel my face fall, but there is nothing I can do to stop that.

When she takes back her camera, our fingers brush, and I feel a spark of electricity shoot through my system. She must have felt it too because she searches my eyes as if needing to see if this was a mutual reaction. It was. And it's fucking new to me, which is why I almost shiver.

"I apologize for taking pictures of it," she says while I place the camera in her hand.

"Why did you?" I ask to distract my mind. I'm also beyond curious. The urge to reach out and tug a strand of her hair behind her ear or twirl it between my fingers consumes me, but I push it away immediately. What the fuck is wrong with me?

"Because I love cars, and I've never seen a Velocità Rossa SUV in real life. It's magnificent," she informs me, and I almost take a step back out of surprise. This gorgeous stranger knows her cars. She just keeps getting hotter, and I barely have the self-control not to beg her to go out with me right now. And I don't fucking beg. Ever.

"It's not mine, it's just a rental," I blurt out because I don't know what else to say.

A moment of silence fills the air between us, but I use that moment to study her, study all of her. Her full lips, the top one slightly bigger than the bottom. Her nose, petite and pointy. Her eyebrows, thick and darker than the shade of her hair. The freckles painted methodically all over her face.

"It's a hell of a rental," she says, and, finally, she smiles before letting out a shaky laugh. Well, fuck it, there goes my ability to breathe.

"If I'd known it would attract a gorgeous woman like you, I'd have bought it instead." My eyes trace her features again.

"Okay then. Again, I'm very sorry about photographing your car, Mister," she says and walks away, leaving me even more confused.

"You don't know who I am?" I blurt out and run to catch up with her.

"Should I?" she challenges, making me grin.

"I guess not."

At her car, I watch her take off her jacket, trying to come up with something else to say. When she turns back to me, I almost fall over. I knew she had curves, I shouldn't be surprised, but the shirt she's wearing is dangerous. It's so tight, her breasts are highlighted so perfectly, I feel myself getting hot all over again, way too fucking hot considering it's minus degrees outside.

"Do you watch Formula One?" I ask, making her wonderful eyes shift back to me.

"I try not to." I almost snort. "Why?"

"Have you ever heard of Adrian Romana?" I manage to ask, my usual confidence somehow still here even though I'm a mess right now.

The beautiful stranger eyes me for a moment, but then simply says, "No, but I've heard of his sister." She gets into her car and I close the door for her, absolutely mesmerized.

"Valentina Romana is the best driver there is so that checks out."

We look at each other for another moment.

"I've got to go," she whispers, biting her bottom lip as I nod in response. It doesn't seem like she wants to leave, and, hell, I don't want her to either. I run my tongue over my bottom lip, catching her eyes in an instant. Instead of getting embarrassed, she fucking smiles.

Fuck, I'm so screwed.

"Will you tell me your name?" I ask, desperate to get anything from her to see her again. I shove my hands into my pockets, stepping away from the car only slightly, enough to allow her to drive away if she wants to.

"I'll make you a deal. If you see me again, I will tell you my name," she replies, and disappointment settles in my chest. She doesn't want to give me her name... it shouldn't sting, but it does, at least a little.

"Okay," I mumble in response and then rub the back of my neck awkwardly. I give her a small wave to say goodbye and then almost slap my forehead.

Did I seriously just fucking wave?

I'm such an idiot.

CHAPTER 29
Nevaeh

ADRIAN HAS A SURPRISE for me.

He hasn't told me where we're going or what we're doing. Only that I'm "about to meet some royalty."

My heart is racing. We don't stop driving until we arrive at a place called *Luz de las Estrellas*. Daniel, Adrian's performance coach, is waiting there for us, a tennis bag over his shoulder.

My body goes into shock, but our conversation from a few weeks ago comes back to me.

"I'm sick of living in the fear of something happening with my shoulder. Will you help me face this fear?"

"Yes, and I know just where to start. Give me a bit of time, and I'll arrange for something, okay?"

Is this what he meant?

And considering I asked him to help me, why is the color draining from my face and why can't I move?

"Nevaeh, I'm not making you play if you don't want to. Thomas Crovetto is a friend of mine, and he asked if I wanted to hit a few balls with him. I suck, but he likes my company. I mean, who doesn't?"

His question pulls me out of my trance of fear, and I almost slap my forehead with the palm of my hand. He lets out a wholehearted laugh, a sound that brings a smile to my face.

"Cocky, cocky, cocky," I mumble.

"How could I not be? I have you," he says, but I just shake my head, my face heated from his words. "Come on, let's not make His Highness wait." I stay seated while he makes his way around his Velocità Rossa, opening the door for me and offering me his hand. I slide mine into his, and he pulls me against his chest, nuzzling my neck and briefly biting the skin there. I giggle and step away with a grin.

"Do I taste good?" I tease, but he gives me a smug smile.

He places both of his hands on each side of me, getting closer until his and my breath are one. His body has trapped mine completely against the car, excitement shooting through me like a shot of adrenaline.

"You, Nevaeh Fuchs, taste like everything sweet in the world. You taste like water after being dehydrated in a desert for days. You taste like happiness and home, and I will never, *ever* get enough of you," he says, claiming my lips and sighing against them. "*Auf geht's,*" he says, the German way of saying *let's go*, and I shake my head.

It should be impossible to fall more in love with someone after reaching the edge of one's capability, but Adrian and I have never conformed to the rules.

Why start now?

My boyfriend leads me to a court where Thomas Crovetto is standing next to... *Santiago Castillo*? Number one tennis player in the world, Santiago Castillo? The guy I played doubles with once during a tournament when we were teenagers?

"I used to know Santiago," I whisper to Adrian, and he looks down at me with surprise in his eyes, so I decide to elaborate. "We played doubles once."

"Did you win?" he asks, smiling now.

"Of course." He snorts at my arrogance but kisses my temple like he couldn't be prouder at the same time.

We close the distance until we're in front of them, Adrian politely shaking the prince's hand. Santiago gives me an amused smile before doing the same with mine.

"It's nice to see you again, Nevaeh," the tennis player says, and I retract my hand with a smile, leaning into Adrian ever so slightly before answering.

"It's nice to see you, too. Win any matches recently?" I ask, and he lets out a small laugh, rubbing the back of his neck with his palm. His hair is dark brown, and he has a wonderful Spanish accent.

"A few, yeah. Piss off any more F1 drivers?" he teases, clearly meaning the time we were playing doubles when Lincoln and I were in a huge fight. At the time, the Brit and I were still best friends.

I burst into laughter at Santiago's question anyway.

"Daily," Adrian replies, and I nudge him in the ribs, but he wraps his arm around me and kisses the top of my head. With our height difference, it's so easy for him to do so. "Okay, I'm ready to get my ass handed to me," he says and releases his hold on me, turning to the professional tennis player. I move in front of Thomas, who holds out his hand to greet me.

"Adrian has talked about you non-stop for months now. I'm thrilled to finally meet you," the future king says, knocking the breath from my chest. There is something about someone else confirming how in love Adrian is with me that makes my heart flutter. "I also watched your career closely a few years ago. You were one of my favorite players to watch," Thomas goes on, which almost makes me let out an awkward, nervous laugh.

"Stop flirting with my woman, Your Highness." Adrian's warning is low, his voice having taken on an edge to sound more threatening, but Thomas merely smirks at my boyfriend.

"Would you rather I flirt with you?" I snort at Thomas' question, but Adrian shakes his head with determination.

"I am a taken man. That means nobody but Nevaeh gets to flirt with me," he says, but he looks so cute with his chin lifted in defiance, I can't help but smile. "Now, I'm ready to show her I'm awesome at tennis, too," Adrian adds, and I thank him with a kiss on his cheek for bringing me here.

Adrian winks at me before grabbing a racket and moving to the side of the court near me. Santiago and I watch from the only bench available, but he keeps his distance from me just like I do mine from him. Adrian is pretty good, but the prince is better. He was training to be a professional tennis player, too—according to Santiago—and I wonder why he never went pro. Maybe his responsibilities as the heir to the Monegasque throne prevented him from following his dreams.

The thought makes me sad for him.

"I'm sorry about your shoulder injury, Nevaeh." Santiago's words aren't meant to make me relive the worst day of my life. They're a way to show sympathy, so I push the uncomfortable feeling in my chest aside.

"Thank you." Santiago's ember eyes find mine, more sympathy in them. "Congratulations on being number one in the world. You deserve it," I say because I remember how hard he works every single day. He's in the best physical shape anyone could ever be, with muscles on top of muscles.

"So would you have," he adds, and I fight back a wave of tears.

My boyfriend pulls me away from the sad feeling lingering inside me when he scores a point and cheers.

"See that, Nevaeh? I'm a natural at this, too." I shake my head and smile at him because his dirty smirk lets me know what the "too" was referring to.

"You know, I tore my meniscus a few years ago. It took me a while to get back into it, to run without the fear of hearing it snap, but it's possible to push past the fear. Beyond difficult, but possible," Santiago says, and my eyes slip to his, meeting an inquiring gaze.

"How? I want to, but I'm terrified. How do I push past it?" I ask, and he leans to the side, picking up his racket and handing it to me.

"Play a few balls against your boyfriend. He's weak enough so it won't hurt," he teases, but Adrian overhears.

"Weak?" he asks with amusement on his face. "Yeah, sure," he adds but nods at the racket to encourage me.

I reach for it without thinking twice, making my way onto the court while mentally patting myself on the back for wearing safety shorts under my skirt today. Thomas moves to the side to give me space, handing me one of the tennis balls simultaneously. I take a deep breath, feeling myself getting anxious now.

"*Mon paradis, inspires profondément.*" I do as he says, inhaling until my lungs can't take more air and then letting everything out again.

I repeat it a few more times, feeling the uneasy feeling linger. It starts to subside when Adrian bounces up and down, imitating what professionals do but in the worst way. I burst into laughter.

"What?" he asks, an innocent smile dancing onto his lips.

"*Je t'aime,*" I simply reply, letting the ball bounce on the ground and then hitting it over the net. My heart skips a beat as soon as the strings connect with it, but I'm forced to focus on Adrian as he hits it back to me. A laugh even escapes me when the ball hits the net because I didn't hit it properly.

"*Merde,*" he curses when he messes up on the next turn, and pure joy consumes me. "Don't give me that grin. I'm just warming up," he complains, so I give him a slight nod as if to say "yeah, sure you are." "*Leck mich,*" he curses in German, and I shake my head with a smile.

Is he learning German?

"I will, baby, all over, but first, let's play," I reply, disregarding the slang meaning of it, "kiss my ass," and focusing on the literal one, "lick me."

"You fucking kill me with that naughty mouth of yours, *mon paradis,*" he says, and my eyes go wide before they shift to Thomas and Santiago.

They're pretending like they didn't hear, but the number one tennis player in the world can't keep the smirk off his face. I frown at my boyfriend.

"What?" he asks again, this time with amusement, so I simply start playing again, the smile creeping onto my face when I realize I'm not scared anymore.

I *want* to play.

I almost burst into tears from the realization. This part of my life isn't gone. It may have changed, but it's still here, and I love it the same as I always have.

My boyfriend gives me a little grin when he wins the point, and another realization dawns on me. I would have never gotten here without him. He created a safe space and atmosphere for me. He made sure I was comfortable, helped me work past my fear.

Adrian Romana, you're the best thing that has ever happened to me.

175

CHAPTER 30
Nevaeh

My boss was so happy with the article I wrote for Valentina after her win in Monaco, as well as the pictures I took, she wrote me a page-long email just praising me. It was... nice. Really nice. At my old job, there were so many people working against me, whether it was Gillian who hated me—which I've long since realized is probably because of the way I got my job—or Cecilia, who made up rules and scolded me based on them, all so I wouldn't be with the man I love.

It's refreshing, and I'm loving every minute of my work.

Cecilia hasn't shown her face again, but that woman has developed a nasty habit of showing up whenever it pleases her.

For this race weekend here in Azerbaijan, Samira has told me to focus entirely on my photography. Of Leonard in his Alfa. Valentina during her track walk, in her car, and pretty much everywhere else she's comfortable with.

It's only Thursday, which means it's media day. Today, I don't have much to do. I've already taken some pictures, but Samira mostly uses the ones I take on Saturdays and Sundays since it's more exciting.

So, I'm sitting with James at a table, waiting for Valentina, Gabriel, Cameron, Adrian, and Leonard to finish their responsibilities and join us. We're all planning to go out for dinner tonight, but I don't mind waiting. I like James, and I enjoy his company a lot.

"How's Damian?" I ask right as he deals us another hand. We're playing a German card game I taught him, and he's been doing incredibly well.

"He's well. I've been missing him quite a bit, though. I've been so busy, I've hardly seen him," he admits, staring down at his cards to avoid looking into my eyes.

"How long has it been since you've spent time with him?"

"We went to the park last week, but I haven't gotten a weekend with him for almost a month now," James explains, sadness covering his features so quickly, I blink and it's everywhere.

"I'm sorry," I say because I can't imagine the toll it must have on someone to be away from their child for so long. Well, at least on someone like James.

"Don't be, love. He's happy, and that is all that truly matters in the end." A smile slips onto my lips before I can stop it. He catches it and returns it, but his features fall in defeat a moment later.

Silence fills the space between us as we both take turns to play. It's not awkward in the least, which makes me happy. I want to get along with James. He's family, and he means the world to Adrian.

"Can I ask you something weird?" James asks after several minutes have passed, and I pull my legs against my chest on the chair.

"Always. I love weird questions. They're so much better than regular ones," I reply, and he gives me a small chuckle.

"Do you think you were meant to meet Adrian? Do you think it was destiny or fate or any of that cheesy stuff people talk about?" His eyes are fixated on his cards again, his cheeks a bright red.

"I've never thought about it that way, but I do believe I was meant to meet him, meant to fall in love with him. We healed each other long before we started dating. His heart is everything to me, it fits like a puzzle piece with mine, and I don't think anything could ever change my mind about that," I explain, so James gives me a look of surprise and awe. I don't know if I gave him the answer he was searching for, but my words make me smile from ear to ear.

"Could you ever move on from him if you felt this way?" is his next question. It wipes the happiness right off my face.

"No," I reply without hesitation. "How could I? He's the love of my life."

His blue eyes shift to my face before they search me with such an intensity, I forget to breathe for a moment.

"How can you be sure he's the one?" he asks, and I finally realize what this is all about. Well, *who* this is all about.

"Because he loves me just as desperately as I love him. Because the thought of spending even a day without him makes me feel sick to my stomach. Because there is only one Adrian Romana out there, and he was always meant to be mine."

Something else occurs to me, a realization I couldn't keep inside even if I tried.

"It's a feeling deep inside, not a thought. It isn't something that appeared in my head and I convinced myself was true. It's something I feel so deeply, so strongly, no thought could ever be strong enough to convince me otherwise."

Tears shoot into his eyes, but he does his best to blink them away as quickly as he possibly can. I place my hand on top of his, careful not to tilt his cards my way. I want to comfort him, not accidentally cheat in the game. Well, at least at first. Once he feels better, I might try to get a peek at them.

"You make it sound like a real-life fairytale," James says, taking my hand and squeezing it.

"Would you believe me if I told you it feels like that sometimes? Only Adrian is the prince and I'm his knight in shining armor, saving him from his massive ego." James and I look at each other for a moment as I do my best to hold back my laughter.

But when he bursts out laughing, so do I.

"There is no more saving him from that, Nevs. He's too far gone," James replies, wiping under his eyes to get rid of the tears of laughter—perhaps even some of the ones he tried to fight back before.

Only once we've both calmed down more do I say the one thing I think he needs to hear the most.

"You are a wonderful person, father, F1 driver, friend, and more. You will find the one person who turns your life into a fairytale, James. I promise. That person is still out there, ready to step into your life when you least expect it." I pause to pick up our cards and shuffle again. "Just ask Adrian. I was unexpected, but he knew the moment he met me that he'd been reserving his heart for me all along," I say, smiling to myself as I remember his words.

His expression turns thoughtful. He runs a hand through his blonde hair a moment later, leaning back in his chair and letting out a breathless laugh.

"That's the difference between my best friend and me. Instead of locking my heart away like him, I gave it away. To the wrong person. And I have no fucking clue how to get it back."

Gabriel snatched pole yesterday with Adrian in second, Lincoln in third, Kyle in fourth followed by James, Val, Cameron, and Leonard.

Adrian hasn't spoken much all day, his concentration mode activated as he prepares himself for the race. He's leading the Drivers' Championship at the moment, and it's putting more pressure on him to keep staying at the top.

Especially with the season coming to an end.

There are only seven races left, and Gabriel and Lincoln are not far behind him in the standings.

The drivers have lined up at the grid, waiting to listen to the national anthem of Azerbaijan and then get back into their cars for the start of the race. I see Adrian from where I'm standing to take pictures of Valentina from the sidelines, talking to Daniel, who hands him his bottle of electrolytes. My boyfriend's eyes go wide, but I'm momentarily distracted by Gabriel and Val, smiling at each other before he pulls her close and gives her a kiss on the forehead. I take a picture, just in case they want a physical reminder of this moment.

They shouldn't be allowed to be so goddamn adorable.

"Nevaeh," Adrian's voice fills my ears, his panic sending a wave of anxiety through me. "*Mon paradis*," he adds when he's close enough, and I furrow both my brows.

"What's wrong, Adrian? What do you need from me?" I ask, scared he's having a panic attack. Adrian takes another three steps toward me, grabbing my face before planting a kiss to my lips. I smile against his mouth, a little giggle leaving me. "Seriously? You worry me for the good luck kiss?" I say when he breaks it but doesn't let go of me.

"It's tradition," he simply replies before kissing me again, and again, and then one more time for good measure. "Thank you, *mon ange*. I have to go now, but I love you endlessly." I say it back, earning the sexiest smile on planet Earth—his smile—before he settles down in his car.

The start of the race has me breathless.

Adrian moves ahead of Gabriel, and Lincoln almost collides with Kyle, giving James the chance to push past them and into third place. My heart is racing as the two Velocità Rossa drivers battle for first, but Gabriel's team soon reminds last year's champion to manage his tires so they can stay ahead of the Grenzenlos and Hawke drivers.

Valentina and Cameron are fighting for sixth place throughout most of the first twenty laps. Both of them pit at the same time, but the Australian's team is faster, allowing him to move ahead of her. They're barely a second apart on the track, and I have to tear my eyes from the screens to breathe.

Adrian is still ahead after he changes his tires, but Gabriel and Lincoln aren't far behind. They're chasing him, putting pressure on him. I wish I was in his garage right now, able to ask Daniel what he's saying, but I have to focus on Valentina.

The screens shift to Gabriel and Adrian's fight, but laps later, everything seems to stop moving for a moment.

Everyone around me gasps.

My gaze shifts back to the screens to see Valentina's car on top of Cameron's, but luckily only on the nose. They are in the barriers, but Val isn't moving. The Australian already got out of his car, running to check on her. My body is paralyzed as I watch him throw the steering wheel away to check on her. I can't see if she's moving.

Then, I hear Gabriel's team radio.

"What's going on with Val? Someone tell me right fucking now before I stop this car where the crash happened and check myself. I've done it before and I will do it again!" No one can tell him yet because they have no idea what's happening. No one is even showing the scene anymore, a common procedure in F1 when they don't know if the driver is okay to prevent the fans at home from seeing anything horrific. "Please, please, someone say she's okay. I'm begging you, please tell me my baby's okay," he says and tears drop down my face.

The red flag is waved, stopping the race at once.

"Scarlette?" I ask, and Val's race engineer turns to me. "Is she going to be okay?" My voice is barely audible.

"She hasn't said anything on the radio, but I can hear her breathing," she assures me at the same moment the screen shows images of Val lifting her arms into the air to show Cameron and the marshals that she's okay. Relief washes over me, and I drop to my knees in response. "The impact must have shocked her," Scar adds, and I nod, trying to calm my heart rate.

Valentina is going to be fine.

All the cars return to the pitlane while the crew cleans up the crash and my friend gets taken to the hospital. Gabriel storms into his garage, arguing with his people about something I can only guess is him wanting to leave to check on his fiancée, which, of course, he can't. He still has to finish the race, something Adrian is aware of as he rushes toward me where I'm standing in his garage. He's not allowed to go into a different one, but I had a feeling he needed me, so I went to his instead.

"Nevaeh," he says, tears streaming down his face. I open my arms for him, and he wraps his around me, sobbing against my shoulder. "I was so scared when she wasn't answering her radio," he admits, his face buried in the crook of my neck. I rub his back, trying to comfort him even though my heart is still racing and the shock hasn't worn off yet. "It threw me back in time to last year, when she was unconscious and they couldn't find her pulse."

"I know," I reply, his uneven breathing hitching even more. "Everything will be okay. Val was already on the radio saying she feels alright, she just got knocked around from the impact," I tell him to try and comfort him, but he holds onto me tighter, his body shaking.

"Don't ever scare me like that," he warns in French, and I'm surprised at how well I understand him. We've been practicing, but Adrian is one hell of a teacher, so I've picked up a lot already.

"I'll do my best not to, *mein Mond*, I promise." Adrian pulls back and slams his lips onto mine, his tears wetting my cheeks.

"I can't lose you," he whispers, his nose brushing over mine. "Not like that, not in any way. You're my everything, Nevaeh."

"And you're mine, Adrian. I'm not going anywhere."

He doesn't let me out of his sight for the entirety of the red flag period. While he talks to his engineers and strategist, I'm right next to him, my hand clasped in his. Adrian needs the comfort of it, and I would never deny him that after what just happened.

This can't be allowed in any way, but he doesn't seem to care.

Eventually, because the crash was so big and is taking a while to clean up, he pulls me to his private room where he drags me to the seating area to place me between his legs and fling his arms around me. We stay cuddled up like that for at least half an hour.

I run my hands through his thick, soft hair, and he traces the infinity sign on my thigh over and over, his eyes closed as he gets some rest.

His phone rings, and he listens closely to Val describe what happened. His hand grabs my thigh harder every so often until his head falls against the wall behind him.

"Careless, Valentina, that was stupid and fucking careless," he says into the phone, and I know without hearing her that she's agreeing. More tears shoot into Adrian's eyes, reddening the white of them and bringing out the light color even more. "I'm glad the doctor cleared you. I love you," he says before hanging up and throwing his phone to the side.

"You're so protective." My smile reveals how sweet I think it is, so he pulls me closer.

"I've lost too much not to be. I have to do my best to shield my family from any harm, I *have* to," he says, and I place a kiss on his cheek.

"I know, but it's a big responsibility, too big for a single person," I almost scold, and he chuckles, the vibration traveling through me.

"Leave me alone. I'm quite content with that weight on my shoulders," he complains and guides me further against him to nibble on my neck. I giggle uncontrollably, although I want to keep talking to him about what he's putting himself through.

"Adrian, the race is restarting soon. Let's get you ready," Daniel says, and my boyfriend gently lifts me off his lap before getting up and placing a kiss on my lips.

"Stay safe and get out of your head," I remind him, and he grins before brushing his nose against mine.

"For you, anything, always," he says, and I hold back a sigh. "Go to my sister. I know you've been dying to," Adrian adds and steps away. I look up at him, guilt on my face.

"I want to be here with you." He gives me a small smile. I do want to go to Val, desperately so. But I also want to be with Adrian for his race.

"I know, but I need you to go and check on her, Nevaeh. Please."

How could I say no to him?

Chapter 31

Neveah

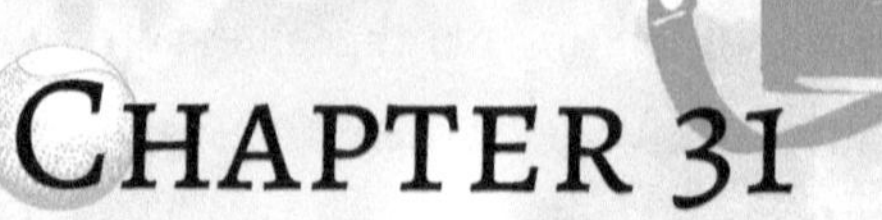

Valentina is sitting in the waiting area of the hospital, her performance coach, Isabella, filling out what I assume is a release form. I rush toward my friend, whose eyes go wide in surprise.

"What the hell are you doing here?" she asks, and I squat down in front of her, my hands moving onto her knees. There is a bruise on her left upper arm, but, other than that, she looks alright to me.

"How is she doing? How's her head?" I say, looking at Isabella because I know Val will downplay how bad her injuries are.

"I'm more than capable of answering those questions myself," she replies, but my attention is on the tall woman next to her.

"Valentina has a mild concussion, bruising on one of her knees and arms, and her left wrist, which was just at one hundred percent after the incident with Eduardo, is now also bruised again." I look at my best friend, a scolding expression on my face.

"Hey, all that matters is that Cameron is fine. The crash was my fault," she says, guilt spilling onto her face and turning her features downward into a frown.

"His safety was not the only thing that mattered when you couldn't move from pain and shock," I say, tears shooting into my eyes before I can stop them. I know if Adrian was here, he'd say the same thing to her. He already told her how careless it was, but the fact her own safety isn't a concern to her would make him furious.

"I know, love, but I'm fine. I promise. This is nothing some rest and Gabriel—" She winks at me. "—can't fix." I let out a small laugh, but Isabella scoffs.

"None of that while you're recovering from your concussion," she says and stands up to hand the nurse the forms. Val leans forward to whisper into my ear.

"She's no fun. Seriously, what's better for your head than getting some, you know, head?" I shouldn't, not right now, but I burst into laughter of relief, amusement, and happiness. This beautiful woman is going to be fine. My outburst turns into a sob, my emotions all over the place after what happened. "Hey, it's okay," she says and slides off the chair to wrap her arms around me.

"Don't scare us like that again," I say, and Valentina chuckles, holding me close while my façade, the one I'd put on for Adrian to be comforting, crumbles into dust until it vanishes completely.

"I'll try my best, I promise." She wipes away my tears, flinging her arm around my shoulder and pulling me against her side.

We stay on the floor for a while, Isabella still arguing with the doctors about the forms. Apparently, there is one aspect she keeps filling out the wrong way, but I'm not listening anymore. All of my attention is on Val's phone as we watch Adrian and Lincoln fighting for first place.

I don't know when I stop breathing, but, eventually, Valentina nudges me in the side to remind me that I need oxygen. It's hard to remember when every time they're battling like this, the Grenzenlos driver can't control his emotions.

"Adrian's got this, Nevs, don't worry," she assures me, but Val has no idea to what lengths Lincoln goes to get what he wants.

They fight for a few more laps until Lincoln moves next to Adrian, pushing him further to the side until he's in the gravel. I sit up straight immediately, but my boyfriend recovers quickly. He moves back onto the track, revenge on his mind.

I can feel it.

"Lincoln has to get a penalty for that," Val almost screams, and I can't help but smile a little. She's so passionate about this sport, it's unmatched. "I will call the FIA personally if they don't," she adds, and I lean my head against her shoulder, grinning at the screen.

Adrian is closing the gap between Lincoln and himself again, but there is no way he can overtake him in the next three laps. His tires are much older than the Grenzenlos driver's. Still, he pushes until he's less than a second behind, putting pressure on Lincoln to get Adrian out of his DRS range. The last thing the Brit needs is for Adrian to have that extra speed advantage. Their roles are reversed now, with Adrian chasing Lincoln, but my ex-best friend has trouble controlling his nerves. He makes a mistake in the tenth corner, going too wide and allowing Adrian to speed past him.

I do my best not to jump up because the race isn't over yet, but Val is cheering beside me.

"Come on, Adrian!" she mumbles.

Her brother speeds down the main straight of the track, finishing in first place. I clap my hands together in joy. Lincoln even gets a time penalty for pushing Adrian off the track, making him drop all the way into fourth place, with James in third and Gabriel in second.

"Yes, *mon amour*! And James. Man, I wish I was there," she says, and I give her a comforting smile.

"I know, but you need to rest." She rolls her eyes at me, but then she drops her head on my shoulder, clearly not one hundred percent okay. No matter how much she tries to hide it, she's in pain.

Valentina needs to rest, and I'll be there for her until she feels well enough to go back to the hotel.

It takes another hour at the hospital to sort out all of Valentina's paperwork, but, finally, I get to drive back to the hotel. Adrian texted me that he will be there soon, too, and I can't wait to see him. It's been a long, scary, successful, and exhausting day for both of us, and there is nothing I want more than to kiss him and cuddle on the bed as we watch a good movie.

I know it's what both of us crave, which is why warmth spreads through me as I walk into the room.

Then, my heart stops beating.

Something is wrong. Someone was in here. I remember Adrian leaving his jacket slung over the chair this morning before grabbing my ass, a thought I'd usually laugh at if I wasn't paralyzed with fear. His jacket is on the table now.

Either our room was broken into, or Adrian had someone come in here, which I doubt considering how particular he is about keeping things a certain way and no one touching his stuff unless absolutely necessary.

Adrian appears next to me before I find a way to move again.

"What's wrong, Nevaeh?" he asks, his lips finding my forehead. I frown at him almost instantly.

"Two things now," I complain, and he chuckles.

"Because I didn't kiss your lips?" Adrian says, and I nod.

"I think someone was in our room, Adrian. You didn't leave your jacket there," I say and point toward it. He tracks the movement of my fingers with his eyes, skipping to where I'm gesturing. He grows tense.

"Fuck."

It takes two hours until the police are done questioning us and we finally get to return to our room to grab our stuff and leave. Adrian booked us an earlier flight home, which leaves in three hours. Neither of us wants to stay here after the break-in. We're supposed to check if anything is missing and report it to the officers, but we all know it's pointless. The security cameras didn't show the face of the robber, and there is no way we'd get anything back.

"Shit, my laptop is gone," Adrian says, and I notice mine has disappeared, too. I tell him as much, but he lets out a small chuckle. "Good riddance. Maybe you'll finally let me buy you one that works properly," he teases, and I frown at him.

There is nothing on the laptop I'm going to miss. All my photos are backed up into my cloud in case of emergency situations like this, and it's not like there is anything... *fuck!*

"Adrian, the photos of us from our photoshoot are on my laptop. What if someone hacks into it and releases them?" I ask, panic filling my chest.

He closes the distance between us, his usual calm demeanor sending warmth through me that relaxes every inch of my body.

"Don't worry. They usually wipe the laptop before reselling it," he says, and I take a deep breath. "I'm sorry I didn't greet you with a kiss on the lips, *mon ange*," he adds before pressing his to mine, all fear vanishing.

My home, my heaven, the love of my life.

A single kiss wakes all of those thoughts, and I smile like I always do when they reappear. He pulls back, returning my happy expression.

"I like forehead kisses, too, but after a proper one," I complain, and he lets out a small laugh. This should be the least of our concerns, but talking about something so small, so silly, makes both of us feel better about what happened. Luckily, they couldn't steal much. The safe in the room kept most of our stuff protected, and I had my camera with me all day.

"You know I'll give you anything and everything you want, Nevaeh Fuchs. I'm glad you tell me when something bothers you so I know not to do it again," he says, and I pull his body against mine by his hips. A surprised gasp leaves him before he claims my lips again.

"Why do these things always happen to us?" I ask when he guides my head against his chest, running his hands over my wavy hair.

"I don't know. Maybe life would be boring without them," he says, and I let out a laugh.

"You're an F1 driver who travels around the world, gets to see and experience everything you desire, and I'm an F1 photographer who gets to do the same. Not to mention, we have assholes as parents, a jealous ex-something of mine that is your rival, siblings we love but want to strangle sometimes because of their actions, and James, who is the wildest out of all of them," I say, teasing James, but Adrian bursts into laughter.

"Yeah, that wild man," he says when he catches himself, pressing his forehead against mine. "You make me happy," Adrian blurts out, and I bring my hands to his strong neck.

"And you me."

But as much as I want to linger on this happiness, something still feels off. Something besides someone breaking in, because what if it wasn't someone random?

That thought scares me more than anything.

Chapter 32

Adrian

"WHY DID I HAVE to come?" James asks as we browse through the rows of laptops. I shoot him an annoyed look.

"Because I wanted to spend time with you," I blurt out, sounding angry. I surprise myself with my level of honesty. James clearly shares the same feeling as he turns to me, shock causing his jaw to hang on the floor.

"Mate, are you bloody alright?" he asks, and I frown.

There is a lot I want to talk to James about, especially after the break-in a few days ago and the email I got this morning, but I haven't built up the courage to speak about any of it yet.

"Leave me be. Let's find my girlfriend a replacement for the garbage she called laptop," I say to change the topic, but James continues to watch me with uncertainty.

I ignore him, asking the saleswoman which model she recommends for everything Nevaeh will need it for, like editing her photos, easy transferring of them from her camera, writing her articles, and more.

"The newest model is one option, but it's a little more expensive. The older one should also work if—" I give her a smile that makes her hesitate.

"The newest is fine. Thank you," I say, and she squints her eyes at me, realization dawning on her.

"Yes, of course, Mr. Romana," she blurts out before hurrying to the back of the store to get me the rose-gold one. It's Nevaeh's favorite color for laptops; she let it slip once when we saw an advertisement at the airport.

"She recognized you but not me? Ouch," James chimes in, and I let out a small laugh.

"Well, have you seen me?" He smacks his forehead with the palm of his hand.

"As humble as ever," he mumbles, and I grab his shoulder, squeezing it once while I let nostalgia wash over me. I miss spending time with him. We're both so busy, we've been drifting apart for a while now, which is one of the reasons I wanted him to go laptop shopping today.

"You love me," I state, but he only rolls his blue eyes in response. "I mean, everyone does. It's hard not to," I say, and he gives me a "seriously?" look.

"Did you forget to take your modesty pills today?" he asks, and I wink at him at the same moment the saleswoman returns with the laptop. I hand her my card and she inserts it into the machine, handing it back to me a moment later.

"Is there anything I can get you, Mr. Landon?" she asks. I can't help but admire the way she keeps her composure, treating us like we're normal customers. We don't often encounter people like that, but I appreciate it more than she will ever know.

"No, thanks, love. I'm all set," he replies, causing her cheeks to heat up in an instant. It's my turn to roll my eyes then, a smile threatening to curl my lips.

"You had to add the 'love,' didn't you" I say, pronouncing it in the same way he does. James gives me a confident smirk.

"Hey, they don't often give me the time of day when I'm with you. It's nice, I liked it, and now, she's going to think about me, at least for a little while." God, I'm rubbing off on him. Soon, he will be just like me, all confidence and no, as he phrased it, modesty.

"Thank you for tagging along," I say when we get back to our cars, James watching me place the bag onto the passenger seat of my Velocità Rossa. He looks over at his car, letting out a sigh.

"I'm going to take your seat at Velocità Rossa just to be gifted one like yours," he complains, and I burst into laughter. It dies out when I realize he gave me the perfect segway to talk about what I found out this morning.

"Between you and me, I'm pretty sure Valentina is going to take my seat next year," I inform him, and he furrows both of his brows.

"Why would you say that?" I smile.

"Because Grenzenlos has offered me a shit-load of money to replace Kyle next year when he retires. Velocità Rossa didn't match the offer, and I'm convinced it's because they want Val instead. Lorenzo doesn't want her to stay at Alfa Adrenalina, he knows it's a waste of her potential," I explain, and James almost loses it.

"And how fucking long have you been sitting on that bus of information, waiting to run me over with it?" he asks, placing his fists on his hips to show how upset he is with me.

"Since this morning, dumbass, and keep your mouth shut. I haven't told anyone else, and I won't. This isn't something to be discussed without me knowing what decision I will make," I say.

"You don't want to leave Velocità Rossa, not even for the money, do you?" This conversation can go two ways. I can either lie to him or be brutally honest with both of us. Before Nevaeh, I probably would have lingered on this decision longer.

"No, I don't. My grandfather and father raced for Velocità Rossa for most of their careers. My plan has always been to stay there for as long as they were willing to have me, but everything's changed now. Val deserves a chance to race for them just like I have for the past two years. I would do this for her, and her alone, but I need some type of guarantee that she'll replace me first," I rant, and my best friend takes two steps toward me, grabs my shoulders, and sighs.

"You have always done everything for Valentina. This? This needs to be a decision you make for yourself, no one else."

"What kind of brother would I be to deny her the fulfillment of her biggest dream?" James watches me with a strange intensity, one that makes me uneasy.

"You need to tell her about this," he says, but I immediately shake my head.

"Are you out of your mind?" I ask, shutting the door of my car and leaning against it. "I'm not going to burden her with this. Don't you ever, ever ask me to do that to my little sister. Do you understand me?" Anger drips from my words, making a compassionate expression replace his surprised one.

"I do, Adrian, I really do, but can you walk away from everything you worked so hard toward?" *No, I don't want to, it's the last thing I want to do when it comes to my future in Formula One, but there will be no choice if Lorenzo Mattia tells me Val will take my seat.*

"I can, and I will." I open my door again, but he shuts it *again*, forcing me to continue this conversation. A groan escapes me before I can hold it back, and James smiles in response.

"Adrian, I'm going to say this once and once only, okay?" he asks, but I roll my eyes.

"Mate, I'm not up for a tough-love talk or any of that shit," I say, and he smacks my shoulder, forcing me to concentrate.

"You are the best brother anyone could ever have. I know because you're mine, too. You're selfless when it comes to the people you love, but this is your career. You have to separate the two," he says, but I give him a serious look, crossing my arms in front of my chest.

"Well, if we forget my feelings, like you say I'm supposed to, then I should take the seat at Grenzenlos. They're offering me more money, more benefits, a strong car, and more I can't disclose. If we disregard my emotional attachment to the team, this is a simple, easy decision." James inhales so deeply, his entire upper body lifts with the motion.

"You're impossible," he complains.

"And you're stupid if you think I'd ever make a decision in my life without thinking about one of the people I love the most in the world. Val deserves the seat more than I ever have, more than I ever will. Now, you either accept this information or leave me alone. Your choice." We both know I'm done speaking about this, but he is unimpressed by my ultimatum.

"No one can deny that Val is a better driver than all of us combined because of her determination, focus, and countless other traits we need to adapt, but there is no such thing as her deserving your shared dream more than you do. I know you're stubborn as hell when you set your mind to something, and sometimes it helps. Sometimes, I even wish I could be like you, but not right now. You're being stupid, and I can't believe you can't see it." He reopens my door.

"You're a pain in my ass," I say because I'm getting all emotional inside, and there is no space for it right now. I need to get home, and in order to do that, I have to get back to Nevaeh.

"Says you." He gives my shoulder one last squeeze, and I shoot him another glare before winking and letting amusement take over.

I get in my car and finally drive back to the apartment.

As difficult as this conversation with James was, it feels like a weight has been lifted off my shoulders. However, it also made me realize I can't talk to Val or Nevaeh about this. I need to speak to someone who understands why this is so hard for me, and who better to tell me what they think than the man who loves my sister more than anyone?

I have to speak to Gabriel.

He will understand me.

CHAPTER 33
Nevaeh

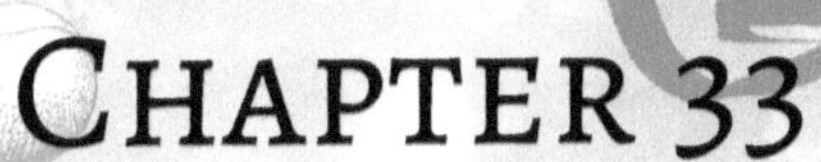

IT'S BEEN OVER A week since the break-in happened, and Adrian and I are on our way to France for the next race of the season. It's only a two-and-a-half-hour drive, so Adrian threw the keys of his Velocità Rossa in my direction, allowing me to get behind the wheel. I can't contain my excitement as I wiggle in the driver's seat, feeling the power of the car under my control when I press harder on the gas pedal. The engine roars wonderfully in response.

I let out a low whistle that makes Adrian chuckle, but his face turns serious as he leans back against the headrest. The sudden change in his mood makes my head spin a little.

"What?" I ask, and he bites down on his bottom lip.

"How would you feel about riding me in my Velocità Rossa, beautiful?" he says, knocking the oxygen out of my body and replacing it with pure, hot, insatiable desire. The ache between my legs snaps to life, and I push my legs together to ease the demanding pressure.

"Right here?" The corner of his mouth twitches, but he bites back his smile.

"Why not?" I can only laugh.

Silence fills the car, so I focus on the road ahead of us, speeding down the highway toward our destination. An image of my family swims into my mind, drowning me in sorrow for a moment. I haven't seen Aileen and Nova in a very long time, but they were able to work past their problems and seemed happy over the phone a few days ago. Mama and I are still not talking. Papa is the only one I saw last weekend at the race and will again in France. However, he was too busy to acknowledge my presence with more than a hug and a quick response to my question about how he was doing.

"Let me distract you from whatever makes you so sad," Adrian says, but I smile.

"I'm not sad. I'm lost in thought." Which is half true, and my smile seems to reassure him.

His hand glides up my leg as his eyes lock onto my face. Heat rushes through me, settling between my legs. He traces the familiar infinity shape on my skin, too close to where my body wants him most. But we have places to be, and if he keeps touching me, I might just pull over.

"Hands off, Romana," I warn, and he immediately retracts his hand, a shocked expression covering his face. He crosses his arms in front of his chest.

"I'm a little hurt," he says, and I burst into laughter when he pushes his bottom lip forward, pouting.

"I need to focus on the street, not your fingers," I explain, and he lets out an *ahh* sound, clicking his tongue with the roof of his mouth.

"That makes more sense. You couldn't resist my touch otherwise," he says with so much arrogance, I can't help the next words spilling from my lips.

"Oh, but I could. Probably longer than you could resist touching me." Adrian leans away, amusement sparkling in his eyes. I see it in my peripheral vision.

"You know I love bets, so I'm going to make one with you now. If I can last longer without touching you than you do me, we'll do that thing I bargained for last time," he says, and the image of the remote-controlled vibrator slips into my head.

"And if I win?" I ask because there is nothing I want that he hasn't already given me.

"You won't," he replies, and I let out a harsh laugh. "But, if by some miracle you do, I'll do anything you want in a situation where I give you a hard no," he offers, but I scrunch my eyebrows together.

"You never give me a hard no," I say, and he shrugs.

"I might, who knows? You can't always get what you want from me," he replies, and I bite down on my bottom lip. We stop at a traffic light, so I hold my hand out for him.

"Fine, you have yourself a deal," I blurt out, and he shakes my hand, electricity shooting through me at the touch. "Last touch, Adrian. Bet starts now." He smiles to himself.

"Alright, you're on. I can't wait to win this one."

The last sentence comes out with so much excitement, it makes my heart vibrate. There is no way either of us will last a long time, but we're both competitive, and I want to win again... *or do I?* I wouldn't hate it if Adrian won. If I'm being honest, it sends a perfect thrill through my system, settling in the tips of my fingers, toes, and stomach to think about doing what he so desperately wants to do.

"You won't win. I'm way too fucking determined," he blurts out after a while of silence, and I chuckle to myself as we pull up to the hotel. "I won't break this time," he says.

"What does the schedule for today look like?" I ask, and he gives me a confused look, probably because I'm changing the conversation without offering a response to his words.

"I have to attend a meeting with my team, but, other than that, nothing. Why?"

"Just curious." I pause for a moment, a naughty thought slipping into my mind. "Would you like to go on a date with me? Dress up and go somewhere fancy?" I ask, and Adrian shifts in his seat, turning his body to face me.

"I would love nothing more," he replies, and a satisfied grin heats up my cheeks, curling my features upward. "I'll make a reservation at *Laurent*. It's fancy. It has three Michelin stars," he says.

I nod, thinking about that orange satin dress I brought with the slit up the side of my left leg. It has a low neckline and hugs my curvy body in the best way. Adrian will be drooling, and he won't be able to keep his hands off me.

I'm sure of it.

"Earth to Nevaeh, did you hear me?" His words pull me back into the moment, and a laugh escapes my throat.

"Yes, I'm paying attention. I'm sorry. What time are we going?"

"Seven, *mon paradis*," he repeats, so I give him one more nod. "You're going to drive me absolutely wild the whole time, aren't you?" I shift my gaze to his gorgeous face.

"You already know the answer to that, my love."

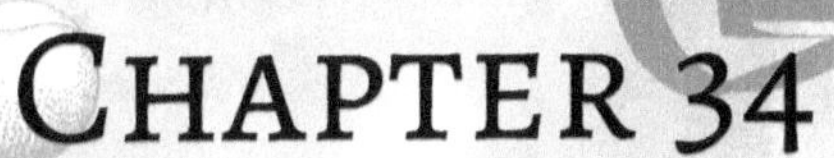

CHAPTER 34

Nevaeh

THE EMAIL ON MY screen sends a bolt of anxiety through me.

Samira Chandra, my boss, has reached out to me, saying that someone from my old job has informed her of certain behaviors that concern her.

There is no doubt in my mind that Cecilia is the one responsible for making Samira aware of these "behaviors," whatever those are.

I don't know what she's up to, but I have a feeling we're about to find out.

I stare at the email for a bit longer, not noticing Adrian walk through the door and toward where I'm sitting until he's in front of me.

My dress catches his attention, and he sucks in a sharp breath, dropping to his knees. A smile I can't hold back slips across my face, and I shut my new laptop—the one he bought me—wanting to leave that trouble behind and focus on the man of my dreams for tonight.

We haven't had much calm recently, and I want us to have a night just for ourselves. And, apparently, our kinky games.

"I don't know how your parents knew, but they named you perfectly, Nevaeh. There is no better name for you, there never will be. You are heaven, *my* heaven." Heat rushes into my cheeks, but I stand up to hide how his words are affecting my whole body.

"And you're mine," I reply as he looks up at me with desire. There is something about having a man like Adrian on his knees for me that excites me.

He stands up slowly, his chest close to mine but not touching. Neither of us is prepared to lose the bet, but I'm almost there. His body looks delicious clad in all black, the fancy clothing making my knees weak. The top three buttons of his dress shirt are open, partially revealing his trained chest. Adrian takes a step toward me, his breath hot on my skin, making mine hitch.

"We should go, *mon ange*," he whispers, and I swallow the lump in my throat, nodding because that's the only response I'm able to give. "Or would you like to stay and admit I have more self-control when it comes to touching you than you do with me?" he asks, and my competitive side takes charge again.

"Let's go," I say with a smile. He attempts to walk away when I call out, "Oh, shoot, hold on," and lift my leg onto the chair next to me.

The slit in my dress exposes my skin all the way to the very top of my thigh while I readjust the clasp from my heels where the band runs around my ankle.

Adrian sucks in another sharp breath and turns away, his head dropping as he inhales.

"What?" I ask with an innocent tone that he doesn't believe for one second.

"Please, let's just go before my dick starts doing all the thinking," he says, and I burst into laughter that doesn't die out until we reach his Velocità Rossa.

Adrian opens the door for me, keeping his body far from mine to ensure he isn't the one to lose by accident. Me, on the other hand, I almost brush against him the whole time. He always turns his head the other way, and I wonder what part drives him the wildest, so I ask.

"Your scent," he admits as he settles down in the driver's seat, gripping the steering wheel harder than necessary. "It draws me in, it has since the day I met you." Adrian lets the engine roar to life, sending a thrill through me.

"It might be my perfume." He shakes his head, his lips pulled into a thin, tight line.

"It's you." My heart rate speeds up, and I welcome the familiarity of it. "Your scent, your body, your smile," he specifies, and I reach for his hand before stopping myself.

"Okay, no more talking! You know physical touch is my love language," I say, and he gives me a wicked grin, revealing how content he is to have made me weak for a moment.

We stay silent the whole ride to the restaurant where Adrian parks his car and then sprints around to my side to open the door again. Usually, he'd even offer me his hand, but not today. He's determined, and I'm already breaking. I want to touch him. I want to feel him pressed against me while he whispers naughty things into my ear.

Adrian leads me into the restaurant where we're greeted by a maitre d' who leads us to a table outside on the veranda. No other guest is present, and I turn to Adrian, shock on my face.

"Do not tell me you reserved the entire restaurant for us," I blurt out.

"What would you like me to tell you instead, *mon paradis*?" he asks, and I stop dead in my tracks, unwilling to go any further.

I cover my mouth with my hands. "Adrian—"

"Laurent is an old friend of mine, now, come, Nevaeh, please. I did something for him so he owed me a favor. I cashed it in for tonight so we can have some privacy."

"You have a lot of people who owe you a favor."

"This business is all about favors. I get his daughters and wife pitlane access to the race on Sunday, and he makes sure no one else is here tonight. That's how it works," he explains, but I'm not satisfied with that answer because I know he paid a lot of money to make this happen.

"You don't need to do extravagant things like this for me, Adrian. I'm more than happy to dress up and go to a pizzeria or something," I say, and his hand twitches, making me realize he wants to touch me more than anything right now.

"I know you don't need it, but I want to give you a life like no other. I want to do both, the fancy and the mundane. I want it all, Nevaeh, everything with you. If this doesn't make you happy, I won't do it again, but, if it does, let me do this for us, for our memories."

"Dammit, Romana," I say and lean my head back to keep the tears at bay. Why does he have to go and say things like that? I can't fall more in love, it's impossible, but then he talks to me this way, making me feel like the queen of the fucking world.

You never realize how deprived of love you really are until the right person loves you more than anything else in the world.

"If you cry, I will touch you and argue that it doesn't count in the bet," he says, and I manage to catch my breath long enough to let out a laugh.

"I'm not crying. Sometimes, I get overwhelmed by how much you love me, what you'd do for me." His hand twitches again.

"Ah, Monsieur Romana, please, have a seat," a man says from behind Adrian in French.

I shift my attention to him right before he shakes my F1 driver's hand. He's a man with pale skin, who must be my father's age, has a full head of hair, ocean blue eyes, and a welcoming smile. I realize this must be Laurent, the chef of the restaurant.

"And this must be your girlfriend Nevaeh. It's a pleasure. My name is Laurent," he goes on. I smile at him, my French coming out surprisingly comprehensible as I tell him the pleasure is all mine. Adrian gives me a proud look. "Sit, please," Laurent says, and we do as we're told. "I'll bring the first course personally in a bit. Enjoy the drink menu."

"*Merci*," I say, and Adrian smirks at me, offering me one of the beverage menus. I take it with a smile, his eyes lingering on my lips for a moment as he holds onto the card, even as I attempt to take it.

"Don't play dirty tricks. Keep your legs on your side and no more seductive smiles," he says to me, and I hold back the chuckle bubbling up in my throat.

"You think all of my smiles are seductive," I counter. "And you, sir, have legs double as long as mine. Keep them on your side," I say, but his shoulders tense at the way I address him.

"Call me 'sir' again, and I'll throw you over my shoulder and carry you out of the restaurant, not giving a single fuck about the bet." Tempting, but I'm not ready for this game to end just yet.

"Yes, si—Adrian," I reply with a wink, but he shakes his head and focuses on his menu, trying to hide his smile by biting down on his bottom lip.

He fails miserably.

By the time dessert comes around, I'm starving. I'm hungry for Adrian's hands on my body, and it's clouding all my senses. We've been having a wonderful conversation about our life together, but he's been quiet for a few minutes, tapping his middle and ring fingers on the table. He runs them in a straight line, back and forth, until I'm pressing my legs shut to ease the ache.

The maitre d' refills my water, a few pieces of ice slipping into my glass and giving me an idea. I watch him walk away before reaching into my water to grab one.

Adrian watches me with curiosity.

"It's so hot out here," I simply say before running the cube over my neck and cleavage to "cool down." The Monegasque leans forward, his breathing heavy now as he follows the drop of water that runs from my neck all the way to the area between my pressed-together tits.

"Nevaeh—" he starts, his voice strained and heavy. He tries to say something else, but it only comes out as a groan.

"You tease me, I tease you. Fair is fair," I state like it's the most logical thing in the world. A laugh, one filled with exertion, leaves his lips, and I bring the cube to my mouth, running it over my bottom lip.

His hands grip the tablecloth before he stands up abruptly and leaves me sitting at the table.

CHAPTER 35

Adrian

I BRIBE EVERY SINGLE person in the restaurant to leave. Laurent is the only one who has to stay, but I trust him to keep his promise to be in his office. With a bottle of whipped cream in my hand, I make my way back outside to Nevaeh, to our table on the veranda overlooking the sea. We're on the second floor of the building, which is located right at the beach. The lights are dimmed, and unless you really look, you wouldn't be able to see us, something I'm counting on.

"Where did you go?" she asks, clearly amused, as I settle back down in my seat.

"We're all alone, Nevaeh. And we're not leaving until one of us loses the bet, and I finally get to fuck you." I love the way a blush turns her cheeks red, the way her chest rises and falls faster from my words.

"What's the whipped cream for?" she asks, bringing a smile to my face. My hands lift to my shirt, undoing the few buttons holding it together. I push it off my chest, taking the whipped cream and placing a single dollop on my naked chest.

"It's for you to lick off me, if you'd like." Nevaeh's on her feet and in front of me within seconds.

"Fuck the bet," she says and drops to her knees, her hands moving onto each of my thighs as she leans forward to lick the whipped cream off my chest.

Only Nevaeh could be on her knees, licking something off my chest, and still hold all the power and control.

My head falls back as a wave of pleasure courses through my system, my skin tingling everywhere her tongue touches me.

Her hand slips onto my naked chest, and all tension leaves my body. Goose-bumps spread over me where her nails touch me. They take hold everywhere, shooting down my arms and only stopping at my wrists. My fingers catch on fire, desperate to transfer it onto her skin in the way that drives her wild. Nevaeh's hands glide all the way to my stomach toward my cock. I almost growl as I grab her hands and stand up, loving the way she grins. My eyes drop to her body, to the way the satin clings to her curves. I wanted to rip it off the second I saw her in it, but I had enough self-control not to.

Until right now.

"I'm going to rip your dress off," I say, my voice low and filled with desire. I want to give her a chance to draw a line or change her mind if this isn't what she wants, but Nevaeh comes closer until her chest brushes mine.

"Do it."

My fingers wrap around the thin fabric, ripping it over her head to reveal she isn't wearing any underwear.

"No panties?" I ask, biting my bottom lip as all the blood in my body rushes to my cock until it presses uncomfortably against my trousers. I don't think I've ever gotten hard so quickly.

"They'd only get in the way," she replies as I trail my hands over her curves, cupping her perfectly big breasts. Her nipples are pebbled, begging for my attention.

She licks her lips, her eyes dropping to my cock.

"Fuck me," she says, running her fingers over my arms. My hands move to her wide hips, digging into her soft skin and lifting her onto the table behind us. "Oh," she says and laughs as her naked body squirms on the table for me. "It's cold," she mumbles and sits up slightly to place her hands back on me, running them over my torso before she unbuttons my pants and pulls my cock out. "Much better," she says with a satisfied moan, but I can't take it anymore. I have to touch her, be inside of her to ease her ache and the pressure in my dick.

"Spread your legs, Nevaeh. Let me see how wet you are for me." Her breathing hitches at my dirty words, but she does as she's told, pushing them apart until I get to see her pretty pussy on display for me, dripping wet.

Fuck me, fuck me, fuck me.

"To your liking?" she asks with a naughty grin, pulling her bottom lip between her teeth.

I need to touch her everywhere, and, for the first time in my life, I have no idea where to start. I've touched Nevaeh so many times, I know all the ways to make her toes curl. I know from where the goosebumps originate and where to put my hands in order to make her tremble.

So, why the hell am I nervous all of a sudden? I know exactly how to pleasure her.

"Adrian, why haven't you touched me yet?" she asks, reaching forward until her fingers hover over my cock. I give her a nod, and she starts pumping me slowly, torturously.

"Fuck, Nevaeh," I moan, grabbing the edge of the table to hold me up. Pleasure sweeps through me, her strokes the source of it all. "You have to let go or I'm going to come in your hand," I blurt out, and she immediately stops her movements.

"No, I don't want that. I want you to come inside me," she says and leans forward, flicking her tongue over my right nipple. I almost fall apart. "I want to feel your hard cock in my needy pussy," she goes on, swiping her tongue across my other nipple. I can't help but wonder where she got her dirty mouth from. Fuck, I hope it's because of me.

"Do you want to go inside?" I manage to croak out, the pressure in my cock building as her tongue moves across my entire torso.

"No, let's stay outside. This is exciting," she says, kissing me all over.

"Lean back," I command, grabbing her wrists to pin them over her head with my hand.

I slide my tongue into her mouth so briefly, I groan as I move down her neck. There is not enough time in the world to savor the way she tastes, but my mouth craves to have her nipple in it, sucking and pulling until she moans for me. Which is exactly what she does when I bite down a little, just enough to make her head spin. My fingers drop to her breasts, cupping and kneading them while I run my tongue all the way down her body. Nevaeh shifts on the table, pressing her thighs together. My head is in the way, but I have no intention of moving it away. I want to taste her. It's one of my favorite things in the world.

"Don't come yet. And tell me 'red' if you want me to stop," I say and wait for her to nod before pressing my lips to her swollen clit. Her head falls backward, her fingers gripping my curls and tugging.

"Adrian!" she screams as I flick my tongue up and down, my hands dropping from her breasts to her hips to hold her down. "Ahh," she moans, her whole body trembling and squirming under my tongue.

Shit, she tastes so good, way too fucking good for me to stop. I've never enjoyed giving a woman head as much as I do with Nevaeh. I want her taste in my mouth. I want to be able to remember how it felt to wrap my lips around her clit and tug until she's begging for her release.

"Please, please, I'm so close," she says, so I stop for a moment, knowing her orgasm will fade for now.

Then, I bring my mouth back to her swollen clit, flicking my tongue over it repeatedly. My hand moves to my desperate cock, and I fuck it roughly, so turned on from having my mouth on Nevaeh's pussy.

I dip my tongue inside her, placing my mouth back on her clit to suck again. She tugs on my hair, trying to keep me in place, but I move back when I feel her legs starting to shake.

"Why? Why can't I come?" she whines, rolling her hips in search of friction.

This woman... she's fucking perfect.

"Because I'm going to give you a mindblowing orgasm now, *mon paradis*, with my cock and fingers, okay?" She nods eagerly, watching me stand upright to align myself with her entrance. So wet, so ready.

"Hurry up," she complains, grabbing her breasts and squeezing her nipples. "I need you," she adds, and I place my hand on her throat, pulling her close to devour her mouth with mine. She moans against my lips, and I become even more desperate.

We're both too needy, so I finally slip inside of her, one hard thrust that makes us gasp in pleasure.

"Fuck, you're so wet," I say, staying all the way inside of her as I fight the urge to fuck her hard and fast and get us both to heaven quickly. Nevaeh deserves for me to take my time with her, she always does, and I refuse to rush this when we have so much time on our hands.

"You're so hard, so perfect," she replies, and my limbs go weak. "Move, my love, please, I need more," she begs, raising her arms over her head and reaching for the edge of the table.

I do exactly as she asked, sliding out of her just enough so that when I thrust back in, she screams in pleasure. I let out my own sounds, knowing full well every moan, groan, and cry pushes her toward her orgasm. Nevaeh is so turned on, all of my thrusts are smooth inside of her, and I have no chance of lasting long, especially when she starts tightening those damn walls of hers around my cock. Heat streams through me, starting in my erection and going all the way into my toes. I feel my orgasm build, but Nevaeh hasn't reached hers yet, so I keep going, keep ignoring the desperation inside of me. It wants the tension gone, wants to be relieved.

"Harder, deeper," Nevaeh demands, and I grab her hips, increasing the aggression of my thrusts. Her breasts bounce with every pump, every hard thrust that makes a clapping noise. Watching her like this... it pushes me too far, too close to the orgasm my bloodstream is demanding to shoot through my body.

"Stand up, please," I say with a nod to the side, and Nevaeh doesn't waste a second.

She already knows what I'm thinking as she walks over to the metal rims of the barrier surrounding the veranda, presenting her ass to me and spreading her legs wide apart, waiting for me to make love to her from behind. I glide my hands over both of her cheeks, grabbing them in my hands before aligning myself again. I thrust back inside of her, ready to get us both to our orgasms. My fingers slide over her back until I reach her hair, wrapping it around my fist.

"Is that okay?" I ask before I proceed with any of my movements. Nevaeh bounces her ass on my dick, and I suck in a sharp breath.

"Pull," she says with a giggle that makes my heart as weak as the rest of my body. I tug a little on her hair, and she screams for me, clearly enjoying everything I'm doing. My eyes shift from her out to the sea for a minute. I lean down then, whispering in her ear.

"Do you like this, *mon ange*? Do you like having sex with a view like this?" I ask, going harder and faster now because I need her to finish at the same time as me. I need to feel her quivering from pleasure as I spill inside of her. "Or do you prefer the thought of being the view for everyone who might see us up here?"

"Oh God," she moans.

"That's not an answer," I say, driving into her even harder.

"You know I do." I'm a fucking goner.

My fingers move between her legs, fingering her clit until she tightens around me again, her orgasm blindsiding both of us. Her entire body shakes, longer than I've ever seen it or felt it, her moans dragged out and low in the quiet night. I'm so surprised, I slow my thrusts, letting her ride out her orgasm for as long as she can.

"Oh my God," she repeats over and over while I run my hands over her ass cheeks, feeling her soft skin in the palms of my hands. "Why aren't you finishing?" she asks moments later, breathless and sweaty. I smile at her as she turns her head to look at me.

"Because I need you to give me one more orgasm, beautiful. I need to watch your body fall apart again," I say, and she bites her bottom lip to hide her smile.

"Okay," is the only thing she replies.

I slide out completely, turning her around and running my cock over her clit and then back inside of her so slowly, it's my own personal torture. But it also helps push my orgasm back to focus on getting her over the edge again.

I repeat the same movement a few more times before slipping deep inside of her. Nevaeh's back arches in response, and I smile to myself as I watch her eyes flutter shut from pleasure.

My moans come out shallow and quick, but she's eating it all up like she's been starving for them her entire life. I know how she feels because it's exactly how I feel.

"You're doing so well, Nevaeh. Tell me you're close." Fuck, I hope she is because I can't last much longer. My balls have drawn so tight, it's painful.

"So close," she moans, and I go faster, deeper, as much as possible.

Then, all the build-up in my body finally releases. I come inside her with my movements slowing, my head floating among the clouds, finding its personal heaven. My cock is throbbing inside of her, pulsating in the same way I feel her walls doing around me. Holy shit, this feels too good, so much so that I can't bring myself to slide out of her for a few minutes.

"Heaven," Nevaeh whispers after a while of silence, her body straightening out until her chest is against mine. I spin her again and wrap my arms around her, resting my hands on her soft stomach as we look out at the sea again.

"And you're mine," I reply, resting my head on top of hers. "*L'amour de ma vie.*"

If only I could freeze time so we could stay like this forever. I don't need more, I never have, and I never will.

CHAPTER 36
Adrian

IT'S NOT AWKWARD TO spend time with Gabriel. It never has been. For some reason, I've always felt comfortable sharing almost anything with him. He has given me a safe space to talk about things I want to get off my chest. It was annoying the shit out of me for a long time, but, right now, I miss how easily I tell him things. I miss words just falling out of my mouth. I'm hesitating. My eyes stare into his as he patiently waits for me to finally talk.

"So, nice weather today," I say, but he merely nods without giving me a verbal response. His face shows hints of amusement, and he crosses his arms in front of his chest, leaning back in his chair. "The tire management is going to be difficult this weekend," I go on, and he gives me another nod.

"Definitely," he says, picking off an imaginary lint from his shirt and flicking it away to show me how bored he is. It's his way of getting me to talk, but I haven't built up the courage.

"Do you think it'll rain on Sunday? I saw the weather report, but—" He cuts me off then.

"Listen, as much as I adore this whole will-he-tell-me-will-he-not-tell-me thing, my patience is running thin. Val is probably waiting for me at our hotel room, just like Nevaeh is waiting for you at yours. Now, get to the fucking point," he says, his smile never fading even as he scolds me. I take in a shaky, deep breath, trying to figure out where to start. Why is this so hard? "Is this about Grenzenlos offering you a seat next season?" he asks, and I forget how to breathe.

"How do you know about that?" Gabriel's green-brown eyes shift to something behind me, then he gives me an unimpressed glance.

"I know everything, Adrian. And if my deductive reasoning skills are as accurate as I know they are, you are struggling with this decision because you don't want to give up your seat at Velocità Rossa, but you know if you do, Val will get it." *What, is this guy fucking psychic?* "And you want me to tell you the right thing to do." It should be a question, but it's not. He knows me so well, it doesn't have to be phrased like one.

"Did James tell you?" It's the only explanation I'm okay with, but Gabriel shakes his head.

"No one had to tell me, mate. It's written all over your face. Not to mention, I know how much you love Val and that you'd do anything for her. It's something we have in common, which is why I also have an answer for your unspoken question," he says, leaning forward on the table to show me he's dead serious.

"Yeah, and what question would that be?" I ask, running a hand through my hair and probably messing it up in the process. On better days, I'd care, but there are more important things on my mind.

"Are you a terrible brother for staying at Velocità Rossa?" Yup, there it is. The one question I didn't dare ask because the answer frightens me so much, it sends an ice-cold shiver down my spine. "Oh, Adrian, you're so stupid sometimes," he says and stands up, starting to collect his stuff.

"Okay, calling me an idiot isn't giving me that perfect answer you promised," I reply, and he lets out a strained breath as he turns to me. He watches me for a brief moment, trying to figure out what to say.

"Do you think Valentina would want that? You giving up your seat at the team both of you love, for her?" he asks, pointing at my chest as he does.

"Of course not, but she's not the one to make this decision. It's mine to make," I defend, and he raises both his eyebrows in response.

"If that is the case, mate, then why is she the main drive behind your decision? Why is she the reason you hesitate?" This shuts me up, halts my argument in my throat. "Velocità Rossa is your home, it's what makes you feel connected to your father and grandfather. No money in the world could give you the same feeling in a different team, and, deep down, you know you'd never give it up. This needs to be a decision about what you desire for once, not Val. Do you understand me?" he asks, and I hold my breath, shaking my head because this isn't something I can do. It's been trained into my brain to do everything in my power to make Valentina's dream come true. I can't just go against it.

"Alright, who the fuck had the genius idea of talking about what I want without me present?" My sister's voice storms into my ears, and Gabriel's eyes light up with love instantly. I wonder if mine do the same when I see Nevaeh. *Ah, who am I kidding? Of course they do.*

"Your brother, the genius," Gabriel says, his gaze fixated on Val as she walks toward him. A smile slips across his face before she gives him a kiss on the lips and then turns to me to smack my forehead. It's so light, I barely feel it, but the point was to tell me I'm an idiot, not to hurt me.

"Why is it that I have to overhear this existential crisis of yours instead of hearing it directly from your mouth?" she complains and leans into Gabriel, who wraps his arms around her in an attempt to calm her. His face moves into the crook of her neck, and the tension fades from my sister's body.

Damn, I'd like to have him around every time she's mad at me.

"To be fair, we thought you were at the hotel already," I defend, but it only makes Val frown until her mouth can't pull down any further. "I'm sorry, I didn't want you to worry about this," I explain, but my sister rolls her eyes. She's about to get mad again when her fiancé rubs her arms with the back of his fingers. It works like magic.

"Adrian, you're not giving up your seat at Velocità Rossa for me, it's not happening. I refuse to let you. As a matter of fact, I won't take your seat, even if it is offered to me. There you go. Now you have no reason to change to Grenzenlos."

She's such a horrible liar. I can see right through her bullshit. Valentina would never turn a seat at Velocità Rossa down, no matter the circumstances.

"Yes, I would," she says, accurately reading my thoughts. "This isn't what Grandpa would have wanted, and you know it. My career mattered to him, my dreams mattered, but so did yours, Adrian. They always came first alongside mine."

Yeah, she's right. Grandpa put just as much time into helping me build connections to get far in this sport as he did Val. When it came to training, she was always more important though. Then again, I wasn't very focused when we were younger. I was stupid and distracted, and it took me a while to find my determination. I got it from watching Val.

"I want you to have a seat there," I blurt out, and my sister's features soften, a small smile now on her lips.

"I haven't even been racing for an entire season. Who knows what the future holds, Adrian? I am in no rush to find out. Let me enjoy my time with the team I have now. They're not looking to get rid of me, and I don't even know if I'm ready to compete for a championship yet. You have to make this decision based on what you want, not what you think I do," she says, and, for the first time since I've been offered the seat at Grenzenlos again, I know exactly what I need to do. I'll turn it down, just like I've wanted to do the entire time. "I love you, Adrian, but I'm all grown up now. You can stop worrying about me, okay?"

No, no, no, no, no. I hate all of it, every single word of that sentence.

"Okay," I lie because I will never stop worrying about her.

The only thing I will start to get better at is putting myself first when it comes to my career. I have to start letting her live her own life without constantly protecting her and fighting with her to make her dream come true. Val has everything under control, and I need to have more faith in her. Plus, she has Gabriel now. He'd do anything to shield her from the things she doesn't want to fight.

"Good. You deserve the world, Adrian, nothing less. Stop trying to give it to me. I'm perfectly happy with the way things are," she says, and I believe her. "Well, except for Cecilia, of course. She's still a fucking pain," my sister says, trying to make it sound like a joke, but we both know she's right.

Cecilia has to leave our lives before things get worse.

"Adrian?" There it is, the best part of my life, the voice I can't wait to grow old listening to, have it be the last thing I hear before I die. I stand up immediately, turning to walk over to where Nevaeh is standing in the door frame. "I'm sorry, I didn't mean to interrupt. Valentina and I were looking for both of you, but I guess she found you," my girlfriend says, a shy smile playing on her full lips. I press my mouth to hers, feeling too happy about things slowly falling back into place to hold back.

"Oh yeah, sorry," Val calls out from behind us, but I don't let Nevaeh answer as I press another kiss to her lips.

"I've missed you," I blurt out, bringing my mouth to her cheek, jaw, and then burying my face in the crook of her neck to inhale the sweet scent coming off her.

"I've missed you, too. That's why I came to look for you." A little laugh leaves her, echoing through my whole body in an instant.

"I'm sorry I made you wait." She steps back to take my chin between her thumb and index finger, a naughty smirk on her face. Nevaeh loves this position so much, she keeps copying it from me.

"I'm happy you did. Now you can make it up to me," she says and grabs my hand, throwing a quick goodbye to the rest of our family before walking me to my car.

I'm so going to marry this woman.

CHAPTER 37
Adrian

Leonard has been staring at me with his lips pulled into a straight, tight line. His grumpy face. I haven't seen it in a while, which is probably why I'm getting punished by it right now. I haven't spent enough time with Leonard, and he's upset about it, I can tell.

I wiggle my eyebrows for him, but he doesn't even flash me a hint of a smile. A sigh escapes me before I can stop it, and still, his expression remains unchanged. His features are hard and angry. This is the Leonard I met years ago. It's the one I had to crack open, and it took me too long for him to give me the same emotionless, cold expression.

"Come on, I didn't work as hard as I did for you to shut me out again, Leonard," I half-tease, trying to get his face to light up a little. He doesn't move an inch, doesn't even show me how my words affect him. I sigh once more. "I'm sorry, mate, I know I haven't been the best of friends recently," I say, sincerity in my voice now. The other approach, the funny one, didn't work. So, I'm going for desperate. "Please, darling, don't be mad." Okay, fine, I'm trying funny again, but it's all I've got. It's my best trait.

"*Hmpf,*" is the only response he gives me before turning to his scooter. I invited him back to the track after the race today—which was uneventful and a shit show with me only coming in fourth, Gabriel winning, Lincoln in second, and Kyle in third—wanting to race around for a little, but he has shown no sign of desiring to do so besides showing up here.

216

"What do you want me to do? Beg? Drop to my knees and ask for forgiveness?" I ask, and he halts his movements, turning his head a little to look at me from the corner of his eye. There is a hint of amusement on his lips now, tugging at the corner of his mouth. Oh yeah, I'm cracking his hard exterior again.

"Try it. Kneel and beg me for it," he replies, but I place my fists on my hips and smile.

"I do kneel, but not for you. Not for anyone who isn't Nevaeh," I blurt out, and he shakes his head with a chuckle. I probably shouldn't have admitted that, but I have no problem with him knowing how wrapped around her finger I am. As a matter of fact, everyone should know.

"God, I was just messing with you. I'm not actually mad," he says, and my jaw drops to the fucking track.

"You were messing with me? You, Leonard Tick, whose sense of humor is as well-rounded as that of a brick, were messing with me?" Leonard scowls, but even as he tries to hide his grin, it takes over as soon as I smile.

"Kiss my arse," Leonard replies, jumping onto his electric scooter and shooting down the track. I step onto mine, trying to catch up with him.

"You're such a cheater!" I call after him, and he flips me off as he takes the first corner.

"You're so slow," Leonard yells back at me, making me laugh out loud.

"Says the grandpa," I tease.

"Grandpa, huh? I think I just won," he says as he brings his scooter to a stop.

We're only at the third corner, but we're both way too tired to do an entire lap around the track. I halt my scooter right next to his, nudging him in the side as I do. Leonard, even though he is shorter than me, flings his arm around my neck, wrestling my head downward until I'm bent over in the most uncomfortable position.

"Okay, okay, you won, you won!" I say, trying to get out of his grasp.

"That's what I thought," he says and pats me on the back with a smile.

"Well, I can still race you back though," I call out and step back onto my scooter, getting the jump on him this time. I make it back first, and by the time we're done, both of us are laughing so hard, my stomach is cramping.

I lean my head back, letting the bright lights around the track shine onto me for a moment. My favorite thing about race weekends is coming to the track when everyone else is gone at night. There is something about seeing it then that sends a comforting warmth through me. The breeze, the feel of the track underneath the tips of my fingers when I bend down, it all feels like... it feels like I am meant to be here. Then, my eyes drift to the stands where Nevaeh is sitting with James, having a thoughtful conversation. I can't help but smile at them.

"What's going through your head?" Leonard asks.

"She just fits into my life, you know? Nevaeh is so perfect for me, she became a part of my family without waiting for permission. Valentina loves her with her whole heart, Gabriel adores her, James is enchanted by her, and I..." I trail off for a moment. "I have no more words for the way I feel about her. There are none in any language to describe how complete she makes me feel. My future is her. My heart is hers. My life is for her. I'm so lost in Nevaeh, I don't ever want to find myself anywhere else again." Leonard's eyes are full of understanding, and a little bit of amusement, too.

"Do you remember that conversation we had when we were in Bali for vacation?" I scrunch my eyebrows together, unsure what he's talking about. "Yeah, I had a feeling you weren't listening. You were pretty busy eye-fucking a woman that caught your attention," he says, and I look away. It's so strange to think about those times now. I don't remember a time I wasn't in love with Nevaeh. It's wild to me that ten months ago, I didn't even know her. Now, I'm probably naïve and stupid, but I don't want to be without her anymore.

"Refresh my memory?" I ask, curious about what he has to say.

"I told you about how training your mind to keep people out, especially ones we fall in love with, is useless. I'm a firm believer of fate. You were meant to meet Nevaeh, meant to fall in love with her, and I told you in Bali that she would come.

I told you no matter what you do, she'd rip down all your walls." It makes sense to me why I don't remember this. I usually filtered these kinds of sentiments out of my brain, unable to believe them, but now?

"I'm sorry I didn't listen to you, Leonard. You were just too wise for me at the time," I reply with a smile, but he's still serious, just like I should be. "Do you think it's ridiculous for me to be so convinced I'm going to marry her one day?" Leonard shakes his head.

"Not at all. My mum used to say it doesn't matter how long you're with the person you'll marry before you have an actual ceremony. Some people get married after years of dating and then get divorced after a month. Others marry after four weeks and die together. I'm not saying get married after four weeks, I'd never do that, but when you know, you *know*, Adrian." Leonard grabs me by the shoulder. "Why do you want to marry her anyway?" he asks, and I smile.

"I want to be able to call her my wife without anyone telling me she isn't. I could start now." I shoot him a look, and he smiles to himself. "But I want it to be true in every single way possible. I want her to be my wife, and I need to be her husband." Fucking hell. Maybe Val's wedding preparations are getting to me.

"Adrian? Where the bloody hell did you go?" Leonard yells, and I smack his stomach.

He laughs at his own joke before nodding his head at something behind me. Seconds later, I feel a body crash against my back. I catch her legs as they wrap around my waist, her arms doing the same around my neck. Nevaeh's lips move onto my cheek, giving me one wet kiss before she giggles.

"Do you only have scooters or also skateboards?" she asks, running her hand down my torso. "I want to race you." I drop her onto her feet to turn around and grab her face.

"Since when do you know how to skateboard?" A wicked grin slips across her face.

"When I was fifteen, I went to skateparks almost every night. I told myself it was part of my training, but I loved the adrenaline. Well, I don't have to explain that to you," she says, and I fall even deeper in love with her.

"I don't know if we have skateboards, but I can che—"

Leonard cuts me off, holding one beside my head. "I am desperate to see you lose, if you couldn't tell," he says, handing Nevaeh a helmet and safety gear. It makes me like him ten times more. He's concerned about Nevaeh's safety, the best trait anyone could have, in my opinion.

"Oh, you will see him lose," Nevaeh assures Leonard as she puts the gear on. I watch her closely, waiting until she's done to offer her my hands and pull her upright. "I'm much faster," she says, and I cock both eyebrows.

"Oh really?" I challenge, and she smiles, tugging on my Velocità Rossa team shirt. James takes out his phone, pointing the camera at us in preparation. I almost laugh at him.

"Yes, my love. I watched you race Leonard earlier, and there is something you're incapable of," she says, causing me to lose my composure. She's really testing *me*, the most competitive person, besides Val, that she will ever meet.

"Enlighten me." She steps on her toes, bringing her lips against mine without kissing me.

"You don't know how *not* to be distracted," she says and grabs the skateboard, racing down the main straight of the track. I race over to my scooter, but she's far gone already, looking hot as hell as she skates away.

That's my girl.

Chapter 38
Nevaeh

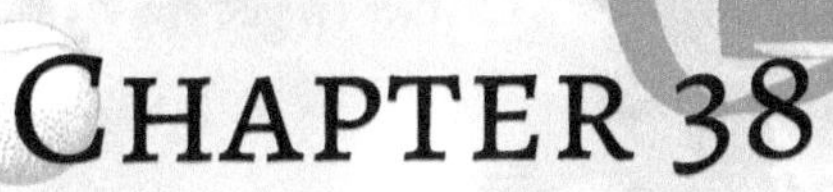

My boss has asked me to meet her in the office today. After that email I received, she told me to only take pictures at the French Grand Prix and then send them to her before our meeting today. She was as kind as always, but something sounded off.

I've been so worried about Adrian's championship lead dwindling down to fifteen points—over Gabriel, twenty-one over Lincoln—that I'd forgotten about the email. It's probably why I didn't tell him about it either. Well, and because he's stressed enough as is. Adrian is always so hard on himself, searching for blame in himself before pointing it at anyone else, and I hate how down he feels because of it.

No sweet, encouraging words help in those moments, so I mostly just hold him.

Or distract him with my mouth.

It depends on what mood he's in.

"Samira is waiting for you. You can go in," Alizia, Samira's assistant, says, and I give them a warm smile before stepping toward my boss' office and—

No.

Fucking.

Way.

My entire body freezes, like it always does when my eyes land on Cecilia fucking Martin.

What is it with this woman and seeking me out? I'm not even her child.

But that's the point, isn't it? I'm not her child, but I am in the way. I'm as much of an obstacle as I am a way for her to get to them. She targets me, and I can either bring her to her children, or she can push me down a cliff and pick up the pieces of their children's heartbreak.

God, I hope my brain only means that figuratively because if I start questioning whether or not Cecilia is capable of physical violence, I might never sleep again.

Me: Cecilia is at my boss' office.

I send the message to Adrian without thinking twice. Without blinking an eye. He should know. As much as I want to protect him, I don't want him to doubt that I'll tell him these things as soon as they happen.

Taking a deep breath, I step inside my boss' office.

"Ms. Chandra. Ms. Martin," I say, the latter I address through gritted teeth.

"Have a seat, Nevaeh," Samira says, a kind smile directed my way.

"I'm assuming Ms. Martin is the person who has made you aware of my concerning behaviors," I say as soon as I'm seated, trying to keep from snarling at Cecilia. She flashes me a vicious smile, sending a wave of shivers down my spine. There is something seriously wrong with this woman.

"Yes. I've been informed that you started dating a Formula One driver despite your contract forbidding you from doing so. I would love to get your side of the story," Samira says while my boyfriend's mother flashes me a daring smile.

Tell her, it says. *Tell her everything and see what she'll think about all of this drama.* Unfortunately for Cecilia, Samira is an amazing person from what I've gathered. She doesn't treat me like the dirt at the bottom of her shoe. She's provided a safe and comfortable work environment.

"I did start dating Adrian while working at *Griffin Sports* and it was against the rules as written in the contract I received from Ms. Martin," I say, focusing entirely on my boss and ignoring the other woman as best as I can with her staring at me. "However, Ms. Martin added that clause on her own because she was meddling in her children's lives." I pause, my eyes meeting Cecilia's. "Adrian and Valentina

Romana." Her face falls at my willingness to share this messiness with my new boss. Then, anger consumes it.

"That had nothing to do with it. It was about staying unbiased," she argues, but I shake my head.

"A good journalist, which I am, reports stories based on facts. Not to mention, I was an assistant for most of the time I was working there. I wasn't writing the big articles you were putting front and center on your website. Whatever bias I had would not have been the make or break of your company." I straighten out my back when Cecilia's expression grows even darker. "Lastly, Mrs. Lu and my father, who was a big part of getting me that job, had no idea about that clause. It was your doing, and yours alone."

"You're just a little bitch, aren't you?" Samira turns her head in complete shock, and I can't help the flood of anxiety hitting my system, but I won't shy away from this confrontation. Cecilia is done messing with my career.

"I was a good worker. Mrs. Lu recommended me highly when I applied for this job. I did everything that was asked of me, but I couldn't stop my heart from falling in love with Adrian. It wasn't a choice I made deliberately to go against the rules. It was simply how I felt, and forcing two people to stay apart when the universe or fate, or whatever you'd like to call it, pushes them together is something not even a little rule can enforce."

Cecilia closes the distance between us so quickly, all I manage to do is stumble out of my seat and step away from her. My breathing hitches as I raise my hands to keep her back. Fear penetrates my system until I'm shaking.

"Ms. Martin, I suggest you back away before I have security escort you," Samira says, standing up and staring at the back of Cecilia's head, but she isn't listening to my boss.

"You've been a thorn in my side since the beginning," she snarls, stepping closer again. My back almost hits the wall, so I step around her and into the middle of the room. "You're ruining all of my carefully crafted plans to earn my children's forgiveness."

"I would never stand in the way of them making up with you, if that is what they wanted, but they don't. They do not want you in their lives. I'm sorry, but that's the truth. They don't want to see you. You are a constant reminder of their childhood trauma, and I will protect them from you as best as I can."

"No, *you're* the one who doesn't want me to see Adrian!" I almost burst into laughter at the absurdity. "You're putting ideas into his head. He wants to see me, I know it. The reason why he won't is you," she says, and I can't hold back a laugh then. It irritates her.

"Madame, I suggest you start seeing things for what they truly are: you abandoned your children. If they ever decide to have a relationship with you, I will one hundred percent support them, but they don't want that right now. Adrian wants you to leave his life, and that is not my fault. It's yours."

Her shoulders sag, defeat coloring her features. I drop my hands, letting my guard down when I see the tears shooting into her eyes.

Never in a million years would I have expected this woman to backhand me for pointing out the truth. Yet, here we are, my cheek burning from the pain of her smack. I barely flinch and tears don't sting my eyes, but the door behind me opens as an angry Adrian steps through.

"Did you. Just. *Fucking* slap. My Nevaeh?" he asks, a deep rage dripping from his words. Relief floods my system when he guides me behind him and towers over Cecilia in such a threatening way, even I take a step away from him.

"She—she—" Cecilia starts but obviously doesn't know where to go from this. "It was her, not me. She pushed me," she says in French, obviously thinking I wouldn't understand.

"I didn't, but I should have," I reply in French.

"You've made one misstep too many. You hurt Nevaeh, and now I will forcefully remove you from my life. You'll never see me again." Adrian's attention drifts to Samira, and she gives him a firm nod. Security steps into the room twenty seconds later, but Cecilia throws me such a vile look as they escort her out, another wave of shivers runs down my spine.

As soon as she's out of the room, I break down into an anxiety attack. My entire body shakes violently, voices sounding distorted as I sink to the floor. Hands find my arms, but I can't stop the buzzing in my ears to filter what Adrian is saying.

"I'm so sorry, *mon paradis*, I'm so fucking sorry," is all I hear Adrian say moments later, but I'm still shaking, hyperventilating.

A cold sweat has broken out across my body, and my limbs are starting to tingle and go numb from the lack of oxygen.

"I'm oka—" I cut off, shuddering. Tears stream down my face and no matter how much I try to slow my breathing, nothing works.

"You anchored me when I had my panic attack. Now let me anchor you."

Adrian places a hand on my chest and then takes my hand to place it on his racing heart. Mine shatters in half at the realization of how terrified he is. It snaps me out of my attack long enough to take a deep breath.

"Good girl. One more deep breath, Nevaeh. You can do it," he encourages me, and I do as I'm told.

But the more my anxiety attack subsides, the more I feel the stinging of Cecilia's slap. Something cold presses against my cheek, and the shock helps me concentrate even more. I take a few more deep breaths, my limp limbs finally regaining some feeling. My eyes drift to Adrian's bright ones, finding worry and heartbreak in them.

"She thinks I'm the reason why you won't see her," I say once I've regained the ability to speak. Adrian lets out a dry laugh.

"I won't see her because she means nothing to me," he explains.

"I know, but she didn't believe me when I said that to her. We're going to have to figure out a way to get her to leave you alone as long as you don't want to see her," I say, and he leans forward to brush his nose over mine before pressing a kiss to my lips.

"I'll take care of that, don't worry." I'm about to complain when he kisses me again, this time not leaning back until we're both out of breath. "I'm so sorry, baby. I can't tell you how sorry I am."

"It's not your fault," I reply, but Adrian shakes his head.

"It is. Everything she does is my fault."

There is no convincing him of the opposite.

Things will only get worse from here. I can feel it deep in my chest.

All I can do now is hope that I'm wrong.

CHAPTER 39

Adrian

I HAVEN'T BEEN ABLE to look at Nevaeh for longer than precisely two seconds since Cecilia slapped her in the face. My eyes dart to my woman's, finding warmth in her gaze, but as soon as I get the slightest glimpse of the mark on her cheek, I can't bear to look at her. It's my fault. She's hurt because of *my mother*, and I cannot forgive myself for it. Cecilia is back because of *me*. She is targeting the woman I love because of *me*, and I have never felt sicker to my stomach.

"My love, do you want to stay in for dinner or go out after we pick Nova up from the airport? Your answer will determine whether I have to put something out of the freezer," Nevaeh says from the kitchen, looking inside the fridge to see what we have.

In this very moment, there is nothing I crave more than to storm over to her, wrap my arms around her from behind and bury my face in her neck, but I don't deserve to do any of that. I still stare at her figure from behind, drinking in as much of it as possible because it's the only part of her I can look at without wanting to crawl into a hole and stay there forever in my shame.

"Do you want to cook?" I ask her, and, as she turns around, I pretend to be busy with something on my phone.

"To be completely honest, no, but I also don't want to be out for longer than it takes to pick up Nova. I'd rather stay in, cuddle, and watch a movie," she says, walking toward where I am and giggling as she stands in front of me, not giving me a choice about looking at her.

Pain seethes through me in an instant. Her lips might be pressed into a smile, but that mark, the one Cecilia put on her, is too fresh for me to ignore. It's a bright, burning red, and it's all my fault. I didn't protect her, just like I didn't protect Val when our aunt abused her all those years.

Don't fucking cry right now, I scold myself and swallow the lump in my throat. *Woman up! Nevaeh isn't crying because of this and neither should you.*

I know I have to be stronger, stop doubting myself, be more like my beautiful Nevaeh, but life keeps telling me how horrible of a partner I am. It keeps testing me, and I lose every single time.

"Then let's stay in. I will go pick up some food. We can keep it in the oven until we're ready to eat," I say, finally breathing properly after I look away from her mark. It's a shit excuse, one that lets me run right now, but I don't care about the food getting soggy.

I can't look at Nevaeh without feeling every type of pain in the world.

I storm over to where my jacket is, and she stays in the same spot, probably watching me with hurt because of how poorly I'm treating her. I didn't even ask if she wanted to come with me.

"Any preference?" I ask as I pull on my shoes.

"Yes, actually," she says, stepping in front of me with her arms crossed under her breasts, pushing them together and tugging on my willpower. "I want you. Forget about the food and take me to our bedroom and make love to me. That's what I want."

And fuck, it's everything I need, but I can't. I can't bring myself to touch or kiss the same face that's hurting because of me.

She places her hands on me, and I can't even step away as they trail down my body. It feels too good, and I know she won't touch me more than this without my consent.

"What are you trying to do?" I ask in French, and she grins because she's so happy she understands me more and more with every day. Our lessons have been paying off, and I wish I could focus on that instead of the shame in my chest.

"I'm trying to get you to touch me," she replies, taking my hands in hers and guiding them toward her tits. Fuck. I take over, cupping them and squeezing. Her head falls backward in response, and I pinch her hard nipples to make her moan. "Oh God." My eyes shift back to the mark on her cheek, and I stop my movements immediately. "Please," she begs, but I grab her face so she opens her eyes to see me shaking my head.

"We have to pick up Nova soon, we don't have time, Nevaeh."

"You haven't touched me since Cecilia slapped me," she almost whispers, and a soft expression takes over my face as I lift my fingers to the mark on her cheek.

"I touch you constantly," I reply, but it only makes her frown.

"Let me rephrase. You haven't fucked me since everything happened," she explains, but I merely shake my head again. It's all I can do to keep from bursting into tears. "Why are you blaming yourself?" My eyes shift away from her at the question.

"We should go," I say, guiding her toward the door.

"I hate that," she blurts out, her face full of determination. "You shutting me out, I hate it. Why do you do that?" My eyes fill with tears, and she closes the distance between us again to place her hands on my face. I grab them in mine to stop her.

"You can't do that. Stop pretending that my mother slapping you isn't my fault. She never would have if it weren't for me, so, please, stop. Stop acting like that mark isn't there because of me, just stop." Nevaeh retracts her hands to cover her mouth. I drop onto the floor, holding my head between my arms.

"Okay, that's enough," she announces and grabs my face before I can stop her again. "This wasn't your fault. She caught me off-guard, but I could have stopped her if she hadn't," she says while more tears shoot into my eyes, but this time, they roll down my cheeks. Nevaeh catches them with her thumbs, wiping them away. "Valentina getting abused was not your fault."

Deep down, I know she's right. This is why Cecilia slapping her hit me so hard. Because I still blame myself for my sister going through years of getting abused without me knowing. Without me taking her out of that abusive household. I take a shaky breath, more physical embodiments of my pain rolling down my cheeks.

"Alright, now you really have to stop. I can't handle this, I can't handle how well you know me," I say and let out a tired laugh, leaning into her touch. "Nevaeh, I'm in so much pain," I admit, and she sinks to her knees in front of me, rubbing my thighs in an attempt to comfort me. My eyes stay on hers the whole time.

"I know. I feel it, my love. Do you know how we can ease it?" I nod, grabbing her chin between my thumb and index finger before pressing my lips to hers.

"You ease it, but not when I push you away." Her cute frown returns at my words.

"Then stop pushing me away when you've done absolutely nothing wrong and neither have I." After another nod and kiss, one where I linger for a moment to feel it spread through my chest, Nevaeh helps me off the ground.

"We have to go pick up Nova," I whisper after a while of us hugging, but I don't let her go. I'm too needy for her comfort.

And, shit, I hope I stop pushing her away because of my trauma. I can't lose Nevaeh under any circumstance.

I wouldn't survive it if I did.

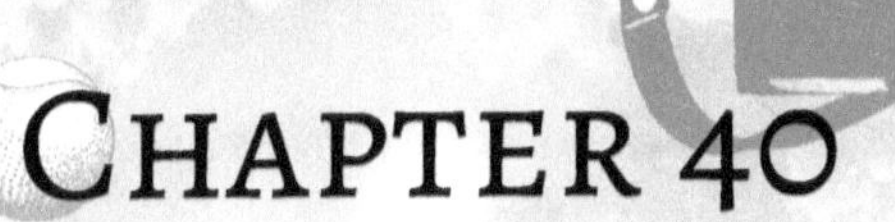

CHAPTER 40

Nevaeh

SAMIRA WAS VERY UNDERSTANDING about the shit show that went down in her office, but she did tell me to take the next race weekend off, and it was non-negotiable. I think she wanted to give this drama a chance to settle and for me to figure out what the hell I'm going to do about Cecilia assaulting me. She gave me other little jobs to do in the meantime, write an article about this here, take some pictures of that there. I don't mind, if I'm being honest. I'm enjoying the slower work so I can spend some time with my friends and family.

Another non-negotiable decision was Adrian buying me a plane ticket to join him in Singapore. It's his birthday during the race weekend, and, even if I'm not working, he wants me there to celebrate it with him. After the cute surprise he had for me on my birthday three months ago—a day filled with all of my favorite things—I want to return the favor.

In order to do that, his favorite thing, which is spending time with me according to him, can only happen if I'm actually there with him.

"Earth to my sister, hello? Where did you go?" I turn to Nova, refocusing on the situation.

We're at a ring store in Monaco, choosing one for Aileen. My sister complete-ly blindsided me with her revelation of wanting to propose in two weeks, but I couldn't be happier for them. Nova has been meaning to pop the question for a year now, but it was never the right time. She finally realized there is no such thing and decided to go for it, as she should. We've all been waiting for a very long time, too long. They're soulmates, they belong together, and if a wedding makes them happy, then they should have one.

"Sorry, I was thinking about work, but that's over with now. I'm yours, one thousand percent," I assure her while my gaze momentarily shifts to Adrian.

For some reason, Nova insisted that he'd come along, but he's been giving us space since we walked into the store. His attention has been on the jewelry in the glass cupboard area, making me lift my hand to the bracelet he gave me. I get distracted by him for a moment, losing myself in how handsome he looks in the blue polo shirt and black jeans he put on this morning. His arms flex as he runs his hand through his hair, staring at something I can't see from where I'm standing.

"You say one thing, but then you do the other," my sister complains, and I let out a small laugh before turning to her again.

"I'm sorry, I'm worried about leaving Adrian in here by himself. I don't want him to get any ideas about something we're not ready for," I tease, but Nova is completely serious.

"When you find your person, Nevi, it doesn't matter how long you're together. I've been dating Aileen for years, but I could have asked her to marry me after the first date. I knew she was it for me." The cynical version of me speaks next.

"Isn't that a naïve way of thinking?" I ask, and Nova cocks an eyebrow.

"No. If you're lucky enough to find your person, which a lot of people aren't, you'll get that gut feeling. It will be the part of you that sees a future only with them," Nova goes on, and, by the way Adrian's left ear and corner of his mouth lift, I'm sure he overheard the whole conversation.

"Is it also that part that tells me to ignore how cocky and full of himself he is?" I challenge to see if he's eavesdropping. A full-on smile spreads over his face.

"Looking like that, I'm not surprised he's full of himself," Nova whispers. I giggle.

"Alright, here you go. This is our least expensive selection," the man helping us out says, pushing the tray with rings toward us. Adrian wraps his arms around me from behind, and I lean into the embrace. His hands rest on my stomach, his chin on the top of my head.

"See anything you like?" he asks in French, and I shift my head so my gaze meets his when he looks down at me.

"You," I simply reply, and surprise washes over his face.

"Nevaeh Fuchs, you just said something cheesy. Careful now, I might enjoy that more than your teasing," he says, and I shake my head, smiling to myself.

"What if I said I don't want to get married?" I tease, feeling Adrian's lips on my neck a moment later.

"I know you want to marry me. From the day I told you '*je t'appartiens*,' you have wanted to spend the rest of your life with me." My heart races uncontrollably from the realization that he's, without a doubt, right. "And one day, I hope you'll marry me not to have a stupid paper that says so, but so we entangle ourselves in this life in every way possible," he goes on, his index finger tracing an infinity symbol on my stomach.

"I hate it when you see right through me."

"No, you don't."

"No, I don't," I agree, refocusing on my sister and leaning further against Adrian.

She spots a ring that isn't on the tray, her eyes lighting up at the sight of it.

"How much is that one?" she asks and points at what she means.

Adrian is busy slipping his hands under my shirt to send thrills through me while I do my best to pay attention to my sister.

"Tell me, Nevaeh. Which one do you like?" he asks, but I shake my head.

"None of these have an infinity symbol," I reply, and he lets out a small chuckle that vibrates through me.

"You're right." He places another kiss on my neck before straightening out to pay attention to Nova, his hand still flat against my stomach to keep me against him.

"It's one thousand-five hundred euros," the man says to my sister, who sucks in a sharp breath.

"It's perfect, but I can't afford it. I'll keep looking," Nova states and walks over to where Adrian was standing before. He presses me even further against his chest, directing his gaze to the salesman.

"Do you take card?" he asks in French, probably thinking I wouldn't be able to understand. I spin around immediately, but he covers my mouth before I can voice a single one of my complaints. I say them against his hand anyway, and he chuckles.

"Yes, sir, we take card," the guy helping us replies, and I step away, out of Adrian's grasp.

"No, you can't do that. It's too expensive," I say in French so my sister doesn't hear. He smiles at me, probably because my pronunciation is off, but I don't care. My brain is in panic mode. I won't let him pay for Aileen's engagement ring. "It's not your responsibility," I whisper in English, and his fingers snake around my hips, guiding me back against his hard chest.

"It's a thank you to Nova for when she used to provide me with the information about your favorite things," he says, his playful smile bringing one to my own lips. "Please, let me do this, I want to. It will make your sister happy, which will make you happy, and that's my goal with everything I do," he says, kissing away the protest that was bubbling up in my throat. I feel one of his hands lift backward into his pocket, and I open my eyes to see him handing his credit card to the salesman.

"Adr—" I start, but he cuts me off. He grabs my face, holding it close to his as he slips his tongue into my mouth to keep me from saying anything.

"Oh my God, get a room," Nova says, a little disgusted by our PDA, and understandably so. He was full-on making out with me, and, as much as I enjoyed it, my sister doesn't need to see this. My eyes shift to her just in time to see hers go wide in shock. "Did you just—" Nova cuts off, watching the salesman hand her the ring inside a velvet box in the shape of a rose.

"Nevaeh will thank me for it later," he teases, and I nudge him in the side, but my sister starts to cry.

"You better be *very appreciative* tonight," she says. Adrian grabs my chin between his thumb and index finger, making me focus on his serious expression.

"That's not why I did this." His French is flawless in my ears. His gaze is fixated entirely on me, and I doubt anything could distract him at this second. He's trying to make sure I don't take this the wrong way. I inhale deeply, his comforting scent filling my nose and spreading through my chest.

"*Je sais*," I reply, and he gives me the slightest of nods.

"Good."

He lets go of my face but grabs my hand to lead us outside. Nova is still staring at the ring, composing herself as she admires it. I've never seen my sister this emotional about a materialistic possession, but I'm convinced it's the meaning behind it. It has to be, otherwise we haven't been spending enough time together and I'm losing touch of who she is becoming. The thought sends a wave of sadness through me.

"You know what? I think you two need to go on a sister date, catch up without me intruding. I have some work to do, so I will see you both later."

I don't know how, I wish I did more than anything, he knows this is exactly what I need. It may have been the change in my mood or facial expression, I'm not sure. Either way, this perfect man always finds a way to give me everything I need without me having to ask for it.

"I love you," he says, pressing his mouth to mine one last time.

"I love you endlessly," I reply.

"In every universe." He steps away, throwing me the keys to his Velocità Rossa. Adrian gives me one last smirk, making my knees weak, before walking back in the direction of the jeweler.

What is he—

"Let me drive," Nova chimes in, pulling me out of my thoughts.

"Over my dead body. Adrian is crazy enough to let me drive it. I won't let him be even more so by giving you the keys." My sister frowns, but I pay no attention to her as I make my way toward the bright red car that costs more than my life.

"Your boyfriend bought me an expensive engagement ring," Nova blurts out, causing me to stop dead in my tracks. "Why?" A smile spreads across my face, and I drop my head to keep the happy expression to myself.

"Because he'd do anything to remind me there will never be another man for me."

And that wasn't even his intention.

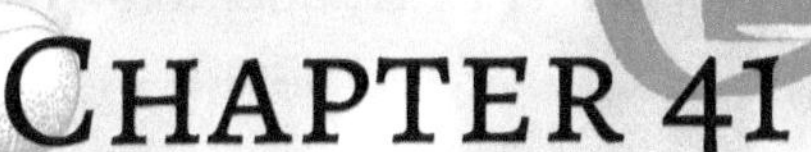

CHAPTER 41
Nevaeh

DAMIAN IS SLEEPING ON my lap, his small right hand clinging to one of my braids and the left one pushing his thumb into his mouth. Domi and Nicolette are on a three-day trip to visit Domi's parents in Italy, which is why the toddler is staying with his dad for a bit. James invited Adrian, Val, Gabriel, and me over for dinner and to spend time with his son. Well, that was his intention, but the little guy refused to go to anyone other than me.

"Do you think I can hold him for a bit?" my best friend asks, and I attempt to remove Damian from my lap, but his grip doesn't loosen. I mouth a "sorry," but she sinks into Gabriel's arms, disappointment curling her lips downward. "I'm his godmother, and he doesn't care about me anymore," she complains, and her fiancé chuckles, pressing a kiss to her temple.

"I'm the shiny new toy, Val. I'm more interesting than you for now, not forever. He'll get bored of me," I explain, and Adrian lets out a snort.

"Yeah, right, like *that's* possible," he blurts out, his eyes going wide at the realization of his words.

Gabriel and Valentina chuckle to themselves while James bursts into laughter. Adrian's cheeks turn a bright red, and he rubs the back of his neck with the palm of his hand. In private or in front of only one of them, he never seems to mind being romantic and corny, but, with all of them in one spot, it makes him blush.

"Don't mind him, he's a dick," I say in French to Adrian, but everyone, except for James, bursts into laughter.

"Very good," Gabriel compliments, and I blush a little.

Adrian's hand slips onto my thigh, his warmth spreading through my chest.

"Alright, give me my son before I start questioning if that stereotype about Germans being rude is true," James says, grabbing Damian and shooting me a glare that turns into a playful smile as he walks away.

Before I know what's happening, Adrian is pulling me toward him, placing me between his legs on the couch and nuzzling his face in the crook of my neck.

"I've been wanting to do this since we sat down," he whispers against my skin, placing a kiss to my neck and sending excited shivers down my spine. It shouldn't feel so good. His body pressed against mine with his lips so close to my soft spot shouldn't be everything I want, especially not in front of our friends. But I don't care anymore when I see them cuddling each other, too. I sink further into Adrian's arms, enjoying the way the tips of his fingers trail the infinity sign just below my belly button.

"*Vorsichtig*," I warn, and his head dips backward so his gaze can meet mine.

"What does that mean?" he asks, curiosity sparkling in his eyes. I shift around so my lips brush the shell of his ear, ensuring he's the only one to hear my next words.

"It means 'careful' because your hand is too close to where I need it most, and I want to stay for dinner." This knocks him completely speechless for a moment. He clears his throat, moving me around in his lap until... oh, he's hard.

"Screw dinner. Let's go home," he says, but the ringing of James' doorbell pulls us out of our moment. Adrian groans against me, the vibration temporarily clouding my senses.

"Cameron must have had time, after all," I say to ease the tension that has me breathless. I walk over to the door, the distance allowing me to think rationally instead of with my body.

I open the door to reveal... fuck no. I try to slam the door shut, but a hand stops me.

"Move out of my way. I want to speak to my children, so I will," Cecilia barks, but Adrian is already pushing me behind him, shielding me with his body. He won't let her hurt me again, and I understand that, but, if anything, I want to be the one to protect him. It shouldn't be this way around.

"Leave," he says, trying to shut the door on her, but she storms into the house before he is able to. His entire body tenses, and when I look over at Valentina, I see Gabriel is shielding her in the same way Adrian is me. These men would never doubt our strength, but they're scared, on high alert. They'd die before they let anything happen to us.

"Please, Adrian, give me one chance, both of you, to explain why I left." I bring my hand to his back, running my fingers down his spine. He relaxes under my touch before leaning into it.

"Fine. Give us your explanation and if we still don't want a relationship with you afterward, you'll never see us again. Yes?" Adrian suggests, and I can hear how tired he is of having to deal with this woman time and time again. Her eyes, the ones she passed onto her children, fixate on me then.

"I want her to leave. She—" Adrian cuts her off.

"*She* has a name, and Nevaeh is my future wife. Start addressing her properly and with more respect."

Never, in all the time I've known him, has Adrian raised his voice to this extent or with this much aggression. Everyone and everything goes silent, except for his heavy breathing, which fills the room. I reach out, lacing my fingers through his and guiding him to my side. Surprised by his own emotional explosion, he lets me, almost welcoming my proximity by stepping behind me and wrapping his arm around my shoulder.

"Sit and explain, Cecilia. Then, leave."

Adrian leads me to the couch, and I sit down beside Valentina, who is doing her best to dial down her angry expression. None of them want this woman here, and I refuse to believe there is one shred of good in their mother. She shouldn't force herself into their lives, she should give them time. Instead, they have to figure out how the fuck to get rid of her without involving the police. That's the last thing Adrian and Valentina want.

The small woman settles down on the sofa in front of us, the one Adrian and I were cuddling on, stuffing her purse against her side. A bright smile reaches her entire face, causing nausea to bubble up in my throat. She's enjoying this. That sick woman is thriving off making her children miserable for an opportunity to explain herself.

"Tini," Cecilia starts, and my best friend shifts in her seat, avoiding eye contact. "I've said it before, and I need to say it again. You've grown up to be more beautiful than I could have ever imagined," she says, and Adrian rearranges us so I'm pressed against him again.

"I'm sorry, I need you close," he whispers, and I'm about to tell him I'd give him anything he wants when Cecilia speaks again.

"And Adrian, you are more handsome—"

"Get to the story, Cecilia. We don't give a fuck what you think about our looks. We're well aware of how attractive we are and compliments from you mean nothing to us."

I was about to laugh at the first half of the last sentence, but the second one made it die out before it even left my lips. Sadness crosses the middle-aged woman's face.

"You have your father's arrogance," Cecilia says with a small smile, and every muscle in Adrian's body goes back to its tense state. He feels like cement next to me.

"As long as I don't have anything from you, I'm fine," he spits, and I slide my hand onto his, guiding his arm around me.

"Cecilia, our patience is running low," Gabriel chimes in, leaning forward on the sofa to get closer to her. "So, either hurry up or leave, your choice." I understand the impatience all of us feel, but rushing this also doesn't seem right for some reason.

"Fine, I'm sorry, I just can't believe I'm sitting with you. After all those years, I'm finally back with my children," she says, wiping under her eyes. *Is she seriously crying right now?* That makes me angry. This woman has no right to cry over something she did, something that hurt two of the people I love most in the world.

"Why did you leave?" Adrian asks, trying to guide the conversation in the right direction. Cecilia shifts uncomfortably, thinking about what to say.

"Your father wasn't the easiest man to live with, you know. He always got drunk."

"We know, Cecilia, you left us alone with him, remember?" Valentina asks, and surprise settles in my chest. I wasn't expecting her to be the one to break the silence.

"I know, but I had to. I couldn't live with that man anymore, and he wouldn't let me divorce him." Val tilts her head, a laugh she doesn't mean escaping her.

"And you thought it would be okay to leave your children with a man like that?" Cecilia ignores the question, focusing on Adrian instead.

"I ran away because I wasn't a good mother anymore. Your father turned me into a scared person, one who couldn't raise two extraordinary children like the two of you. All I thought about was myself, my safety, and I realized how messed up that was. What kind of mother was more concerned for her own well-being than her babies'?"

"The kind you are. The kind that has been harassing us since you returned, forcing yourself into our lives to tell us a sad story about a father we lost. The only parent that stayed in some way, mind you. Yes, he was horrible and neglected us, but he stayed. He always came home, made sure we were fed, clothed, going to school, and so much more. His career meant everything to him, but he at least came home after dropping us off at our grandfather's house for however long he was gone."

I look at the man I love, tears stinging my eyes at the pain in his voice.

"I'm sorry about what you went through, truly, but have you got any idea what happened after you left?" Cecilia shakes her head, guilt on her face. "Our grandmother died. Then, our father, who sent us to your sister, for some inexplicable reason, also died. Our aunt *physically* abused 'your daughter.' Then our grandfather died. Valentina endured more abuse, years of it, all because you fucking left." Adrian stands up to get back to the front door. "You have shared nothing with us that could justify why you left us, more than anything, now I wonder how you possibly could have let your children endure such an insufferable, terrible man." He shakes his head and opens the door, signaling for her to get out. "Don't come near us again. Don't even breathe in our direction. We don't want you, we never have. We were fine without you, but your presence makes us miserable. You want to be a good mother? Get out of our lives."

Cecilia hasn't stood up or even attempted to leave. She merely watches her son, trying to find a way to convince him she should stay and talk things through with them.

"I came back because I went to therapy. I worked on myself and have finally become the mother you deserve," she says, and Adrian slams the door shut.

"And it took you almost two decades to do that? Don't bullshit me, Cecilia. You came back because, like the gold-digger you are, you've probably run out of the money you stole from Dad when you left." She's about to respond when he raises his hand, telling her to stay quiet. "Please, don't try to deny it. Do you honestly think Grandfather wouldn't tell me that you only started showing interest in my father when he became famous, not the ten years you were in school with him? Do you think Dad wouldn't tell me you stole from him?" he asks, and I wish I could unfreeze my limbs to comfort him, but there's nothing left for me to do except listen.

"That's not fair," Cecilia mumbles, making him laugh dryly.

"You know what's not fair? Blaming yourself for your mother's abandonment for years until Nevaeh showed me it wasn't my fault. You know what's also not fair? Losing almost every single person you've ever loved and then getting abused by the only other blood relative you have apart from your brother!" Gabriel pulls Valentina close, but she looks ready to step in and fight Cecilia with Adrian.

"That wasn't my fault!" Cecilia counters, but Adrian storms toward her and grabs her by the arm, leading her to the door.

"We had a deal. Now, get out. We're done with you, for good."

He pries the door open, shoving her outside with so much care, I'm surprised he is able to control himself while anger pulsates through his body. He shuts the door again before she can say anything else and then storms toward Valentina, pulling her into his arms.

"I'm sorry I brought up what happened with Carolina. I just needed to make Cecilia understand we will never forgive her," he says in a rushed voice, but she shakes her head.

"It's okay, if I had found my voice, I would have said the same," she replies, and I rub my face with my hand, feeling someone grab my other one. I turn to see Gabriel giving me a comforting look and squeezing my fingers to assure me everything will be fine.

If only I believed him.

CHAPTER 42
Adrian

Singapore is beautiful.

I've been here more than half a dozen times, but I'll never get sick of this place. Especially Sentosa, the smaller island connected to the bigger one, where Universal Studios is, along with beautiful beaches and other fun activities like zip lining and indoor skydiving. I took Nevaeh to all of it.

We arrived in Singapore several days before the start of the race weekend, which allowed us enough time to do it all. Well, everything I put on my bucket list. Singapore might be tiny, but there's a lot to do here.

We even celebrated my birthday yesterday by going on the Singapore Flyer, where I may or may not have spent the entire time kissing Nevaeh instead of admiring the beautiful skyline. There is nothing and no one more beautiful than her.

It helps distract all of us from Cecilia forcing herself back into our lives, too.

My responsibilities are the only reason I'm not currently spending the day with Nevaeh at the beach, ogling her half-naked body—respectfully, of course—and letting her distract me.

Today is media day.

Val, Gabriel, Leonard, Lincoln, and I were chosen for the press conference, and I'm not looking forward to being in a room with Lincoln again. He's been keeping his distance since I punched him in his dumb face, but we're the biggest competitors for the championship, so we get thrown together a lot.

"Try not to punch Lincoln again," Val says with a grin, and I flash her the most arrogant smile I have.

"Have you seen the video of it online? It was a perfect punch. I'd love to give the fans a part two," I reply.

And I know you'd enjoy seeing me beat his ass again, too.

"As entertaining as that might be, kiddo, I'm in no mood to break up a fight today," Leonard says, grabbing my shoulder and giving it a squeeze. It's meant as a warning, but I direct my smile his way anyway.

"Then don't break it up. He doesn't stand a chance against me." Leonard rolls his eyes, but I can see the hint of a smile he always offers me curling the side of his mouth.

"One day, that cockiness is going to get you into serious trouble," Gabriel chimes in, grabbing Val's hand and pulling her to the seating area at the front of the room.

"It already got me into trouble, and her name is Nevaeh," I tell Leonard, who snorts and shakes his head. Then, his frown returns as he grabs my arm to stop me from walking toward the couches as well.

"Listen, there is something serious I want to discuss with you before the press conference today," Leonard says, sending a wave of concern through me. "I said serious, not bad," he adds when he notices my expression.

"What is it?"

"I'm retiring at the end of this season." This is the Leonard I'm used to. No bullshit. No pretty words to dampen the burning of the band-aid getting ripped off.

"Oh," is all I manage to say. His news shouldn't send a wave of stinging pain through my chest, but trying to picture this sport without Leonard in it when he's been here since my first day makes me feel uneasy. "I'll miss you," I admit, another realization washing over me. I won't see Leonard as much anymore.

Fuck, why do I feel like crying now?

"I'm sorry, kiddo, but it's time. I'm tired. I've achieved everything I wanted to, and I want to spend more time with my wife and little girl." I can't blame him. If I had to be away from Nevaeh every race weekend, I'd consider retiring as well.

"I completely understand. It won't be the same without you, but I get it. I'm happy for you," I say, meaning every word. I *am* happy for him, but I can be happy and sad at the same time. "You're going to announce it now, aren't you? That's why you told me." Leonard nods, his warm brown eyes full of sadness. "Let's end this season on a fucking high, shall we?" I suggest, bringing a soft smile to his lips.

"Sounds good."

We join Val and Gabriel at the front, and I almost snarl at Lincoln when he steps through the door. He avoids eye contact with all of us, and I almost smile when he sits as far away from me as possible.

As promised, Leonard tells the first reporter who asks him about his plans for next season that he's retiring. The room goes silent, shock covering their faces. Valentina looks unsurprised, which makes me realize Leonard probably spoke to her about it a while ago. They're teammates and business partners, so it makes sense.

I'm still a little jealous that Val knew it before me.

"The next question is for Adrian, Gabriel, and Lincoln. With the season coming to a close and the championship standings amongst the three of you being so close, how do you feel?" Beside me, Val snorts a little. I can't help but smile at her as she plays it off as a cough, but Gillian, the asshole who asked the question, won't let it go. "Is there something funny about my question?" he asks, but my sister merely gives him an unimpressed look.

"You know there is tension between Adrian and Lincoln, and yet you still went with that question. Are you trying to start a fight?"

Gillian's jaw drops to the floor while Gabriel leans his head back to keep everyone from seeing his smile. Leonard directs an unsure look at Val, but there is a hint of amusement in it, too. Even Lincoln smirks to himself.

I focus back on Gillian, gesturing toward him and saying, "Well, answer the question." Leaning forward, my elbows on my knees, I intertwine my fingers and place my chin on top of them.

"I think it's a fair question to ask," Gillian sputters, and my eyes drift to Gabriel. His meet mine, and I give him a small nod, telling him to answer first.

"Naturally, I think all of us are very nervous and determined to get this championship title. We're working hard, and we'll fight this out until the last race of the season," he says, concise, straight to the point, and polite.

Lincoln hasn't learned that approach yet.

"Nothing's been decided. I will still win that championship, so I'm happy and secure at this stage of the season." Cocky. I give him a thumbs-up for his answer, but he merely shoots me a glare.

"I think that the next four races are going to be filled with drama and excitement, so, yeah, I'm nervous, but I'm looking forward to showing everyone some great racing," I say, flashing a fake smile at Gillian.

"Next question is for Valentina," another reporter says, and I lean back in my seat, draping an arm over the back of the couch and placing my left ankle on my right knee. "Ever since you won the Monaco Grand Prix, have you felt more expectation from your team and fans to win again?" a female reporter says, and I appreciate the way she treats my sister like any other driver. A lot of the male reporters have yet to dial back their sexism when addressing Val, but at least my sister, being the badass that she is, handles every question well.

"Definitely. I think as soon as everyone realized that it *is* possible for a midfield car like my Alfa Adrenalina to win, they've started hoping I could pull it off again. Especially at another street circuit like the one here in Singapore, I've gotten a lot of messages and comments from fans hoping I'll snatch my second win," she replies with a grin, truly filled with joy because of how far she's gotten.

I'm so, so proud of her.

"Thank you," the reporter says.

"This question is for Adrian. There have been rumors circulating about you having a panic attack before the last race ahead of the summer break. Care to comment on what people are saying about your ability as a race car driver who suffers from these kinds of attacks?"

The question catches me completely off guard. I haven't heard any of these rumors, but I've also done my best to stay off social media since Nevaeh and I announced our relationship. I don't want to see any negativity thrown her way. So, I've barely been on social media, but I regret it now. If I'd been more present, I'd have seen the rumors. I wouldn't have been caught by surprise now.

I attempt to answer, but my throat goes dry. This question is so very personal, and all I can hear is Nevaeh's words repeating in my head.

"Do you know how people look at you when they find out you have a mental illness like anxiety, depression, ADHD, or any of the other ones? They look at you like you're not a human being. They view you as incapable, less than."

That's exactly what people are saying now that they heard about my panic attacks. They're wondering about my ability to do my job.

Nevaeh is right.

And now, so many people are looking at me, it's my job to make sure everyone knows that a person's mental illnesses and struggles do not define them or their ability to do anything they put their minds to.

"Yes, I have panic attacks sometimes, but they don't affect my ability to race. I think it's ridiculous to make it a rumor and put so much shame around it. A person's mental health is first and foremost none of anyone's business until that person opens up about it. Secondly, there is *nothing* to be ashamed of if you have panic attacks, anxiety, depression, or anything else."

The reporter who asked the question looks downright embarrassed for putting me on the spot like this. Good. Maybe he'll learn.

"As a society, we need to do better. Stop shaming people for their mental health. *Stop* thinking that whatever mental illness one has automatically makes them incapable of doing their job. *Start* offering accommodations for people who have mental illnesses. Society spends so much time dissecting a person like me and my mental health when that energy could be put into making sure we feel comfortable enough to open up and discuss our mental health struggles. But instead, here we are, shaming yet another person for something I have no control over. It's quite disappointing really."

My rant comes to an end, and the entire room falls silent. Nevaeh would be so proud of me for speaking out about this, and I can't help but think of her and her anxiety. Of how people have been treating her whenever they find out about it. How she has to hide it because she trusted people with the knowledge of her anxiety and they have used it against her in the past.

That's not the kind of society I want for my angel. I want to make it a better place for her.

And to do that, I'll have to do more than just call out one reporter.

I'll have to do something bigger and more impactful.

They ask us another ten questions before all of us get released from this tiresome meeting. Then, I make my way back to the hotel.

Back to Nevaeh.

CHAPTER 43
Nevaeh

"I don't like those at all," Gabriel says, and I can't help but grin at him. "Sunflowers, *ma chérie*, that's the only type of flower I want at our wedding. Nothing else."

Valentina closes the folder with the other kinds of flowers, leaning over to plant her lips on Gabriel's. They're planning on having the ceremony in five weeks, but we've already planned out pretty much everything there is to plan. Now it's only the small details like what cake they want and what time the wedding should be. Since they want to have it in Italy before the last race of the season, most of the people they would like to be attending will be able to come. Gabriel's aunts, Damian, and Jean will drive down, and Evangelin and Carlos will fly. Other than that, the rest of the guests—James, Leonard, Chiara, Leonora, Cameron, Scarlette, Julián, and me—will already be there to set everything up days in advance.

Italy is a special place for Val and Gabriel, so Chiara and Leonard offered for them to have their wedding on their private island called 'De Luca.'

"Okay, that's enough wedding planning for today. I wanted this to be a small ceremony, not a big ordeal," Val says while Gabriel frowns at her.

"I see how it is. Our wedding means nothing to you," he teases, winking at me as he pretends to be mortally wounded. He bursts into laughter from his own joke a second later, and Val smacks her forehead with the palm of her hand, a chuckle shaking her shoulders.

"You're so weird," she says, but he pulls her onto his lap to tickle her for that comment. Valentina squeals, for the first time since I've known her she squeals, and

I can't keep my jaw from dropping a little. "Okay, I'm sorry, I'm sorry," she giggles, and Gabriel releases her, but not before claiming her mouth again.

I instinctively look over at the empty seat beside me. Adrian is working late tonight, and I hate how much I miss him.

"I'm going to head to my room, okay? You both need to get some sleep before Qualifying tomorrow, and I want to take a bath in that luxurious tub. I've dreamt about doing so since we arrived three days ago," I explain while gathering my things and heading for the door. They both give me a smile and a "bye" before turning back to each other, hunger in their eyes.

Alright then, I think to myself while heading toward my room.

This hotel is too fancy. There are cameras everywhere, ensuring both the safety of the guests and that crime stays at a minimum. That's why Singapore is so safe and clean. You even get fined for throwing a cigarette bud on the floor, and the punishments for committing any kind of crime are harsh. I've never felt so safe in any country.

Adrian took me to the beach a few days ago, and I never wanted to leave. The water was clear and warm, it was peaceful since not a lot of people were there, and we could really enjoy having a moment of quiet.

I almost run into my door because I'm so lost inside of my head, I don't even realize my key card didn't swipe properly. It's still early, and my stomach is turning and spinning from hunger. I plan to text Adrian and see if he wants to go out for dinner, but, once I'm in the bathtub, every single thought leaves my head. They drift away into the water, and I don't hold on as all worries subside, too. I've forgotten how relaxing a bath can be, how it can heal your soul, even if it's only by a little... and not for long.

Every worry comes crashing back. I think about what I'd do if I lost my job, if Cecilia succeeded in messing with my career to get me fired... again. There is no way I could stay in Monaco. It wasn't an option when I lost my job at *Griffin Sports*, and it wouldn't be one now. I saved some money, but it's not nearly enough. Adrian would never let me move out because of something like money, but I'm already relying on him to pay our rent. I pay for some things, groceries and dinner sometimes, but I don't make enough money to contribute more. If I lost my job, it'd be even less.

Then I think about what my father would say.

"You lost another job, Nevaeh? Are you kidding me?"

He'd be so disappointed in me. Nova wouldn't care. She's been jumping from one job to the other, never sure what she enjoys enough to continue. Aileen is on my team no matter what happens. And Mama? I have no idea how she'd react. Losing my job over a man—because, let's face it, my relationship with Adrian put me on his mother's radar, so Mama would always blame him—would push her even further away from me. I don't see it like that. I'd never, ever blame Adrian for his mother's actions, but I know Mama. And she'll be disappointed, just like Papa would be.

I let my head sink below the surface for a brief moment, welcoming the warmth of the water before my head spirals again.

What if Cecilia does something worse?

Will Adrian leave me?

Could I *ever leave* him?

No. Not after everything I've felt, everything he's made me feel. Not after he told me I'm the love of his life and I realized he's mine.

What if you don't have a choice? my head asks, and my heart rips open.

It feels like my soul is catching fire. My limbs freeze as ice travels through my veins.

I lift my head out of the water again, taking several deep breaths to calm myself.

"Nevaeh? *Mon ange?*" That voice. It holds everything I could ever want. "Are you okay?" he asks, his hand grazing my cheek.

His touch. I only ever want his skin against mine.

"You look a little pale," he says, and I shift my gaze to his.

His body. It's the only one I ever want to look at, study it until I've memorized every detail. I want to stare into his eyes until they have swept me up and away from everything else.

"Kiss me," I blurt out, and he obeys without a moment of hesitation.

His taste. He tastes like home and mine and happiness all at once.

His scent. It fills my nose, the comfort of it running through me. He smells like everything good and joyful. Like a summer day at the beach with him by my side and my camera in my hands. Like a forest after rain. Like heaven in a person.

"Don't leave me." I don't know where the words come from, I didn't even think them, but they spill from my lips anyway.

"I could never," Adrian says, wiping away my tears. "Never," he repeats so softly, it turns my insides into mush. His lips find mine one more time before he leans back, sucking in a sharp breath as his gaze trails down my naked body, which isn't covered by anything other than clear water. "Are you almost finished with your bath? I want to take you to dinner," he says sweetly, his attention fixed on my eyes.

"Oh, I thought you were going to join me," I reply, and he lets out a shaky breath.

"I want to, more than anything, but you haven't eaten yet, and I won't have my woman run on no food," he says, determination replacing his desire to be in this tub with me, to feel his naked body envelop mine.

"Okay, give me five minutes to dry off and get dressed," I assure him, and he hesitates for a moment before nodding and walking out of the bathroom.

I put on a short, orange, curve-hugging dress, knowing it will drive him absolutely wild. My scar is on display for everyone to see, but I only briefly acknowledge it before finishing a simple makeup look and meeting Adrian in our hotel room.

He changed into a black dress shirt, which is tucked into matching dress pants. His all-black outfit is finished with a pair of fancy shoes. He's wearing rings on eight of his ten fingers for the first time since he came into my life, along with a watch from one of his sponsors. My mouth starts drooling at how handsome he looks.

His eyes fixate on my appearance then, stopping at the bracelet he gave me and then dropping down all the way. I do a little spin for him, and he's already there to catch me when I face him again. Adrian's arms fling around my waist, pulling me against his chest as his mouth drops to my scar. He traces the mark, his lips grazing the skin so softly, so carefully.

"Beautiful," he says to it and then looks directly into my eyes as he adds, "Drop-dead gorgeous. Stunning. Sexy. Ravishing. Mesmerizing beyond words." I smile at him, his fingers snaking around my hips to guide my lower body against his.

"Careful, Adrian, I'm already all yours. I don't know what else to give you," I reply, grinning because, in all of the chaos, I'm so happy. I've never been this happy.

"*Je t'appartiens*, Nevaeh, for now and forever. I belong to you." He kisses my lips once, then steps back. "I don't want anything more from you. You've already given me everything, *mon paradis*." I never would have expected my name, a tool to be used by others more than myself, to turn into the sweetest pet name anyone could have ever given me.

Adrian takes me to the top of the Marina Bay Sands, and I take in the sight in front of me. Tall buildings, The Financial District stares at us, pointing toward the sky at the same time. I can see the ocean from here, where hundreds of boats and ships are docked or passing by. People look like ants from this height, and I smile when a warm breeze swipes over me. Adrian pushes my dress down before it lifts too high, pressing his body against mine from behind and sliding his hands onto my stomach.

"Propose to me here," I blurt out, catching both of us completely off-guard. "Or I will propose to you here, either works for me," I clarify, not stopping my words, even though I probably should. Adrian stays silent, and I raise my hand to the charms hanging from my bracelet. "It's so beautiful," I whisper at the skyline, but he brings me closer.

"Tell me when you're ready, and I'll bring us back here, Nevaeh."

One day, I will be ready, and he's the only one I'll ever want to say "I do" to.

CHAPTER 44

Adrian

I BRING NEVAEH CLOSER against my chest, resting my cheek on the top of her head while my fingers trace an infinity shape along her stomach. The Singapore skyline has been a favorite of mine since I raced here years ago for the first time. Knowing she adores it as much as I do makes the ring I bought her weigh heavy in my pocket. If it were up to me, I'd drop to my knee right this second. I'd tell her she's everything to me, my whole life, and I'd ask her to be mine in every way a person can be. I'd ask her to be my wife so I can become her husband.

"Should we go ask for a table?" Nevaeh asks, but I'm not ready to leave this moment yet. For once, everything seems so peaceful. We don't have a care in the world up here, every problem is a tiny fleck at the bottom, and I need us to stay here for a little longer.

"If you want," I reply because she must be starving, but Nevaeh shakes her head. Her hands slip on top of mine, and, for a brief second, my heart stops beating.

"Not yet."

God, she's perfect. She feels everything I do, wants the same things I do, has me breathless in the best ways, but is also the breath in my lungs at the same time.

Fucking hell, I'm starting to become poetic in my love for her.

I almost smile to myself.

If only we could stay like this forever.

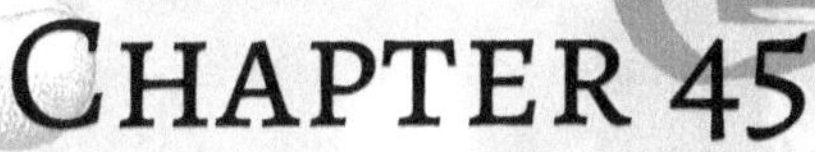

CHAPTER 45
Nevaeh

QUALIFYING STARTS IN TEN minutes. Adrian is running around in his garage, trying to find Daniel, but he's nowhere to be seen. He presses a sloppy kiss to my lips for good luck before cursing and getting into his car. I assure him I'll check on his performance coach, but I doubt he can hear him in his daze of stress and confusion. It's not like Daniel to simply vanish, especially not right before Quali. I check the private room in Adrian's garage, knock on the men's washroom, and then ask a few people, but none of them have seen him.

Luckily, he comes shooting past me a few minutes ahead of the start, and I let out the breath of worry I was holding.

"Sorry, sorry, sorry," he mumbles to a furious Adrian. They are as close as a driver can be with their performance coach. "I know, my bad, man," he says, running around to grab Adrian's gloves.

"Stop apologizing. Just get me my things, please!" I hear Adrian yell, and I almost burst into laughter. Even when he's pissed, he's using the word "please" when asking for something. God, he's too cute sometimes.

"Hey, Nevaeh, you should go watch from where Lorenzo is. He asked for you to sit with him. I promise you won't regret it," Chloe says, and I give her a warm smile before walking toward him. I'm convinced everyone on the Velocità Rossa team, Adrian's side of it anyway, knows who I am. He's made sure they do so I'm always looked after when he doesn't have time.

The team principal gives me a brief smile before placing a pair of headphones on my ears and telling me to watch the monitors with him. I'm convinced this isn't allowed, but it gives me a great idea for an article.

Maybe Samira can help me give it to the Velocità Rossa publicity team.

I take notes of everything Lorenzo is in charge of, trying to understand the depth of his responsibilities. After Q1, I briefly get distracted by how bright the lights outside shine in the darkness of the night. I love night races, and, on top of that, it's a street circuit in the most beautiful country I've ever visited. The weather is tropically warm and the people cheering their favorite drivers on makes me happy.

"Come, Nevaeh, look here. I want to show you how well Adrian did in Q1," Lorenzo says, and I spin back around to face him with a grin.

I listen attentively as he shares how well my boyfriend has been doing and explains the strategy of what will happen now in Q2 and Q3. I almost bounce up and down from excitement. He's going to get pole, I know he is. He will get pole at one of his favorite street circuits, and it will make him really happy, which is all I want. Adrian full of joy is one of my favorite things in the entire world.

I only wish it could stay this way for a whi—

Then, I see Cecilia. She's staring at me, cocking her head to the side to signal for me to go with her. But I don't. I hesitate. No interaction with this woman has ever given me anything positive, and I don't want to be near her without Adrian again. Looking at her, the determination set in her eyes, I realize I have no choice. She will find a way to be alone with me, whether I like it or not. She won't stop.

So, I step toward her, strut right past her and into the bathroom.

"How did you get into Adrian's garage?" is my first question. Cecilia gives me a dangerous smile as she leans against the door of the bathroom.

"I have my ways. I'm a very influential woman, as you may know," she says, and I almost shudder.

"What do you want from me?" I spit the words. Surprise shoots onto her face for a second, but she refocuses so quickly, it scares me a little.

"Break up with my son," she says, draining the color from my face.

I'm about to protest when she raises her phone to show me the photos Adrian and I took in our jeans, no shirts on our bodies. Cecilia scrolls through all of them while I try to process the fact that *she* broke into our hotel room. She stole my laptop and had someone hack into it to get these pictures. To blackmail me.

I'm going to be sick.

"Break up with him, or I will leak these," she adds, and nausea overwhelms me to the point where my head starts spinning and a cold sweat starts running down my spine.

"You broke into our hotel room," I blurt out because her threat hasn't settled in completely. My mind is stuck on her committing a crime other than blackmail. It's stuck on the fact that she really did it. I had my suspicions, but this? This is all the confirmation I needed.

"No, doll, I had someone break into your hotel room. You see, I was looking through your camera bag that weekend, but you had nothing I could use to extort you on there," she explains, walking toward me to wrap one of my curls around her fingers. If my body wasn't paralyzed with fear, I'd slap her hand away, but I can't move.

Why can't I fucking move?

"Sorry to disappoint," I snarl, glad my voice is showing more strength than my limbs. "I can't believe how far you'd go to tear us apart." I didn't even know she was there that weekend. That she went through my things to get to my camera and look through it.

"Not to worry, pretty girl. I have enough now," she says, pulling on my hair until I groan from pain. I regain enough strength to shove her away from me. "Break up with Adrian. I will release these photos if you don't. You've seen what I've done so far. I have cracked the foundation of every part of your life. Your family, your career, even your relationship with my son. This?" She points at the screen of her phone. "This will break everything, dear, and I won't give a single shit what it costs to get my son back." I can read in her eyes that she means every single word. There will be no regret from her.

"Okay, Cecilia, I will break up with him. I can't let you destroy my life, so I'll do it."

Over my dead body. I just need to buy a little time.

"Just give me until tomorrow, okay?" Desperation slips into my tone, trying to make her believe me. Her eyes scan my face, silence filling the bathroom. I need to figure out a way to get these photos back or come up with another option.

"You have twelve hours. If you don't text me before then, I will release the photos." I shake my head, disbelief settling in my chest.

"Why are you trying to break Adrian's heart? You're supposed to be his mother and protect him from harm," I say, but Cecilia shakes off my comment with a shrug of her shoulders.

"Once he's heartbroken, he will need me. He will *want* me in his life. Not to mention, I know you're the one keeping me from him." Her hand reaches for the handle of the door, but my words stop her.

"I know you don't have any idea what kind of a person I am, but there is nothing in this world I wouldn't do to make Adrian happy. If a relationship with you would do that, I'd be the first person to push him toward you, but it's not."

I stop abruptly because I won't go down this path again. Cecilia heard it enough times from me now, and if it still hasn't gotten through to her, it never will.

"We will see. After all, it won't be your problem by then anymore," she says, and I suppress the urge to slap her, shake her by the shoulders, tell her she's officially the worst person on the planet. I do none of these things and simply watch her walk away before I sink to the ground.

Fear comes crashing into my body, tearing me down until I can't breathe properly.

What the hell am I going to do now?

She will release the photos, intimate photos Adrian and I took for ourselves. I pull my phone out of my pocket, skimming through the photos to see if there is anything too inappropriate about them. Adrian is covering my breasts in all of them. The pictures are no more revealing than the jeans commercial known worldwide by a very famous company, and I won't let them be the reason Adrian and I break up.

Shit, I really have to talk to Adrian.

I need to tell him my plan.

CHAPTER 46
Adrian

Pole.

I got fucking pole.

Adrenaline has consumed me as happiness rushes into my chest in unstoppable waves. I drive my car to the first position sign in the middle of the track, between the start and finish line. Gabriel came in third, and, unfortunately, Lincoln is second. He was only a hundredth off my time, which is way too close for my liking.

For now, I push the thought aside, focusing on getting out of my car. I remove the steering wheel before standing up and placing it back in its proper spot. My legs, tired but vibrating from excitement, bring me to the nose of my car at the very top where I celebrate by punching the air with my fist. I know it's only pole, I haven't won the race yet, but this is the first time in my Formula One career I've gotten pole in Singapore.

It means a lot to me.

My eyes scan my team's crowd for Nevaeh, but she's nowhere to be seen. Worry immediately consumes me. It's unlike her not to be here to celebrate with me, and it's unsettling. The urge to drop everything and find her is overwhelming, but Gabriel wraps his arm around my shoulders and taps his helmet against mine.

"Interviews first," he reminds me, letting go a second later to walk toward where the towels, caps, and water are for the top three drivers.

I join him, after letting myself be weighed, removing my helmet and placing it on the table area next to the water bottle. Gabriel throws a towel at my head and laughs, something I would usually find very amusing, but I can't right now, not while I have no idea what has happened to Nevaeh.

It must have been Cecilia.

Dammit, this is why I tried to get her banned from coming to races. This continued harassment cannot go on like this. She's hurting my family, and I refuse to race for this sport any longer while she messes with my relationship when I can't be there for Nevaeh. *Fuck!* I'm so angry right now I can't even think properly at this point.

I have to find my angel.

"Adrian, hey, what's wrong?" Gabriel asks, but I don't manage to respond. My blood has turned to ice. It's preventing me from moving.

"Nothing," I lie because there are cameras on us from every angle and keeping up a pretense of excitement is crucial.

"Bullshit, but okay. Tell me later," Gabriel replies, and we both turn just in time to see Lincoln grabbing his bottle of water from the table beside us.

"Sorry, I didn't mean to interrupt you," he says, his accent thick and his voice full of sincerity. I've never felt as much pity for him as I do at this moment. He looks broken.

"Adrian Romana," someone calls out, and I realize it's Herb Lint, former F1 World Champion. He's the one doing the interviews today, but I've never liked him. He dragged my name through the mud a few years ago, spreading rumors about things I didn't do. It's why forcing a smile becomes ten times more difficult.

I can't catch a fucking break.

I've looked everywhere, searched every room and every corner, but Nevaeh has vanished. Even my calls go directly to voicemail. I'm starting to panic.

My phone rings after a minute of me trying to slow my breathing, and a sliver of hope slices through me when I read my sister's name on the screen.

"Did you find her?" I ask, desperate to get any information.

"Yeah, she's in your private room. She needs you," Val says, and I sprint toward where they are. My heart is racing so quickly, I'm convinced it's going to burst out of my chest.

I rip the door open, spotting Nevaeh sitting in the corner and talking to Val with tears streaming down her face. It's my fault. Immediately, I know it's my fault because Cecilia did this. Causing Nevaeh pain is her favorite pastime, which is why I know she's responsible. It almost makes me fucking explode. Instead, I focus on soothing my girlfriend and thanking my sister for helping me track her down.

Val leaves the room so I can turn to Nevaeh and wrap her in my arms. Her legs move to each side of my hips while I hold onto hers.

"Where were you? I checked in here ten minutes ago, but you weren't here," I say, wiping away her tears with the back of my hand. She sucks in a sharp breath, her throat working as she swallows the lump there.

"The bathroom," she says, and I caress the skin on her legs to get her tense body to loosen up, even if it's just a little.

"What did she do? Tell me," I urge because I have to know what happened. I have to know so I can find a way to fix it, fix everything.

"She hired someone to break into our hotel room, steal my laptop, and then hack into it to blackmail me with these photos." Nevaeh holds up her phone, and I stare at our half-naked bodies entangled in one another's. "She said if I didn't break up with you, she would spread them everywhere," she goes on, and I do my best not to fall backward from shock.

It all makes so much sense now. It wasn't a random break-in. It was Cecilia. It was on purpose; all of it was on purpose and part of her master plan to break Nevaeh and me up.

Anger courses through my veins until it fuels me. There is no way I will let Cecilia win. I will go to the police, I will break into her hotel to steal her phone, whatever it takes. She will not be the reason why Nevaeh and I end.

It's not going to happen.

It can't happen.

I won't let it.

"Come back to me," Nevaeh says, and I refocus my blurred gaze on her until all I see is her eyes, the ones I fell in love with the day I first saw them. "I have a plan," she says, wiping her own tears and kissing me until the pain vanishes. "She won't rip us apart, I promise." I'm supposed to be the one reassuring her, not the other way around, not when I'm the reason everything is getting so fucked up.

"Nevaeh, your career. We have to be very careful how we handle this situation," I say, but she gives me another kiss. "I love you so much, but kissing won't make this go away," I remind her after leaning back.

"We need to post them first, Adrian. We have to put them into the world before she can, take charge of the narrative. This needs to be a beautiful thing. Maybe we will say it's a photography project of mine," she explains, but I shake my head.

"There is so much uncertainty about how people will react, how your boss will react. I'm terrified this will do more harm than good."

"It's our only choice that doesn't involve you and I ending things," she says and grabs my face, but no part of me likes this.

We took these photos for fun, for memories. We never thought they would get out into the world, because they were never meant to. They are intimate, beautiful, and *private*, a concept that monster I once called "mother" clearly doesn't understand. I've never been so fucking frustrated, but I see no way for her to get out of our lives that doesn't involve her leaving voluntarily.

"What if it makes everything worse?" I ask, but Nevaeh simply tilts her head to the side, studying my face before using her thumb to trace my features. I try to stay on high alert, focused, tense, but it all washes away under her touch.

"Then we will deal with it."

I almost roll my eyes at her optimism. She cocks an eyebrow, challenging me to do it. Yeah, there is no way I'd ever roll my eyes at her. I don't think I'm even capable of doing it. My brain has a latch that physically prevents me from invalidating her words or feelings.

"You know I'm right," she says, tucking her slightly thinner bottom lip between her teeth. I lean forward, my thumb pulling her chin down to let it bounce free again only to bite down on it myself.

"Fine, you're right." One of my lesser qualities is my inability to admit when someone else is right and I'm wrong, but it comes easy with Nevaeh. "We have to spin the narrative the way we want it to go, and making it your photography project is a good way to do so," I say, but her face lights up with another idea.

"Unless we get the brand of the jeans to sponsor us, too!" she blurts out, reaching for my phone and shoving it into my hands. "Problem solved. Neither my boss nor yours can say anything about that," she says, excitement now consuming her as she wiggles on my lap.

"Okay, I will make some calls," I say, and she stands up, giving me room to breathe and focus. "How long do we have until she leaks them?" Nevaeh sucks in a sharp breath.

"Eleven hours," she replies, and I shake my head. If I manage to pull this off, it will be the quickest sponsorship deal in the history of mankind. "Unless I tell her we've broken up," Nevaeh interrupts my thoughts.

"No, that's not happening. We're not going to let her think she won for any longer than is necessary," I reply, finding the contact number of *Blazing Jeans Co.* and praying they will accept this deal.

"I'm sorry for all of this chaos," she says after a moment of silence, and my gaze shoots to her in surprise.

"You're apologizing for the shit my mother is pulling?" She gives me a sad nod, and I shake my head. "This is all my fault, Nevaeh. Everything that's happening is my fault. I'm the one who's sorry." Her lips part like she wants to argue, but I kiss them until her argument dies out.

Because it is my fault.

All of this is on me.

And now it's time to get to work.

Chapter 47
Nevaeh

It's been two hours.

Adrian stepped outside a while ago, arguing with someone over the phone. Valentina has been cuddling with me on the sofa, watching a movie neither one of us is paying attention to. We're both trying to listen for any update. I shift in her arms, thankful for her warmth and comfort. The last time I cuddled with anyone who isn't Adrian was a year ago when I was sick and Nova was taking care of me. Since then, I haven't had anyone else wrap their arms around me while we did something as simple as watching television. I also didn't need it. Adrian has given me everything, but after the day I've had, and the fact that he's busy right now, I'm so grateful for Val's embrace.

"He will convince them. You'll see," Val says, so I look up at her. She gives me a small smile, an expression that reminds me so much of her brother, and I lean my head against her side.

"Some things not even Adrian can achieve," I reply because, no matter how hard he's been trying, he hasn't been able to get rid of Cecilia, either. Some things are just out of our control, and I don't want him to destroy himself over them.

It's not his fault, but I know he blames himself.

"*Ooff*, do not say those words to my brother. He will implode," Val teases, and I let out a laugh. "You know, he's always found a way to make life easier for me. He's helped me fight and given me courage when I lost my own. I doubt there is anything he can't do," she says, and I chuckle at the thought crossing my mind.

"Take quick showers, actually. He's in there for at least half an hour," I reply, and Valentina rolls her eyes, laughing at my response.

"I was trying to cheer you up, love, but never mind. You're too stubborn," she complains, and I tickle her sides. She squeals, standing up to put some distance between us. I roll onto my back on the couch, bursting into laughter.

"I'm sorry," I blurt out, covering my face while the remnants of amusement shake my body.

"Yeah, sure you are. You're a mean woman," she complains. I shift my position and find her watching me, her hands placed on her hips and a grin on her lips. The humor dies out quickly when we notice Adrian dropping his head and slamming his hands against the railing of the balcony. "Let me go speak to him," Val interrupts my thoughts, and I give her a small, strained nod.

"Okay," I mumble to myself. After a few more repetitions of the same word, I finally stand up, my vibrating legs no longer capable of keeping me sitting.

Adrian is arguing with Val about something I wish I could hear, but eavesdropping has never been appealing to me. He will tell me when he's ready.

There is a knock on the door, startling me. My heart races in my chest while I step toward it, looking through the peephole to see who is intruding. My father's green eyes stare at the door, his patience running thin. I can see it by the way his foot is tapping the ground. Great, things are about to get a whole lot more difficult. My father would never risk messing up his sleep schedule on a race weekend, but here he is, at one in the morning, knocking on my hotel room door. I debate ignoring him, dealing with the consequences of it in the morning. Then, he knocks again, this time longer and harder, and I know there is no avoiding this man when he's on a mission.

"Hi, Papa," I say once I've opened the door, but he does something completely unexpected. My father's arms warp around my torso, bringing me close to his chest.

"Why didn't you tell me what's happening? Why have you kept this a secret?" he asks, and I swallow back the tears. There is something about my father showing me a comforting side that makes my emotional barriers crumble down into a pile of nothing.

"I'm not sure what you're talking about," I reply because there is no way he could know what Cecilia has been putting Adrian, Val, Gabriel, and me through.

"Adrian told me. He asked me to help him find a way to ban her from the races," he explains, and I raise both my eyebrows as he steps back to show him the surprise settling in my chest. Papa grabs my shoulders and shakes his head. "You don't have to hide these things from me." A laugh I don't mean leaves me.

"Of course I do. I don't want you to be disappointed in me," I say, stepping away from his grasp and further into my hotel room. Papa shakes his head in response.

"Cecilia is trying to ruin your career. That is not your fault," he says, but it frustrates me more. "I'm so sorry you're going through all of this. Let me be there for you, Vaeh. I can help get this situation under control, make sure Cecilia doesn't come near you again," he says, but his words aren't comforting. They don't make me hopeful or happy.

If anything, they make me feel the opposite.

"We've tried, Papa, but she broke into our hotel room. She stole our things, blackmailed me, keeps showing up at our houses, and is probably stalking us. And she always makes sure there is no evidence, makes sure we can't link those things to her. It's our word against hers. We can't do anything to make her stop," I explain while my father pays close attention, nodding along to my words as a way of acknowledging them. He walks inside where he sinks down on the couch.

"Have you tried going to the police?" I shake my head.

"Like I said, it's her word against ours," I reply at the same moment Adrian and Val walk back into the room. She gives my shoulder a quick squeeze and leaves.

"Oh, son, you need to get some sleep," Papa says when he sees how tired Adrian is. "I just wanted to see how you were doing, but it's clear you need to be alone."

"Thank you for coming, sir," Adrian says right as my father walks out the door. He gives him a quick nod before replying.

"Call me if there is anything I can do to help," he says.

Once we're alone, Adrian turns to me, wraps his arms tightly around my body, and exhales until there is no more air left in his lungs. He inhales deeply a second later, his body shuddering ever so slightly.

"I did it. I told them what happened, and they agreed. They're going to sponsor us. We just have to sign a few things in an hour and then we're safe," he says, and the weight, which was resting on my shoulders, finally lifts off.

"Thank you. And I'm sorry I wasn't of any help," I say, guilt now consuming me. Adrian steps out of the hug so quickly, it almost knocks the air out of me.

"Help? Nevaeh, I'm the reason your career is hanging on by a thread. I'm the reason everything has gotten so messy and complicated. You shouldn't have to do anything. This isn't your battle to fight, it's mine," he says, his legs giving out until he's sitting on the couch with his face in his hands. A sigh escapes his perfectly full lips, and I reach out to trace the shape of them.

"Your battles are my battles. We're in this together, my love. Next time, let me do more. Give me contact numbers and e-mail addresses, and I will do it all," I say, rubbing my hands over his thighs. He grabs my wrists, pulling me on top of his lap.

"You've done more than enough. You came up with the idea. I was just the executioner." I let out a little gasp when he rolls my hips forward. "You're brilliant in every single way a person can be. I need you to remember that," he whispers, guiding my hips forward once more.

"You need to rest," I manage to croak out, but Adrian shakes his head.

"I need *you*. I need to know you don't resent me for everything that's happening."

He needs intimacy right now. This isn't going to be about pleasure, not entirely, and I understand.

I understand it so well, I rip my shirt over my head without hesitation.

CHAPTER 48
Adrian

I PLAY WITH NEVAEH'S hair, dragging her against my chest while she's deep asleep. A small smile is on her lips from after we made love and then signed the contracts that saved her reputation. I fucking hate how she's the only one affected. My body gets sick at the thought. No matter the public statements I make, not a single person is going to care about me. It's more appealing for them to ruin Nevaeh's life.

"Adrian?" she whispers.

"Sleep, *mon paradis,*" I whisper and press a kiss to her lips. She smiles more brightly for a moment and then her breathing becomes steady and even again.

I don't know what to do anymore. I'm lost. Cecilia has spun everything out of control, and I can't fucking breathe properly anymore. I wish there was someone to help me figure this mess out, assure me Nevaeh and I will be fine, but I'm not so sure anymore.

Our relationship is hurting her career.

If I was less selfish, I'd let her go, but I could never do that. She claims it would hurt her more if I broke up with her, but I know better. I know she'd recover from this heartbreak, but not from losing everything else she's worked so hard toward. And yet, I can't bring myself to push her away. She's my fuel, my pit crew, the engine powering my body. She's everything to me.

I bite back the sob in the back of my throat, unwilling to let my emotional turmoil wake her.

"I'm the cause of all your problems," I whisper, but by the way Nevaeh moves, I realize she's awake enough to hear me.

"No, you're not," she says. "You're the cause of all my happiness," Nevaeh adds, so sleepy and honest, it makes tears shoot into my eyes. "All mine." She snuggles closer against me, her nose brushing over the side of my neck before she inhales.

If my body could, it would turn into a puddle because those words tug at my heartstrings. Nevaeh makes me feel like I'm the best thing in the world to her, completely disregarding how upside down my mother has turned her life. Her family might be complicated, but, except for Val, mine is really fucked up. My father was an alcoholic and neglected his children for years. My mother abandoned us entirely.

"Okay, I'm awake," she says, sitting up in bed and rubbing her eyes. "You're overthinking. Why, my love?" she asks, her hand slipping onto my cheek.

"I'm scared and tired and you're going to leave me or I will have to leave you because of Cecilia, and it's terrifying the living shit out of me because you're everything to me and—" I cut off, realizing my run-on sentence will only get worse if I don't stop.

Nevaeh lets out a long breath before offering me a small smile.

"I'm not leaving you. You're not leaving me. We will figure out a way to get her out of our lives somehow. Until then, she has nothing more to blackmail us with. So, don't worry," she says and grabs my chin between her thumb and index finger. Her eyes stare into mine as she leans closer, her breath hot on my skin. "Now, go to sleep. You need to rest for tomorrow." Her lips press against mine, making me sigh.

"Okay," is all I can respond because, as much as I'd like to believe this is the end of Cecilia's master plan, I have a feeling she's not finished with us just yet.

CHAPTER 49
Nevaeh

I FEEL UNEASY. As a matter of fact, I've never felt so unsettled in my life. Adrian has been leading the race since the start forty laps ago, but only by a couple of seconds. My boss has asked to speak to me after the race. Papa wants to see me tonight to discuss what has happened. And, if all of that wasn't enough, everyone around us keeps giving *me* strange looks since our pictures went out in the world.

Not Adrian.

Just me.

Fucking double standards.

I focus on the screens again, watching the last twenty laps while my heart does somersaults. Adrian's tires are losing grip. Gabriel is catching up to him, and with every lap, the gap between them closes. Val is doing amazing. She's been in fourth place for most of the race, but James is fighting her for it. Lincoln is in third, following closely behind the two Velocità Rossas.

My foot bounces up and down when Gabriel is only half a second behind Adrian with four laps remaining. They've been given the green light by Lorenzo to battle for first as long as they're careful and don't risk losing the one-two finish.

"I don't have any grip! I don't think I can hold him off." Adrian says over his team radio, something I get to listen to through the headphones on my head.

"You've also been given a warning for track limits, Adrian," his strategist says, and my boyfriend swears loudly. "Okay, try to—" He cuts Chloe off.

"Leave me to it."

I hold my breath. Adrian needs this win to expand his championship lead, but he's struggling. Gabriel overtakes him at the beginning of lap sixty, and I groan so loudly, Daniel gives my shoulder a quick pat. Then, Adrian overtakes his almost brother-in-law again, moving back into first place. I clap my hands together and then cover my mouth, unable to keep my body still. This is unbearable. My chest feels tight from both fear and excitement.

By the time lap sixty-two, the last one, comes around, I'm sweating. I'm glued to the screens, watching Adrian defend against Gabriel to the best of his abilities. They pass corner one, Adrian is ahead. Corner two, Gabriel is right next to Adrian. Corner three, he has overtaken Adrian. Corner five, six, seven, and eight, Gabriel is ahead, but only slightly. He has also started losing grip. Then, Gabriel takes corner nine too wide, allowing Adrian to race past him and back into first place. He breezes through the remainder of the lap, flying over the finish line moments later.

Daniel and I start celebrating with the rest of Adrian's team, cheering at the top of our lungs. This was one of the most phenomenal drives I've ever witnessed, and I've been watching Formula One since I was in diapers. Adrian is going to be a world champion this year, I have an undeniable gut feeling about it.

I sprint outside, waiting for him with a vibrating heart and happy tears falling from the corners of my eyes. His joy, his victorious emotion, courses through me until I'm floating on cloud nine. I love being connected to him like this. I love feeling everything he does in such a supernatural way. I am overcome by happiness because he has won the Singapore Grand Prix for the first time in his career. My fingers instinctively lift to the bracelet he gave me, squeezing the charm with his number tightly while I wait.

Adrian drives his car to the first place sign, removes his steering wheel, and then steps out of the cockpit. He stands on the nose, punching the air with his fists before jumping down and running straight for me. He rips his helmet off, which Daniel takes from him, before grabbing my face and kissing me all over. I taste my tears on his lips when he wraps them around mine.

"I won, *mon paradis*," he whispers when he steps back, his forehead pressing against mine.

"I saw, *mein Mond*. I'm so proud of you," I say, my fingers moving to his neck. He grins at me from ear to ear before brushing his nose over mine and walking over to the person that has to weigh him.

Three races to go.

Adrian is leading the championship.

Cecilia couldn't blackmail us into breaking up.

We'll have the next two weeks to recover from the whirlwind that was this weekend.

Maybe things are starting to look up, after all.

CHAPTER 50

Nevaeh

EVERYTHING'S BEEN UNUSUALLY QUIET since Adrian and I came back from Singapore a few days ago. No new attacks from Cecilia. Samira messaged me saying she loved the photoshoot Adrian and I posted and would send the article I wrote on Lorenzo Mattia to his team. Most of my family is excited for us to come visit them for a week starting tomorrow, and Val and Gabriel will already fly to Italy to start preparing for the wedding.

I can't believe they're getting married in a few weeks.

Adrian and I have been silently packing for half an hour now, shooting each other challenging looks. We're leaving for England in the morning, and I'm a bit nervous about how everything is going to go. Nova and Aileen, the newly engaged, are excited I'm coming, and so is Papa, but Mama is not a fan of having Adrian and me staying in one room under her roof. But Mama is Mama, and at this point, I really don't care what she throws at my head.

"Are you excited to see your family?" Adrian asks after a while, and I fold one of my dresses so I can pack it neatly in my luggage. I notice him doing the same thing to one of his shirts and almost smile.

"Yes. I can't wait to spend time with Aileen and Nova, especially." Adrian flashes me a bright smile, and I return it without hesitation.

We go back to packing, organizing our suitcases together like we have for every race since we started living together. He refuses to do so without me anymore, but I also enjoy the way silence feels between us. It's not awkward or uncomfortable. It's the opposite. It's safe and makes me happy all at once.

"Shit, James is going to be here in a couple of minutes to drop my phone off. Do you think you could go down and get it for me, please? I haven't finished packing," he says right as I zip up my luggage, and I give him a sly grin. He left his phone at James' place this morning, so his best friend offered to drop it off.

"Of course. While I'm already down there, I'll grab us some *pain au chocolat* from the café across the street. I've been craving some for days," I say and make my way toward the door when he stops me.

"Let me come with you then. I don't want you to go alone," he says and grabs his wallet, but I snatch it and throw it across the room, onto the couch.

"Stay here. It's a five-minute walk. And finish packing," I scold and leave the room before he can respond. He loves to be protective, but there's no reason to be.

James is already waiting downstairs in his car, staring down at his phone. When he sees me, his face lights up for a fraction of a second before the corners of his mouth drop again.

"Hi, love, I'm sorry, I'm afraid I have no time to chat. Damian is waiting for me to take him home for a few days," he says and holds out Adrian's phone for me.

"No worries. I was on my way to the café anyway," I assure him while giving him a kiss on the cheek and grabbing Adrian's telephone.

"Have a great time in England," he says before driving off again.

I make my way to the coffee shop, challenging myself to only speak French to the person at the counter. Additionally to Adrian teaching me, Gabriel has offered to give me some lessons every Wednesday evening while Adrian and Val take that time to hang out together. I know it's hard for both of them to live in separate houses after sharing the same home for most of their lives. I know how they feel because I've felt the same about Nova since I left her months ago.

Ever since I was a child, I dreamed of the day I would move out, become independent because my family's money weighed me down more than it ever helped me. I hoped to feel freer, more accomplished on my own, which I do. Even though I'm living with Adrian, my life has become something I can be proud of. I'm a successful journalist, who established her good reputation by writing articles like no one else.

I somehow managed to make the most beautiful human being, inside and out, fall in love with me. I'm a good friend, who has found another family in Monaco.

I am happy.

If it weren't for the painful twitch in my heart whenever I think about the mess Cecilia is responsible for, I'd have no worries in the world. I'd be carefree.

Someone taps me on the shoulder as I wait for my order. I turn around to see a young woman, a few years younger than me maybe, trying to get my attention. Her green eyes are glowing with fascination, making me realize she knows exactly who I am.

"I'm sorry to bother you, Ms. Fuchs, but I'm a huge fan of yours!" she says, holding up her camera to show me. "I'm also a photographer, and I was wondering if you had any tips on how to take pictures of fast-moving objects." My face lights up instantly.

"Yes, sure."

I do my best to explain everything I've learned over the years, but I'm pulled out of my rant when the server calls my name to let me know my order is ready.

"Wait, please, you haven't finished your explanation," the girl says, and as much as I'd like to continue speaking to her, considering this is a pleasant interaction, Adrian will worry about me if I take too long.

"I have to leave, but it was nice meeting you," I say, attempting to walk away, but she follows me out of the café.

"Do you use a specific lens depending on what type of object you're photographing?" she asks, and I stop dead in my tracks, uncomfortable with the thought of her knowing where Adrian and I live. I should probably go somewhere else first.

"Yes, but I really should go. Have a good day."

She grabs my arm.

I tense.

"Please, one more question, then I will leave you alone. I promise," she says, and I have a feeling she means it. I doubt she means any harm, even if she has made me incredibly uncomfortable by following me out of the café.

"Alright, one more question."

Her face darkens. She takes rigid steps toward me, and I back away from her immediately.

"What are you doing?" I ask, taking more steps backward, away from her.

"You see, I don't want anything from you. I was told to do one thing and one thing only," she says, coming closer and closer to me. I'm still stepping back, not realizing that I'm at the edge of the sidewalk until I almost fall onto the street. "And I want my money," she adds, pushing me onto the street right as a car comes rushing at me.

I scream at my body to move, but fear has paralyzed me. Everything seems to happen both in slow motion and too fast for my brain to handle. My heartbeat is in my ears, and my breathing is uneven. Still, I cannot move a centimeter.

I'm frozen.

The blood in my veins has turned to ice, keeping me standing in the way of the vehicle, which isn't slowing down despite my presence either. This was all planned. The woman speaking to me in the café, asking me all of those questions, pretending to be nice but then following me to freak me out, it was all so I would be right here, waiting to be run over.

I beg my body to move one last time, beg the survival instinct inside of me to melt my frozen blood, but it doesn't.

I stare into the eyes of Adrian's mother as her car races toward me, numbing my limbs even further.

And that's when I hear him scream my name.

This moment feels like an eternity, even though I know it's only a few seconds.

A few seconds until the car is hardly a meter away from me.

And then...

CHAPTER 51

Adrian

I'M RUNNING. I'VE NEVER run this fast in my life. My lungs are burning as I scream Nevaeh's name. She cannot die. I won't survive it. I've survived every other death, but I won't be able to live with hers. Nevaeh's my soulmate. If she dies, I die. Simple as that. So, I run. As quickly as my limbs can carry me, but it's not fast enough. I know there's no way I will reach her in time, but I try anyway. I have to make it. I have to save her.

I have to—

Someone grabs her by the waist, dragging her off the street before the car hits her and onto the sidewalk where they stay on top of Nevaeh to protect her from the rest of the world. It takes me a moment before I realize who it is. The hair, the back, the watch around the wrist. All of it is so familiar to me, but it doesn't stop my breathing from hitching.

It's Lincoln.

"Nevs, please, oh God, please tell me you're okay," he says as he grabs her face, checking her head for injuries.

"Lincoln?" she asks, her eyes wide and full of panic. "What—what are you doing here?" Her voice is barely audible.

She's terrified, and I haven't found a way to speak yet. I'm right behind them, but the image in front of me, Lincoln saving her because I couldn't, hurts me.

"I came to speak to you and then some woman tried to run you over," Lincoln explains, and I sink to the ground next to them.

My phone rings at the same moment, and I pick up, answering the call from an Unknown number because I know it's *her*.

"End it or next time, she won't be so lucky, Adrian." Then, she hangs up, and I almost throw my phone on the ground.

No, no, no, no, no. It was my mother. My mother tried to kill Nevaeh. This is my fault. She almost died because of me. Oh my God. I cannot breathe. I endanger her life, Lincoln saves it. No, I can't process this. No part of me can process this.

"Adrian?" So soft. Why is her voice always so soft and perfect when she says my name?

I break down in tears, the urge to comfort her taking over. But I can't. This is all my fault. Cecilia coming after her is on me. This wouldn't have happened if she wasn't with me.

I'm going to be sick.

"No, my love, it's okay. I'm okay. I promise. Don't—This wasn't your fault," she says, but I can't hear anything after that. My ears are ringing while I fight the need to touch her, to feel she's okay. I can't do that anymore. I can't touch her, shouldn't. Things have gotten out of hand.

"Mate, it's alright," Lincoln says. My eyes fixate on the image in front of me again.

One of his arms is still around my Nevaeh. He saved her life. I'm so grateful and angry at the same time, it's messing with my fucking head. It's spinning. I'm spiraling. I can't breathe.

"Please, Adrian, I can't feel my legs yet, but come to me. Feel me. I'm alright," Nevaeh says, and I regain my ability to think about something other than the fact everything is my fault. That she'll try something like this again.

"Thanks, Lincoln. I got it from here," I say, my voice monotone, distant, and cold.

My feet bring me to her, and I lift her, wrapping my arm around her waist to stabilize her. I lead her all the way into the building, my emotions numbing my mind, soul, and body on the way to our apartment. I place her down on the couch, putting as much distance between us as the small living room allows. Her eyes watch me, her shaking hands still figuring out a way to stop. I wish I could make them stop. I wish her near-death experience could be wiped clean off her mind forever.

This isn't fair. None of this is fair. Nevaeh is not the one who should have to suffer because of my fucking mother.

My mother, the monster, almost killed the love of my life.

Lincoln saved her.

I have to break up with her. She isn't safe around me anymore, and I won't have that. I won't allow her to risk her life by being with me.

Her job is one thing, but her life is another.

Her life is *at risk*. I can't be selfish anymore. Not while Cecilia is in the picture.

"Please don't," Nevaeh cries, tears streaming down her face. I realize my facial expression has hardened from the numbing happening inside of me. "Please don't leave me. This was not your fault," she says.

If I could feel anything right now, I'd probably drop to my knees, but my emotions have shut off. How? I wish I had a clue. I should feel something, anything, but I know if I let myself feel, I will break in half.

"I need you to grab your suitcase and stay with Val for the night. Then, you have to fly to your parents. You can have the apartment when you come back," I say, my voice harsh and cold. Nevaeh manages to stand up, tears rolling down her cheeks as she makes her way toward me on shaky legs.

"I'm not taking the apartment, Adrian. Listen, we will figure this out. We will find a way to make Cecilia leave us al—" I cut her off.

"That's what we've been trying to do since she returned, Nevaeh. And it hasn't been fucking working, has it? Now she tried to *run you over*! Yes, Nevaeh, kill you. We don't have any proof, we can't go to the police without it, and everything is a fucking mess. You need to leave. You need to be as far away from me as possible because I can't get rid of her. I don't know how!"

I'm screaming.

I'm screaming at the woman I love because I've never been so terrified in my entire life. I watched my grandfather and grandmother die, witnessed paramedics drag my father's lifeless body from the car crash into our living room, but none of the fear I felt then compares to the one I'm experiencing right now.

"Please don't make me leave," she cries, and tears fall from my eyes.

"You have to."

Never leave me. I can't survive without you. You're everything to me, my future and all my desires. I never, ever want to lose you.

"Cecilia has lost her mind, and you need to stay as far away from me as possible. Now grab your suitcase and go."

Please don't go. I'll die without you. Darkness will envelop me, I know it, because you are my light. I will burn in hell without you, my heaven.

"Adrian, look at me," she says and grabs my face, forcing me to stare at her tear-stained face. "I know you're scared, but I'm asking you not to do this, my love."

Do you really think I want to do this? Do you think this is easy for me? My mother tried to kill you! You can't be with me anymore.

"Leave," I say softly, taking her wrists to remove her hands from my face. It'll keep my heart from hoping we could still find a way to make this work.

"No. You love me. You don't want me to leave." She's so fucking right, I almost nod.

"Nevaeh, you can't be with me anymore. You need to run before she succeeds next time. So, I'm asking you to please leave. Go to your parents. Far away from me where you will be safe."

I feel it creeping into my chest long before my hands start to shake. I can't breathe properly anymore. Sweat starts collecting at the back of my neck. Panic attack. Fuck me.

"I understand why you're doing this, baby. It's okay. Just tell me this isn't forever. Tell me this is only until we find a way to get rid of Cecilia," she says, and I want to tell her "yes."

I want to scream that as soon as I find a way, I will throw her over my shoulder, carry her into our bedroom, and keep her wrapped in my arms forever. But I can't make that promise when I don't know if Cecilia will ever leave us alone. I also can't speak anymore. The panic attack has completely taken over now, ripping the ability to talk from my vocal cords.

"Okay. I see." She moves toward me, steps on her tiptoes, and kisses me. She kisses me until all my walls shatter, emotions come crashing back inside of me, and a sob leaves me. "I know, I know," she coos, flinging her arms around my neck and comforting me.

"You have to leave me," I cry, and Nevaeh nods, rubbing the back of my head. "I'm sorry it has to be now, after everything that just happened."

"I know," she repeats. "I will, but only if you remember this wasn't your fault. None of it. Please don't forget that, ever." She waits for me to acknowledge her words before she steps back.

"Just until she's gone. Until I've found a way to keep you safe," I finally say, and she nods. "I can't live in a world without you in it, Nevaeh, and I'm so scared of what she'll do next." More tears fall from both our eyes.

"I know that, too," she replies, taking a deep breath.

"This is not forever. It can't be." Nevaeh doesn't say anything to that. She merely steps into our bedroom and leaves me to sob by myself.

When she reappears in the living room, she's carrying her backpack and suitcase. Her phone is pressed against her ear as she speaks to someone, probably Val to let her know she's coming. Oh God, this is really happening. I'm losing my future. I'm dying. I need to sit down.

My body slumps onto the coffee table in front of the couch while I watch her step toward the front door. I should peel my eyes off her, but part of me thinks I deserve the pain of witnessing her walk out of the door, out of my life.

"Adrian?" she says right before opening the door. Since I'm already looking at her, she gives me a little smile. "No matter what, you're the love of my life. You know what that means?"

"Tell me," I say, digging my nails into the palms of my hands to feel anything other than my heart ripping into shreds.

"It means there'll never be anyone I'll love more than you. We will find our way back to each other, I'm sure of it."

She leaves the apartment before I can tell her I hope she's right.

Deep down, I know my mother has lost her mind too much to ever leave me alone again.

Cecilia has finally done it.

She's cost me everything.

Which is exactly what I text the same number that called me earlier. I tell her I broke up with Nevaeh, hoping Cecilia will finally leave her alone.

I did what she wanted, after all.

I broke myself into infinite pieces that keep shattering every time I think about Nevaeh.

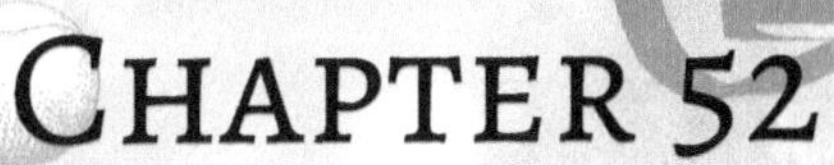

CHAPTER 52
Nevaeh

ADRIAN AND I ARE broken up. Cecilia almost ran me over with a car. Lincoln saved my life. Nothing makes sense anymore, which is exactly what I tell my best friend while she holds me in her arms and lets me cry until no tears are left. I don't even know why I'm crying. We will find our way back to each other. We have to. Neither one of us did anything wrong. We didn't fall out of love. We didn't have a big fight. Neither one of us cheated or betrayed the other's trust.

The root of all our problems is Cecilia.

"I can't believe she'd try to—God, I can't even say it," Gabriel says, grabbing my hand and squeezing it.

Val pulls me against her, tears slipping down her face now. Even Chase rubs his head against my leg in comfort.

"I'm so glad you're okay, but I should go see if Adrian needs me. If that's alright with you," he goes on, and I give him a quick nod.

The Monegasque says something in Italian to his fiancée, and she quickly replies before running her hand over my arm.

"I'll drive you to the airport tomorrow, Nevaeh, okay?" he asks me, and I nod again.

Gabriel leaves the room moments later, phone pressed against his ear and shoulders tense.

"Nevaeh?" Valentina says, running her hand over my head to caress it. "I'm so, so sorry, love. I have no words for how sorry I am about Cecilia. She ruined everything now, for you and for Adrian, I'm just—I can't—" She feels guilty, too. Like her brother, Val feels guilty for things she's not responsible for, and I hate it.

When will they stop blaming themselves?

"It's not your fault," I scold.

"Stop that. Stop pretending you didn't get caught up in this mess because of us. I will get very angry with you, and the bride shouldn't fight with her maid of honor this close to her wedding date," she says, and I lean away from her to see the fire in her eyes. "Adrian was right to distance himself from you, at least for now. You have to disappear out of her direct line of vision for a while so she can see you're not the reason behind our refusal to have a relationship with her. It's good you're going to your parents. When you return, everything will be better," she assures me, but doubts infiltrate my brain.

"She's too persistent, Val. She won't leave you alone. You have to find a better way. Promise me you will find a better way so that all of you can have some peace of mind," I reply and grab her shoulders, making sure she understands how important this is for me.

"I promise I will bring Adrian back to you," she says and my limbs turn to cement.

The exhaustion of the day, the adrenaline rush subsiding slowly now, it's all dragging me down into the darkness of sleep. But I don't want to sleep, not without Adrian. I won't be able to either. I can already feel my heart fighting the urge to rest. It won't feel safe until he's here, which is why it's beating at an abnormal speed, sending waves of panic through me. Its shield, Adrian's heart, has vanished. So, it beats faster and faster, reminding me how vulnerable it is without its other half.

"Let me make you some food," Val says, and I whisper a "thank you" I'm not sure she can even hear.

Where is he? My heart is screaming at me. *Where is my other piece?* I wish I could assure it everything will work out how it's meant to, but hope has left me. *I won't survive on my own, will I?* The answer should be simple: of course you will. You were beating just fine before he came into our life, and you will work just as well now that he's gone. But heartbreak isn't merely an emotional pain. I feel my chest tightening unbearably, feel a stinging pain shoot through it every single time I see Adrian's face in my mind. My heart may have worked before Adrian, but it's incomplete without him, without his heart.

Then, Adrian's words echo in my ears.

Je t'appartiens, mon paradis.

He belongs to me. I belong to him.

I almost hear his heart screaming at me inside of my chest then.

I haven't disappeared. I'm still here. I'm yours, forever.

CHAPTER 53
Adrian

Someone's knocking on my door, but I can't fucking move. I've been stuck in my panic attack for the past... I don't know how many minutes, and I don't think I'll snap out of it any time soon. My entire body is shaking. I'm sweating profusely. My heart is racing. I'm pretty sure I've lost myself completely, and there is no saving me.

"Alright, mate, I've got you now."

"Go away," I manage to croak out, but his arms are already around me, holding me to keep my limbs from shaking. "Stop. Touching. Me." He doesn't listen. Of course he doesn't listen. It's Gabriel. He wants to make sure I'm okay, and I accidentally let it slip once that when a panic attack happens to me, I enjoy being held by Nevaeh.

"Don't be so stubborn and breathe. You're not breathing," he scolds, still holding me close to his chest. Annoyingly enough, his warmth is helping.

"Leave me alone to die," I say, my voice shaky.

God, I'm so fucking tired. I'm sick of these attacks and the toll they have on me. I'm sick of always ending up alone. And, most of all, I'm sick of losing the people I love. I love Nevaeh so much. I want her back. I need her back. It's been an hour, but that's already too much time lost. I don't want to lose any I could spend with her, not anymore. We've already lost so much.

"Don't be so dramatic. You're not dying," Gabriel says, pulling me back into reality where I'm still shaking and succumbing to panic. "Want me to tell you a story to take your mind off it?" His question reminds me of Nevaeh and the way she always told me stories when I was in this state.

"I hate you," I say instead of answering, and Gabriel chuckles against my arm.

"We both know I'm one of your favorite people. Don't pretend I'm not," he replies and taps my arm in a very specific pattern: *tap tap-tap tap.* He is one of my favorite people, and I have no words for how thankful I am that he's here with me at the moment. I don't want to be alone, not while my hollow chest is heaving in pain.

"I can't make it stop, Gabriel. I can't make it stop," I repeat, over and over, my words breathless and quiet in the silent room.

"You have to snap out of it. We have to find a way to get you back to Nevaeh, *mon frère.*"

"How? How the fuck do I do that? I've been trying to get Cecilia out of our lives for months, and I've been everything but successful! So, tell me, oh so wise Mr. Biancheri, how the hell can I get Nevaeh back when Cecilia will not vanish from our lives again?"

My anger is helping me out of my panic attack, but it's also frustrating me. I slip my hand into my jeans pocket, pull out my wallet, and then grab the ring I've been carrying around in the slit where my money is.

"I can't live without her," I say and reveal the ring to him. I haven't shown it to anyone, not James or Val. Gabriel is the first person.

"Holy shit. I mean, hearing you say these things is one thing, but this? This is unbelievable," he blurts out, attempting to take the ring from me, but I snatch it out of his reach. "Sorry," he says and raises his hands in mock surrender while I study the simple silver band with two infinity signs meeting in the middle, at the orange diamond.

"I want to give this to her." Gabriel's green-brown eyes stare into mine.

"You will."

I barely hold myself back from slapping him across the face for being so fucking optimistic during the most hopeless time in my life. He smacks the back of my head when I roll my eyes at him.

"Listen, you little shit, I'm not going to be part of this pity party you're throwing for yourself. Either you fight for the woman you love, or I will hit you over the head again, this time with something more painful than my hand," he warns, and I almost smile at him.

Almost.

"Okay, where do we start?"

You got any idea?

CHAPTER 54
Adrian

MY EYELIDS FEEL HEAVY when I wake up the next morning. A yawn slips past my lips while I reach over to place my hand on... She's not here. Nevaeh isn't here, but I'm reaching for her anyway, muscle memory the responsible cause. It shatters my soul into more pieces, if that was even possible. I grab her pillow, burying my face in it to fill my nose with her coconut scent. If there were any tears left in my eyes, I'd cry, but I'm all dried out. I'm hollow. Empty. Broken. Destroyed. Lonely.

"You are one fucking idiot. What the hell did I tell you just a few weeks ago?" someone says, and I shoot up in bed, the color draining from my face as all my defense modes activate. My breathing manages to slow only when I realize my sister is the intruder. "Don't push her away. Don't let her go no matter how hard things get because there is nothing you couldn't figure out together. How fucking difficult was it to understand that? Should I have said it in French for better comprehension?" Oh. She's mad. She's really upset with me, and I can't blame her. I've never hated myself more than I do currently.

"Cecilia tried to run her over because she's dating me, and I was supposed to stay with her? Keep her at risk? Do you honestly think I could ever be so selfish?" Her expression saddens.

"No, of course not. You always give other people what they need, but I have a feeling this time, it wasn't the right decision. Nevaeh would have always chosen you, no matter the danger."

And that's the problem. That's why I had to be the strong one with a clear mind. Cecilia has lost it. I need to get rid of her, and then bring Nevaeh home.

"Instead of telling me everything I've done wrong, why don't you try to help me fix it, huh?" I challenge, misdirecting my anger. I have to watch my mouth around Val. She's done nothing wrong, but it's hard to yell at myself while she's here.

"Please, I'm so far ahead of you already, it's embarrassing," she says and grabs her purse, pulling out a folder. I laugh at the same time as my phone screen lights up. *Nevaeh.*

Nevaeh: I'm sorry I'm texting you. I know you told me to stay away, that this is what needs to happen while Cecilia is forcing herself into your life, but I couldn't sleep last night knowing you're blaming yourself for what happened. It's not your fault. I know why I had to leave. Please don't blame yourself. We will fight for our way back to each other. I know we will.

Tears shoot into my eyes as I read over her message over and over again.

Me: I love you so much.

I don't think before sending the message. I just do it. Because it'll never not be true.

Nevaeh: I know. I love you endlessly, mein Mond. In every universe.

"Adrian, what's happening?" Val asks, and I realize I've just successfully pushed myself into a panic attack with my sister around. Fantastic. Not only am I the worst boyfriend in the history of mankind, now I'm also the worst brother.

Someone shoot me.

"Nothing," I lie, but my body is shutting down.

"Are you having a panic attack?" she asks, hovering over me.

"No." Another thing I'm the worst at: lying.

"God, you're infuriating. Just admit you're having a panic attack, it's not a bad thing!" Val complains, wrapping her arms around me and pulling me against her warm chest. Comfort. Yeah, I need my sister's comfort. I don't think I've ever needed it so much. It calms me more quickly than Gabriel could yesterday, but not nearly as fast as Nevaeh does.

"Thanks," I say after a while of silence. Val pushes my hair off my sweaty forehead.

"What triggered this one?" she asks, and I sit up, putting some distance between us.

"My mind has been all over the place since Cecilia returned. I've lost my temper with Nevaeh, blamed her for things she never did, and we fought because I couldn't control my demons. Maybe part of me knows letting her go should be forever. I haven't been good for her, not the way I'm supposed to be. Then again, maybe part of me is just terrified because every time I've lost myself, Nevaeh brought me back. I got drunk? She took care of me. I yelled at her? She didn't leave me but fought it out with me. I hid things from her? She understood that I wasn't ready to address the broken boy inside of me. You see, Val, I'm in a constant state of panic now. That's what happens when people lose their life, home, and future all because she walked out the door."

I don't have to tell her most of this. My sister knows me better than anyone, and she's experienced heartbreak long before I ever gave my heart away. But I need to share how I'm feeling. I need to hear her say my emotions are valid. Otherwise, I'll not only feel distant from Nevaeh, but I will feel distant from everyone in the entire world for feeling a way no one else has before.

"What if I told you I have a plan to get her to confess to everything and all it takes is for us to do exactly what she wants?" I cock an eyebrow, uncertainty settling in my chest.

"You really are way ahead of me, aren't you?" I ask, and my sister winks at me.

"When am I not?"

For the first time in hours, I let out a short laugh.

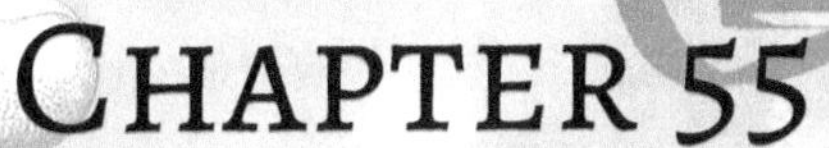

CHAPTER 55
Nevaeh

IT'S BEEN SEVEN DAYS. I've felt cold for seven days. My body keeps shivering uncontrollably, even when I'm sitting outside in the burning sun. Everything's cold. Emptiness has settled in my head, but I've been doing my best to push it away to appreciate the time I'm spending with my family.

Mama and Papa have been attentive, understanding, and sympathizing with my heartbreak. Aileen and Nova keep me distracted by taking me camera equipment shopping and talking to me about everything except Adrian. They know better than to bring him up because I shut down on them every single time they do.

When I'm around my family, I don't feel quite as empty as I do the moment I'm alone.

Like right now.

There are no distractions except for the new camera lens I bought today. Under different circumstances, I'd be thrilled to try it out and take lots of pictures. Today, I can't even bring myself to take it out of the box it came in. Nothing motivates me. I feel exhausted, although I haven't done anything except work from home, editing my pictures and finishing up the article Samira asked me to write. My entire being is falling apart under the emotional pain leaving Adrian has inflicted.

I never knew just how powerful it was.

Emotional pain.

I've experienced a fair share of physical pain when my injury happened. It was hot as it seared through my shoulder, causing a scream to leave me on the tennis court. But it wasn't everywhere. It was in my shoulder, rooted there forever. Emotional pain is worse. It's long-lasting. It's everywhere inside of me. It's hidden and right in my face at the same time. I can't locate it yet feel it from head to toe. I can't make it stop as it slowly gets more unbearable. I feel worse with every breath even though there is nothing physically wrong with me.

Nothing has ever torn me down this much.

My fingers glide over the box with the camera lens while I think about taking it out and twisting it on. I also know it would cheer me up, at least until I look at the pictures, accidentally go back too far, and see the photos of Adrian I took. After seven days, I'm pretty sure I will break if I see a picture of him right now.

I miss him so much. I miss every little thing about him. His dirty blonde locks as I run my fingers through them. His green-blue-brown eyes as they study my face until he's had enough, which never happens. His sweet words as they fill my ears. I miss his laugh and his cocky comments. I miss the way he holds me and fulfills me. I miss the way he smiles when he plays the piano and makes up new melodies for me to enjoy.

I bring the back of my hand to my cheek, wiping away the rogue tear.

Seven days.

They've felt like hell.

Seven days.

And I feel like I've died a million times only to come back to my personal torture chamber in hell.

Seven days.

I can't take any more of this.

I can't be apart from him for any longer. It makes me look at the pictures before I can stop myself.

He's half asleep, naked from the waist up, on my torso. His ear is pressed against my chest as he listens to our hearts beat inside of me. A smirk lingers on his full lips, the ones I've kissed endless times. They're the only ones I ever want to have on mine.

After I took the photo, he looked up at me and smiled so brightly.

"Why do you take so many photos of me?" he asked. I returned his happy expression, staring at him through the lens of my camera.

"Because you're the sexiest, most beautiful person on the entire planet, and I want to capture it so I can admire you even when we're not together," I replied. Adrian's face turned serious then.

"I don't like the thought of us not being together, for any reason." I almost laughed.

"Well, we can't always be on top of each other, so I need them." Adrian placed his lips on my naked breast, kissing his way up to my nipple.

"I love being naked with you so much. I think we should always be without clothes," he said while trailing his lips toward my other nipple.

"We're not even completely naked," I complained, and he pushed off me to rip his pants and boxers off in record time. He slid back between my thighs, guiding my underwear down to my ankles and then throwing them to the floor.

"Much better," he said, trailing his hands over my thighs. His head rested on my stomach, and I laughed so whole-heartedly, it made him smile, too.

"Now you undressed me and won't kiss me?" I asked, and he went straight between my legs, sensing exactly what I wanted from him.

That was one of the best things about our relationship. We always just knew what the other needed. We gave it to each other without hesitation. It's the reason why I know we're soulmates, why he's the love of my life and I am the love of his.

And I'm crying again.

Cecilia is still in the way, and with every day we spend apart, I grow angrier with him for telling me to leave. I don't want to be upset with him. I know he did it to protect me. I know watching a car race toward the person you love terrifies you like nothing else, especially if your estranged mother is behind the wheel. Although all of this makes logical sense and I understand him perfectly, I'm a little angry with him. I shouldn't be, but I want him to hold me right now and the fact that he isn't drives me to anger.

It's infuriating. All of my feelings are at this point. It's the reason I keep crying and crying until everything hurts even more than before. And then I do something I know will only make me feel worse.

I wonder how Adrian is doing.

I hope he's getting sleep. I hope he doesn't experience the same pain I am. No matter what, I never, ever want him to feel this way, but, deep down, I know he feels a thousand times worse than me. He's the one who ended things because of his mother. He's the one who had to make this painful decision, and knowing how much he loves me, I can't imagine the guilt he feels now.

Worst of all, however, is that I know he feels even emptier than I do.

Because I still have his heart, and I'm never giving it back.

Chapter 56
Adrian

I'M DEAD. I MUST be. This is exactly what I've always imagined how a body would feel after the life has been sucked out of it. With my heart gone and my soul shattered, the hollowness inside reminds me of how the house of a snail must feel when its host disappears. I'm a Formula One car without tires, fuel, and an engine. I'm an ocean without water, a beach without sand, a forest without trees and other living organisms.

I'm dead.

Yup.

Hollowed out and dead.

Maybe I'm a zombie.

Nope, just a fucking idiot.

It's been seven days since I told Nevaeh to leave. Seven days since I've been anything other than a mess of emotions no one could ever figure out how to put back together. I've lost a lot of people in my life, people I've loved more than anything else. Their deaths brought me unbearable pain. But this? It's so different. It's so... so much worse. The thought sends a shiver through me because it feels wrong to even think that, but I can't help it.

When Grandpa, Grandma, and Dad died, I didn't die with them. My future was still intact. I knew I could move on with my life, especially because I was motivated to stay strong for Val. But what I'm feeling right now is the complete opposite. I don't have to be strong, so I've collapsed into myself. I can't move on because I don't know how anyone could. I don't even know how I've made it through these seven days.

The first three, I actually managed to get myself out of bed. I went to the police with my sister, asked what our options were. There are none. Without proof of what happened or any of the harassment she's been putting us through, they cannot do anything. It doesn't matter that she had someone break into our hotel room, stole from us, blackmailed us, and tried to kill my reason to live. I have no proof for any of it, and the woman who pushed Nevaeh onto the street is nowhere to be found. I've never felt so hopeless in my whole life. It's the reason why the past four days, I've been in bed, hugging Nevaeh's pillow like my life depends on it. I haven't showered, I've barely eaten, and the only thing I do regularly is brush my teeth and drink water.

My fingers lift to the stubble growing on my face. Never, ever in my life have I let it get this long. I like the lower half of my face to be free of any hair. It's something I've been meticulous about since I hit puberty. But I'm no longer motivated to do anything. Who do I have to be clean for? Myself? I don't deserve to feel that level of comfort.

God, I'm wallowing in self-pity, and I can't fucking stop.

A knock on my front door shakes my whole apartment, but I have no plans of letting in whoever is bothering me. It can't be Val. She was supposed to fly to Italy yesterday, not that I have any idea if she really went. I haven't spoken to anyone since the police told me there is nothing they can do to help me get rid of Cecilia. She'll still be there, at every race, COO of *Griffin Sports*, tormenting her children.

Unless... unless Val's plan to get her to confess works, but neither of us has had the courage to actually go through with it yet.

We're dreading it.

"Okay, you stubborn son of a bitch, next time I knock, fucking open the door." James? What the hell is he doing here? I didn't tell anyone about Nevaeh and me.

"Leave me alone," I say, my voice cracking because I haven't spoken in days.

"No way. Val sent me here to pick you up, and I'm not leaving without you," he replies, ripping the blanket off my body. I cling to Nevaeh's pillow, not ready for her scent to be ripped from me. Unfortunately, my best friend doesn't give me a choice. He snatches it out of my weak arms and throws it to the ground.

Yeah, I'm angry now.

"I told you to leave me the fuck alone. Now, give me back my goddamn pillow and let me sleep," I growl, but James isn't having any of it as he makes his way into my closet and grabs a towel. He throws it at my head before ripping my curtains wide open. The sun is so bright, it takes me several moments until my eyes have adjusted to the light again.

"Go shower. You stink worse than a pile of horse shit." Ouch. But I almost laugh. If I wasn't dead inside, I probably would.

"If I may ask, what is the point? My mother will only torture me if I leave the house, just like the thought of knowing no matter where I go, I will never go there again with Nevaeh." James stays silent for a moment, arms crossed in front of his chest and disbelief all over his face.

"Are you bloody joking? Have you lost the plot?" he asks, and I roll my eyes. "No, seriously, mate, are you stupid?" Okay, getting angry again.

"I know you could never understand true heartbreak, but it doesn't give you the right to treat me like this," I reply.

"I don't understand true heartbreak?" His shoulders tense at the last two words. "I watched the woman I thought was the love of my life fall in love with hers. I watched her be happy every single day with him for the past year. That's first of all. Second of all, I share custody of my son with two other women, wonderful people, but nonetheless, I have to share him because his mother abandoned us. I had to make a decision that ripped my heart into shreds. Last but not least, I experience heartbreak every single time my son looks at me, and I remember I don't get to see him a lot, something he'll probably ask me about when he's older. Do you know what that feels like?"

I shake my head, shame settling in my chest.

"That's what I bloody thought. So, get off your lazy arse, shower, and let's go to Val. She invited Cecilia over for dinner. She wants to start the plan tonight," he says so nonchalantly, I want to punch him in the face.

"What do you mean? Tonight? At dinner?" I ask, stunned and a little upset I have to find out like this.

"Yes, tonight, at dinner, because what better way to bond than over a meal?" James points at the bathroom without saying another word, and I stumble into it.

Fuck it.

Let's try it my sister's way.

"Thank you for inviting me," the attempted murderer says before taking a spoonful of Valentina's lasagna into her mouth.

I suggested poisoning her plate, but Val smacked my arm and told me to put on my best smile. We need to make it seem like we want to have a relationship with her, make her vulnerable so she lets it slip what she's done. Val already hit record on her phone, but there is no way Cecilia would be stupid enough to admit anything. She's a fucking mastermind and all just to have a relationship with the children she abandoned in the first place.

"Well, to be honest, we're getting a little sick and tired of all this drama happening around us. We thought maybe you could tell us why having us back is so important to you now," my sister says, and I shoot her an unsure look. I have no idea what she's trying to do, but she's treading carefully, making sure not to break any of the eggshells we're walking on.

"I regret what I've done. I can't imagine how difficult it must have been for the two of you to grow up without a mother, and I would like to try and make things right. You can understand that, right?" she asks, and my sister gives her an acknowledging nod.

"Yes, of course. I remember you said how difficult it was to be married to our father. I can't imagine how hard it must have been to make the decision to leave us behind to save yourself," Val says, and I almost laugh at the sincerity in her tone. She's pretending to mean it, but I know there are a million tons of sarcasm coated around the words. Cecilia doesn't detect it.

"Yes! Yes, exactly. I'm so glad you finally understand me. I knew once Nevaeh was out of the picture you would come to your senses." My nails dig into the palms of my hands until I feel my skin starting to give way under the pressure. I shove a spoonful of food into my mouth to keep from saying things that would ruin this evening. My mother shoots me a comforting look, knowing damn well I broke up with Nevaeh because of what she's done.

Val's voice fills the uncomfortable silence.

"Actually, I wanted to talk to you about that. Nevaeh was the one who encouraged us to give our relationship with you another try."

What the fuck is she trying to accomplish? I'm usually very good at sensing what my sister is thinking and feeling, but, right now, I'm lost.

Then, it occurs to me.

Val wants to make Cecilia feel guilty.

"Oh, really?" Could it be? Does my mother feel remorse? "She's the reason we're having dinner?" Val nods in response. Cecilia stares at her plate. "Then, how come she isn't here?"

I was trying my very best. For the record, I lasted a full hour, but I can't swallow back the words before they spill from my lips.

"Because you tried to run her over with your car." Gabriel drops his fork into his plate, Val's mouth falls wide open, and James runs his hand over his face. Cecilia, on the other hand, looks inhumanly calm.

"She was keeping you from me," she replies with a shrug, not caring that she tried to *take another person's life*. "I did what I had to do." I have to keep her talking.

"Like breaking into our hotel room? Stealing from her? Blackmailing her? *Killing* her?" I stand up, anger seeping from my words.

"I did what I had to!" she repeats, getting up to face me. It's not a confession. I need her to say the words, to have undeniable proof.

"Killing my girlfriend is what you had to do, Cecilia Martin?" I scream, desperate and in pain. The thought makes me feel sick.

"Well, I wasn't very successful, was I?" she yells, and I shoot Gabriel a look, telling him to call the police. "Great, isn't this just fantastic? And here I thought we could have a civil conversation."

The next thing I know, her fist connects with my jaw before she throws the veranda table over and on top of Val, James, and Gabriel. I fall to the floor, shock and panic consuming me.

I try to refocus quickly, but Cecilia is long gone.

Fuck, I just made things ten times worse, didn't I?

Chapter 57

Nevaeh

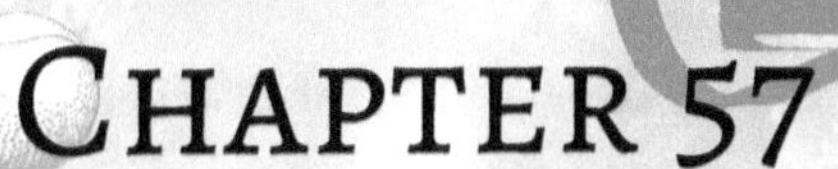

TEN DAYS. I CAN'T believe I've gone ten days without speaking to Adrian, but now we're going to be running into each other again at the upcoming race weekend. Nova has been trying to prepare me for how it will feel to see him, but how could she ever understand? She and Aileen have had one fight in the duration of their relationship, and now they're happily engaged. My sister has never experienced any other type of heartbreak except a brief two-day one she was responsible for. Her lies caused their fight. Not a criminal mother.

She could never understand.

"Vaeh?" my father's voice fills my ears, and I turn my head to him.

He insisted on driving me to the airport because, according to him, we didn't spend enough time together.

"Honey?" Papa says, reminding me he just tried to get my attention.

"Yeah, sorry. What's wrong?" I ask, shifting my eyes to his face.

He looks older. There are more lines around his eyes and mouth now. His hair is turning gray everywhere. The bags under his eyes have gotten bigger. He's starting to look his age.

"Will you be alright?" His question knocks me breathless for a second. I think about lying to him because what would be the point of telling him the truth? It would only make him worry, and he has enough of that to do with his team. The season is coming to an end, and he's been stressed about the Constructors' and Drivers' Championships results.

"I'll be fine, Papa, don't worry," I assure him, managing to bring a smile to my face. It drops soon.

"Are you sure? You're going to be—" I cut him off before he can hurt my feelings.

"I'll be fine!" There is no way he'll believe that.

"Okay," he says, his eyes trained on the road. "Would you like to talk about that—" He searches for a word. "—reaction?" he finishes, and I wipe my eyes. God, I'm so tired.

"Not really," I reply, wrapping my arms around my legs.

"Holding back will only make you feel worse," he says. I turn to him, crossing my arms in front of my chest.

"Alright, fine. I'm pretty sure I won't be able to handle seeing him. I am dreading this week more than anything because there is no way I won't break down at the sight of him," I rant, and he shoots me a side glance filled with worry.

"What is it about Adrian that makes this heartbreak so horrible for you?" he asks, and I almost laugh again.

What isn't it about Adrian?

"We have something most people never even attempt to search for because they think it's unreachable."

"And what is that?" he asks.

"It doesn't have a name, I don't think it should ever get one. It's so much more than true love or any other concept society has come up with. It's real. It's hard work. It's priceless. It's raw happiness and joy, even in the hardest times. I want to fight for him, for us, because sleeping in his arms is where I'm home. There is love in everything we do, even when we fight. What Adrian and I have is *everything*. It's a reason to breathe. It's a reason to try our hardest. It's a reason to be free of our demons."

I stare at my hands, not quite finished talking.

"I was so reserved when we first met. I told myself it was my job forbidding it, but, deep down, I knew he was it for me forever. I wasn't quite ready at first. So many people fall out of love, and I was scared I'd fall out of love with Adrian or he with me. That's why I told myself I hadn't already flown in love with him. But I had. I also realized that if I was ever sure of one thing, it was that I could never, ever fall out of love with him again. He's tattooed on my heart, skin, and soul, and there will never be a way to erase him."

I'm breathless.

My emotions have spilled everywhere. My father and I have never been the best at sharing our feelings with each other. With him always being gone for work and me learning to grow up without him present, it became hard to have a close bond. It's why we always fight and struggle to communicate things that have to be said. But not anymore. I have offered him a piece of myself, whether he wanted me to or not.

It's up to him now to not make me regret it.

"You truly feel this way about him?" he asks, and my features soften instantly. Tension leaves my shoulders, and I even manage to smile, somewhat.

"Yes. Do you understand me a bit better now?" I say, and my father takes my hand in his, squeezing it tightly.

"Not really, Vaeh, but only because I never felt this way about anyone. Not even your mother." He drops his head, sucking in a sharp breath. I know they don't have the happiest of marriages, but hearing him say something like that makes me pity him a little. "You're not going to give up fighting for him, are you?"

"Never," I reply without hesitation. "But he's not the problem. Cecilia is. His mother is the reason we broke up, remember?" I shared the story of what happened with my parents the day I arrived at home. They were both beside themselves when they heard what type of monster my boyfriend's... ex-boyfriend's, *ouch*, mother is.

"Right..." my father replies. "Are you sure it's a good idea for you to stay with Valentina? What if she sees you with her and then tries to do something to you again?" He's worried. I am a little, too.

"Cecilia doesn't seem to have a problem with my friendship with Val. Her biggest issue is—was my relationship with Adrian. So, don't worry. It'll be okay. I will make sure never to be alone in case she's lurking in the shadows," I try to joke, but my voice cracks, revealing how scared I am that this is a possibility. "Everything will be fine. You'll see," I assure him, my words stronger this time to take away some of his worry.

"If anything happens, I will lock you in our house and never let you out," he warns, and I lean my head against the padding of the seat, allowing my tired eyes to flutter shut for the rest of the drive.

"Sure, Papa, you've got yourself a deal," I say, going along with his joke before an anxious feeling settles in my chest again.

After ten days, I'm going to see Adrian again.

After ten days, my home will be within reach.

After ten days, we're no closer to getting back to heaven than we were when I left.

That thought alone makes me feel so sick to my stomach, I make a plan in my head to avoid Adrian at all costs. I can't do it. I can't face him yet. I feel raw, too much so to see the cause of my heartbreak.

CHAPTER 58

Adrian

CECILIA HAS DISAPPEARED AGAIN.

I don't know what's worse, when she's gone and plotting, or when she's right in our faces.

At least the police believed us now, after listening to the recording, and have opened a case on her. They're looking for her, and I've officially hired security to follow everyone I care about. But they're discreet, so I doubt anyone has even noticed. Nevaeh certainly hasn't, otherwise she would have reached out to me again. At least, I hope so. I miss her so much. It's been three weeks since I told her to leave, and we're two races away from the end of the season. She had Val pick up some of her things, but not everything. Nevaeh is as ready to move on from me as I am from her. Not at all.

It shouldn't give me hope, not with Cecilia still around, but it does. It means she understands why I asked her to leave. Why things need to be this way for now.

Last race weekend, Nevaeh did her best to stay as far away from me as possible, only spending time in Valentina and Leonard's garage to do her job. And I did fucking horribly in the race. I came tenth while Gabriel and Lincoln took first and second place. Gabriel is only eight points behind me now, and Lincoln is a close third with merely fifteen points behind me.

Valentina and Gabriel are getting married next week.

My head is spinning, unable to keep up with everything it's trying to process. And I have no time for any of it. I have to stop overthinking to focus entirely on racing.

I'm starting from pole with Lincoln in second, James in third, Gabriel in fourth, and Valentina in fifth. She's done extraordinarily in her first season in F1.

I was expecting nothing less, but I'm still so fucking proud.

"Hey," Daniel says, and I shift my attention from the car to him.

He's offering me my balaclava and helmet, and I take them from him with an appreciative nod. Ever since Nevaeh and I broke up, he's been gentler with me. Less jokes, more focus on work. The entire world seems to be concerned about me. The sunshine of Formula One, the cocky playboy, looks down in every interview, hardly answers questions, doesn't even smile anymore. It's so unlike me, I've even worried Lorenzo. I think he's convinced that my performance at the last race was influenced by my emotions, but if anything, I'm so angry at the world, I race harder, more recklessly, but in a good way. Well, maybe not *good* exactly, but I did get pole because of it yesterday, so it can't be bad.

Right?

"Yeah?" I ask when Daniel doesn't say anything else.

"I know you're hurting right now, but Nevaeh is waiting for you. The only way to get back to her is to be safe out there." Tears shoot into my eyes without my permission.

"I know."

"Do you? Because you've been driving like a fucking idiot, no offense."

"I'm just doing my job," I reply with a glare, but Daniel merely shakes his head.

"If you won't listen to me, maybe you'll listen to him," he says a second before a hand appears on my shoulder, squeezing in a way I'm too familiar with. The tears reappear in my eyes, but I'm not fast enough to swallow them down this time.

"Hey, kiddo," Leonard says, and I almost break down all over again. I've been avoiding him for this very reason. I knew as soon as he talked to me, I'd feel everything I'm trying not to feel. "Come with me for a moment," he says, so we walk off the track and toward the Grenzenlos bathroom area. As soon as we're alone, he wraps his arms around me.

I break down immediately. Sobs turn into more sobs. Tears stream down my face as all the pain of the last few weeks comes crashing into me like a train, racing straight into the place where my heart used to be before I gave it to Nevaeh.

"I've got you, kiddo," Leonard promises, tightening his hold on me. "We will get her back to you. We will find a way to get rid of Cecilia for good. You will be back in Nevaeh's arms where you belong in no time, okay? I promise." And I believe him. I truly do believe him because if I didn't, I don't think I'd ever recover.

As soon as the lights vanish, I shoot forward, Lincoln right beside me. I don't mean to hold my breath as we make it into the first corner, so the burning in my lungs surprises me. I fight him off, unwilling to let that little shit claim first place.

A little shit who saved Nevaeh's life after you endangered it, my subconscious reminds me, and I let out a groan so loud, it vibrates through my helmet.

"Focus," Chloe reminds me, and I realize I accidentally pressed my radio button and everyone probably heard me.

"Trying," I say through gritted teeth as I fight Lincoln off in the third corner.

Shit hits the fan pretty quickly after that.

His front wing touches my right rear tire as we head into the tenth corner of the second lap, Lincoln pushing me onto the gravel. My tire explodes. My car slows. Everyone else zooms past me, including Lincoln. Somehow, I make it back to the pits where my crew is already waiting for me, but by the time I come back out on track, I'm last.

Fucking last.

"Tell me they're investigating that asshole," I say to Chloe, my blood boiling in my veins.

"I'm on it," she replies, and I leave her to do her job while I focus on doing mine. Climbing back up the ranks and ending the race somewhere that won't make me fall into second or third place in the championship.

I have to make my way back up to third place, and only if Lincoln stays first and Gabriel doesn't win. But even then, we'll all be equal.

"Fuck!" I make sure not to accidentally hit the radio this time and speed down the main straight of the track, chasing the Klein car that's in nineteenth.

Twenty laps later, I'm fucking sweating, so much so it's dripping into my eyes, but at least I'm back in the points. I'm in tenth place. I've got this.

"Lincoln has been given a five-second penalty for forcing you off the track and causing a collision," Chloe says, and I practically jump in my seat from joy.

"How far ahead is he?"

"He's got four and a half seconds on James."

Fucking hell, James, pick up the damn pace.

"Okay. And Gabriel?"

"Gabriel is chasing James, but he's struggling with his tire compound," Chloe explains, and I nod several times even though no one can see me.

Another ten laps pass, but I'm only in fifth when our second pitstop happens—the first for every other driver—and I end up back in eighth place.

I hate everything about this cursed race.

"Lincoln served his time penalty during his pitstop, but he came back out in first place." Of course he did.

This race is a one-stop race, unless people like Lincoln crash into you, so all that's left now is just hoping I can fight my way back into the top three places.

"Gabriel has overtaken James as well. He is now chasing Lincoln." On one hand, I'd rather have Gabriel overtake Lincoln and win, but if he does, we will go into the last race of the season with my brother leading the championship. If Lincoln wins, it'll equalize us. None of these options are fucking ideal, but there is no way I'm going to win today.

"Who do I have left to overtake to get into third?"

"Cameron, then Leonard, Kyle, Valentina, and James."

"Thanks."

Cameron fights me a little in the corners, but as soon as we get to the straight, his Spark doesn't have the speed to keep me away. The same goes for Leonard. Kyle is harder to overtake in his Grenzenlos, but he takes a corner too wide, letting me take the inside line and shoot past him. My sister is the hardest to overtake. She may not have a fast car, but the way she drives that Alfa Adrenalina makes it seem like she's actually in a Velocità Rossa. I almost give her a thumbs up as I finally manage to race by her, just because she's done such an outstanding job.

The last one I *need* to overtake is James, which will be even harder. His Hawke has been quick all weekend.

"You're the fastest car on track. Overtake James, then go for the fastest lap for the extra point at the end," Chloe says, her voice firm but gentle.

"Got it."

The last few laps are hell. James doesn't give up, and I only manage to overtake him four laps before the end because I dive down the inside and push him a little wider. He stays on the track, something Lincoln should learn from, but I shoot ahead of him, using the next three laps to recharge my battery so I can use it on the last lap to get the fastest one of the race. I may have old tires, but Chloe said I'm the fastest car on track. So, I'll be the fastest car on track.

"Come on, Adrian," she says as I rush down the straight, right over the finish line. The lap time starts counting. I focus on my heavy breathing, trying to get it under control. Gabriel still hasn't overtaken Lincoln, but he's in DRS range, according to my race engineer, so he still has one lap to get the Brit.

"You've almost got it," Chloe says, and I push even harder, groaning at the exhaustion I feel in every centimeter of my body. "You got it! Fastest lap, well done."

I know she's trying to cheer me up, but it's not working because Gabriel didn't overtake the rookie. He and Lincoln now have the same amount of points, and I'm only one point ahead of them. We're entering the last race of the season head-to-fucking-head, and before I can even worry about that event in two weeks, I'm thinking about what's happening next week.

Valentina and Gabriel's wedding. Seeing Nevaeh. Being unable to avoid her, not that I would want to, but not even *she* can avoid *me* like she's done for the last few weeks.

It feels like I'm going to die all over again.

Chapter 59

Adrian

"OH MY GOD, STOP freaking out, mate," James scolds while Cameron nudges me in the side to get my attention.

We're all sitting at the table for the rehearsal dinner, waiting for my sister and Nevaeh to arrive.

Okay, we all know I'm mostly waiting for Nevaeh.

Every part of me craves to see her, touch her, be with her. It's been twenty-four soul-crushing days.

"You can get her back now, you know? Cecilia has disappeared." I might punch James for being such an idiot.

"While the police are searching for Cecilia, do you think it's a good idea to expose Nevaeh to more danger?" I retort, and he flinches when he sees how angry I've gotten.

"But don't you think her being here doesn't already put her at risk? Do you think begging her to get back with you will make Cecilia any angrier?"

Don't punch your best friend at your sister's rehearsal dinner. Don't do it. It's not his fault he's stupid.

"Do I look like the type of man that wants to risk it?" I ask, my eye twitching slightly. "Not to mention, Cecilia always had more of a problem with Nevaeh being my girlfriend than Val's best friend." Leonard, Cameron, James, and Gabriel all lean away from me in response to my—probably—wild facial expression.

"Cecilia is gone, Adrian. She hasn't shown up in weeks, and she won't again. She'd never risk jail just to force herself to be part of her children's lives when they so clearly don't want her to be in them," Cameron replies, and I reach out to take a sip of my water.

"You all are very stupid if you think we've seen the last of Cecilia. Nevaeh will be safer if she's not with me. If you saw what I saw over three weeks ago, you would understand why I can't endanger her life for my own selfish needs again. And, by the way, you should be proud that the guy who is in love with himself can be so selfless," I rant, and their eyes go even wider.

"Adrian, you might be arrogant, but you are the most selfless guy in our entire friendship group. But we do think it's part of the problem. You're so set on what you think she *needs*, you haven't stopped once to wonder what she wants. Any fool can see you're the one Nevaeh can't live without. Don't you think you owe it to her to try and protect her to the best of your ability *while* you're together," Leonard says, and I wish I could be angry with him like I was with James, but there is something about him saying it that shuts me up.

Damn Leonard and my respect for him.

"We're just saying, man. You're deteriorating without her," Cameron says, and I smile at him for a fraction of a second.

"That's a big word, Cam. Did you finally start using the Word-of-the-Day calendar I bought you?" The Australian lets out a *hmpf* before grabbing his beer.

"I'm going to let that one slip because I know you're in pain. Under different circumstances, you wouldn't be so lucky," he says before taking a sip of the liquid I only ever liked when Nevaeh drank it and kissed me after.

"I can't risk it. I'm too scared," I admit, my gaze fixated on the serviette lying on my plate.

"Are you sure?" James whispers right as Nevaeh steps into the restaurant.

God, she's so beautiful. I never forgot, but the reminder hits me in the chest with so much force, the air is knocked out of me. She cut her hair, but only a few centimeters. Her body is still so perfect and curvy. Her honey-brown eyes stand out more now that the usual white of her eyes has turned a deep pink from exhaustion and potentially crying. Her freckles are wonderfully painted on her face. Her lips, the top one a bit fuller than the bottom, are painted a deep red, the same color as my Formula One team. Her curves are getting hugged by a black dress with spaghetti straps and a low cleavage line, tugging at my willpower.

Then, her eyes meet mine. Pain fills my body from the top of my head, spilling all the way into my toes. I stand up without realizing, the desperation to touch her pushing me toward her, even though I know I shouldn't. I know this is painful for both of us and that me keeping my distance would be the respectful thing to do, but, shit, I miss her so much.

I also don't want the first words I say to her to be a spectacle for everyone at the table.

Nevaeh watches me with confusion as I take quick strides toward her. I don't even know what the hell I'm trying to achieve. We can't get back together, not while Cecilia is still out there plotting her revenge. The police are searching, but they also told us she could be anywhere. The only thing keeping us safe are the bodyguards I hired for protection, but I can't be certain they will be enough. I'm too fucking scared. I'm too terrified of getting back with Nevaeh when, at any moment, my mother could try to take her from me.

When I reach her, I'm so out of breath, anyone would assume I just ran up a hundred flights of stairs. My fingertips are vibrating, begging me to touch her, embrace her, and bury my face in the crook of her neck. My nose tingles, desperate to take in her scent and feel whole again. For the first time in twenty-four days, I feel the proximity of my heart, and my hollow chest doesn't feel quite as empty anymore. But I can't have her. I can't put her in more danger.

I find the bracelet I gave her safely wrapped around her wrist, and I want to cry my eyes out. She's wearing it. She didn't take it off. Nevaeh is still mine, like I am hers: forever. I'm overcome by both joy and an immense amount of sadness. I wish my fucking mind could focus on one emotion at a time for once.

Finally, I fixate on her worried expression.

"Oh, Adrian, what happened to your face?" she asks with worry, her hand reaching out to touch the fading bruise on my cheek and jaw, the one I'd completely forgotten about until this very second. She stops herself a centimeter before her fingers touch my skin, and I do my best not to whimper when she retracts her hand again. "Sorry," she mumbles, staring at the floor. Fuck, I wanna reach out, grab her chin between my fingers, and make her look at me so badly.

"Cecilia punched me," I blurt out while she wraps her arms around herself, and I wonder if she's doing it to keep from touching me. It's the reason why I shoved my hands into my pants pockets.

"Oh my God, how? When?" She's so worried about me. Tears shoot into my eyes from the need to kiss her.

"A few weeks ago, but the bruise hasn't been healing well," I say before giving her a brief summary of our plan and how much it backfired.

"So, the police are looking for her now?" Nevaeh asks, and I give her a nod. "And the bodyguards are here for our protection?" Again, I nod. "So, why aren't you touching me?" Her question leaves me breathless.

"Because I can't lose you to death, not like everyone else," I admit, and, for the first time since that disastrous dinner with Cecilia, I realize this is the true reason I keep pushing her away.

At first, I was scared my mother would try to hurt her again, if not worse, but now? Now I know logically that the bodyguards will be able to do their jobs and protect us. It's what I hired them to do. But I'm still terrified of Nevaeh getting caught in any type of crossfire I'm responsible for. The people around me die. She cannot die. I can't drag her into my life where death is an old friend I never wanted to get close to. What if I'm the magnet for it?

"Adrian," she says, her fingers getting close to me again. I step away from her, straightening out my back while I try to bring back the version of myself I used when I told her to leave. I bring back the numb me.

"We should go sit down and eat. We don't want to keep the happy couple waiting."

I couldn't care less if they started eating without us. Val would want Nevaeh and me to work this out, but I'm burdened with my trauma, more so than I ever have been before.

What kind of a person does that make me? A broken one? A scared one? A hopeless case? I want to say all of those things because I know how good I was when I was with Nevaeh. I know the person I am when my friends are with me, but does that make me the right man for my Nevaeh?

"I can't do this," the love of my life says, stopping me before I can walk back to the table. "I know you love me. I know I'm everything to you. I know you want me. Stop fighting us. Stop pushing me away. And, for the love of God, stop pretending to be someone you're not. You said when we fight we resolve it one of three ways," she starts and takes a step toward me. My body is paralyzed by the desire to be close to her. "'Number one: we sit down and speak about it until the conflict is resolved. Number two: we take some time to cool off but only with the promise of going to dinner after. And number three: we fuck our anger away.' Those are your rules, *our* rules. Why are you breaking them?"

Her body is almost touching mine, *almost*, and it drives me absolutely wild. This distance between us frustrates me more than anything has ever frustrated me.

"Because we're not fighting, *mon paradis*. We didn't break up because we were angry with each other. We broke up so you'd be safe." I turn around to walk away, but she grabs my arm. Life courses through me, waking me up cell by cell until my whole body catches on fire.

Alive. I'm alive again.

"What if I told you that no risk in the world is too great for us to be together? What if I told you I'm slowly dying without you? And I don't care how fucking dramatic that sounds. I can't eat. I can't sleep. I try because I want to be strong, but I can't. What Cecilia did wasn't your fault, but this is. The both of us being in excruciating pain now is your fault," she says, and the tears drop down my face when she lets go of me and my body sinks back into death.

I'm unable to respond for a moment, and she beats me to speaking before I manage to croak out an answer.

"Take your heart back, Adrian. I can't stand this heartless version of you," Nevaeh says, and my brain jumps awake again.

"Don't you dare give me back what's yours." She almost stumbles backward from my fast words.

"Then where do we go from here? I'll never want anyone but you. You'll never want anyone but me. You have the resources to have security around us all the time. I don't understand where the problem lies," she admits and runs her hands through her beautiful locks. The urge to do the same overwhelms me.

"I'm lost," I reply, and Nevaeh lets out a sigh filled with pain.

"I know you are, and we both know you'd find yourself with me, but you don't want that. And I'm done putting our hearts on the line when you don't know how to be with me anymore." I shake my head immediately.

"Don't say that. I know how to be with you. Fuck, being with you is the easiest thing in my life, but that's not the problem. I'm overcome with fear. I'm scared Cecilia will hurt you, terrified death surrounds me and anyone that comes close to me will die because of it, and I'm terrified of being wrong for you. All at once, everything, it's scaring me, and I don't know how to ease it."

Nevaeh steps beside me then, looking up at me before she responds.

"Instead of spending all your time in the land of fears, why don't you rejoin me in the land of the living, my love?" And I'm speechless again. She raises her hand to my left pec, sending a jolt of life through me. "I understand your feelings, but I can't wait forever."

She walks away, to the table where the rest of our family is. I watch after her, wiping my tears and doing my best to keep the rest of them inside. I still haven't touched her. She touched me twice, and I didn't take the chance to do it even once.

Man, I'm a fucking idiot.

A lost, broken, stupid idiot.

Whose only way to feel whole again just walked away like the goddess she is.

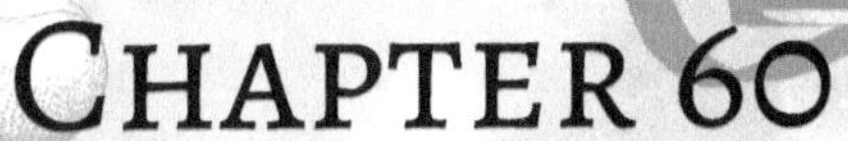

CHAPTER 60
Nevaeh

TEARS STREAMED DOWN HIS face. He showed me how deeply he's hurting, and there is nothing I wanted more than to comfort him. One simple hug would have been enough to bring him back to me, to break down his restraints, but it's not up to me anymore. He's the one who has to accept his fears. Cecilia is gone, at least somewhat. So, why can't we be together?

Because Cecilia isn't really gone, my subconscious reminds me. *And he almost watched you die, so he's terrified now.* If only I knew how to reassure him everything will be fine. We could come up with a plan to make sure I'm not alone like I was last time. I want to scream at him for thinking he's wrong for me, that he always goes back to this thinking when he's the best thing to have ever happened to me. I'll never be able to show him he's not the cause of death in his family, but I hope he will realize it before it breaks him.

"You look beautiful," Cameron whispers after the food is placed in front of us, and I tilt my head in his direction to show him my smile.

"Thank you. As always, you look stunning," I reply and admire the way his blue dress shirt hugs his muscular torso. His pants fit snugly, showing off his thick, trained thighs too. Cameron is a work of art, without a doubt, but my eyes always drift right back to Adrian, who is sitting diagonally across from me.

He's dressed in all black—dress shirt, pants, and shoes—with his fingers covered in rings, a bracelet around his wrist, and a matching silver necklace to finish off the look. This outfit is very similar to the one he wore in Singapore when we went to the rooftop bar of the MBS, and the memory sends a stinging pain through me. It hurts me how gorgeous he is, that he's still mine in almost every way possible, but I can't touch him. I can't take away his worries or his fears.

"I'm so glad you're here," Val says. "How do you feel? I know this must be hard," she adds and takes my hand from beside me. I look into her eyes, pure agony ripping through me. Her eyes, her face, her smile, they are too similar to Adrian's. So, I focus on her floor-length red dress that shimmers when the light hits it just right instead. The way it hugs her curves but is flowy at the same time. I look at Gabriel's suit, loving the way his dress shirt is the same color as her dress.

"I'm fine," I lie, but I do it well enough to surprise her. Her eyebrows shoot up on her forehead and her lips part ever so slightly.

"Oh, that's good. I'm glad to hear," she says and squeezes my hand once more before turning to her fiancé. Gabriel grabs her face and plants his lips on hers so quickly, Val giggles.

I have to shift my gaze away, but it drifts to Adrian before I can stop it. He's already looking at me, and I can see in his eyes that he wants that to be us. Kissing and laughing, he wants us to go back, and so do I. It's all I've wanted since the day he told me to leave.

Adrian can't bring himself to look away and neither can I, even as Domi and Nicolette join our table with an excited Damian in their arms. James stands up to greet his son, who wraps his arms around his father without hesitation.

"Daddy, daddy, daddy," he screams, wiggling from side to side.

"Hi, bud, I've missed you," James replies, planting a kiss on his son's cheek.

"Auntie, auntie," Damian cheers next, and I turn to Val, who is pouting now. I don't understand her upset expression until I see Damian reaching for me. "Nevi," he says, and everything inside of me melts. James places his son in my arms before we all sit down. I bounce Damian up and down on my leg, my dinner completely forgotten.

"You can give him back to me, if you'd like to finish your food," Domi says, but I hold onto the happy toddler.

Normally, I'm not very good with children. They're sticky and loud, but Damian is none of those things. He's well-behaved, happy, and not sticky, at least most of the time. He's also a comfort I need right now. He has no idea how painful this world can be yet, and I envy that. I wish I could be clueless like him again.

"I'm okay, thank you. Please, eat. I will take care of him," I assure Gabriel's aunt while James and Cameron switch places so the Brit can be close to his child.

"Hey, little warrior," James says, letting Damian take his index finger. "He loves you," he adds, looking at me, and I smile at the child on my lap.

"Yeah, he seems to," I reply with half a grin, still bouncing my legs to make Damian giggle from joy.

"I didn't mean Damian, love. It's obvious my son adores you, but you need to be reminded that, even as Adrian pushes you away, he loves you more than he'll ever understand." James gives my hand a comforting squeeze, and I watch curiosity slip across Adrian's face. He can't hear us, but he must suspect what his best friend is saying is about him.

"He could love me more than anyone's ever loved someone, but if he doesn't realize pushing me away is only hurting both of us soon, no amount of love will be able to repair the damage," I say and hand James his son, excusing myself to go to the bathroom.

This is getting ridiculous. There are so many emotions inside of me, and I can't deal with any of them. They're too overwhelming. I can't breathe with them weighing heavy on my chest, and all I want to do is finally let the scream rip from my lips. I've been holding it back for a very long time now, but it has to break free. If not, I'll never be able to get myself under control again. I think about screaming into my hands right here and now. The only thing stopping me is the thought of anyone hearing my pain, and, with anyone, I mean specifically Adrian.

"Love? Are you okay?" Val asks, knocking on the bathroom door.

"No, I'm really not," I whisper, hugging myself as tears stream down my face. "I'm fine, just one minute," I yell back so she can hear me.

"May I come in?"

"No," I say quickly, not willing to let her see me like this.

"Please, I really need to pee," she says, and I let out a short laugh before wiping away my emotional betrayal and opening the door. A comforting smile slips onto her face. "I don't actually have to pee," she says, and I give her a small nod.

"I had a feeling," I reply while she flings her arms around me. I bury my face in her neck while she rubs my back.

"And I had a feeling you needed me. I guess we were both right," she says, stepping back to run her fingers under my eyes. "Waterproof mascara?" Val asks, and a genuine laugh falls from my lips.

"Of course. I knew I'd cry sometime tonight," I say, making my friend chuckle.

"Smart," she replies and leads me to the sink.

"Can you knock some sense into your brother? He's not listening to me. He's set on believing I'm safer and better off without him," I explain while Val wets a napkin and hands it to me.

"I wish I could. I wish I could shake him, punch him so hard he'll see we're safe now, but with Cecilia still out there, he won't be able to rest. Just... be a little more patient," she says to me, and I wipe under my eyes and over my face.

"I want to be, but it's painful. Seeing him and reliving the memories of being with him and not getting to have the same now, it hurts more than anything I've ever experienced." Val leans against the sink, her red dress swaying with the movement. She's so effortlessly beautiful... just like her brother.

"After Gabriel ended things between us a while ago, I felt the same. I had to see him after the summer break every single day of the race weekend. It was excruciating. Remembering the way his body felt pressed against mine or how he loved me so fully, it tore me apart. But now, here we are, getting married in two days and hosting our rehearsal dinner. It seemed hopeless for us at one point, too, but soulmates always find their way back to each other," she says, but it's not as simple as that, is it?

"You know what? You're right. I'm going to stop worrying about anything other than your bachelorette party tomorrow." I throw the paper towel into the garbage can, forcing a bright smile to my face.

"You don't have to come if you're not feeling up for it," she says, and I offer her a fake excited expression.

"Of course I'll come. I'd never miss it. Plus, I have to make sure everything goes smoothly. I did plan it for the past month," I reply, and she flashes me a grin of happiness.

"Great. And I promise, if you want a stripper, we can still arrange for one," she jokes, and a chuckle vibrates off my chest.

CHAPTER 61

Adrian

Gabriel won't let me skip his stupid party.

After I watched Nevaeh disappear into the bathroom at dinner yesterday, I ran out of the restaurant. She couldn't bear looking at me anymore, and I didn't want to make things even harder for her. So, I ran out of there without saying a single word to anyone else. My family didn't like that. As a matter of fact, Gabriel was so pissed at me, he told me to stop hiding from my feelings and just get my woman back. When I yelled back at him, he walked away from me, told me to go to his party and be the best man I promised I'd be.

I've always cared more about how other people feel. My own emotions are important to me, but they always come second to those of the ones I love the most. That's why I've managed to put on a pair of blue jeans and a white dress shirt, leaving the top five buttons undone to look more casual. My hair is curly and all over the place, but I give up trying to control it.

Who am I trying to look attractive for anyway?

Nevaeh.

Fuck. I run my hands through it a few more times until it looks somewhat decent. I adjust my shirt, and then make sure everything else is in order on my body and face. Stupid fucking bachelor parties. I want to smack the person who invented them. If you've found the person you love, why do you even need to have the whole 'last night of freedom' thing? I never felt freer than I did when I was with Nevaeh. Then again, Gabriel and Val are mostly doing this because they love throwing parties, not because of the symbolism society has given these events.

I make my way toward the stairs of the house Val and Gabriel rented for yesterday and today before we all head to Chiara and Leonard's island tomorrow. Not everyone is sleeping here, only the happy couple, James, Cameron, Leonard, Domi, Nicolette, Damian, me, and Nevaeh. Julián, Scarlette, Evangelin, Carlos, Chiara, and Leonora are only coming tomorrow when we get to the island.

I've done my best to avoid Nevaeh to the very best of my ability, which is why I want to kick myself in the ass when I run into her at the bottom of the staircase. I was stuck in my head, not looking where I was going, and now I'm catching her before she falls. My arms are around her perfectly wide hips, my fingers digging into her soft curves as I press her chest against mine.

Everything is on fire.

Flames lick up my spine until shivers run down it. Heat spreads through my veins, lighting my blood on fire. I'm alive. I'm breathing heavily, but for the first time since we broke up, I'm getting enough oxygen to my brain. I can feel my heart again. It's racing from having her so close to me. My eyes close involuntarily at the coconut scent coming off her. The feeling of returning to heaven after weeks of hell fills me with so much life, I'm vibrating.

"Adrian," Nevaeh whispers, and I snap out of my trance. Touching her is dangerous. I shouldn't be touching her. It tears down my walls to the point of no redemption.

"I'm sorry," I say and step away, my body slumping back into its familiar undead state.

"Don't be," she replies, her hands slipping onto my chest. I suck in a sharp breath, the need to pin her against the wall, to lose myself completely inside of her, knocks the air out of me. "Hey, it's okay," she says, grabbing my face and tilting my head down. "You can touch me." And fuck do I want to. There is nothing I've wanted more in my entire life than to run my hands all over her while she assures me we will be fine.

"I shouldn't," I say and step back, breaking her hold on me.

"I hope you realize this is the second time you've rejected my touch in the past twenty-four hours, Adrian. Twice you've stepped away. I won't offer you the chance to do it a third time. I can't," she says and walks away while my hands reach out to hold onto her. They grab the air, nothing more.

"Sir, may we have a word?" one of the bodyguards, Armando, says, and I shift my attention to him, swallowing back the lump in my throat.

All Armando tells me is that they will be stationed everywhere at the club tonight to make sure no one goes in and out without their say-so. Apparently, the club owner wasn't too happy about it, but after explaining the situation, he was convinced that extra security he didn't have to pay for wasn't a bad idea.

I shake my head with a laugh I don't mean when I walk toward my soon-to-be brother-in-law, unable to believe what our lives have come to. First, Eduardo, and now Cecilia? I might actually fucking implode from anger.

"I saw what happened with Nevaeh," Gabriel says, so I try to walk away again. He grabs my hand before I have the chance to avoid this conversation. "Listen to me, you stubborn man, something like that, stepping away from her, it's one of the worst things you could ever do, you hear me? You *rejected* her." There is something about him using the same word as Nevaeh that makes me feel like death incarnate. "She might be understanding of your fears and trauma, but if you keep doing it, her anger will shift from Cecilia, the person who is actually responsible, to you, the person who is giving up without fighting for her."

I really shouldn't, I know better, but I push him backward anyway. Gabriel doesn't even stumble, despite me being taller and possibly stronger than him. Well, apparently not stronger.

"You've got no fucking idea what I'm going through. You broke up with my sister to play happy family with people you didn't even fucking know." Yeah, I just somehow made it even worse.

First, I push him and then I point out the worst mistake he's ever made, something he still hates himself for? What the hell is wrong with me? He seems to be thinking the same thing, I can tell by the way he looks at me.

"Okay, we're done with kindness? Fine by me. I've been wanting to tell you this for weeks now and I'm not going to hold back anymore. You have fucking lost it if you think you will ever be capable of being a decent human being, let alone a functioning one, without Nevaeh by your side. Cecilia may have tried to run her over with a car, but you're the one who told her to leave right after! What the fuck is wrong with you? You should have held her after, taken care of her. Instead, you told her to leave. Now count yourself fucking lucky she's not flipping you off and telling you to never speak to her again. That means she loves you, but every human has limits. We can only take so much pain, and Nevaeh will push you away the more you hurt her. I'm done telling you I understand how you feel when you don't even understand your own emotions. *Fix this.* Cecilia might come back, but you'll both be stronger to fight her together, for fuck's sake."

I have no words as I take three steps away from him, but he closes the distance between us again. His hand slips into my back pocket, ripping my wallet from it and pushing it open to take out the engagement ring I bought for Nevaeh.

"You were ready to be her husband, Adrian, but you're not acting like one right now. Through sickness and health. Through all the good and the bad, you stand together. You bought this because you want to marry her, but you're not ready, not until you stop letting your past determine your future. Now, you either get her back, or I don't want to hear a single fucking word out of your mouth about Nevaeh again."

The thought sends a stinging fear through me.

"But... what if Cecilia shows up and tries to hurt her again? It will be my fault. If I let her go, Nevaeh won't be on Cecilia's radar anymore," I say, but it only makes Gabriel angrier.

"Nevaeh is already on her radar, Adrian! Get that through your head. What you're trying to do, as selfless as it might seem, is just plain stupid. If I were you, I'd start figuring out a way to apologize for being the dumbest person alive."

And that's it. He leaves me without letting me respond. He leaves before I can tell him how sorry I am about the way I behaved toward him just now. He leaves before I can thank him for taking the burden off my shoulders.

"I've never seen him so angry and frustrated," James says, and I jump at his voice coming from behind me in the kitchen.

"Well, I've never been such an asshole to him," I reply and rub my face.

"What the hell is this?" I look up to see my best friend holding the engagement ring into the light to study it. I try to snatch it out of his hand, but he smacks mine away before I can do so. "Were you going to bloody propose before everything happened?" he asks, and I feel my stomach twirl.

"Yes. Give it back," I say, but James shakes his head.

"No, I'm intrigued now. You were going to propose and didn't tell me?" I cock an eyebrow.

"I wasn't going to tell anyone before I told Nevaeh." Am I meant to? Shouldn't she be the first one to hear it?

"Damn, alright then. Do you still want to? Propose, I mean," he clarifies, and I frown.

"Of course. I want nothing more than to call her my wife," I blurt out.

The sound of two water bottles hitting the ground behind us sends a wave of panic through me, spinning me around. Leonard and Cameron stare at me in disbelief. Then they bombard me with questions.

Yeah, this was my fault. I shouldn't have opened my mouth in the middle of the kitchen where everyone would be able to hear me. Their questions are my fault, but I have no choice. I have to answer them all while fighting the urge to run away and find Nevaeh.

Actually, I'm fighting the urge to snatch the ring from James' hand, run to her, and propose to her on the spot. I can't do this anymore. I can't be apart from her any longer.

In sickness and in health.

I'm ready.

"Okay, enough of your questions. Where did Nevaeh go?"

Chapter 62
Nevaeh

"Val, I left my wallet in my room. I'll be right back." Valentina and I were about to step into our taxi to head to the location of the bachelorette party.

"Hurry up," she says with a smile, so I rush back into the house, glad I chose to wear flats instead of heels today.

I push the door to my room open, freezing in place when I see—

"Adrian," I gasp, my lips parting in surprise. He's on his knees, his palms resting on his thighs. His head hangs low as he surrenders himself to me.

I shoot Val a quick text, telling her to leave without me. This is going to take some time, and I won't have anyone rushing us as we find our way back to each other.

"I'm so sorry," is the first thing that comes out of his mouth. "For everything." My knees weaken in response, so I lean against the door frame, my hands clasped in front of me.

This is it, the moment I've been waiting for since he told me to leave our apartment. He's finally ready to talk, and I suck in a sharp breath to keep my heart from stumbling with hope.

"I don't want you to be sorry for everything," I say, which finally makes him look at me. "I know why you told me to leave. I'm not angry with you for it. You did what you thought was best, and I can't deny that Cecilia has left me alone for the past few weeks because we weren't together anymore. So, truly, I get it."

Tears stream down his face while I speak, so I take several steps toward him.

"I even understand your fear of loss terrifying you. But now you have security. You have a team constantly following us. Now we can be safe as the police are finally investigating Cecilia. You don't need to push me away anymore, Adrian. You don't need to reject my touch," I say, stopping right in front of him. His hands clench like he's still holding himself back from touching me. "I'm yours, *mein Mond*, and I will only ever be yours."

"But I don't deserve you," he mumbles, dropping his head again. I reach out, grabbing his chin between my thumb and index finger.

"You deserve everything good in this world. You deserve *me*, and anyone who tells you differently answers to me." More tears fall from his eyes as he looks up at me. "Now, touch me, Adrian. Touch me until you're sick of it."

There is so much hope in my chest. He's coming back to me. We're so close. I'm touching him again. After weeks of taking so many steps away from each other, we're moving toward one another again.

"I'll never be sick of you, *mon paradis*." His hands finally—*finally*—move to my hips again, and I drop to my knees to fling my arms around him. "I love you so much. I'm so sorry," he says, repeating the same thing over and over at least a hundred times. "Forgive me, *mon ange*. Forgive me for being the biggest idiot on the planet."

"I forgive you, but I want you to tell me what changed in the last twenty minutes. Tell me why you went from stepping away from my touch to going to my room to apologize," I say, so Adrian leans back and cups my face, making sure I pay close attention to his next words.

"Because I couldn't do it anymore. I thought I was being selfless, but I've been repeatedly told I'm just being stupid. Because I love you more than life itself and being away from you is like inhaling shards of glass with every breath. Because you're my life, and I want to marry you."

I kiss him. Right as he finishes talking, I press my mouth to his without thinking. Adrian practically whimpers at the contact before kissing me back even harder. The sound sends both of us into a frenzy. He slips his tongue into my mouth as I palm his hardening cock through his dress pants. His hands find my ass, guiding me onto his lap to grind my aching pussy against his erection.

"I've missed you so much, Adrian," I say between moans while he nips at the soft spot on my neck.

"I've been dying without you, Nevaeh." He runs his tongue over my neck and then pushes me backward until my back is flat against the floor and he can move between my legs. "I've also been dying to rip this tease of a dress off you since you put it on," he says, tugging at the hem of my very short orange dress.

Valentina helped me choose it weeks ago. I was between a velvet one that was much longer and this sparkly, short one that barely covers my ass and tits.

"Tell me you're wearing panties," Adrian adds, but when he looks down and sees my bare pussy, he sucks in a sharp breath. "You're my naughty girl, aren't you?" he asks with a little smirk, and I'm so happy to see it, I smile brightly at him.

"Well, I was hoping you'd drag me into the nearest dark corner, lift my dress, and fuck me at the party tonight." Adrian's eyes turn molten with desire.

"Is that right?"

"Yes," I admit, my chest rising and falling so quickly with shallow breaths, Adrian places a hand on my sternum to steady me. "I knew you'd like this dress too much not to touch it."

"You do know me better than anyone else." His grin makes my heart flutter. It fades a moment later, his hand still on me. "You're my home," he says, his emotions flitting through his eyes, too many to focus on one.

"And you're mine. Now, please, fuck me. Slip inside me and make us feel whole again."

Adrian doesn't need more encouragement. He lowers his pants just enough to take his cock out, then spreads my legs even wider before sinking deep inside of me. We both gasp as soon as he's seated all the way, Adrian's arms shaking as he tries to hold himself up. I fling my arms around his neck, my hands moving onto his nape and the back of his head to guide his mouth back onto mine.

"God, you're fucking perfect, Nevaeh." He drives into me so hard, I see stars. "The way I was made for you will never get boring." I'd agree if only I could do anything other than scream his name. "That's it, beautiful, you take my cock so well."

It's messy and fast and both of us tumble over the edge into the most blissful of orgasms before we want to, but it's perfect. We're both breathless as he pumps me full of his cum, our bodies shaking in perfect harmony. He keeps slipping in and out long after both our highs have faded, but I love that he needs more time just being like this with me.

"I fucking love make up sex," he says, and I can't help but burst into laughter.

"Me, too." His mouth glides over mine again, tasting me and making him groan.

"I'm so sorry," he repeats, nuzzling his face into the crook of my neck again.

"Stop apologizing, Adrian, or I'll be the one to spank you." This makes him chuckle.

"Yes, ma'am."

"Good boy," I praise, and he practically shivers in my arms.

"I'm never letting you go again."

CHAPTER 63
Nevaeh

THE BACHELOR/BACHELORETTE PARTY—COMBINED AS per Valentina and Gabriel's request—is so much fun. We're all dancing and drinking, except Adrian who merely stays behind me and grinds against me while we're on the dance floor. It's perfect. I'm so happy to be back in his arms, I let my guard down.

It's always when I let my guard down that the worst things happen.

My phone dings with a message.

I'm drunk and therefore hallucinating. It's the only explanation I'm willing to accept because this cannot be. The message I just received... it can't be reality. I refuse to believe this is truly happening. It can't. Please, this cannot be true. Out of all the things she could have done, this is by far the worst.

Unknown: Meet me at the house in fifteen minutes. If you say anything to anyone, you will never see Damian again. Understood?

She also sent me a photo. That sick woman sent me a photo of little Damian playing with his toys, and I feel sick to my stomach.

Unknown: I promise he will be just fine. Damian isn't the one I want to punish for my son's mistakes. You are. Come to the house alone, and I will ensure nothing happens to this sweet little boy.

She's lost her mind. But I have no choice but to do what she says, do I? If I try anything, it will be Damian who gets hurt, and I will only let that happen over my dead body.

Fear strikes me in waves. This type of shit isn't supposed to happen. People like Cecilia shouldn't be real. They should be the villains in detective shows or some bullshit, but not in our lives.

I have no idea what to do except follow Cecilia's instructions. I have to cling to the hope that hurting a child is too far for her. I have to hope she will let him go when I get there, but, first, I need to find a way to slip out of the club without anyone noticing. Especially those two bodyguards at the entrance.

I look around for Adrian, but Cameron, Leonard, and James whisked him away a few minutes ago, wanting to show him something "fucking awesome," as Cameron put it.

"Nevaeh, come look at this!" Val squeals as she uncovers a baby photo of Gabriel and Jean. I see her fiancé's face drop at the mention of his brother's name, the brother who couldn't make it to his bachelor party because he has a seminar to attend at his university.

"Very cute," I say after I've looked at the picture. "I'm just going to head to the bathroom, I'll be right back." It's a good, believable lie that no one questions. However, Adam, my personal bodyguard as Adrian has informed me, stays right behind me on my way there. "You don't have to follow me to the bathroom," I say, but he frowns down at me.

"Miss, I'm specifically hired to oversee your protection," he replies, and I feel my heart sink into my stomach. I look back over to my family, where two other bodyguards are. Then, I bring my eyes back to Adam.

"Okay. I'll stay right here but could you maybe get my purse? I'm pretty sure I just got my period and there are some tampons in there," I lie, crossing my legs a bit to make it more believable.

Without questioning it, Adam walks back toward the VIP area, and I shake my head. Period reasons really are the best in situations when you don't want any questions asked, especially from men.

I make a run for it. I run toward the exit, but two bodies move in front of me, blocking my way. I look up at the bodyguards, my heart racing at an abnormal speed. I have to get out of here. With every minute Cecilia spends alone with Damian, he is in more danger of her doing something unthinkable.

"Valentina collapsed on the dance floor, please go help her. Adrian told me to come get you." I should get an award for how well I'm lying, even if the lies are terrible, horrible things I shouldn't even put out in the universe.

"Miss, you have to come with us," one of the bodyguards says, and I nod, pointing in the direction.

Not thinking I would ever leave, they run forward, assuming I will be right behind them. It's almost too perfect, but, then again, this was never supposed to be the hard part.

Facing Cecilia will be. Managing to get Damian to safety will be. Fighting for my life will be.

I rush toward the taxi line, opening one of the doors to a car and telling the driver the address to the house. He gives me a simple nod, obviously not in the talking mood.

I can't linger on my panic. I can't even begin to think about how Adrian will feel when he realizes I'm gone.

My only priority is getting to Damian.

My head spins a bit from the remnants of the alcohol in my system, but the messages Cecilia sent have mostly sobered me up. I no longer find things, the most ridiculous things, funny, and my buzz has drifted into the night sky. Fear is the antidote to being tipsy. Well, fear and panic. They have pushed all other feelings out of my body. I'm terrified, more so than I've ever been. I know what Cecilia is capable of. She tried to kill me because she wants me out of the way. She will attempt it again, I have no doubt.

Another text message lights up my screen.

Unknown: Tick tock, dear. Tick tock. You have seven minutes left to get here.

She's sick and twisted, and I have no idea how to breathe anymore when she sends me a picture of her holding Damian. Cecilia is smiling in the fucking picture, too. Smiling like she isn't threatening a child's life.

What the fuck is wrong with her?

"Excuse me, how much longer is the drive?" I ask because I can't, for the love of God, remember how long it took to get to the club. Adrian kept me too distracted by kissing me all over.

"About six minutes," the driver replies, his accent thicker than anyone I've ever met in my whole life.

"Thanks," I say breathlessly, unable to calm the fear spreading into every cell of my body. It's in my bloodstream now, but so is adrenaline.

I have to save Damian.

Whatever it takes, I will get him back to his family safely.

Now I only need to figure out how to outsmart someone with a criminal masterplan.

CHAPTER 64

Adrian

"WHAT THE FUCK DO you mean she's gone?" I ask, panic slicing through me, threatening to bring me to my knees.

"She distracted us and left," Armando says, and I'm close to strangling him. I'm beyond furious. I'm enraged.

"I hired you to do one simple task: *do not let her out of your sight*! How difficult was it to understand that?" There are a million insults flying through my head at the moment, but yelling at him will not solve the most important problem. Where the fuck is Nevaeh?

I feel sick to my stomach. This, her vanishing into thin air, is my biggest fear. All of the horrible thoughts and scenarios of what may have happened flood my mind, but I cannot stop them. They overwhelm me, pushing me closer to a panic attack I know I won't come out of unless I see her in front of me without a scratch on her.

"*Find her!*" I yell when the bodyguards simply stand in front of me, not doing a single thing to make sure she is safe.

I could be overreacting. But why wouldn't she have told anyone? Why would she have just left? Nevaeh can't be that drunk to not realize how terrifying it is for her to simply disappear after everything that happened with Cecilia.

The bodyguards I apparently overpaid scatter around the club, and I cover my stomach with my hand, trying to keep the nausea down. Then it hits me. Breathlessness. It overwhelms me until I'm heaving to try and bring oxygen to my lungs. I collapse forward on the floor while Valentina's hands slip onto my back, running her fingers along my spine to calm me. Under different circumstances, it might have worked, but right now, I'm too terrified to do anything but succumb to this weakness inside of me.

"Come on, Adrian, we will find her, I promise, but you have to stay strong for us to do that," Gabriel says, and I realize he's right in front of me. Val is trying to call someone, I'm assuming Nevaeh, but I haven't figured out how to slow my spiraling mind yet.

"Okay, okay," I repeat over and over, trying my absolute best to snap out of the attack.

"You can do this. Breathe. Fixate on finding Nevaeh," he says, and embarrassment settles in my cheeks when I realize I've almost fallen into a panic attack in front of everyone.

"I'm fine," I assure them and stand up, the feeling of shame overpowering fear.

"She's not answering her phone," Val says to James, but I hear her anyway.

"Maybe she went back to the house? How long has she been gone?" My best friend is staying surprisingly calm and rational despite his drunken state.

"I saw her last twenty minutes ago, but I don't know how she could have called a taxi while she's so tipsy. Even if, she would have told me. This all seems very wrong."

I couldn't agree more with my sister. This seems like a trap. But what the hell could possibly motivate Nevaeh to step into it? Everyone's here. She was safe around her bodyguards. There is no reason, no motivation that should be strong enough to allow her to be so reckless. I don't understand.

Everyone is here...

Oh my God.

Oh my god!

No, no, no fucking way. She's psychotic, but this is a whole new level.

"Gabriel, call the babysitter," I say in Italian because I don't want to frighten James unless I have to. I could be very wrong, fuck, I hope I'm wrong.

His eyes go wide in response, and he fumbles around in his pocket so quickly, it almost makes me dizzy. Then, I watch him hold his phone to his ear, and wait and wait and wait. The color drains from my face with every second the babysitter doesn't respond. Sweat starts collecting on the back of my neck, and fear shuts down my nervous system.

Gabriel lowers the phone, drops it to the ground.

"He didn't respond," he says to me in Italian, the same fear washing through his eyes.

"Cecilia has Damian," I blurt out in English, and my best friend turns to me.

"What the fuck do you mean Cecilia has my son?"

CHAPTER 65

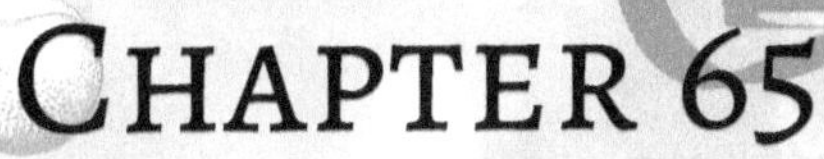

Nevaeh

I SPRINT OUT OF the taxi, running up the staircase. I rip the door open, and there she is, standing in the middle of the living room with a crying Damian in her arms. My body feels paralyzed for the briefest moment, but the instinct to protect the little child pressed against her side is stronger than anything I've ever felt. It pushes me forward until I'm standing in front of her, legs weak and hands shaking.

Her eyes catch mine before a content smile covers her face. A shiver, the worst type I've ever felt, trickles down my spine. She's enjoying this. She's enjoying every moment of me doing exactly what she wants. She's twisted and sadistic and I have no more words. I have nothing I want to say to her at this moment. I just want Damian to be out of this house, which I now realize smells stranger than it did the first time I stepped foot in it.

It smells like gas and... like something's on fire. The scent of burning wood and fabric fills the small living room, and I freeze in place as I watch her smile at my realization.

She's set the house on fire.

Upstairs.

I watch the smoke snake down the stairs. She must have disabled the smoke detectors because there is no alarm going off, nothing warning the neighbors and the people inside of the house that there is a fire.

"Please, take Damian outside. Please. He shouldn't inhale the smoke," I plead, but she bounces him up and down on her hip, smiling at me.

"Not yet, dear. First, I need you to do something for me." Cecilia puts Damian on the couch, and he starts screaming at the top of his lungs for the same reason my eyes are starting to tear up.

The smoke is starting to burn our senses.

"First take him out of here, and then—" She cuts me off, screaming at me.

"NO. You will do exactly as I say or I'm going to have to stop playing nice." She takes out a knife from her back pocket, holds it up at me. "Now, take these, put one side around your wrist and the other around the railing of the staircase." Cecilia throws a pair of metal handcuffs at me, but I don't manage to catch them. They drop to the floor, angering her. "Pick them up. You have ten seconds to do as I said or I am going to use this knife," she threatens, and I hurry over to the staircase, fastening the handcuff around my wrist.

Tears stream from my eyes as the burning gets worse. I cough and cough, my lungs begging me to go outside and get cleaner oxygen, but I can't do any of it. Even as the smell of the house slowly burning down intensifies. My senses are on high alert, the adrenaline coursing through my veins bringing pain to my limbs. Sitting down while it tells me to run and fight brings agony to my muscles.

"Why? Why are you going through all this trouble to punish your son?" I ask because it's obvious that it's exactly what she's trying to do. Cecilia runs the blade over my cheek, the cool metal so sharp against my soft skin, I freeze to ensure it doesn't cut me by accident.

"Would you like to know the real reason I returned?" she asks while tears fall from my eyes from the smoke. She wipes one of them away with the tip of the blade, but she pushes so hard, my skin splits open.

I grind my teeth together as I groan through the pain.

"To be honest, if I'm going to die, I'd rather the fire takes me out instead of your boring story." She slaps me across the face.

"Careful, dear. You still want me to carry Damian to safety, don't you?" The knife glides toward my throat, and I tilt my head in response, trying to get away. I'm unsuccessful as she pushes the weapon against me.

"Please, the fire is spreading. He needs to get out of here. The fire will be down here soon and—"

I'm cut off by the sound of something exploding in the kitchen right behind me. The fire is already down here, grabbing onto the edges of the house. The stairs above me catch fire, the flames dropping down and making me move to the other side of the railing. Heat fills the room, and I'm sweating instantly.

"Please, please get Damian out of here."

The toddler is screaming at the top of his lungs. The fire hasn't spread to where he is on the couch yet, but it's on the curtains around him, getting too close to him. Panic causes more tears to fall from my eyes, but luckily, Cecilia steps away, taking away the weight of fear on my chest from the knife.

"I came back because when I left the first time, I stole millions from my husband. Millions. But they can only last so long, you know. So, I had to find someone else, a new source who would be able to provide me with a comfortable life. That is where my children come into play," she says while I pull on the handcuffs, trying to get free. "Stop that!" she barks at me, but I don't.

"Only when you take Damian outside," I yell back, tugging and ripping to get free.

I watch orange, yellow, and red flames diffuse and tear down everything in their wake. The house is creaking and squeaking as it dies, and I keep pulling. But there is no use. Absolutely none. Not unless the fire burns away the wood I placed the other half of the handcuff around, and that would ultimately result in me getting my hand burned off.

"Actually, I would like to finish my story," she says, and I snarl at her, the handcuffs, and the fire. Someone has to see what's happening, won't they? One of the neighbors will call the police and firemen, and we will be saved, right?

"Please." I'm begging again because fighting my restraints isn't working. "You can tell me after you take Damian to safety," I say, but she's ignoring me, desperate to finish her story.

She sits down on the edge of the couch, stroking Damian's hair to soothe him. He clings to her arm, not realizing she's the one who's endangering his life.

"My children have so much money, and I was hoping if I got close to them, they would support me. The only reason I became COO was to get close to them, not because I enjoy working. I never thought they would greet me with so much hostility, but that was your fault, wasn't it? You filled their heads with lies because you knew if I came back into their lives, into Adrian's, you'd have to share my son's money with me, didn't you?"

I can't help myself. I burst into laughter at her accusation.

"You think I was with Adrian because of his money? Do you have any fucking idea how reserved I was to be with him because of it, because of our jobs? I am *not* you, Cecilia, and I never will be. Do not compare your motives to mine. You want money, I want love. That's it."

My eyes stay on her, watching darkness take over her features. I've angered her, but before I can linger on that fact, I feel a burning sensation on my back. I jolt upright, trying to get away from the flames assaulting my body, but there is nowhere to run. The fire is almost everywhere now. The living room is the only area not consumed yet, but where I am, there is only a little patch where I am on the marble floor that hasn't caught fire yet. It won't stay like this for long, I know it, but there is nowhere to run. I'm going to die here, swallowed by fire.

"Well, it's too bad love can't save you from this," she says, striding back over to where I am with her knife. "In fact, I think I will stay here with you. Death seems a whole lot better than jail, don't you think?" she asks, cocking the knife as a way of getting ready to kill me with it.

I keep struggling against the handcuffs, not willing to die like this, not when my career has only started. Not with my whole life still ahead of me. Not when Adrian just admitted he still wants to marry me. And most certainly not while Damian isn't safe yet.

"Wait, hold on now, if you kill me, you won't get the satisfaction of watching me slowly burn to death. Think this through. You won't get to hear my screams," I suggest, playing on how fucked up she is as a way to keep me alive.

I need to find a way to get Damian out of here.

"Yeah, but I kind of want to be the one to rip the life from you." She raises the knife again, and I can tell this is it. This is how I die, by her hand, again. "Goodbye, Nevaeh. It was not a pleasure knowing you," she says, and I close my eyes, unwilling to see anything but Adrian's face in my mind as the last image.

I love you, Adrian.

CHAPTER 66

Adrian

I'M SPEEDING DOWN THE empty road. Cecilia has Nevaeh and Damian, and I'm dying. I haven't taken a proper breath in minutes, but I couldn't care less about the burning in my lungs at the moment.

"We will get to them in time, I'm sure of it," Val says, trying to reassure the both of us. It doesn't work, not for either of us.

I floor it. I don't care if the police try to pull me over. If anything, getting their attention is good. I want them to get to the house, if the other police cars aren't there yet. Fuck, what if they aren't there yet? What if it will be too late? Who knows what Cecilia could have done to them already. Fuck, fuck, fuck. Please, please don't let them be dead. Please. I won't survive it if anything happens to either of them, none of us will.

"Adrian, I think it's best if we swap seats. You're going way too fast, it's dangerous," Val says, but I'm not listening to her. I do slow down, but only ever so slightly.

"I can't lose her, and we can't lose Damian," I whisper into the car, my eyes drifting to the inside mirror to see Gabriel, James, Domi, and Nicolette right behind us in their car. Gabriel doesn't seem to give a shit about speed limits anymore either, and I want to hug him for it.

"We won't lose them, but if you crash before we get there, we can't save them either," my sister says, and I suck in a sharp breath.

She is right, but I'm a skilled driver.

Hell, I do it for a fucking living.

"How can you be sure it isn't already too late, huh?" I challenge, going faster again.

"Because Grandma, Grandpa, and Dad won't let that happen. They're protecting them, I know they are."

Her optimism is almost heartwarming, and I know it's also exactly what Gabriel is thinking right now, but I'm neither of them. I don't believe in those sorts of things. I can't let myself, not while everything is on the line.

I press down even harder on the gas pedal.

Almost there, Nevaeh and Damian, just hold on.

CHAPTER 67

Nevaeh

Someone knocks Cecilia to the ground.

It happens so fast, I don't have time to catch up when the knife clatters to the floor. I jump toward it, unsure what I would even do once I have it, but getting it away from Cecilia is extremely appealing. I reach for it, crying out because my arm isn't long enough. Only a few centimeters. I'm only missing a few centimeters.

The knife is kicked toward me, and I look up, trying to see who the hell is in this burning house, fighting for Damian's and my safety.

Then I see him.

Adam.

The man hired to protect me.

"Nevaeh!" he calls out, and I refocus on what's important.

I try to cut through the wood to get free, but it's thick and would take me hours to slice open with this simple kitchen blade. It's useless. I look around, searching for anything that has caught on fire, anything I can use to light up this wooden railing to weaken its structure. More coughs escape me, the smoke filling my lungs too quickly now. My eyes shift to Damian, who is crying and screaming for help.

"I'm coming, Damian!"

I scream, kicking at the wood, over and over, ignoring the heat on my skin and stinging pain on my wrist as the handcuff cuts me open. I keep kicking, barely watching Cecilia and Adam fight each other. I don't pay too much attention until I see her holding his gun, aiming it at him, and then, a gunshot. It's deafening. It makes me stop my movements to see Adam falling to his knees, blood seeping from the wound right above his hip. He growls, kicking away her legs and making the gun drop to the floor. I can't linger on what they're doing. I just continue kicking, continue fighting to get free.

And then.

The wood splinters.

Breaks.

I keep going until I finally manage to split it in half, guiding the handcuffs through the opening. My feet attempt to bring me to Damian, but Cecilia grabs my ankle, tearing me to the floor. I fall right in front of the flames but manage to wiggle away before they can burn me. My mind is set on survival mode, and it almost feels like everything is running on autopilot because of it. I don't have time to wonder about what happens if I don't make it to Damian in time, if I die first before I have the chance to save him. I just get back on my feet, jumping over the flames covering the floor.

"It's okay, I've got you," I say once he's safely wrapped in my arms. The toddler coughs and cries. "I know, buddy, I know," I coo, trying to figure out a way to get out of here. Everything's on fire, ceiling pieces dropping to the floor.

Another gunshot fills the room, and I freeze for a fraction of a second. Then, I quickly scan Damian for an injury, but there are none. Thank God. He's fine. He's completely fine.

"Nevaeh!" Adam screams, and I realize there is a burning sensation spreading down my arm. Not fire burning, but pain burning. Open wound, blood flowing down kind of burning. I stare down at my left arm, watching the red color drip to the floor.

My eyes shift to Adam then to Cecilia, and I realize she's pointing the gun at me. She shot me. She shot me, but the bullet only seems to have grazed me, and it's driving her mad, I can hear it by the way she screams into the burning room. Adam, bleeding himself, throws his body at her, but then I hear it.

One more gunshot.

I cover Damian's body with my own, but the bullet didn't hit me this time. I spin around, watching Cecilia's eyes go wide with shock. Adam is pointing the gun at her chest, but it's already done. He shot her. She's dropping to the floor, death consuming her until her eyes flutter shut and she simply lies there, not moving a centimeter.

"We have to go," Adam calls out, more blood seeping through the bullet wound on his hip. I jump over the flames again to get to him, and he takes Damian from my arms because of the awkward way I'm holding him with the cuff still on my wrist, bolting for the door. I'm right behind him, but something grabs hold of my ankle again.

She isn't dead yet.

She isn't dead and she's pulling on my legs until I fall face-first onto the burning ground, something she did only minutes earlier. My head hits the floor, and this time, everything goes blurry. My ears vibrate.

And then, darkness consumes me.

Everything vanishes.

CHAPTER 68

Adrian

THE HOUSE IS ON fire. Windows explode. Glass shatters everywhere. The structure ripples apart, one brick at a time. Flames are everywhere. They've infiltrated every area of the house, the fire acting as a diffuser of the smoke, and I'm running toward it faster than I've ever gone before. Nevaeh can't be in there. It's not possible. Cecilia must have taken her somewhere else along with Damian. They can't all be in there. I refuse to believe it.

But then I see Adam running out the front door with a screaming Damian in his arms. From what I can see, he's unharmed, unlike the person who is carrying him. Blood is dripping down Adam's thigh and his shirt clings to the wound just below his waist.

I feel sick to my stomach.

Sirens sound in the distance, but I couldn't care less right now. I'm running toward Adam, grabbing Damian from his arms a second before he kneels on the ground, holding his hand over his wound. Val appears next to me, and I hand her the screaming toddler to bend down next to Adam.

"Where is she?" I ask, and his eyes go wide in shock. He spins around abruptly, cursing under his breath at the fast movement that probably brought him a lot of pain.

"She was right behind me, I swear. She must have gotten stuck inside," he says, and every organ inside of my body shuts down.

I don't think. I pay no attention to the pain seeping through my entire body, grabbing hold of every cell. I simply run. Into the burning house. Without a second of hesitation. Nevaeh isn't going to die like this, not here. The only place I will allow her to die is safely in my arms while I pass away too so we can always be together. So we can be ghosts for the rest of eternity, pulling funny haunting pranks on our children and their children. So I can love her until the end of time and then after that, too.

My feet bring me to the front door, and I kick it open. Part of the ceiling, burning and surrounded by flames, is blocking the way to where I see her lying. Two bodies. One is Cecilia, the other is...

God, I can't even think it.

"Nevaeh!" I scream, but she doesn't respond, she doesn't even flinch.

Adrenaline pushes into my chest so violently, it knocks the breath from my lungs for a moment, not long enough to keep me from pushing the wooden piece out of the way with my foot. I feel my torso burning from the inhalation of the smoke, but I push past the feeling to get to her.

I have to save her.

"Come on!" I cry because another piece of the ceiling stands in the way between me and my everything. I kick it, it doesn't budge. I kick it again, nothing. "Nevaeh. Please, *mon paradis*. Wake up. You have to meet me halfway," I call to her, but she doesn't wake up.

Fuck. I don't know how I'm going to get to her. Not alone. I'm not strong enough.

"What are you just standing around for, you bloody wanker?" James says, and I watch Gabriel, Leonard, and Cameron join him inside.

They start kicking at the wood, and I don't have time to tell them all how stupid they are for running into a burning house. I know they'd do it again and again if it meant saving someone they care about, just like I would do it for them every single time. That's what family does, and I'm the luckiest man in the world to have one like no other.

We manage to knock the wood out of the way, and all five of us sprint to where Nevaeh and Cecilia are on the floor. I pull the love of my life into my arms while

Leonard and Cameron pick up my mother. Neither of them is moving or showing any signs of life. Neither of them seems to breathe. All the color drains from my face. Sweat is running in waves down my back from both the heat of the fire and the nervousness settling in my chest.

Every single one of us makes it out of the house right before something explodes inside. I don't turn around to check what's happening. I don't give a single shit about anything other than feeling Nevaeh's pulse right now because she has to have one.

She just has to.

I lie her down on the grass, far enough from the fire that the firemen are now rushing to put out. Police are everywhere, but no paramedics yet. Fuck. Why are they not the first ones here? They have to help her. They have to make her stop bleeding. No, no, no, why is she bleeding? I lift my bloody hand, watching it as it starts to shake.

"Please, *mon ange*, please stay with me. Please, please, please. I'm begging you. Don't leave me. Don't, you can't."

She doesn't move. I press my hands to her throat, trying to find a pulse, but I can't feel it. Oh God, I can't feel her pulse. Please tell me I'm just too stupid to press down properly.

"Nevaeh, wake up. Please. You're not stubborn, don't start that shit with me now. I'm the stubborn one out of the two of us," I croak out, tears falling from my cheeks and onto hers. I grab her face, tilting it to me. "Please. Please, Nevaeh. I want to come home. I don't want to be in hell anymore. I just want to come home," I beg, but she doesn't respond. "HELP! Please, anyone!" I scream, and Val rushes toward me, dropping down beside my lifeless Nevaeh. "I can't feel her pulse," I cry, and my sister's fingers slip onto the side of my life's neck. She readjusts her fingers several times before she drops her head.

"She has a pulse," Val says, and I drop backward, letting the sobs of relief fall from my lips. Val takes my hand, guides it to Nevaeh's throat and then I feel it. Strong, healthy almost. "She will be okay. She probably just got knocked out," my sister assures me while I keep crying.

"Thank you," I mumble, and she jumps to her feet to talk to one of the police officers. I stare down at Nevaeh's face, still sobbing violently. "You can't do this to me, Nevaeh Romana. Never again," I cry, dropping my head onto her chest. I press my ear to her breast, listening to the steady beat of her heart.

"Nevaeh Fuchs-Romana," she says, her voice weak. I jolt backward, watching her eyes flutter open, barely. "I want to keep my name," she croaks out, but I'm not listening to her anymore.

I'm pressing my lips to hers, my tears salty between us.

"I'm sorry," I say once I lean back, but she pulls my head down again, capturing my lips with hers.

"Don't ever let me go," she says, wrapping her arms around my neck. I slide mine around her, pressing her body against my chest.

"Never again, *mon paradis.*"

Nevaeh is fine.

The hospital released her a few hours ago after they stitched her up and checked her head for any internal bleeding, which there was luckily none. They assured us that with a little bit of rest, she should heal alright. Damian is, although still crying, unharmed. Out of everyone, he got the least of it all, nothing except the fright of his life. I'm sure he'll never remember this, but it doesn't make it any less horrifying. Domi and Nicolette have asked James to stay with them for tonight, and he agreed straight away. He doesn't want to be apart from his son any more than Damian wants to be away from his father.

Adam was also taken to the hospital and Armando and the other bodyguards went with him to make sure he's okay. Now that the reason why I hired them is… dead, I no longer need them.

Cecilia is dead.

And I have no idea how I'm supposed to feel. Part of me is so relieved she's gone for good, that she can never harm Nevaeh or any of us ever again. Another part of me doesn't think she deserved to die like this, even if it was her own fault. My mind is having a strange battle between feeling bad for her, grieving the mother I wish I could have had, and being glad she's gone.

It makes my head spin for a moment.

"*Mein Mond?*" Her voice. Oh God, it feels so good to hear her address me like this, to know we're going to be just fine.

"Yes, *mon ange?*" I say and look at the small cut on her cheek. Anger briefly courses through me, but when she smiles that smile I love more than anything, I lose track of the rest of the world.

"I'm hungry. Actually, I'm starving," she says with a little chuckle and there it is. I feel my heart beating again. Being this close to her, I feel it as it races uncontrollably from her presence.

"We will get some food," I promise her, running the backs of my fingers over the length of her other cheek. Her eyes close in response. "I love you endlessly, Nevaeh. I will forever love you endlessly. In every universe. I hope you know that. I hope you can feel it." Nevaeh's face turns serious.

"I felt it even when we were apart. Because I took this with me," she says and points at her chest. "I wasn't planning on ever giving it back," she informs me with a smile.

"Good because it isn't mine."

My fingers slip to each side of her face, cupping it in my hands.

"It hasn't been since the day I laid my eyes on you."

I lean down, allowing our mouths to melt together.

Home.

I'm finally home.

CHAPTER 69

Adrian

WE ALL AGREED THAT after what happened three days ago, we would not cancel Gabriel and Val's wedding. We postponed it to today, desperate to have some positivity after all the shit that went down. The last race weekend of the season starts in four days, but, for the first time in my life, I'm not looking forward to getting back into the car. I want to do what Nevaeh and I have been doing—staying in bed, making love, cuddling, being naked with each other—for a while longer. I knew how much I missed her, missed being with her in a way I've never been with anyone else, but my brain couldn't fathom how much that was until I was completely lost in her again.

I trace my lips for a moment, the feel of hers against them so burned into my mind, it's almost as if I'm constantly kissing her, kissing the memory of her. The need to go check on her in the bathroom, watch her while she gets ready for the wedding, overwhelms me until my feet carry me there.

I knock on the door, waiting for her soft voice to assure me I can come in, which she does. I open the door to find her standing in front of the mirror, applying some blush with a ridiculously large brush. Her body is only covered in a pair of panties and a matching bra, making it wildly impossible for my body not to react instantly.

I lean against the door frame, crossing my arms in front of my chest as I watch her be so perfect without having to try. She just is. In everything she does, I find perfection, and I will never stop seeing it. How could I? Nevaeh shows me every single day that she doesn't possess flaws, at least not in my eyes. I don't deserve her, hell, I probably never will, but it is my mission to give her everything she desires in this lifetime. It is my mission to have her love me so much, she will choose me again in the next lifetime. And the one after that.

For a moment, I allow myself to study the cut on her cheek, the bandage around the wound on her left arm. I tried everything to keep her safe, pushed her away from me to make sure this wouldn't happen, but it was useless. All of it was useless. Cecilia still went after her. She almost died. It was all for nothing. Nevaeh wasn't safe, and I caused both of us so much pain.

But we talked properly. We spoke for hours and hours at dinner, about everything both of us needed to get off our chests. And we realized one thing. We don't work well without each other. We can function without each other, but we need each other to live, that's what those weeks have taught us. No one else will ever fulfill us the way we do. It was almost impossible to focus on anything apart from how lost we were when we were apart.

I refocus on my beautiful girlfriend, hopefully soon-to-be wife, watching her glide the brush over her cheeks. I rest my head against the door frame too, managing to bring a smile to my face.

"Are you enjoying yourself, *mein Mond*?" she teases and turns her body in my direction.

I can't help myself. My eyes drop to her breasts, studying the way the thin fabric of her bra barely covers them. Her nipples are hard as they push against the thing standing between them and their freedom, and it makes my bottom lip slip between my teeth. She's so damn sexy, if we didn't have to go to my sister's wedding, I would ask her to stay with me in this room in Leonard and Chiara's villa on their island for the rest of the day, preferably without her wearing any clothes.

"Always when I'm looking at you," I reply. Nevaeh takes three steps toward me, placing her hands on my chest.

"I love it when you wear black. It suits you well," she says, running her fingers over my black shirt with a smile. I already knew she felt this way, I could see it in her eyes whenever I put on an all-black suit. "Then again, everything suits you," she adds, and I'm a goner again.

I have been since I first met her, since she first teased me, and I saw she was everything I've never thought to look for. I didn't think she'd exist, but I like the thought of being made for someone the way I am for Nevaeh.

"Everything suits *you*," I say, and a blush settles on her cheeks, heating up her face until it's a warm shade of red.

"You flatter me, Mr. Romana," she says, so my fingers wrap around her neck, tilting her head back.

"You complete me, Mrs. Romana." A brighter red replaces the subtler one on her cheeks. I brush my thumbs over them, enjoying the way her soft skin feels against mine.

"It's still Ms. Fuchs to you," she teases, but I shake my head.

"It hasn't been, not for a very long time."

I'm used to it now. The words falling from my lips so effortlessly makes me realize I'm used to it. As a matter of fact, I love it. I considered it garbage, all the romance and cheesy stuff, but this makes me happy. Seeing her eyes light up because I say these words and mean every single one of them makes me happy.

"Let me get dressed. We don't want to be late for the wedding," she whispers as I lean down, my mouth getting closer to hers.

"I would offer to help you, but I prefer taking clothes off you, not putting them on," I say, watching her breathing hitch from my words.

"Well, I do need help with the zipper in the back, so you don't have a choice," she replies with a naughty grin. I can almost feel my knees turn to putty as she runs her hands up the length of my torso just to drop them to the waistband of my pants. "But I promise, you will get to take it off again after," she adds, and I don't waste another second.

I place my lips on hers, letting my teeth tug on her bottom one for a moment. Her fingers dig into my biceps, a whimper slipping past her lips. My hands move to her ass before I lift her onto the sink. I move between her legs, my kiss growing hungrier by the second. She tastes so good, so much like home. I bring my mouth to her cheek, jaw, and then neck, sucking on her sensitive skin there until I hear the familiar moan fall from her lips.

"You have to let me get ready," Nevaeh says. I can't help but groan against her neck.

"Fine," I grumble, stepping back reluctantly with a pout.

"So dramatic," she says with a laugh that makes my body tingle. "I love you," she adds, placing one last kiss on my lips before getting up and rushing into the bedroom.

"*Je t'appartiens*," I whisper even though she can't hear me anymore.

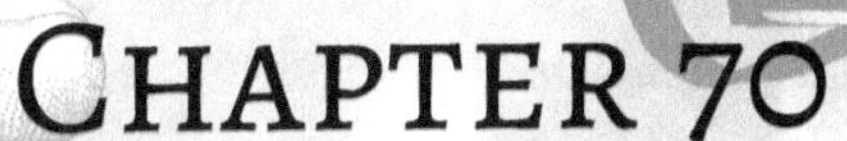

CHAPTER 70
Nevaeh

THE CEREMONY WAS BEAUTIFUL. Val and Gabriel decided to have their wedding on the beach on Chiara and Leonard's island with Chase sitting right beside them at the altar.

Leonard married them and now we're all sitting at the tables Adrian and I arranged to have at the beach, eating the food Evangelin volunteered to make. It's the simplest wedding I've ever had the honor of attending, but it's definitely my favorite.

They look so happy. Gabriel keeps kissing Val when she least expects it, and it makes her smile every time. I watch them every so often, wondering how Adrian will react when I walk down the aisle. I wonder if he will have the same look in his eyes that Gabriel had. I wonder if he will stand there, emotion weighing so heavy on him, he has to let out a deep breath to collect himself like Gabriel did. I wonder too if I will be like Val, walking gracefully down the aisle, smiling at her husband as if nothing else mattered in the world.

Of course I will because, in that moment, nothing else will matter. The only thing I will have eyes for will be his green-blue-brown ones and the way he smirks at me. The way I know nothing will change except the fact that I get to call him my husband and he will call me his wife. We will be tied to each other in yet another way, and as much as the thought has scared me in the past, now it settles me into a comfortable happiness.

"What are you thinking about?" he asks, his thumb trailing over the corner of my mouth.

"You, us, our future. And I'm wondering how many more of those fried mozzarella balls Cameron will manage to inhale," I reply, catching the Australian's attention. He winks at me from across the table.

"I could eat them all, gorgeous. As a matter of fact, let's see how many I can put in my mouth at once," he says, reaching for the plate with them on it. Leonard slaps his hand away, scolding him with one look. "Fine, Jesus. You're so serious, mate," he complains, but as soon as Leonard looks away again, he reaches for the plate and starts shoving them into his mouth. I can't contain my laughter, no matter how hard I try.

"Okay, I have an announcement to make," Gabriel says, standing up to face everyone at the table. He takes Valentina's hand, staring down at her while he gets ready to tell us his news. "Next season, I will replace Kyle Hughes at Grenzenlos."

My boyfriend instantly freezes.

"Valentina, *mon tournesol*, you will be offered my seat at Velocità Rossa." This is her biggest dream besides winning a championship. It's what she's always dreamed of, to step into her father's, grandfather's, and big brother's footsteps. I'm about to start crying when she covers her mouth, tears streaming down her cheeks.

"Are you serious?" she asks, and Gabriel leans down, pressing his lips to hers.

"Everyone, please raise a toast to our future World Champion. Valentina Romana-Biancheri." All of us raise our glasses while she flings her arms around her husband. I turn to Adrian, who is staring at the table with shock and underlying happiness.

A while ago, he was struggling with whether he should give up his seat at Velocità Rossa to allow Val to take his place. I can't imagine what a relief it must be for him that even though he's keeping his seat, his sister is getting her own chance to live the dream they share.

I reach out to run my thumb over his cheek and ear, smiling at him when he turns his head in my direction, tears glistening in his eyes. I can sense he needs a moment, so I focus my attention on Leonard and Cameron, who are now arguing over who they think could win the championship the following year. I don't think there is much to argue about. Valentina, then racing in a top championship-competing car, will kick all of their asses.

"Come dance with me, *mon paradis,*" Adrian whispers into my ear, his lips brushing over the shell of it as he stands up. He smiles at the goosebumps trailing down my arms as he takes my hand and leads me closer to where the speaker is.

Dylan Scott's song 'Look At Us Now' is flowing from the speaker, and I can't help but grin at Adrian when I realize he put this song on before we went to dance. His hands slide onto my back until he's pulled me against his chest, his cheek pressed against mine. He hums the melody of the song into my ear, making me close my eyes while I enjoy the way it sounds. Adrian has a beautiful singing voice. Sometimes when he plays the piano, composing his own melody, he will sing some lyrics he made up for it. Every single time, I close my eyes, listening in awe to how beautiful it sounds.

"What are we going to do when you win the championship this year?" I ask after another song starts playing and Adrian stops singing. He steps back a little, smiling as he stares into my eyes.

"Get married," he replies, and I let out a little laugh.

"Only if you win?" I challenge, but he shakes his head immediately.

"No, but when I do, I will slip the ring I bought you months ago on your finger because winning means nothing without you in my life to celebrate with me. I want to tie myself to you in that moment, and then I will take you to Singapore to do all of this properly. To give you the proposal you deserve," he says, turning me speechless.

Adrian has a ring for me. A ring he bought months ago. He wants to slip it onto my finger after he wins the championship, something I know he is very capable of doing. This is a lot of information to process at once, but I lean my head against his shoulder, letting the tears of happiness fall from my eyes.

"You don't need to take me to Singapore. I don't need a fancy moment for it to mean everything," I assure him, and he spins me around once, bringing me back against his chest once I'm in front of him again.

"I want it to be a moment you will never forget, *mon ange.*"

"Any moment with you is one I will never forget," I reply, making him smile.

Adrian seals this moment, just like every other, with a kiss to my lips and the smile I've memorized so well, it's been burned into my memories.

My happiness, my home, my heaven.

Epilogue

Adrian

W E ' R E   I N   A B U   D H A B I for the last race of the season.

Everything is on the line.

I'm leading the championship by one point and one point only.

I have to win today, which is going to be difficult considering I only qualified third, with Lincoln in first and Gabriel in second.

This is going to be the hardest race of the season.

"Deep breath," Nevaeh says as we warm up together in my private room. We're bouncing on our heels while she helps me work through my nervosity. "You will win today. You are going to get that title. You will be champion of the world," she adds as we roll our shoulders at the same time.

"I will be champion of the world," I echo, watching her smile proudly at me.

"That's right. You're almost there."

I'm almost there.

"You going to win for me, future husband?" she asks, taking a couple of tennis balls from Daniel for our next warm-up. Testing my reaction time.

"Yes, my beautiful wife. I'll win for you." She rolls her eyes at my complete dismissal of the word future, but I merely grab her by her hips to pull her against me and capture her mouth with mine.

I'm going to win for Nevaeh.

And for everyone else I've ever loved.

After we're done warming up, Daniel ushers me toward the door, saying, "Let's go, Adrian. We have to get the car to the grid." I nod, turning to Nevaeh one last time to press my nose to hers.

"Breathe, race, win," we say together. "As long as it doesn't cost you a limb." I press my mouth back onto hers, tasting how much she loves me on her lips.

"I love you, *mon paradis.*"

"I love you endlessly, *mein Mond.*"

"In every universe."

Things move faster than ever after that. Before I know it, we're taking our formation lap. Lincoln lines up on his spot on the grid, followed by Gabriel, me, Kyle, James, Val, and the rest of them. My heart is racing, but I hear Nevaeh's voice in my head, reminding me to take deep breaths.

The title is on the line, but I'm worthy of it.

She told me I'm worthy of all the good things in the world, and, for the first time in my life, I truly believe it.

"Remember everything we discussed," Chloe says, and I let out a short laugh as we wait for the rest of the drivers to make it back to the grid.

I touch my helmet where I've made a very big change recently to the design.

The words "Let's Talk About Mental Health & Spread Awareness Instead Of Shame" are written across my helmet, big enough for people to see when the camera zooms in on it.

I've become an advocate for mental health this season, and it's something I'm very proud of.

"Yeah, yeah, no fucking up for shits and giggles. I understood you," I tease, but all it earns me is a snort and silence.

This is up to me now, no matter how big of a part Chloe plays in everything going smoothly. I'm in the car. I have to be one with it and drown out the rest of the world to the best of my ability.

The lights finally turn on, one by one, until all five bulbs glow red above us. I blow out a breath at the same moment the lights disappear, pressing down on the throttle and shifting the car into gear.

Gabriel has a slow start, but Lincoln pushes ahead, leaving me to fight my brother for second place. I slip past him two laps later and groan when I notice Lincoln disappearing from my line of sight as he takes a corner at least two seconds ahead of me.

"Tell me," I say to Chloe.

"Two point nine seconds. Get him," my race engineer says, but I'm still fighting Gabriel off, and I can't ignore him to chase Lincoln, not while he's in DRS range.

Only five laps in, I'm already sweating profusely.

"Two point six, Adrian. Keep pushing," Chloe says a lap later. "Try to do that again. Whatever you just did."

"Chloe, I'm doing the same thing every lap, what are you talking about?" She doesn't answer me right away, so I just keep driving, keep trusting myself to do what needs to be done to catch up to Lincoln.

"Your management in turn six, seven, and eight was better. Keep doing it."

I listen to my race engineer, and a few laps later, I'm in DRS range.

Now, onto the hard part: overtaking Lincoln without him running into me and ending my race.

"Keep an eye on Lincoln. I don't want him to pull any shit with me," I tell Chloe, not giving a fuck who can hear me.

"On it, Adrian," she assures me, and I take several deep breaths to slow my racing heart. I have to stay in control of my emotions for this next part to avoid any mistakes.

I'm so close to winning the championship, I can almost taste it. Lincoln is right in front of me, not even half a second ahead. This season is supposed to be mine.

I take a deep breath as we rush over the finish line. My body is running on pure adrenaline now, pushing me to go further, faster, and approach this situation more strategically than I ever have. I have to wait for the main straight. Our car is quicker on the straights, and I need to be patient, not reckless.

I'm still right behind Lincoln, in a good position to overtake him when it comes to it.

"His tires are losing grip, Adrian." If his tires are losing grip, then they're going to slow him down. Good. It gives me, considering my tires are still in good condition, an advantage.

For a second, my mind drifts to Nevaeh, who is probably taking hundreds of notes right now for the article she's writing to distract herself from how nervous she is. Hell, I'm fucking nervous.

Breathe, race, win.

All the voices of my family members, alive and gone, echo in my ears, calming my nerves. I can do this. I will be the champion of the world. I will make my father proud. I will make my grandfather proud. They can't be here for this, but this would mean everything to them, so I will give it my all.

I stay close behind Lincoln, and then, when the main straight comes into sight, I take another deep breath. I open the DRS flap, getting that extra push of speed, and race past him into first place.

Lincoln fights me, his Grenzenlos faster in the corners. He overtakes me and moves into first place again.

"Okay, plan B, Adrian," Chloe says laps later when I still haven't gotten the chance to move back into first place.

I smile at her words.

"Got it."

Plan B means undercut.

We're going to undercut the shit out of Lincoln and the Grenzenlos team.

I can practically hear everyone gasp when I drive into the pits, stopping for hard tires because they will last until the end of the race. My pitstop goes smoothly, and it seems like the fastest one we've had all season, which is a major advantage. Now we just need Lincoln's pitstop to be slower than mine, and he will rejoin the track behind me, leaving me to take first place.

Which is exactly what happens.

Three laps later, I watch him drive out of the pits as I shoot down the track and away from him.

The rest of the grid follows, and I end up in first place, just as planned.

"Keep it up. All you have to do now is bring it home."

A laugh slips out of me at her casual words.

Just bring it home, Adrian, no big deal.

Except, in the last few laps, Gabriel, Lincoln, and I are all less than a second apart. Gabriel is fighting Lincoln. Lincoln is fighting me. And I'm hanging on for dear life.

"Three laps. Hold on," Chloe says. I groan through gritted teeth.

Three laps.

I defend through the next lap, but Gabriel distracts Lincoln by trying to go down on the inside of the third corner.

I get away.

I manage to get out of Lincoln's DRS range while he defends his place, but ultimately loses it to Gabriel, who slips into second place.

Just a lap longer.

I can taste victory. Fans are cheering my name already. I'm so fucking close.

I—

I'm the champion of the world.

Fireworks go off, I'm over the line, and I managed to hold onto first place.

I did it.

I fucking did it.

"You've done it, Adrian. You're the champion," Chloe says, and I scream at the top of my lungs.

Pure joy floods my bloodstream, replacing everything inside of me until I'm running on happiness. Tears stream down my face under the helmet, but I'm rushing to get to Nevaeh and the rest of my team.

Gabriel and I take our cool down lap and drive back to the finish line where we nod at each other before turning our steering wheels all the way, spinning in circles. We do a few more donuts before Chloe tells me I have to stop.

Even Lincoln appears beside us to join our donuts, and I can't even be mad at Robert for helping Lincoln get a seat at another F1 team. He's turned his act around in the past few races and left Nevaeh alone since... well, since everything happened.

He's removed himself from our lives as best as possible, so there is no reason for him to be kicked out of the sport for good.

I drive my car to the first place sign, watching the fireworks for a moment longer before I get out of my car, ripping off my helmet and throwing it in the cockpit. I wrap my arms around Nevaeh, the rest of my team crowding around us, celebrating with us. We jump up and down together for a moment until they step back and I kiss Nevaeh more fiercely than ever before.

I reach for the ring where I hid it in my race suit and slip it onto her finger, just like I promised her I would.

"I'm going to be the wife of a Formula One World Champion," she says with a giggle, kissing me firmly once again. Tears stream down both of our faces, and I linger for a bit longer before going back to hugging her and the rest of my team.

Nevaeh doesn't realize that she already is.

She's my wife in every way but legally, and I cannot wait until we finally make it official.

For now, I'm going to get my trophy, listen to my country's anthem, and slam my champagne bottle on the podium the way I've done all season.

I'm going to celebrate my dreams coming true, each and every one of them.

I did it Dad, Grandpa, and Grandma.

I have everything you've ever wished for me.

I'm happy.

The End

Adrian and Nevaeh will return in future novels.

Spicy Bonus Epilogue

ADRIAN

I've been waiting for this day for over a year.

Nevaeh is going to be wearing a remote-controlled vibrator—the controller being an app on my phone—while we're at work. A few months ago, on the anniversary of our first kiss, Nevaeh and I got married, and I love the way I get to call her "my wife" without anyone telling me she isn't.

Like right now.

"You're my wife," I say as I approach her with the toy. "My beautiful, perfect wife. And I'm going to enjoy making you come all day long with this toy." Nevaeh smirks at me, jutting her chin out defiantly.

"If you can," she teases, and fuck, I do love it when she teases me.

"Spread your legs, wife. Let me push this inside my pretty pussy." I've become as possessive as Leonard.

"I'd rather it was *my* cock slipping inside of me," she replies and reaches for my hardening dick, but I interrupt her by pushing the toy all the way inside her. She's so wet for me, it slips in with ease. It's designed in a way so part of it presses against her clit while the rest of it fits inside her snugly. "Fuck," she moans, and I capture her mouth, smiling against it.

If we could, I'd take my time with her first, but we have to be at the track in twenty minutes.

"Be my good girl and don't let anyone know we're playing today, okay?" Nevaeh nods with a grin.

"Yes, sir."

I kiss her once more before we make our way to the car I rented. It's just Nevaeh and me, so I use that time to try out the toy.

"Adrian," she gasps when I turn it on using my phone, but I keep my eyes trained on the road. "Oh, that feels so good," she says, rolling her hips even though the toy is pressing against her clit already.

"Yeah? Want more, beautiful?"

She nods, so I make it go faster, turning my head to see her grab the door handle. Her knuckles turn white as her head falls against the headrest, her lips wonderfully parted as she moans breathlessly over and over.

"Come, Nevaeh, come all over the toy." It's like my words have enough power to get her over the edge, an orgasm making her entire body vibrate. "That's my girl," I praise, loving the way a blush has taken over her face and chest.

"How am I going to pretend I don't have this toy inside of me if it makes me have such intense orgasms?" she asks, but I merely shrug.

"As soon as anyone notices, I'm dragging you to the nearest bathroom, taking that toy out of you, and replacing it with my cock." I love the way my wife smiles in anticipation.

"Deal."

We make it to the track a second orgasm later, and I chuckle when I open her door, holding my hand out for her because she said her legs feel like jelly already. She leans against the car a little when we get out, the blush still on her cheeks.

"Remember your safe word," I whisper into her ear, pressing a kiss to her forehead before we head toward the motorhome.

Today is only media day, so I have some time to play with my wife's control to keep anyone from noticing. Daniel already gives her a suspicious look when we make our way into the motorhome, but she merely offers him a cheerful smile as she greets him.

I spend the next hour turning the toy on and off, edging her without giving her the release she's looking for. She flashes me a warning glare when I do it again.

So, I give in, turning up the speed and making her cross her legs and gasp in surprise. She's standing in the corner to look over the photos she just took, and she almost drops her camera as she spins around to hide her face.

Daniel approaches her, so I turn off the toy again, too scared he'll hear anything. He taps Nevaeh on the shoulder, making her turn her head to look at him. Her chest is rising and falling abruptly as they exchange a few sentences that make my wife laugh and shake her head.

My performance coach turns his earlier suspicious look on me, which is my cue to get Nevaeh out of here.

"My wife and I have somewhere to be. I'll be right back," I tell Daniel as I grab Nevaeh's hand and lead her to the nearest bathroom.

Finally.

NEVAEH

Adrian rips his shirt off and places it on the sink in the bathroom he dragged me into, his mouth moving back onto mine.

"Need to fuck you so badly," Adrian says, lifting me onto his shirt and spreading my legs. He moves between them, trapping me between him and the mirror with his arms. "I'm so hard for you, my beautiful wife, I need to bury myself inside of you," he goes on, brushing his fingers over the droplets of sweat that are running down my cleavage from all the edging he did with me.

My knees dig into his hips, trying to guide him closer. His face moves to my neck, his nose swiping over the skin before he inhales deeply.

"Your scent is my personal heaven," he says before gliding his tongue over my skin. "And so is the way you taste. You're mine, all mine." I am, irrevocably so, too. His hands slip onto my ass, guiding me to the edge to pull my underwear to the side and the toy out, then thrusting himself against me. A wave of pleasure sends a low moan from my lips. "God, I can make you moan so easily," he groans after another thrust.

"Undress me," I moan, almost whining at this point. I'm desperate, too, just like him. He rubs his hard dick against me again, and I barely hold myself together. Every cell, every nerve ending, all of it catches on fire. My system is overloading, asking to be released from this ache between my legs. "Husband, please," I beg, and he slides his fingers into the waistband of my underwear.

"Lift your hips up a little, *déesse*," he instructs, and I don't waste a second before I push off the sink, letting him slide my underwear down. "My pretty *petit paradis*," he mumbles, and I bite down on my bottom lip before letting my head fall backward. "Fuck, I need to feel you," he says, the muscles on his arm flexing.

I reach out to play with him through his pants, but he stops me.

"I won't last, Nevaeh, not if you touch me right now." Adrian has no self-control with me. A single touch could make him fall apart. I smile at the thought. "Don't give me that smile. You're just as needy for me," he reminds me, thrusting his still covered erection against my clit again.

All my strength leaves, my body turning into a mush of pleasure. His lips attach to my neck, tilting my head to the side. Then, he rubs up and down, over and over. It pushes me so close to the edge, I grab his hips to stop him. He edged me for an hour, and I only want to come with him inside of me now.

"Put your cock in me," I demand, and he chuckles against my neck.

"So bossy," he says with a click of his tongue. "Your pussy craves me, doesn't it?" Adrian's fingers glide toward my breasts, cupping them through my t-shirt.

"Yes," I croak out, my mind fogging up.

"Needs my cock to come on, doesn't it?" I nod because he's rubbing again, and words have left me. "Okay, *mon ange*."

Adrian pulls his cock out of his pants. He spreads my legs as wide as possible, aligning himself with my entrance but only pushing inside a little.

"This will be fast and hard, okay?" I nod because that's exactly what I want right now.

I shudder, forcing him to slip inside of me completely. We both gasp from pleasure before laughing breathlessly. Adrian shuts both of us up with another hard thrust inside of me, hitting that perfect spot and making me scream. He presses his hand against my mouth to keep anyone else from hearing, a chuckle leaving him.

"You need to be quiet, Nevaeh."

I nod, but we both know if he repeats the same movement, his hips pushing his cock inside of me with so much force, I will make that sound again. I press his hand further against my lips, telling him to keep it there while he fucks me.

His other hand digs into my hips, keeping me in place as he slides back inside of me, making me scream against his palm. He's going so deep and so fast, the friction makes me weak. The pleasure is spreading, settling in my lower stomach along with the familiar build-up. His groans push me closer to the edge, his quick movements giving me my usual high.

He grabs his phone and hands it to me before picking up the vibrator again, pressing it against my clit.

"Turn it on, Nevaeh," he instructs, and I do as I'm told, the vibrations combined with his hard thrusts making me scream even more. "That's it. You're doing so well," he praises.

It pushes me right over the edge, my orgasm coming forcefully into my body. It lifts me straight into the heaven Adrian has designed for me, and I float there for a while, not paying too much attention to his slowing movements as he spills inside of me. All I hear is his moan, and I smile at the sweet sound, one of my favorites in the world. Adrian's hand drops from my face, grabbing onto the edge where my legs are dangling over.

"I guess we can cross that off our list of sex things to do," I say after a moment of silence between us, and he chuckles.

My fingers slip into his hair, tugging on the roots to get him to look at me, which he does without hesitation.

"I want to have all your remaining firsts with you," I add, and he grabs my chin between his two fingers, leaning down to press a soft kiss to my lips.

"You can have them all. They're yours for the taking," he replies.

"And mine are yours. For the rest of this lifetime, and all the next ones. I'm yours, Adrian Romana."

"And I'm yours, Nevaeh Fuchs-Romana."

Bonus Chapter

Adrian

"Do you think they'll like me? I know how much Carlos means to you, and I'm scared he won't," Nevaeh says, tugging on the hem of her dress to stretch it longer.

She doesn't want her outfit to be inappropriate—it's the reason she changed four times before we left—but, if it were up to me, she could wear whatever she wants. Hell, she could have put on a pair of sweatpants or sweatshorts, and I would be the proudest man in the world to call her mine.

"He will adore you. How could he not? You're *my* girlfriend, and he loves me," I tease because I know it will take some of the tension off her shoulders. For once, it doesn't work.

"I know you're trying to do that cocky thing to make me feel better, but I feel sick to my stomach." This is the first time since I've known her that a slight German accent has slipped through her American one.

"You can still change your mind. No one will be upset." I know her anxiety doesn't make these social situations easy for her, so I want her to know she always has a choice with me without any consequences or questions asked.

"Not changing my mind. I just want you to know if I run to the bathroom, *don't follow me.*" I kiss her temple, shaking my head. I know anxiety has all kinds of effects on people. Sweating, handshaking, nausea, vomiting, and so on. I would never let her go through any of it by herself. But if that's what she wants, I will respect it.

"Okay," is what I respond because I don't want to argue with her when it comes to her anxiety. She set a boundary. I won't step over it.

We're already in front of Carlos Klein's house. He's my idol, the man I spent most of my childhood studying, admiring. He still holds the title for the youngest man in the history of F1 to get a championship title. Tonight means a lot to all of us, but I'm not nervous, not even in the slightest. Having dinner with him, Evangelin, Val, and Gabriel was my idea, after all. This is a part of my life I haven't introduced her to yet.

It's about time I do.

"I don't want to make a terrible impression, *mein Mond*," she says, turning to me when we stop in front of the door. I'm momentarily distracted by the high the words "my love" out of her mouth take me on, but I refocus quickly enough.

"Listen to me, *mon ange*, you are..." I trail off, unsure how to proceed, what part of my view of her to share to reassure her. "A bright light in a dark world. Everyone on this planet would be lucky to know you. Do you understand me?" I ask, making her features soften. She leans into my touch as soon as I bring my hands to her face, almost forcing a sigh out of me.

"Yes," she whispers, and all of my muscles turn to putty.

"Good."

I can't resist her or the coconut scent I smell coming from her lips before I even bend down to press my mouth onto hers. She melts against me, her chest pressing against mine and her hands slipping to the back of my neck. Nevaeh is tilting it further down, the height difference between us making me smile.

"I should knock, Nevaeh," I say, but she holds my mouth captive for a moment longer. If it were up to me, she could keep it forever.

"You always say my full name, never Nevs or Nevi or anything else I've been called," she points out, the tips of her fingers sliding over my ears. Shivers run down my spine. "Why?" she asks, pulling me back into the moment and away from how good her touch feels.

"Because Nevaeh is a beautiful name. I don't want to take away from its meaning, away from your value in any way, even if it's just your name." *God, I'm such a fucking sap.*

"Why are you so perfect?" I almost laugh at her question.

"I'm not. I'm so far from it, it's terrifying." She shakes her head with so much determination, I can't help but smile.

"You're perfect *to me. For me.* You're everything I've ever wanted put into one person. It's incredible," she says, and I suck in a sharp breath. *Just so you know, I'd be on the floor crying right now if I didn't want to look tough in front of Nevaeh.* "Let's go. We don't want to be late." She knocks on the door while I try to compose myself.

Carlos opens the door, smiling so wide, I don't think I've ever seen him this excited before. He takes my girlfriend's hand, placing a kiss to the back of it and grinning as he tells her what a pleasure it is to meet her. He turns to me after, offering me his hand to shake, just like I always do to greet him.

"Come in, both of you. Valentina and Gabriel are setting the table right now. Evangelin and I have almost finished preparing the meal," he informs us as we walk through the door, leading us outside onto his veranda so we can enjoy the summer day while we eat.

"Thank you for having us and all the trouble you're going through," Nevaeh says, but Carlos waves her gratitude away with a flick of his wrist.

"We're excited to have you here. Adrian has never brought anyone over." I don't know why, but warmth spreads through me.

Carlos and Evangelin are the closest people I have left that resemble what parents would be like. I'm bringing a girl over. It's strange how fulfilling this is.

"I'm honored to be the first person then," Nevaeh replies, sliding her hand into mine so our fingers can intertwine. The comfort of her touch immediately sweeps through me.

"You should be. He's the best guy I've ever known, along with Gabriel." Carlos swoons, and I smile at the back of his head, his white hair carefully combed over the bald spot.

"Uh oh, don't flatter him too much. If his head gets any bigger, he won't be able to fit it in his car later," Nevaeh jokes, and I chuckle as Carlos walks away. Fuck, I love it when she teases me.

I love it so much, I grab her by the hips and pull her against my front.

"Careful now. You're going to get me all hot and bothered," I say, pushing my groin against her a little. She gasps so quietly, only I can hear the little sound.

"*Going to*? Aren't you always when you're around me?" she replies. I'm about to excuse us and give Carlos some bullshit reason why Nevaeh and I need to leave when Valentina flings her arms around her.

"How are you, love?" My sister leads my girlfriend away before I have a chance to stop her. I almost growl when Val looks over her shoulder and sticks out her tongue.

She's got to stop trying to steal my girlfriend.

Gabriel appears next to me, handing me a glass of water while he sips his beer.

"The introduction went well, I assume?" he asks, and I give him a slight smirk.

"Are you underestimating the power of Nevaeh's charm? She didn't even have to say anything for Carlos to adore her." Gabriel cocks an eyebrow, then raises his hands in mock surrender.

"Hey, I never, ever doubted her ability to make a good impression. However, I always doubt your ability not to fuck things up." I frown instantly. "I'm joking. God, I thought you get all *hot and bothered* when you get teased," he says with a wink, and I choke on the sip of water I just took.

"You heard that? I whispered it," I blurt out once I'm able to speak again. Gabriel bursts into laughter.

"Not quietly enough," he replies, smacking my back and then grabbing my shoulder. "It's okay, I don't judge. Whatever gets you going, mate, good for you." He attempts to walk away to join the others, but I hold onto his wrist for a moment.

"You tell anyone, and I will let them all know you get hard from winning a Grand Prix," I say, cringing at the fact that I know this. It's a little hard not to notice *it* when we're in the cool-down room. Gabriel tilts his head to the side, licks his lips, then responds.

"Winning isn't what makes me hard, Adrian." I scrunch my eyebrows together, confused both because I'm curious and also because I really don't want to have this conversation. I wait for an explanation. "Do you really want to know?" he asks with an awkward laugh, and I suck in a sharp breath.

"Unfortunately, my mind won't let it go now unless you tell me," I reply, and he rubs the back of his neck with his hand.

"Valentina and I have a thing now after every race I win where she—" I cut him off immediately.

"Ahhh, no, thank you. I don't want to know what kinky games you play with my sister. That's enough." I shudder at the thought, pushing it away as quickly as humanly possible. "*Ugh.*" Gabriel chuckles, sipping his beer.

"You asked. I was happy not sharing." Yeah, he's got a point there.

Without lingering on this conversation any longer than necessary, we join everyone else at the table.

I pull Nevaeh close to my side, my lips finding her temple. There is a need deep inside of me, always pushing at me to touch her and be close to her. It appeared the day I met her and hasn't made any effort to leave. If anything, the claws keep sinking deeper into me, and I want them to. I want her hold on me to increase, no matter how fucking terrified I am every single time I realize how in love I am.

In love... what a strange concept.

Meeting someone, figuring out they're perfect for you in every way, wanting to spend every free moment with them, and then becoming fully aware they're the love of your life is... beautiful. You start to plan a life with them until it consumes your every thought, and you don't ever want to let them go.

I don't want to let it go.

I'd fall in love with Nevaeh in every single lifetime, in every different universe.

"What are you thinking about?" she asks, so I lean my forehead against hers.

"Ripping this skin-tight dress off your body," I lie, but it makes her giggle.

She pokes my side, and I tickle her until she begs for mercy. I claim her lips one more time before Evangelin tells us to sit. Nevaeh and I complain at the same time, asking what we can do to help. The elderly woman looks between us with a small grin, clearly amused by the synchronization.

"Sit. There is nothing else to be done," she assures us, so I merely pull out a chair for Nevaeh.

"Such a gentleman, even with that dirty mouth," she whispers, and I smirk to myself.

"You love my mouth, you fuck it almost every morning," I reply, and her jaw drops to the floor. I close it for her, leaning down to kiss her lips and settling down in my own seat.

Surprise lingers on her features for a few moments longer until Carlos grabs her attention and bombards her with hundreds of questions, which she answers honestly and without hesitation.

Val shoots me an amused look, and I cock an eyebrow at her.

"What?" I mouth, and she forms a heart with her fingers before pointing at her eyes. She's telling me I have heart-eyes for Nevaeh. I almost laugh at my sister.

Without a single doubt, I know she's right. I know I've always looked at Nevaeh that way, and I don't think it will ever change.
Val mouths, "You love her," and I know she'd sing it if she were saying these words out loud.

"You're annoying," is all I mouth back, but she's grinning at me.

Gabriel shifts her focus to him, twisting the engagement ring on her finger into its proper place on her hand. I instantly stare down at Nevaeh's naked finger, overwhelming thoughts flooding my mind.

"Careful, don't hurt yourself," Nevaeh says with a whisper. I turn to her with half a smile, half a confused frown.

"What?" I reply, waiting for an explanation.

"It looks like you're thinking really hard about something. Don't hurt yourself," she teases, and my heart starts racing against my ribcage.

"Second time, Nevaeh, second time," I warn, but she pretends to pout.

"What are you going to do about it?" I take the glass in front of me, sipping the water.

"Nothing here, but at home?" I let out a small chuckle. "I'll *do something about it.*"

I watch different scenarios cross over her face until her chest rises and falls more abruptly.

My perfect woman is getting all hot from everything she knows I'm going to do to her later.

Sneak Peek

Prologue

James

I'VE MADE MANY MISTAKES in my life. Falling in love with my best friend was the biggest. Not only is she now happily married to a man I cannot fucking stand for the life of me, but I'm also a part-time father and full-time Formula One driver. Love isn't in the cards for me. Maybe it never has been and never will be. It feels like I'm slowly getting over my feelings for Val, but I'm also acutely aware that no one will ever *be her*. It doesn't matter how much time passes or how often I tell myself there will be someone else who is even more amazing for me than the woman I've been pining after most of my life.

How pathetic.

I know it is. I don't need to be told I should move on from Valentina. People don't realize how fucking difficult that is when you've spent your entire existence imagining a life with someone. Growing old with the person you've loved more than anything else. My son, Damian, has long taken that spot, but she's still in second place.

Married.

She's married.

And if that isn't like a bullet to the chest, one that peels itself out of me only so I can get shot again every time I think about it, then I don't know what is. As I said, people don't realize what it means to let go of the kind of love I hold for her when I've been carrying it around since I can remember. Watching her get married shattered something inside of me. Hearts can't break, but they can tear, and she tore mine into a million shreds when she whispered "I do" to a man who isn't me.

Again, pathetic, I know.

But it only just happened, too. I'm allowed to wallow in self-pity for a little, right? No one would expect me to simply be happy for her when she was my happy ending for so long. Choices have consequences. I chose not to tell her how I felt. I made that mistake, not Valentina. She isn't the one to blame. She didn't pretend she had feelings for me. She always called me exactly what I am to her. Her best friend. If my head came up with delusions, then that's on me.

Then again, I wish it was her fault so I could be angry with her. So she wouldn't seem so perfect to me, including all of her imperfections.

"Hey," Adrian, my best friend, says as he stands beside me on my veranda. He came over to have dinner with me, but I've been in such a pissy mood, I've hardly spoken. "How are you doing?" he asks, his hand moving to my shoulder and giving it a comforting squeeze. My gaze shifts to the night sky, the light pollution too strong where I live in Monaco for me to see stars.

"I wish I could see the stars shine," I blurt out, and Adrian looks up, too.

"Yeah, so do I," he replies.

Silence fills the space between us until I break it again.

"You've shut yourself off from love before. How did you do it?" I hear myself saying, but it feels like my soul has left my body as I contemplate how the fuck I'm going to keep my chest from aching.

"I didn't have Nevaeh, so there was no reason to open my heart to love like the one you're talking about. Once she stepped into my life, she split me wide open, entangled her soul with mine, and that was it. She is it for me." I nod along to his words, feeling a stinging pain tugging on that fucked up organ in my chest.

"So, you're saying I'm screwed because Val already split me open and now closed me off from everyone else?" I ask, but instead of laughing at how dramatic I'm being, my best friend steps in front of me. He grabs both of my shoulders, his eyes, the same as Val's, staring deeply into mine.

"I'm saying you may love my sister, but she was never meant to be yours. Stop trying to convince yourself she was and open your eyes. There is a whole world out there, a sky full of beautiful stars, even if you can't see them now. Val may have been your first love, but she wasn't your star. You're going to find your own shining bright light, I know you will," Adrian says before letting go of me and pointing at my chest. "Your heart is still in your chest, James, that's why you're hurting right now. If Valentina was meant to be yours, she would have taken it, but she didn't. She left it for someone else to have one day."

"Who?" I ask, tears jumping into my eyes.

"Your happy ending, James."

Acknowledgements

Diffuse was a difficult book for me to write. I was doubting myself, scared the story would not live up to how loved Reserved's story is. And while I still doubt myself, seeing how adored this story was by my amazing beta readers and ARC readers made me so emotional in the best way.

So, I would like to thank all of my beta and ARC readers who commented their thoughts and emotions as they went through the story. I want to thank Jess, Solène, Amélie, Gemma, Michelle, Rukhshar, Melanie, Emma, Tanisha, Kayla, Makayla, Ainsley, Stepahnie, Vicky, and many more.

I would also like to thank the people who've been by my side for a very long time, who have supported me and shown me love beyond all measure for as long.

Drew, thank you for reading Diffuse in two days and taking most of my fear of the story not being good enough. I will never be able to express how much that means to me, nor will I be able to express what our friendship means to me. Ams, thank you for sticking by my side and helping me perfect the stories I am so scared to share. I don't know what I'd do without you. Teigan, thank you for always helping me reach my dream. I'm so eternally grateful for you. Emma, thank you for reading everything I write. Natalia, thank you for helping me become the writer I am today.

I want to give a special thank you to the readers who have become friends after reading my books and shouting about them from the rooftops. Halie, Sophie, Sami, Martina, Alyssa, Apoorva, Beth, Hali, Renee, Mais, Hannah, Allyson, and so many more. I am so grateful for you and honored to have amazing people like you cheering me on every single day. It means more than words will ever be able to explain.

To my fellow author friends, I have a few words to say, too. Esha, you are absolutely amazing and I aspire to become as brilliant of a writer as you. Ruby, I'm so proud of you and so thankful for always having you in my corner when I need someone. Samantha, you are so strong, and it is that strength that inspires me every day. Rosaline, you are an absolute ray of sunshine, and you brighten up my life every day.

Most importantly, I need to thank my sister. If you've read my acknowledgments before, you know she does everything. She formats the book, she makes the covers, she edits it, she takes photos for my social media with me, and, and, and. Without her, I'd be as lost as Adrian would be without Val and vice versa. She's my favorite person in the entire world, and the best business partner anyone could have ever asked for.

Lastly, I always want to thank my grandparents, mom, and Robyn and Miriam for being there every step of the way and being the kind of emotional support system everyone should have because it is the best thing in the world.

I love you all, and I'm so very grateful you continue to read my books.

All my love,

Bridget

About the Author

BRIDGET L. ROSE IS a half-German, half-Italian author, who was born and raised in Germany until the age of thirteen. She fell in love with books from a young age, and soon discovered her passion for writing as well. She likes to spend her free time with her family, reading a book, or writing one herself. She also adores the sport Formula One, which led her to write her Pitstop Series.

Books by Bridget L. Rose

The Pitstop Series

Jump-Start

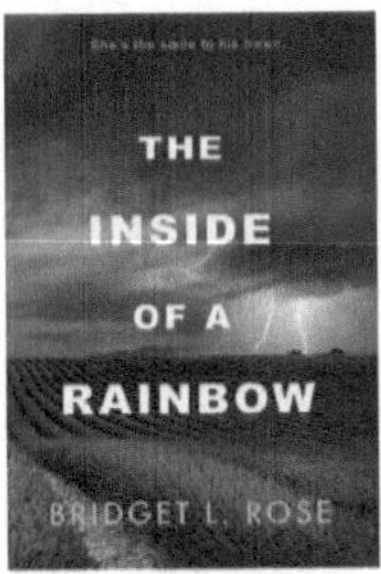

The Inside of a Rainbow

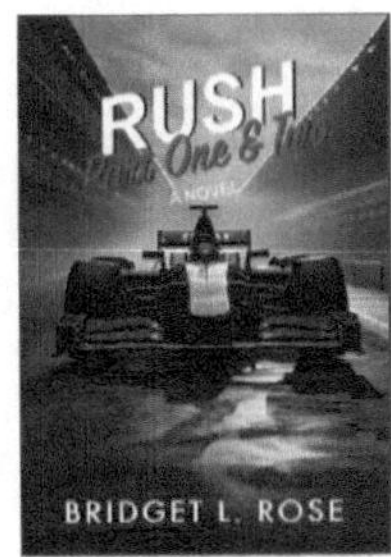

Rush: Part One & Two

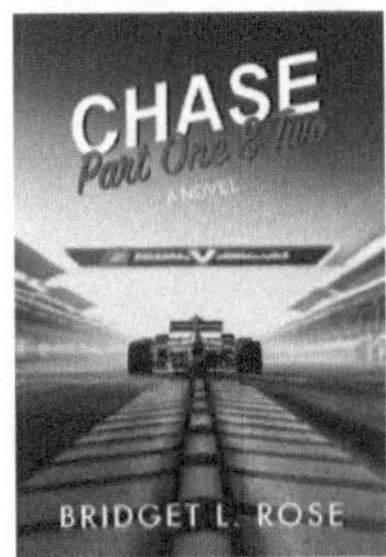

Chase: Part One & Two

Reserved

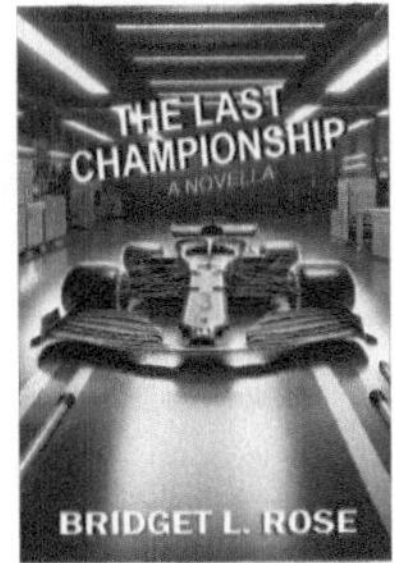

The Last Championship (Novella)

From Angels to Devils Series

From Devils to Angels